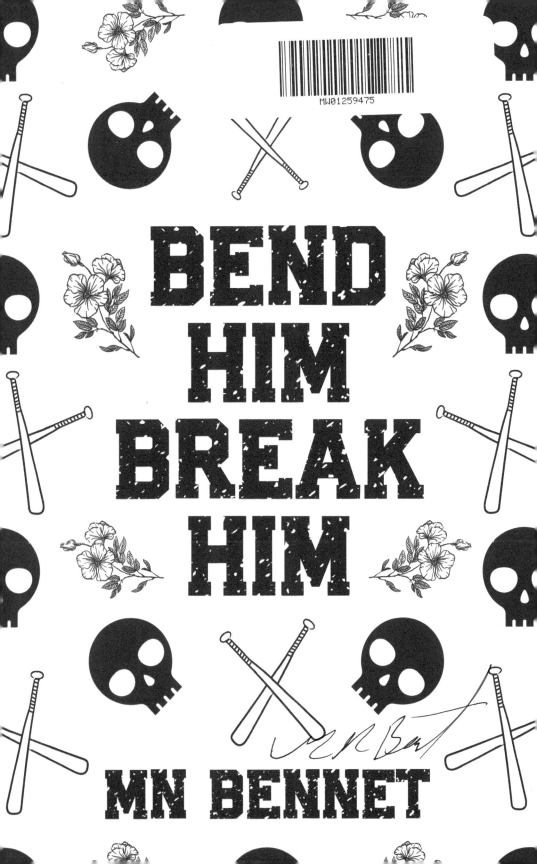

BEND HIM BREAK HIM

MN BENNET

Hardback ISBN: 978-1-967397-09-9
Paperback ISBN: 978-1-967397-08-2
Ebook ISBN: 979-8-9901493-8-0

Edited by Charlie Knight (https://cknightwrites.carrd.co/)
Cover art by Lina Ganef (https://linaganef-eng.carrd.co/)
Formatting by Mayonaka Designs (https://mayonakadesigns.com/)

www.mnbennet.com/

AUTHOR'S NOTE

Like most of my stories there are some lighthearted moments with humor wrapped into several scenes, however, this is also a dark romance. Very dark at times. Please consider checking the tropes and content warnings below.

Thank you so much for considering Colton and Isaac's story. I truly hope you enjoy meeting these two and following their twisted little journey.

TROPES:

Dark Bully Romance
Enemies-to-Lovers
Revenge/Redemption
Grumpy/Sunshine
Hurt/Comfort
AITA Vibes
Dom/Sub
Hate Fucking

CONTENT WARNINGS:

Toxic Romance
Bullying
Teasing
Hazing
Blackmail
Homophobia
Queerphobia

Toxic Masculinity
Smoking
Alcohol Use
Profanity
Exhibitionism
Humiliation
Public humiliation
Violence and fighting
Threats
Paranoia
Anxiety
Depression
Suicidal ideation (off page and prior to the start of the story)
Emotional assault
Drugging
Attempted SA (on page)
Physical assault (on page)
Hospitalization
Family abandonment

This is an open-door romance so there is a lot of graphic sex between adults: Dubcon, CNC, oral, face fucking, throat fucking, gagging, choking, spit, grinding, anal, rough top, praise/degradation, first times, D/s dynamic, spanking, fingering, toy play, public play, rimming, cum play/sucking/swallowing.

Please remember your mental health is important and if this story isn't for you that's completely okay. Your comfort matters. Your joy matters. You matter.

This is for all the folks who love toxic guys, dubious arrangements, and unhinged romances. May this twisted story feed the beast in your soul.

CHAPTER 01
COLTON

COLTON raced across campus, weaving around every carefree student who hadn't overslept for the third time this week. Pulling the straps of his book bag tight helped lessen the jostling smack against his back. He started to sweat through the University of Clinton Lloyd Institute of Technology hoodie he'd tossed on, thinking the storm clouds meant cool weather. They did not. The trek and outfit left him so exhausted first thing in the morning that he couldn't even laugh at the sea of CLIT merchandise he darted between on his way to class.

Oversleeping had already gotten him a letter grade deduction in his history course, and he couldn't also afford his composition course knocking down his score this close to the end of the semester. As he reached the English building, he darted inside and apologized to every person he nearly knocked over on his way to the auditorium. Taking a deep breath, Colton wiped the sweat from his brow and quietly made his way inside.

"You're late," Isaac hissed as Colton skirted around the grumpy goth guy and ducked low to walk the length of the auditorium.

Professor Howard didn't scold people for tardiness—not that she needed to when she had a TA like Isaac standing at the door, ready to shame anyone and everyone—but she did make certain they regretted whatever decision led to them showing up late.

Every door leading into the auditorium was locked except for the front entrance, where Professor Howard positioned her podium and table while presenting lectures.

Colton not-so-stealthily made his way past her and to the opposite side of the auditorium where he sat. Not that they had assigned seats, but he and his teammates had always perched up in the middle edge, allowing them leg room by the steps, far away enough to avoid being asked questions and central enough to draw the attention of any curious classmates who wanted the eye candy of the varsity baseball team members.

"Looks like your boyfriend's mad," Leon whispered when Colton took his seat.

Colton's attention immediately went to Isaac, who shot daggers at the jock and the other members chuckling at Colton's late arrival. Leon leaned in, gesturing lewdly in Isaac's direction with a jacking motion and drawing a larger laugh than Colton preferred.

He smiled at his teammates and pretended to find Leon's jokes hilarious, even if he wanted to punch the big brute in the face.

If it were anyone else, Colton would've considered it a playful joke, but Leon had a tendency to make gay jabs on a regular basis, pulling other team members in and reminding everyone of Colton's queer status and recent outing last spring.

Leon was the epitome of keeping your friends close and enemies closer. Not that Colton wanted Leon around. But no matter what Colton did, he couldn't shake Leon, who presented himself as a diehard friend but was always ready to stab Colton in the back so he could be the new starting pitcher. Leon practically flipped his schedule so he could stay close to Colton, which he tried not to complain about too much, given a lot of the team tried to group up so they could all work on classes together.

"Oh, I bet you can pull from your essay last year," Leon said, nodding to the ongoing lecture and nudging Colton to remind him how he'd already failed this course.

It sucked being the only non-freshmen in the comp course. Well, that

Colton knew of. Surely, he couldn't have been the only person here who tanked a few classes last year. Still, he was the only baseball team member who wasn't a freshman in this course, something Leon's calculated jabs always found a way to bring up.

Leon had obsessed over Colton since he joined the team, doing everything in his power to outdo him. It didn't help that Leon had a bigger and taller build, but it did help that Leon's pitches lacked the same precision or flair, no matter how much harder he trained.

Ignoring Leon, Colton pretended to focus on the lecture and the upcoming final essay, but his eyes wandered over to Isaac, who continued glaring at him with a sour expression and a clamped jaw. Isaac was the only person who knew Colton before coming to college, and damn if he wasn't the last person Colton wanted to see after high school.

Isaac's style had shifted since high school, no longer the gothic-esque getup adding flair to his school uniforms. Instead, he'd dived headlong into a full-blown dark phase. The heavy eyeliner, mascara, and eyeshadow made the blue of his eyes pop from across the auditorium, but they also enhanced his angry expression. No longer bound by private school standards, Isaac had bleached his shaggy hair white, added faded purple streaks throughout, and now sported tons of piercings and tattoos.

Last Colton had counted, Isaac had nine piercings. Visible ones, anyway. The tongue piercing was Colton's favorite and one he certainly wished Isaac had gotten in high school. Then, he had two piercings on each ear with studs in all except for the lower left, where he sported a dangling cross. His upper right ear had an industrial piercing that balanced out the left eyebrow ring, left nose piercing, and right lower lip piercing. It had this weird zigzag effect running across Isaac's face that sometimes made Colton smirk.

He often found himself smirking when he thought about Isaac when he reminisced and ignored where everything went wrong.

Colton pulled out his laptop and signed into the classroom dashboard, doing his best to follow along with the lecture and adjoining slideshow. But try as he might, Colton could never pay attention very long during class lectures, especially when he wondered how many tattoos were under Isaac's outfit.

Sure, he wore a button-up with long sleeves for classes, went with slacks instead of those baggy Tripp pants or ripped jeans, and he even added a small tie, but the look still screamed goth. The tie was usually his only outlandish thing. Today, Isaac had sported a white tie with blood splatter that popped so much brighter against his black ensemble.

Isaac only ever dressed up for his TA gig, which Colton assumed had to do with some personal style instead of Professor Howard's mandates since some of the other TAs showed up however they wanted, including in pajamas.

Occasionally, Colton would see Isaac outside of classes, dragged to some party or campus event, and he usually dressed in a more traditional goth getup. Or at least what Colton assumed was traditional based on movies and such.

The two of them had completely different styles. Colton had gotten one piercing back in middle school, which someone said was on the gay ear, so he removed it and never wanted another one again. His wardrobe consisted of polos, expensive jeans, workout clothes, and a few tight outfits meant to show off his muscles when going out for an evening.

Colton kept his fashion very conservative, very in line with the rest of his teammates, because he was already different enough as the only openly queer member.

"Ooop," Leon whispered. "Boyfriend alert."

It didn't take long for Leon to make a deep-throat gesture while adding gagging noises. Given the way Leon joked, Colton suspected he wasn't the only pitcher with bi tendencies.

Leon coughed a bit as Isaac walked the length of the auditorium, making his way toward their ascending stairs.

Colton studied Isaac for a moment, noting no changes in the visible tattoos and figuring they were the real reason behind why Isaac dressed the way he did. Not that it hid them all. Flames from something on Isaac's chest covered his lower neck, almost like he was on fire. He had a butterfly on his left hand, which seemed quite contradictory to Isaac's demeanor or the other tattoos on his hand, from the silly stick figure smiley and frowny faces on his thumbs to the boldly written "D E A D S O U L" etched across his knuckles.

"You guys should talk less and focus more," Isaac whispered. "I'm sure giggling about whose bat is bigger is quite enthralling, but maybe y'all can pay the fuck attention."

"Whoops." Leon loudly shushed himself. "We're so sorry."

"Whatever." Isaac's glare hung on Leon for a moment but quickly found its way back to Colton as it always did. "It's just some students should probably focus more on the lecture since their grades are borderline, and they've already failed the course."

Colton glared, ignoring the wheezing laughter coming from Leon and the other members, who also 'oooooed' at the cutting comment. Considering Isaac spent most of their time together on his knees, he sure did like riding Colton's ass every chance he had, reminding him how much power he had over Colton's academic standing.

"Take a hint and ride someone else's dick during class," Colton snapped, glaring back at Isaac in equal measure.

Isaac's eyes widened in shock, the sharp blue glossing over slightly. The sharpness of Colton's attitude twisted his stomach in knots, leaving him remorseful but unwilling to show it.

Leon's lewd gagging and gurgling noises only added to the tension until, finally, Isaac abandoned the baseball team and returned to the front of the auditorium. While Leon—or anyone for that matter—didn't have an inkling of a clue about Colton's history with Isaac, he did have a knack for making folks uncomfortable with his constant belligerent behavior. Something Colton greatly accepted from Leon right now to get Isaac off his back.

It was hard enough for Colton to give a fuck about classes, but when the dude who literally embodied all of Colton's shame waltzed about the classroom of three hundred-plus students with his piercing blue eyes locked onto Colton, it made it impossible to focus.

Every part of Colton wanted to drop the course, but his academic probation prohibited him from such things. He'd already bombed the class last year, bombed a few classes, honestly. He couldn't afford to fail any courses this year. Switching his schedule would've been preferable, but his athletic schedule made it damn near impossible to find courses that fit together.

Ultimately, Colton had to suffer the guilt of his high school hookup's icy stare every time they crossed paths. His hate was more deeply rooted than screwing around, though, and Colton knew that. He'd mocked Isaac for years, teased him relentlessly, then used him for his own experimental pleasures, and finally broke him to save his reputation.

Christ, he would never live down what happened between them, no matter what he did to make amends. Not that Colton had tried an apology. How would someone even begin to apologize for half the things he did to Isaac? For what he caused? For what he instigated? Allowed? Used to shield his own secrets?

And it wasn't like Isaac was searching for an apology. No, he was a vindictive, spiteful prick who had it out for Colton.

Colton had barely maintained a C minus the entirety of the semester, thanks to Isaac's harsh grading. And he knew it was Isaac who graded all his work even if the professor said all her TAs impartially graded the papers, blindly picking from the stacks and often not even checking names when running through work. That minus was below academic standards, and if he didn't remove it, Colton would be in breach of his probation.

Given all his other faults, other incidents, he knew the disciplinary panel wouldn't care for his excuses. He'd had too many already from the on-campus drinking tickets, the fighting, and the possible-sort-of-maybe-just-a-little-bit-of hazing that happened to some of the more unfortunate freshmen last year. Colton didn't feel culpable for that incident. He either joined the team in their playful targeting, or he would've ended up a target. He swallowed hard at that, reminded of using a similar excuse when it came to Isaac.

This was why he needed his final paper to be perfect. Scrolling through his computer, he let his eyes gloss over a folder holding the file that'd save his ass this semester. Thankfully, he'd found a perfect essay. Not an easy feat since he already had a plagiarism scare last year, part of what put him on academic probation.

But it just so happened that this final exam essay involved career research, and his cousin had a similar one from his senior year. Colton couldn't use his own senior year career essay since he bullshitted the entirety of it and everything senior year after getting his acceptance letters. His cousin's essay was strong, though, even with Isaac's asshole grading scale, Colton knew he could challenge the harsh scoring if it dropped his class grade. And the essay wasn't floating around online, so Colton didn't have to worry about plagiarism.

Colton could breathe easy once the fall semester ended. He'd keep his grades above the C average he was required, knock out this minus currently holding him back, and go into the spring semester ready to finish strong. Once this class ended, it'd be a breeze to finish out the spring semester on a high note, passing his courses and getting off academic probation once and for all.

CHAPTER 02
ISAAC

DID Isaac glare at Colton and the baseball team for the remainder of the lecture? Yes. Did he realize it was spiteful and unproductive? Absolutely. Did he give a fuck? Nope.

Isaac tried his hardest to endure Colton's presence. But it was difficult to tolerate the guy who made life worth living while simultaneously ruining it. When Isaac escaped their small, conservative town of Straight Arrow, he hoped to move past the ironic homophobia. But then Colton had to choose to attend the same college. Of all the schools in the world, Colton's decision felt blatantly intentional, even if no one knew where Isaac had fled. Every time he saw the budding baseball pro, Isaac struggled with the feelings that still lingered deep in his core.

When class came to an end, Isaac handed in some late papers to Professor Howard, turning on his heel to leave before she could complain. There was a lot about Professor Howard he enjoyed, but her incessant requirement for punctuality on assignments wasn't one of them. He intended to skirt her questions and dodge her accusations about the papers until she broke down and put the scores into her gradebook.

If she pressed too hard, Isaac would lie and say he fell behind on his grading goals instead of admitting the students failed to meet the absurd mandated deadlines. It was easier for Isaac to take the blame on the assignments, which never hurt his standing as a TA. The problem was that Howard didn't fuck around when it came to grading, clawing her way from an adjunct professor to head of the department. Part of that came with a need to be ruthless, which Isaac normally respected; hence, the appeal to major in English and embrace his love for literature. Well, double major since he knew there was literally zero profit when it came to reading and writing, so he needed a real degree if he wanted cash flow after his grant money dried up.

The moment Isaac stepped outside the classroom, he nearly bumped into Colton, who lingered near the doorway at a table that wasn't supposed to be there.

Isaac glared at the green-eyed, black-haired, chiseled jock who stood there looking annoyingly gorgeous with his perfectly tan skin, sharp features, muscular body, and perfectly fitting hoodie and tight jeans despite also appearing frumpy. How could someone be this hot in a wrinkled outfit that looked like they'd just tossed on?

"Excuse you!" Isaac glared.

"You're excused, sweetie." Mina snapped her fingers from behind the unsanctioned table and waved Isaac off before handing Colton a flyer to the GSA club meetings.

Mina's dark brown skin popped, complimented by her baggy sky-blue blouse that hung off her shoulders and exposed her stomach. Her unrelenting bright, white smile matched the walls where she'd posted up to promote the queer club. When a few guys paused, Mina leaned forward, encouraging them to linger as she passed out flyers. Her makeup was perfectly composed, matching her shirt and complementing the starry night polish of her nails she'd gone with this month.

Beside Mina, Jazz did her best to ensure every single student who exited the auditorium had a flyer for the next GSA club meeting. It wasn't uncommon for the president and vice president of the queer campus club to post up and hand out flyers to draw in a bigger crowd, but they usually set up in more populated areas, not a random English course that happened to have

Isaac in attendance.

Jazz wore her very daring 'I eat CLIT' hoodie, which had tiny text to make it appropriate if anyone dared question her school spirit for Clinton Lloyd Institute of Technology. 'I eat *at* CLIT *Café*' was the full text, not that anyone could see the at or café portion, but it worked for her, and the university fed into the clit jokes to up their merchandise sales.

Jazz's smile filled her entire face, making her chubby cheeks rise high. The only chubby thing on her, in fact, since she was almost as tiny as Mina, despite the fact Jazz dressed in baggy shirts and jeans she needed a belt pulled to the hilt in order to keep them up. Jazz had a bleach blonde buzzcut and a light brown tawny complexion. While she carried herself aggressively, she was butch in aesthetic only, walking around like a goddamn golden retriever in Isaac's opinion. Jazz struck up three conversations at once in the time Isaac spent gawking at his GSA friends.

Jazz encouraged Isaac to join her at her makeshift booth, where she passed out flyers for the next club meeting. Unfortunately, Jazz had this annoyingly convincing attitude that Isaac hadn't been able to escape since he met her. Isaac rolled his eyes and locked them on Mina, who brushed her fingers through her long, waist-length box braids, doing her best to appear dainty despite being known for her zero tolerance on bullshit attitude.

The two of them hadn't come because of Isaac's presence in the class, which should've been a win for him, but knowing they came here to reel Colton back into attendance only managed to piss Isaac off more.

"We'd love to see you again," Mina said with an obnoxious amount of enthusiasm.

Isaac huffed at the phony cheer oozing off her.

"Yeah, bro," Cunt-A-Saurous Leon Coleman shouted with a flippant attitude. "*They* wanna see you *there* again."

Leon put a heavy emphasis on the pronouns, mockingly, of course, because he was a cunt that Isaac wanted to throat punch on a regular basis. Every time the douchebag spoke, Isaac cracked his knuckles and reminded himself that unless he had the pleasure of finding Leon without witnesses, he shouldn't swing first.

"Shut the fuck up, dude." Colton cast his eyes down and crumpled the flyer up before leading his baseball team members away.

Leon turned back and cheered for Pride sarcastically until his team cut the corner.

"He's a piece of work," Mina said without missing a beat and flipping off Leon.

"What the fuck are y'all doing here?" Isaac asked, unconcerned by the interested new members of GSA hovering nearby.

As the secretary of the club, Isaac often took notes on future agendas, and nothing said his fellow board representatives would be lurking outside his class.

"We're recruiting new members," Jazz said as the bulk of the crowd cleared out after a meager five minutes.

"Yeah, and your reason for posting up here?" Isaac stared, unblinking.

"Thought we'd persuade the campus hottie with a bi body to speak again," Mina said, still eyeing the direction Colton had walked off in.

It annoyed Isaac how the one club, the one place, refuge, sanctuary, he'd found had opened its doors for Colton motherfucking Lennox like he was some damn hero.

"You realize he's not that special," Isaac snapped. "Just some annoying jock who likes dick occasionally."

"He'd make a huge difference in attendance," Jazz said, her brown eyes turning into some annoying pleading expression.

"Everyone loves a hero." Mina led the way toward the student court-yard.

"Hero?" Isaac snapped. "He got fucking outed. That's not heroic. It's sloppy—just ask your local senator."

Okay, normally, Isaac would hold more sympathy. In fact, he had held more sympathy by keeping Colton's DL queer status to himself all through high school despite how it might've benefited Isaac to snitch on everyone's favorite jock for being a big ole homo.

"Do you know how brave it is to own your queer identity when being outed?" Mina leapt to Colton's defense. "As a bi, masculine athlete, he could've easily denied the allegations."

"Not that easy, given the cumming out factor," Isaac said, alluding to the rumors Colton was caught mid-blowjob, which supposedly forced his hand to come out before those photos came out.

There was something super infuriating about Colton being praised as a queer idol, a hero for his bravery in coming out. Isaac knew Colton long before this bullshit. He wasn't heroic, and chances were he tried to throw someone else under the bus to salvage his reputation before being forced to embrace his homo status.

Every time someone praised Colton, congratulated him for his bravery, Isaac was reminded of every year he'd weathered the hatred of his peers by coming out in high school. No one offered him a medal, no one demanded Isaac speak at club events, no one made reels by the tens of thousands about him. Though, honestly, Isaac was grateful for that factor. Part of him empathized—as best he could—for Colton when the online baseball gay pitcher posts started up with everyone giving their opinion on the bi batter with a bad attitude.

"I just think his popularity is overrated and fizzling out," Isaac said, hoping his fellow GSA representatives would realize they were wasting their time on recruiting Colton as a member or a speaker. "He's not that special."

"Oh, but he's so hot," Mina whined.

"He really isn't," Isaac said too quickly, then went quiet to throw off suspicion.

"You know, normally, I don't go for that whole macho brute thing," Mina continued on her campaign to defend Colton's honor. "But last year, he fought two guys to protect the honor of a girl he was dating."

"Yeah…" Jazz cringed. "But he did put one in the hospital."

"So hot, I know," Mina swooned. "Total bi daddy gentleman vibes all the way. And I would let him go all the way and further."

"You know, they weren't actually dating," Isaac clarified because, of course, he had to drop the fact that he secretly knew everything about Colton. Everything he could learn without going stalker mode, at least. Okay, without going full-blown stalker mode. "Your Prince Uncharming was flirting with the girl when the other guys started hitting on her, too. It wasn't chivalry; it was caveman mentality."

"Not caveman—so dated."

"And sexist," Jazz added with a smirk, only intending to pile on to the Isaac-being-wrong stack, not actually out to make a point. She allowed Mina to take charge of the lecture during their walk.

"Colton's more of an alphahole," Mina said with a shudder of intoxication like the word itself boozed her up.

Isaac let out a scoff snort combo.

"And what the fuck is an alphahole?" he asked with a bitter edge in his voice as his mind swirled to a particular type of hole he might enjoy from a so-called alpha.

"OhMyGod," Mina blurted with unmatched enthusiasm, drawing the attention of others walking through the courtyard. "They are the epitome of baddie bossy boys. I mean, controlling, strong, aggressive, cunning, calculating, irritating, all wrapped up in the hottest fucking bods a girl could ask for. Well, anyone could ask for, really. We all wanna ride that alpha dick at one point or another."

"Not all of us," Jazz clarified, but Mina was too lost in her swooning to notice.

"So, they're just good-looking assholes?" Isaac tilted his head side-to-side because he could a appreciate a good-looking asshole—literally and personality-wise.

"No, hun. You're an asshole." Mina pointed a finger at him, nearly jabbing him with the sharp stiletto tip. "An alphahole is a completely different beast, emphasis on the beast. Especially in the sheets."

"I get no complaints."

"Of course not." Mina shrugged. "Who doesn't love an angry angsty power bottom twink who dresses edgy because it matches the color of his soul?"

Isaac rolled his eyes at Mina's dramatic flair when acting out her most emo boy impersonation before correcting herself from sad sack to grumpy goth. "Because you're not like other middle-class white boys with a darkness inside them."

"Upper middle-class," Isaac playfully corrected.

Mina nodded at that, continuing her best, intentionally worst, Isaac impersonation. "You're angry and filled with purpose. Rawr."

"He's filled with something all right," Jazz chuckled.

"Exactly!" Mina clapped her hands, dropping the impersonation and returning to her explanation. "An alphahole is a dom, an assertive daddy who knows how to make his baby purr."

"So, how are assholes and alphaholes different again?" Jazz asked, then winked at Isaac to remind him this was all playful banter.

Jazz had a tendency to emotionally check in on her friends, even discreetly, to make sure no conversation or topic steered too far. She hated hurt feelings and hated being the cause of upsetting someone, even unintentionally. When Isaac grinned, he knew it reassured her that he enjoyed the nonsense teasing.

"An asshole is a beta bitch boy posturing to be in charge to prove his anger is more than bluster." Mina gestured to Isaac as a grand example. "Sorry, Izzy. I don't make the rules, but you have masochistic hedonist sub written all over that pretty face."

"Well, as long as I don't have cum on my face, I guess it's an improvement."

Jazz and Mina burst into laughter, keeling over as they walked and dragging Isaac into the giggle fit himself. This was why he tolerated GSA. This was why he made time for his friends. They pulled him out of the darkness, the constant anger that consumed him, and helped him make fun of his own audacious rage.

Isaac didn't contest the bottom boy assumptions, preferring not to disclose his bedroom intimacy more than what anyone already knew based on the occasional two-in-the-morning hookup they'd see slink out of his dorm room.

Since Isaac's tastes steered exclusively toward jocky frat boys, most folks assumed his hookups used him for easy ass, which was the furthest thing from the truth. Isaac didn't sub for anyone ever, not since spending five months with his mouth practically glued to Colton's cock junior year. The idea of submitting, of serving someone else entirely, made Isaac queasy. He did his best to be a generous partner but always on his terms. His discretion, his control. He would never hand the reins over to another person. Not ever again.

Isaac was the furthest thing from a submissive beta boy. Hell, he usually broke those so-called alphahole guys in himself, finding eager and curious fellas on campus ready to serve. Though, given Mina's explanation, maybe he'd been fucking assholes in the asshole this entire time.

During the rest of the walk through the student courtyard, Isaac tried to subtly convince his friends that the GSA Club didn't need some random varsity baseball pitcher to improve their membership engagement.

CHAPTER 03
COLTON

COLTON checked his emails to find a politely composed message from the GSA Club inviting him to once again be a special speaker. Becoming the queer icon at Clinton University wasn't what he'd signed up for, especially as the freshman starting pitcher on the varsity baseball team. He wasn't the only open athlete—well, maybe he was at his college—but treading that line of being out and proud while still athletically conservative for the sake of an audience made Colton unsettled most days.

It didn't help the choice had fallen from his hands. Last year, he got a little too wild with his freedom, and his grades suffered. That probably had to do with all the parties and drinking and other hijinks the campus frowned upon. Like they didn't know it was all happening. But Colton never registered that just because they didn't write up every drinking incident or party didn't mean he had to flaunt his behavior everywhere he went.

That bad boy behavior nearly cost him everything when his hookups became more rampant, and a reporter got ahold of pictures of Colton getting a blowjob from another guy. There was no dodging that news headline, so Colton did the only thing he could think of at the time: he steered into the scandal and gave them a positive coming-out journey.

His mother always taught him it was best to lean into a story instead of running from it. However, his parents weren't fond of his experimental phase, as they put it—in regards to his open bisexuality and his baseball dreams. That was why it was important Colton maintained his sports scholarships. Yes, his parents could pay any tuition fees to any college in the world, but their assistance came with strings and requirements and expectations he'd gone his entire life trying to escape.

If he floundered at Clinton University, then his freedom, his dreams, would come to an end. He'd be tossed onto that pathway his father had been trying to drag him back onto since the day Colton got his acceptance letter.

Colton replied to the GSA email, agreeing to do another speech. He still had a lot of community service hours, and technically speaking, this extracurricular counted toward community outreach interventions. Plus, it was important for him to alibi himself for at least a few hours. Most of his time spent giving back to the community came from JV players presenting themselves as Colton and getting his form signed off at soup kitchens, shelters, donation centers, or wherever the hell folks went when trying to give back to the community due to obligations.

GSA didn't feel like an obligation for Colton. His newly found queer celebrity status wouldn't last forever, and admittedly, it'd spared him from the worst of his troubles last year. Being the iconic bi pitcher on social media had a few perks, which Colton leaned into in order to avoid expulsion for his stack of freshman antics. Since his parents wouldn't bail him out on this endeavor of independence and his trust fund didn't have nearly enough zeros to offer a proper apology to the university, Colton had to get craftier in order to force the disciplinary committee to show him leniency.

Colton had agreed to speak at the last GSA meeting before winter break, which had been scheduled for a Monday instead of their usual Wednesday evening gatherings since student attendance dropped fast once most turned in their semester finals. As Colton dragged himself from one class to the next, he regretted his decisions. Staying up late to drink with the team. Waiting until the literal last minute to study for his science final. Agreeing to go to the GSA on a Monday night when all he wanted to do after classes was curl up in his bed and play video games.

"Remember to email me a copy of your final essay as well," Professor Howard instructed as she wrapped up her last lecture for the semester.

Well, not her last lecture, but as if Colton would show up Wednesday or Friday for fun chitchat and extra learning opportunities. He had his essay, his cousin's foolproof essay, and he wanted to put this class behind him once and for all.

Seeing Isaac three days a week made for grueling reminders of Colton's guilt, and he hoped Isaac wouldn't be a TA in any of the Composition II courses. Even outside of class, it seemed like Isaac lurked around campus, always standing out from the crowd, always glaring at Colton. Maybe it seemed like Isaac prowled the campus grounds because of his haunting goth appearance, or maybe it had to do with the anchor of guilt that weighed on Colton's chest every time he saw the guy. He hoped by next semester, he'd stop having run-ins with Isaac and could finally move forward with his life.

"You sure you don't want any help on the essay?" Leon asked as if Colton would be foolish enough to accept his help.

"Got it covered." Colton beamed, leading the group of players out of the lecture hall and toward the dining building for an early lunch.

"Hey hey hey!" Tim shouted from the other end of the quad, bringing a slew of teammates with him as the baseball members funneled inside to discuss break and how hyped they were for the upcoming season.

"Howdy ho!" Tim slapped a hand on Colton and Leon's backs, shoving his way between the pair.

"Hey," Leon said, attempting to make a bit more room for himself as Tim's angled walk slowly pushed Leon against the wall.

"Ha! You're a hoe." Tim snorted, mocking the fact Leon responded to his earlier comment, one Colton had learned to avoid last year.

Tim was an acquired taste, given his love for terrible puns, dad jokes, and the worst kind of innuendoes. But he was a good guy. The fiery redhead with a loud mouth and unyielding smile had befriended Colton during his first month in college and stuck by him throughout everything.

He was also the first baseball team member to have Colton's back after his outing scandal hit. Tim's attitude never wavered. When Colton's bisexuality became literal front-page news on campus, Tim didn't hesitate in the locker room, afraid of Colton's supposedly lecherous gay gaze. Tim didn't back out of the on-campus apartment they'd decided to room together in after their freshman year—unlike their other teammate, who suddenly remembered his girlfriend wanted to get an off-campus place together. Tim never allowed Leon's slights and jabs to go unchallenged, always there to cut him off. Colton wished he had more classes with Tim, but unlike Colton, Tim didn't fail his courses their first year.

"Oh, my fucking god, dude, you would not believe..." Tim rambled on, slinging an arm over Colton's shoulder and dragging him away from Leon and his crew while the pair grabbed trays and talked about nonsense.

Tim and Colton chatted until they'd drawn a big enough crowd to fill their table and leave unwanted guests to sit elsewhere.

The rest of the day flew by, and before Colton realized it, he had arrived at the GSA meeting that evening, getting there early to beat the members. The meeting was held in one of the office club rooms above the student center. A collection of tables lined from one end of the room to the other formed a squarish circle for those in attendance. It seemed like way too much space considering the last time Colton arrived, there were maybe twenty people, including the GSA leadership, and these tables could easily hold fifty or more.

Up at the front of the room was a podium where Colton would stand during his little Q&A session. Currently, only the representatives of the GSA were here. The Pride president, Jazz Hendrex, rushed toward Colton, greeting him and introducing him to the other representatives. She was a small woman who wore a suit and tie, definitely bringing a more formal aesthetic to the meeting.

"Why hello there." Mina Robinson introduced herself, reminding Colton she was the vice president. Much to Colton's surprise, she boldly flirted with him, and while his mind lingered on allies being part of the club, he quickly remembered his own bi identity, which he and Mina clearly had in common. Maybe. The more she talked, the less he thought she was flirting, and the more he figured she just liked being the center of attention since she didn't let anyone get a word in edge-wise for the next five minutes.

"This is Will," Jazz finally interrupted Mina, pushing her aside and nodding to the next club representative.

"Club treasurer," he waved.

"Nice to meet you again." Colton gave Will a strained smile, trying not to make it obvious the two knew each other outside of the handful of GSA meetings he'd attended.

Colton had hooked up with the theatre twink several times last year. Though, after his outing, Colton kept a much lower profile—not that it did him any good since the world already knew.

"William Richard Cox." Will took a dramatic bow, showing off more flair than he ever had during their hookups. "It's like my parents were trying to fulfill a prophecy."

Colton cocked his head. "Huh?"

"Willy, Dick, Cock." Will shrugged nonchalantly.

"Oh." Colton blanched. "That's something for sure."

"Not that I'm complaining." Will winked, too suggestive, too obvious, so Colton averted his gaze back to Mina. "I can't get enough of any of them, but I just wish my folks weren't so on the nose with the gay jokes."

"Wait." Mina perked up at the comment. "Did they seriously name you that, knowing…you know?"

"They claim it's family name traditions, but like, it would've been less gay if they'd named me after my grandmothers."

"And this is Carlos," Jazz said, still laughing at Will's name origins but trying to usher through the meet and greet, likely wanting Colton to have an idea of who's who before the rest of the members arrived.

"Nice to see you again." Carlos extended a hand, which Colton shook.

Carlos was the biggest person here, built like a linebacker, but with a face that made him look like he still belonged in high school. The wispy mustache and goatee helped a bit, but he still looked very young. Carlos was trans masc and used he/they pronouns based on the signature from his most recent email invitation to GSA.

"Hope you had a chance to review the questions," Carlos said. "We'll try to keep the random musings to a minimum, but some folks will definitely have questions they didn't submit prior."

"Not a problem." Colton smiled, fake and bright like he'd used a thousand times before during pre- and post-game interviews.

"Gotta love our event strategist." Jazz squeezed Carlos' shoulders.

"And web coordinator," Carlos added. "And pretty much everything around here the rest of these slackers aren't clever enough to handle."

That got a lot of offended "hey!" from the group until a small laughter broke out.

Colton could almost see himself getting lost in this group, in this carefree dynamic. Baseball used to be like that for him until his junior year. Then it turned into a messy match of hiding who he was and staying one step ahead of his friends, his teammates, his competition. College ended up being more of the same, only once he was out, it turned into careful steps to remain on top while not appearing like he wanted to top any of his teammates. An easy enough thing since there were plenty of hot guys and gals elsewhere, but it didn't help when the rumor mill rotated, and he had to downplay his sexuality so others would be comfortable. So much of his time was spent making himself smaller so others felt content.

Colton spent more time putting out fires than he did enjoying the game he wanted to make his life. Here, though, in this silly room with this silly group, he wondered why he didn't carve out a bit more time for the GSA Club. In the few minutes since he'd arrived, he already felt he could breathe easy.

"Are we done rolling out the red carpet?" Isaac practically snarled, his icy stare shooting daggers at Colton and reminding the jock why the GSA Club wouldn't work as a sanctuary for him to relax.

This place, this organization, belonged to Isaac, and Colton wouldn't push to take it from him. He didn't deserve it; he knew that.

"And here is our surly secretary." Carlos gestured to Isaac, who stayed seated and simply scowled. "He's an acquired taste."

"Oh, I know," Colton blurted before he realized, and suddenly, everyone's eyes fell onto him.

"That's right," Jazz said. "You're from the same hometown, right? So wild."

"Wait, really?" Mina asked wide-eyed. "I thought y'all just had class together."

They didn't have any classes together since Colton had failed most of his freshman year and was spending his second year retaking the basics, while Isaac had graduated a year early from high school, which put him in his third year of college courses.

"No, they're from… Oh, what's the name?" Jazz snapped her fingers as if the click would trigger her memory. "It's funny and fucked up and flipping ironic. What is it?"

"Straight Arrow," Colton and Isaac said nearly in unison, even their beleaguered sigh for the horrible town name.

Everyone burst into laughter.

"So, you both left the town of hetero roadmaps," Mina said while wheezing, "so you could attend the literal university of clit, and then both decided to be into guys instead?"

"I was into guys while I lived in Shitstain Arrow," Isaac hissed, cutting his gaze to Colton.

"And I'm planning on majoring in clit with a minor in dudes," Colton said with a chuckle to lighten the mood again.

While the name rang through with the same humor as their college, Colton and Isaac both understood there was no joy to be found in Straight Arrow. A tiny conservative town with residents who had enough money to make the world a better place, but instead, they banded together to isolate themselves and uphold values meant to diminish anyone who dared to be different. Colton and Isaac attended a private school that cost more a semester than a Clinton University degree. Each of them should've been enrolled at an Ivy League, following their family's designated path, but they cut their strings instead.

Well, Isaac had cut his if the rumors were true. Supposedly, he'd surrendered his trust fund and forged his own path. Colton hadn't been nearly as bold. He kept his money, his family, his life for the most part, but he'd been forced to make certain sacrifices to follow his dream. He couldn't fathom how Isaac walked away from his family without so much as glancing back once. Not for his parents. Not for his siblings. Not for anyone or anything in the town of Straight Arrow.

Okay, Colton had some ideas. He knew what he did played a role in Isaac's vanishing act. He knew his cruelty made it that much easier for Isaac to sever the bonds of family and abandon his life in Straight Arrow.

"We're hoping you'll go over your coming out story again," Carlos said, steering the discussion back to the meeting ahead. "I'm sure you're a little tired of discussing it again and again, but I was thinking maybe you could elaborate less on when you came out and more on how life is settling in since you took this bold step."

"Bold step?" Colton knew the answer but still found himself asking.

Carlos politely explained—the same way everyone did—how his role as a star athlete put him in a unique position. Basically, everyone wanted to believe anyone could be themselves and whoever they wanted and that the journey would be easy.

It wasn't easy, though. Since coming out, Colton had to watch his back more times than he could count. He had to let bridges of so-called friendships burn so he could forge ahead. He had to ignore cutting comments and slurs—when it'd be so much easier to knock someone on their asses. That last part had more to do with his long-standing track record of violence and the fact the disciplinary committee wouldn't tolerate any more of his physical outbursts.

"I can share the story," Colton said. "It definitely wasn't an easy choice coming forward and coming out, but there's been a lot of cool stuff since then."

"You make it sound like you planned the press conference." Isaac scoffed, seething at how everyone fawned over Colton's story, Colton's bravery. The rage was easy for Colton to identify, even without Isaac's elaboration, but he could feel more heated words on the verge of spilling. "Here, I thought you only came out because you got caught shoving your dick down some dude's throat. Not quite the heroic retelling everyone is prancing on about."

Will coughed outlandish at that, followed by Mina and Carlos. Only Jazz remained silent during Isaac's bitch fit.

Colton blushed, face burning hot. "Um, well, yeah… Ugh, there's a lot of moving components which all, um, played a role in the decision making behind my decision making for the important decision, but um…"

"Ignore him," Mina said, wrapping an arm around Colton's and escorting him past Isaac and to the front of the meeting room. "He's a sassy bitch, but he means neutral."

Colton quirked a brow in confusion. "Do you mean well? As in, he means well?"

"Oh, God no," Mina continued. "Isaac's a cunt bag for sure and never means anyone well. Neutral for the most part, ill will to all the bigots of the world, anyone who annoys him, and probably the children. Maybe that last bit is just me. But they're messy and loud. Disgusting. What about you? How do you feel about kids?"

And like that, Mina had washed away the tension between Isaac and Colton and dragged the jock down a rabbit hole of a dozen different questions, leading the conversation in more directions than he could keep up. His perplexed stare and slow blinks didn't seem to deter Mina as she laughed at her own comments and continued pushing more random topics.

Everyone chatted until the rest of the GSA members arrived, and Colton did his best to not look in Isaac's direction, feeling his icy stare the entire time. Colton couldn't have this life, this club, but he could do his best to enjoy the evening and make room for a few nice memories of what life could've been like if he'd made better choices.

CHAPTER 04

ISAAC

ISAAC drowned out Colton's grating voice by focusing on the stack of essays he needed to get through. Professor Howard had been kind enough to place Colton's essay among the set Isaac had to grade. She didn't need the story or want it, but she did spiteful as well as the next person and made room for Isaac's vindictive nature so long as he didn't cross the line. Hell hath no fury like a scorned woman who understood the need for petty vengeance and justified suffering.

Screwing with Colton in the form of grading him too severely wasn't much in terms of revenge, but it helped make the semester more bearable for Isaac. If he had to endure the absolute worst person in the world, then at least he could make Colton's life miserable, too.

"...and admittedly, last year got away from me," Colton said with a boyish chuckle, the kind that made everyone in the room join in for a laugh, too. "But it was a learning experience for sure. That's why I've tried putting my best foot forward this year."

Isaac scoffed. As if Colton had ever made a genuine effort with his academics. He used to threaten Isaac in middle school to help him on assignments, or he'd kick his ass. It was more of the same in high school, using his alpha meathead ego to knock Isaac around while simultaneously keeping the creepy goth kid close to him. With a purpose, of course. The threats of kicking Isaac's ass eventually shifted to promises to pound it instead.

They'd never gotten past oral before Colton broke things off. Maybe Isaac had broken them off. It was difficult to know for sure who officially ended the arrangement, only that after what Colton did, Isaac never wanted him back.

"Let me just say that while you're searching for yourself, don't let your grades slip," Colton said, reluctantly drawing Isaac's attention. "Trust me, it's an exhausting mountain to climb when you find yourself on academic probation."

Colton's grades suffered because he was lazy and used to other people handling his work. People like Isaac. And while keeping Colton's semester grade at a C- offered Isaac pleasure, he knew in the end he'd have to let Colton pass and maintain his academic standing. It was satisfying watching Colton squirm in class, always so frustrated by the red ink Isaac covered his papers in but unable to argue the need for improvement.

But Isaac didn't have any intention of pushing to fail Colton; he knew if the guy appealed it with the academic panel, they'd question the lower curve Isaac had thrown on his scores. Isaac didn't need to lose his TA position or any of his grant money for misconduct, but he deserved to get a bit of revenge, all things considered.

Since drowning out Colton seemed utterly impossible, Isaac decided to take a look at the jock's final essay. Hope that he'd turn in something dreadful quickly washed away when he spotted how clean and composed the introduction paragraph was written.

"Impossible," Isaac muttered, biting his pen and retrieving his laptop.

No way, absolutely no way possible, could Colton write such a well-crafted essay. It had to be plagiarized. He went to Howard's digital classroom and grabbed Colton's emailed essay to run through a plagiarism checker all the professors utilized.

Nothing. Not a goddamn thing aside from the standard ten percent of quoted materials, which didn't count since Colton had cited them all correctly. Well, all except for two. They were even in a different font from the others.

It was like Colton had grabbed a good essay and added a few last-minute touches to prove he used relevant on-campus sources in his evidence. The other sources seemed dated yet familiar.

"Reflecting on last year, how do you feel being out now versus when your story first broke?" a GSA member asked. "Obviously, the choice was taken from you, but now that you have time to reflect on it, do you feel better being yourself?"

"Whoa, that's a hard one." Colton braced against the podium like he might end up swept away by a tornado. "That's what she said."

The silly joke brought cheap laughs and gave Colton a minute to compose his response.

"Being outed is definitely not the way I wanted to come out, but then again, I never really planned on coming out," Colton explained, a sad half smile on his face while he pondered his next words. "It forced me to really reflect on the type of person I was before being honest with myself and the world. I look back on the jerk I was and cringe."

Colton paused at that, a playful expression to show how much he hated looking back at his brutish former self. Isaac hated who Colton used to be, too. Hated him with a passion.

"But every misstep got me to this point, and my hope is now that I'm here and queer," Colton said with a laugh that brought out more laughter from the audience. "My hope is that I can start taking the right steps, that I can continue growing and help others grow into themselves whenever they're ready."

Isaac tsked while all the GSA members swooned for Colton's bravery like tragic little sycophants hoping to carve their way into the jock's life.

Isaac couldn't help but wonder how much respect folks would lose if they knew the truth about Colton. Oh yeah, tons of heteronormative queers were pricks and bullies before they finally came out of the closet, but Colton took things to a whole other level.

If they knew what Colton had done to Isaac back in high school, would they still clamor over his every word? Or would they even care? What was in the past was in the past, after all. And Isaac knew all too well how no one at his school had cared what happened; no one in his town, not even his family, offered more than backhanded pity.

Everyone blamed Isaac, accused him of acting out and buying into the obvious lies he'd done this for attention. It was easier than supporting him.

Isaac rolled his eyes up to the ceiling to fight back the tears as the horrifying memory surfaced. It took work to keep himself composed on the outside as he fought a battle with his mind.

Isaac had hated Colton for years. He'd spent most of his youth being teased by Colton and his friends. Then, when everyone found out Isaac was gay, the teasing turned into hateful bullying. Colton was the worst about it until junior year. Something in Colton changed, but not really. Colton followed Isaac on his walk home so closely that Isaac was convinced Colton planned to jump him when he cut through the woods.

Colton had stalked closer, shoved Isaac against a tree, and went to kiss him. It was the most startling *almost* in Isaac's life. Colton couldn't bring his lips to meet Isaac's; instead, he'd buried his face in the crook of Isaac's neck and grinded against him.

"You like this, don't you?" Colton panted and pressed his body harder, rippling muscles working Isaac over as the hard bark of a tree clawed at his back. "You want me?"

Isaac nodded, unable to speak.

When Colton whipped out his dick, Isaac didn't even hesitate. He started stroking the jock immediately.

"On your fucking knees." Colton's firm hand pushed down on Isaac's shoulder, and he obediently dropped down.

He'd never done anything with anyone up until that point, but he sucked Colton off until he shot his load in Isaac's mouth.

Isaac could still recall how it felt to choke on Colton's cock. Day after day, he serviced him, talked with him briefly before and after, and in some foolish idiocy, Isaac convinced himself there was something between them. The only thing between Isaac and Colton was cum. Colton's cum to be clear. He wanted a mouth to use and a throat to abuse, and Isaac willingly took his dick day after day for the better part of the school year without complaint or expectations.

Isaac refused to see this arrangement for what it was, refused to believe he was just an easy lay meant to suck the star pitcher's cock when it was convenient for Colton.

At the time, Isaac hadn't realized how much happier he appeared even when being used as a personal cum dumpster for the guy he liked, by the bully who had a secret soft spot for him. It blinded Isaac to the threats and dangers surrounding him.

At a young age, Isaac had learned to be hyper-aware of the dangers other people presented. Years of taunting, teasing, harassing, mockery, and assault had taught Isaac to always stay vigilant. Colton had washed away those securities. Colton's cock had left Isaac drunk on lust and lost in fantasies of what might be. What would never be.

When Colton invited Isaac into the custodian closet during school, Isaac prepared for another brutal face fucking, eagerly hoping this would be the one that led to something more. This would be the one where Colton finally kissed him afterward. Maybe this would be the one that made Colton realize he wanted more than a secret relationship; maybe he'd finally see Isaac as someone worth showing off and coming out for. Isaac knew he was a delusional fool for such fantasies, but they kept him happy every time he dropped to his knees to take Colton's cock.

There was no blowjob that day, though. Colton craved something more. Alone in the closet away from the world, Colton caressed Isaac in a way he rarely did, in a way that sparked Isaac's desires until all logic fell away. When Colton demanded Isaac strip, he obeyed, standing stark naked and ready to please Colton in any way he could. After five months, Isaac believed they were going to finally take the next step. But it wasn't pleasure Colton craved—it was control, humiliation, and destruction.

The closet door whipped open, and the cameras flashed. Isaac's entire body erupted in icy goosebumps and burning embarrassment, his stomach churning somersaults. More jocks than Isaac could count rushed into the closet, calling Isaac slurs and smacking him with belts and towels and even their fists. It was brutal and bloody, and most of the memory during those awful ten minutes of physical torment only came back as searing flashes. Isaac didn't wanna remember the sounds of their laughs, the wicked smiles on their faces, the loud tears he cried as they kept pelting him, kept striking him, kept demanding he beg.

When a few jocks grabbed his arms and yanked him out of the closet, Isaac froze. Part of him was terrified, but another part was relieved to be freed from the closet before they could hurt him more. He stood naked in the hallway, lost in the taunting words, the booming laughter, the cutting remarks, and the flashes. They were still taking pictures.

Isaac fled. Lost in a blur of tears and hyperventilating, he nearly collapsed in the crowded hallway as he bolted to the office. Of course, the jocks had timed the humiliation right as the second bell of the morning went off.

When the time came to answer questions, Isaac revealed everything. Well, not everything. He said Colton had lured him into the custodian's closet, but not how he'd done it. Despite all the hate he held for Colton now, back then, a secret part of him still yearned to keep Colton's secret. A part of him clung to the sad, broken expression Colton made in the closet while his teammates beat Isaac relentlessly.

No one believed Isaac's story. No one wanted to believe their star golden boy would do something so awful. No one wanted to believe the best athletes in a decade had hazed Isaac. Colton's story of the team in the weight room went unchallenged. Even their coach backed up the tale, not an ounce of hesitation when he entered the dean's office with Isaac and his parents and confirmed he saw all the athletes working out. He even gave a bullshit story on how he took a mental headcount of everyone there.

Oh, how furious Isaac's parents were at that statement. Not with the school. With Isaac. No matter what happened, his perverse desires led him down this path in some way, or so his mother muttered passive aggressively for the days that followed Isaac's 'incident.' If Isaac just didn't need to parade himself around, this would've never happened. His father was more convinced Isaac was pulling some political queer stunt than he was about Isaac being lured into the custodian closet by the star pitcher.

BEND HIM BREAK HIM

The pictures had disappeared from the jocks' phones—but a few nudes they'd taken still floated around Snapchat and group chats and DMs. Isaac knew those were the pictures the jocks had taken, the angles perfectly aligned with the custodian closet he'd been thrown out of. But the administration claimed anyone could've taken those pictures since Isaac ran naked through the hallways.

Isaac knew, though. Isaac knew the truth. But Isaac didn't know why Colton did it. He didn't know why Colton betrayed him, abandoned him to the wolves, and broke him in front of everyone.

Every part of Isaac wanted to die. He hated being around people, he hated being by himself, and he hated every waking moment of his life up until winter break when he used the isolation of the holiday to plan an escape. Running away from his problems would get him nowhere. That'd been a lesson he learned while naked in the halls of his school. Fleeing only delayed the pain. No, Isaac didn't want to run from his problems; he wanted to run toward his solution.

From freshman year, he'd taken extra classes and maintained a high GPA while performing extracurricular activities, hoping to have the best senior application in his school district. He hoped his junior year marks would be enough to stand out when he decided to graduate early and apply to colleges.

It worked. Isaac got accepted to the University of Clinton, packed up everything he could fit in the '76 station wagon he bought off some elderly woman online, and drove to college. He'd never turned back. Isaac didn't come home, didn't call his parents, didn't message his siblings, didn't miss his family. He simply disappeared from their lives, and they seemed okay with it. No animosity either way. Just silence met with surrender. They cut off his trust fund and pretended he didn't exist.

Isaac had spent his childhood too vocal about science, too bold about politics, and too proud of his homosexuality. While his family tolerated him, they didn't accept him, so when he finally cut that cord, he realized they'd already severed the thread from their end, too. No bridge to mend, so he let it burn and focused on finding a new life on his own.

"Thank you again for sharing your story," Jazz said, reeling Isaac from his memories as she led the applause that everyone quickly joined in on. Everyone except for Isaac, who glared at Colton's smiling face as the jock basked in the flattery of the audience.

Isaac hated Colton so much and hated the pedestal of Pride they threw him on. Yes, everyone deserved to come out on their own terms, their own time, but bigots didn't deserve to be praised for finally owning up to the sexuality others around them were brave enough to accept before them.

It wasn't fair.

But Isaac remembered nothing in his life had ever been fair. He cut out of the meeting early without a single word and went back to his dorm to finish grading papers. Mostly, he wanted to inspect Colton's paper more.

If it was really plagiarized, then Colton would be automatically failed from his Comp course. If he tanked this class, he'd be in violation of his academic probation. If he violated his probation, he'd be kicked out of the university. And if he was kicked out, Isaac could finally breathe easy again without the constant reminders of the man he loved to hate and hated to love.

Knowing Colton cheated was easy, proving it took more work, but Isaac had spite to motivate him, hate to fuel him, and a vindictive mind to help him search for answers. He worked tirelessly through the night until he found the answers he was looking for and could easily out Colton's actions. He just couldn't decide how he wanted to go about it. Destroying Colton required a level of savoring. Isaac would only get to play this hand once before he ignited Colton's world, so he wanted to make sure he had the right seats to enjoy the flames.

Isaac composed a very formal email to Colton, requesting he meet him in the auditorium tomorrow evening. What better way to destroy Colton's life than by presenting a farewell lecture he'd be forced to finally pay attention to?

CHAPTER 05
COLTON

COLTON arrived at the English building and swiped his card to get in with no luck. Of course, the building had timed access to ensure whoever wanted inside couldn't just waltz in whenever. He went to respond to Isaac's email, the one requesting his presence, the curt message that'd made Colton's stomach twist with curious and confused knots. When a small group of students exited out of the automatic handicap door, Colton tucked away his phone and slipped inside unseen. He made his way through empty hallways and toward the auditorium.

It was an unsettling feeling, being summoned by Isaac to meet so late. Colton's mind couldn't help but pop with ideas, believing perhaps an olive branch was going to be extended. Perhaps something would be extended. While he was certain Isaac hated him beyond measure, Colton's ego grew along with another part of him, believing this might be Isaac's attempt to bury the animosity between them. And yes, there was so much hatred after everything that went down before the winter formal. But it'd been three years.

Maybe Isaac had finally moved beyond what happened in high school. Maybe Isaac listened to Colton's speech during the GSA meeting, and it roused some feelings, reminded him what they had, what they could have.

The last time Colton attended the club meeting, Isaac stormed out for an indefinite smoke break. This time, he stayed close, even if he pretended to grade papers while Colton shared his coming out experience. Colton often assumed the best because no matter what hurdles he was thrown, most situations worked out in his favor, so it was difficult for him not to assume.

Besides, this definitely wasn't a standard meeting. He would've gone to an office, not a classroom. He would've gone during office hours, not on the cusp of night, and if it was course-related, Professor Howard would've set the meeting, not her grumpy goth TA.

Alarm bells never really rang for Colton, always considering himself too strong for any potential threats, so while he strolled up to the auditorium doors, he shrugged off the sketchy vibes crawling on his skin. Instead, he favored the intrigue of possibility. After all, Isaac hadn't directly spoken to him without hurling a backhanded insult on classroom etiquette since he started college. Part of him always missed Isaac, missed what they had before he screwed things up. Now that they'd escaped the tiny conservative town of Straight Arrow, perhaps they could pick up where they left off, explore each other the same way they used to. Isaac used to love servicing Colton, and he missed that absolute authority.

The *possibly* idea was easy to circulate, thanks to the drinks he'd had prior to this meeting. A little liquid encouragement because while Colton often remained optimistic for the best outcome, Isaac had certainly changed. Besides, his roommate Tim was throwing a party, and there was no way he'd slip out without having a few shots beforehand. If he tried, Tim would've asked him a thousand and one questions. Colton didn't exactly have any answers to tonight's whatever this was…he simply had his own questions.

Isaac had gotten creepier since they parted, since he got into college, so Colton ignored the flair for mystique and wondered if Isaac missed the fun they used to have together. Wondered if Isaac could wash away the sour past between them.

Isaac stood in his usual spot, off to the side of the main desk and podium where their instructor set up. "You came."

"I often do." Colton smirked, gauging how flirty to make his face based on Isaac's reaction.

No stern scowl, but also no half smile. It was neutral, but Colton could work with neutral; it was already an improvement to the daggers Isaac usually shot.

Isaac focused on his laptop, retrieving a controller, and turned on the projection screen. He worked silently, not seeming to pay Colton much mind, despite having called him to the auditorium at this hour.

Since this wasn't class, Isaac didn't wear his standard gothy casual suit-style outfit. Instead, he had on short sleeves that exposed his arms. His left arm was bare, aside from the butterfly tattoo on his hand and the finger tattoos. But his right arm had an exquisite sleeve tattoo that Colton had never seen before.

A wilted black rose was inked on the inside of his forearm while vibrantly colorful petals fluttered around like they were caught in a breeze. Colton didn't know much about the countless queer flags, but he recognized the bi flag, the trans flag, and maybe the lesbian one too. The president of the GSA wore a similarly colored pendant during the meetings Colton rarely attended. It seemed Isaac had tried to get every possible queer flag as a rose petal.

Above his wrist, which Isaac kept covered with dangling mesh stockings, was a barbwire tattoo serving as the roots of the black rose. A quote was etched in the inked blood dripping from the sharp spikes: 'Learn to Thrive Without the Roots.' Poetic and morbid and a little fascinating.

"You know, you're lucky I'm resourceful," Colton said, unable to bear the silence much longer and hoping to ease the tension with some humor. "You realize the building's locked, right?"

"Oh, yeah." Isaac continued clicking away at his computer. "Resourceful. Hmmm. That's one way to put it."

This was as awkward as the very first time Colton flirted with Isaac, doing his best to remain subtle about his interests while blunt about his desires. No, this was much harder. Isaac hated Colton now—and for good reason. Before, despite all the years of bullying, Isaac hadn't hated Colton, merely loathed the jock. Colton knew that and managed to wedge himself into Isaac's thoughts.

He began to think the same scenario hadn't occurred a second time.

"Why'd you call me here?"

"I summoned you so that I could personally congratulate you on such an amazing essay." Isaac tapped a button on his laptop and pulled up Colton's final exam.

His stomach dropped, immediately nervous but curious about the minimal red markings.

"It was so spectacular," Isaac said with a big smile, a phony smile.

It was scary, the way Isaac locked his eyes onto Colton, the way his teeth filled his face, the way the light from above cast shadows on his features and added a glint to the many piercings on Isaac's face.

"So spectacular, in fact, I just knew it couldn't be yours." Isaac nodded affirmatively. "What does one do when they suspect cheating? Well, they search the web for lifted materials, they run the text through AI analysis software, they do all the things to check off their list of copied work."

"It's not plagiarized."

"Really?" Isaac scratched his chin like he was deep in thought.

Colton suspected Isaac was, in fact, not thinking deeply.

"One might think that, especially if they looked as thoroughly as I did and came up with nothing," Isaac continued. "But there was something off about it. None of the words matched your style remotely. Your prose is sloppy but decent. This was too eloquent, yet also tastefully watered down in sections, almost intentionally simplifying itself to go undetected."

Colton only understood about half of what Isaac said at this point.

"It was also very familiar in this gnawing sort of way." Isaac tapped a button and pulled up a digital copy of the original essay.

Colton scrunched his face. How did Isaac have the essay Colton's cousin had turned in?

"Now, I don't have the original," Isaac explained. "But I bet if I called good ole Ms. Farmer, she probably still has it filed away somewhere. She used to horde student projects to keep siblings from recycling each other's work. Or, in your case, cousin's work."

"How did you…" Colton stared at the giant screen of the two essays side by side, not requiring Isaac to scroll through them. He'd only added a few new quotes so he could include on-campus resources, which he mostly fudged to begin with.

"Who do you think did the essay to begin with?"

"What?" Colton stared wide-eyed.

"It can't be a surprise," Isaac said. "I used to do your work all the time. Granted, the only thing I got in exchange was a dick down my throat, but most of my clientele offered pretty nice payments for a solid B paper."

"It wasn't really plagiarizing. It's not like I stole it from some published work," Colton said, mostly reassuring himself.

Isaac pulled up a new screen to display a few of the academic guidelines and definitions in the student handbook.

Plagiarism, in its most basic form, was an act of theft without providing proper credit for someone else's ideas or work. Using his cousin's words—his cousin's paper—was the same as looking at someone else's test and writing down their answers.

"I have a friend who is part of the student disciplinary panel." Isaac tsked and shook his head. "They say you're quite the troublemaker, always just barely escaping the chopping block."

Fear washed over Colton, making his body warm and queasy while a cold wave of terror trailed along his skin, giving him goosebumps.

"Fighting, drinking, academic dishonesty." Isaac clicked through his slideshow, letting the words pop up in bold bubble letters. "Quite the list it took to land on academic probation. Hell, half of this alone would get most students suspended."

"It's not what…" Colton struggled to speak, to defend himself, to argue against the truths Isaac gleefully hurled.

"But plagiarizing in Professor Howard's course will not be swept away. The woman's a force of nature and doesn't let athletes—or anyone, quite frankly—walk over the academic integrity of her department."

Colton couldn't move, couldn't think, could barely fathom the basic function of breathing as dread seemed to close his throat.

"Even if the school doesn't enforce the expulsion policy because of the plagiarism, Professor Howard will enforce the automatic zero and write up for it. This is the final exam. It's your whole fucking grade, which means you'll fail this class."

Colton didn't need the explanation, understanding his situation all too well, but he suspected Isaac took some sadistic pleasure in beating Colton over the head with the details.

"That breaks the rules on your academic probation." Isaac began counting off on his fingers. "Not eligible to play sports ball games, GPA too low for academic standing, and the grace period on your probation running short means you'll be kicked out for that."

"You're just gonna destroy my whole life, and for what?"

"For what?" Isaac nearly ran up on Colton, stopping short of slamming into the jock. "Don't you dare turn me into the villain of this story. This isn't villainy. This is justified. You're the fucking criminal who broke me, ruined me, humiliated me, and got away with it."

"I'm… I'm…" Colton choked on his apology as he had a thousand times before when rehearsing it. "What happened was awful, but you came back stronger. If you do this, it'll destroy my chances at any school. You don't just walk off an expulsion."

"You think I just walked off what you and your buddies did?" Isaac glared. "You think I had a little therapy and talked about my feelings and got over the fact I was stripped and beaten and thrown out naked for the school to see?"

"No, I didn't mean—"

"You think I just walked off the idea of my first lo…crush, lustful whatever, dude I was sucking off's betrayal?" Isaac tilted his head, locking his icy blue eyes onto Colton's. "That fucked my head beyond repair. I don't do relationships—not even many hookups—because all I think about is how you took my trust and spit it back into my face, how you shattered my fucking identity so a couple of homophobes could have a laugh at my expense."

Colton remained silent as Isaac's speech turned more into profane comments than a list of all the horrors he endured.

"What do you want?" Colton asked, voice cracking and eyes glossy. There had to be something he could offer, something Isaac craved more than his suffering. After all, he brought him here.

"Personally, I would love to slit your fucking throat, but I'll settle for burning your future to the ground."

Colton took a deep breath, biting back the building fury inside him. Isaac's nonchalant and brutal sarcasm wasn't helping to keep him in check. In this instance, Colton was as angry as he was frightened, and when he found himself feeling this way, it usually helped to punch something…or someone.

It quickly occurred to Colton that Isaac intended to use this as blackmail. He hadn't disclosed that part yet, but it was obvious enough.

"Besides ruining me, what do you want?"

"Want? I want to see you broken." Isaac grinned. "That's all I've ever wanted."

Colton's nostrils flared, and the building tears illuminated the fury in his green eyes.

"There it is," Isaac said with this sadistic smugness, a voice which grated on Colton's ears. "The fractured realization of defeat. The entitled ego still desperately searching for an answer. But I broke you. I broke the arrogant alphahole who thinks he runs everything just because—"

"You wanna see something broken?" Colton bolted toward Isaac and went to punch him.

But then Isaac did the impossible; he weaved around Colton, caught his arm, and hurled him over his shoulder.

Colton stared at the ceiling in bewilderment. The shine of the lights bearing down stung his eyes, but Isaac's head helped block the inferno of brightness when he leaned over.

"I'm not the punching bag you and your friends had in high school," Isaac explained. "If you think I'll just take an ass kicking like back then, you're even dumber than I thought."

Colton swallowed his rage and sat up. "You can't do this."

"Really?" Isaac posed, practically prancing back to the podium. "Pretty sure I can. Pretty sure I did."

"You sent it already?" Colton asked, unable to hide the quiver in his voice as he scrambled to his feet.

"All in good time." Isaac grinned. "It's not like I can barge into Howard's office and demand she meet me now. I planned on telling her in person—better than an email—but I also know how to cover my bases."

Colton still had a chance. A chance to stop this. He couldn't grasp why Isaac would confront him, though. It was foolish and arrogant and cocky in a way Isaac professed to be so above.

"Why bring me here? If not to blackmail me, what the hell do you have to gain by confronting me?"

"Blackmail you?" Isaac chuckled. "How retro."

"Why bring me here?" Colton asked again. He wanted to add the risk Isaac took in doing so, but he'd realized the skinny guy did a lot better defending himself now than he ever had before.

"I thought about waiting, lighting the match and savoring the look of defeat on your face after the fire burned down your life." Isaac slinked toward Colton again, a serpent's gaze as he circled the jock. "Then I thought how delectable it would be to show you the matchstick before I ignited everything. To watch you scramble and struggle and try to blow out the fire to no avail."

"You're a fucking psycho."

"How would you know?" Isaac gestured dramatically, wiggling his fingers with flair. The black polish glistened under the lights and swift movement. "It's not like you paid attention in your Psych 101 course. I can almost guarantee you cheated your way through that one, too."

Colton's face burned, the shame of Isaac's spot-on accuracy. He'd never done well in classes, struggling a bit more every single year. The more his athleticism improved, the worse his academic performance became.

By the time he reached freshman year and made the varsity team of three sports, he'd learned charm and confidence were the only things he needed to pass a class. Either he would sweet talk a teacher into altering a score, find an eager 'friend' willing to help him study by which they'd finish the work, or complain to a coach until they put a bit of school spirit weight on the back of the reluctant teacher's neck. In any case, that was really the only thing Colton ever had to learn in high school.

"You're a lazy, entitled, hot-headed, smug piece of shit," Isaac said. "You get all the accolades. Brave queer athlete. Trailblazer. The world wouldn't think you were so amazing if they knew how awful you were while hiding in the closet."

"If you do this, I will fucking kill you."

"There it is." Isaac's expression turned chaotic, inviting Colton's ruthlessness.

Colton would deliver it, too, but he wouldn't be swept into another basic defensive counter by Isaac. He rushed forward, snatching Isaac by his shirt. The necklaces around Isaac's neck clicked against each other, and the patter of his heart skipped a beat from the jolt of Colton's actions.

"I will make you suffer." Colton pulled back a fist. "I will beat you until—"

"Please." Isaac fumed, hands gripping Colton's wrists tightly like he was ready to snap them.

There was no fear in his expression or his voice. There was only an invitation, he wanted Colton to swing, and it took everything in Colton to pause and think. If he struck Isaac, it wouldn't solve anything. Colton knew he'd only further play into Isaac's hand.

"You think after everything you did to me in high school, death scares me?" Isaac leaned in closer to Colton's face, his breath pressed against Colton's lips as only an inch of space divided them. "Do your fucking worst. I have my emails scheduled and ready to bomb your life the same way you ruined mine."

Colton's anger fractured, and he knew Isaac saw the look of devastation that swept across his face. He released Isaac, eyes flitting down to the baggy mesh sleeves held in place by the spiked bracelets. Isaac obviously didn't want to explain his scars to anyone on campus, so he'd turned them into a fashion statement most folks never suspected. Colton knew about them, though, knew about them like everyone else in Isaac's hometown. He knew the lengths Isaac had taken to escape the pain Colton had caused, had allowed.

The care and concern on Colton's face must've confused Isaac because his rage dissipated, and he shoved the jock away from him. Colton didn't apologize because that would be selfish. He'd already spent too many years being selfish at Isaac's expense. The way he bullied and beat Isaac for years. The way he used Isaac for months to get off with his own curiosities. Colton suspected that maybe he deserved this, deserved the hate and judgment and punishment, but he wasn't ready to surrender the life he'd spent his entire life clawing at.

Colton sacrificed all his personal freedoms to train and become the best; he'd put his life on hold for years just so he could build a life outside his parents' vision. Would it really all come to an end here and now?

"Must be hard knowing there's nothing you can do to stop this from happening." Isaac's expression of twisted delight had washed away, replaced by this vacant contemplation. "Imagine, fighting against that all-consuming sinking dread, yet knowing nothing you do will stop it. You're gonna drown. No one is gonna care. The golden boy charm and arrogant attitude won't get you out of this one."

Colton tried to speak, tried to beg, tried to think of something—anything—he could say, but the words remained stuck in his throat.

"Enjoy your last week before winter break." Isaac turned on his heel and headed for the doors. "I suspect they'll have you booted before the kickoff of spring semester."

Colton stood frozen, thinking of what he could offer, what he could do. Beating Isaac wouldn't get rid of the evidence. Pleading with his humanity wouldn't work either. Colton

"Damn." Isaac smacked his forehead. "Y'all don't kick in baseball, do you? That pun would've been better when you still played football."

Colton huffed because while there was a kicker in football, it wasn't Colton's position. Isaac had paid so much attention to Colton's schedule their junior year, attending all his sporting events from game nights to practices, all so he could discreetly service Colton afterward. Still, he never learned a goddamn thing about the games, sitting in the stands and sulking like the weird gothy gay guy he was.

"Wait." Colton chased Isaac into the empty hallway. "There has to be something you want."

"Nothing, dude." Isaac practically floated, appearing so much taller as Colton hunched, the defeat finally registering.

"Everyone wants something," Colton continued, unrelenting because it couldn't end this way. "Tell me what I have to do."

"Oh, suck my dick, prick." Isaac snatched his arm away. "There's not a goddamn thing I want from you. And if you touch me again, I will break that fucking arm."

"Fine, I understand." Colton nodded, finally grasping what he had to offer, a way out, a humiliation he didn't dwell on for very long before accepting this as his best chance. "I will."

"Thank you," Isaac said with heavy emphasis and complete sarcasm as he strutted away. "Finally, taking a hint."

"No. I'll do it." Colton jerked Isaac's shoulder and shoved him against the wall.

"Motherfucker." Isaac grabbed Colton's wrist and twisted. "What did I just say?"

Colton ground his teeth, fighting back a shout and keeping his gaze on Isaac's calm blue eyes. There was no malice in his violence, just a measure of protection.

"I said I'll do it," Colton said through gritted teeth. "I'll give you what you want."

"What I want?" Isaac scoffed. "I already told you I don't want anything."

"Yes, you do."

"The only thing I want is to see you lose, see you suffer, see you fall to your knees in defeat." Isaac twisted Colton's wrist harder while also moving his foot between Colton's legs and wrapping his heel behind Colton's leg in preparation to sweep the jock off his feet. He could feel the pressure, physical and emotional.

"I'll give you what you really want." Colton embraced the throbbing pain in his arm, he accepted the weight of crushing defeat pressed against his lungs. It helped him accept what came next. "I'll do it. Here and now if that's what it takes."

"Do what?"

"Suck your dick," Colton blurted, and all the color from Isaac's face washed away.

Isaac released Colton and stared at the jock with wide eyes.

"That's what this is about, right?" Colton's Adam's apple bulged as he swallowed hard, the words edged out nervously, and he felt queasy at his own proposition. A proposition Isaac didn't fully grasp based on his unblinking stare. "You want control. Power. Take it. Fuck my face the same way I did to you in high school. Take back your power. Just...just don't take my future. My life."

"Not taking your life," Isaac said with a huff. "You did that all on your own, prick."

"Please." Colton dropped to his knees, begging. "Please, Isaac. I can't be kicked out. I can't lose everything because of one fucking paper."

It wasn't one paper, though. It was a mountain of bad behavior. Drinking on campus, fighting off campus, speculations of hazing, and so many failed courses his freshman year. Colton had used up every excuse he'd pleaded with last year, he'd watched his coaches pull the last strings they could to keep him on the team, and he knew he'd reached his last straw with the disciplinary committee. If they learned about this paper, learned he cheated on his final exam, they'd burn him to cinders.

"You really think sucking my dick will just make up for everything?" Isaac glared down at Colton, appearing disgusted by the jock and the proposition, but Colton could see the sly smile nearly creeping up across Isaac's face.

He knew a secret part of Isaac relished how the jock looked on his knees, relished the power he held, and Colton hoped this sacrifice would clear the board between them.

"I think you want me defeated, put in my place," Colton said looking up at Isaac. "I think you're obsessed with control."

"Oh?" Isaac scoffed. "As I recall, controlling was more your thing."

Colton nodded. "But you could've turned the exam in right away. You didn't want that, though. You wanted to control how I learned about my defeat."

"And I got that. I don't need to degrade you to win."

"But you want to," Colton said.

Isaac's expression turned pensive, clearly lost in thought and contemplation. Colton knew he wanted this. Knew he could offer this piece of himself to steer away from the fire that'd destroy his future.

"Whatever on-the-spot twisted game you're playing, I'm not that stupid seventeen-year-old boy anymore." Isaac shoved Colton back and skirted around him.

Of course, Isaac suspected a trick. The last time Colton had come on to him, had flirted and lured him someplace secluded, it ended up being the worst day of Isaac's life. Well, Colton couldn't know for certain if that was the truth, though he found it difficult to think of Isaac having worse days than what happened in the custodian closet, what happened in the hallways afterward. It may or may not have been Isaac's worst day ever, but it was certainly Colton's worst.

A memory that still marred his memories of high school when he looked back. An emptiness of shame and guilt and regret he could never fill or fully ignore.

"It's not a trick." Colton's voice cracked with desperation and the sadness of his past haunting him. "It's my way to offer…I don't know. Control, power, revenge all wrapped into one thing. A way to not lose everything in the process. And a way to apologize."

Isaac laughed. "You really think sucking my dick is the best way to say sorry?"

"No." Colton shook his head. "But would you accept an actual apology?"

"Never." Isaac glared, approaching Colton once again. "You ever suck dick before, Colt?"

He shook his head. It hadn't been part of the arrangement between him and Isaac. When the thoughts of men—thoughts of mostly Isaac—crossed his mind, all Colton wanted to do was maintain his masculinity. He wanted to stay in control, even if his sexuality deviated from what he wanted. The same arrangement blossomed with other men here and there, though few and far between since he'd waited until college before hooking up with a guy again. After what happened to Isaac, Colton shut that part of himself down until he graduated and escaped his small town.

The only thing Colton had ever done with a dude was oral and anal. Mostly oral and always receiving. Anal a few times—surprisingly, more with girls since he'd tried to bury his bi tendencies most days—and he always played pitcher. Colton had almost kissed one guy but found himself shoving the guy to his knees and ramming his dick down his throat first. By the time he came, the urge to kiss had faded.

"All right, screw it." Isaac shrugged. "Let's fuck that pretty face of yours."

Colton gulped, green eyes wide with shock. He had no idea what to do, how to get out of this arrangement he'd foolishly walked directly into. But Colton couldn't do anything with Isaac holding the threat of expulsion over him.

CHAPTER 06
ISAAC

ISAAC took pleasure in Colton's anxiety, the way his eyes darted back and forth down the hallway. There was a sadistic craving building deep inside Isaac's lungs, making each breath harder as he sought to let this scene play out. This wicked desire. When Colton reluctantly leaned forward, Isaac gripped his zipper.

"Not here, you perv." Isaac chuckled as Colton broke out in a nervous sweat.

He couldn't do this. Not seriously do this. Isaac wanted to do a lot of things to Colton, including hate screw him, but the idea of actually fulfilling the fantasy created too many questionable thoughts. Isaac didn't consider himself very ethical or unethical, but if there were a line he knew he shouldn't cross, it probably involved blackmailing the dude he hated into getting skull fucked by Isaac's dick. Yeah, that was definitely a line he couldn't cross. Probably.

Then why couldn't he just say no? Why couldn't he just laugh in Colton's face and say no deal? Why couldn't he speak at all? His mind swam in the fantasy, clung to the desire, and made it impossible for Isaac to let go.

"It's late, I unloaded a lot of info on you," Isaac said with a feigned exasperated exhale. "So, before I unload anything else on you, in you, whatever, maybe we should take a day to reflect."

Isaac dug into his satchel and retrieved a pen and paper to scribble his number.

"Take a few, in fact." Isaac handed the paper to Colton, dropping it to the floor as the jock went to retrieve it.

Was it petty? Yes. Juvenile? Totally. Enjoyable? Absolutely.

"If you're serious about this proposition, you can text me when you're sober," Isaac commented, noting the potent smell of gasoline on Colton's breath. It must've been cheap booze, for sure.

"I had two shots," Colton replied as if that mattered. Though, from what Isaac noted, it didn't affect his speech or behavior. However, he suspected it played a role in Colton's decision-making skills, even mildly.

"Whatever. I'd prefer you have a clear head if you're gonna give me head."

Isaac had a major lack of interest in drunk guys, finding they came in two particularly annoying varieties. Either he dealt with homophobic jerks who'd lost their filter and felt the need to comment every offensive thought that crossed their minds, or he ended up with hyper-masculine DL cock hungry duds. He'd had more than his fair share of eager-to-please frat boys his freshman year. They were all the same in demanding discretion and requiring liquid courage when texting Isaac at two in the morning so they could get pounded out.

"Wrap up your finals—try not to cheat on the rest of them—and meet me at my place Friday evening."

"Ugh, I'm supposed to drive home after classes."

Isaac merely glowered. A tiny part of him forgot most people used their break to visit home.

"I can just head back Saturday morning." Colton shrugged.

"Be seeing you around, Colt." Isaac walked away, a swagger in his step and a rush that left him buzzing more than any high he'd experienced.

This had really happened. Colton fuckwad Lennox had dropped to his knees and begged for Isaac's mercy. He'd offered himself up, fulfilling the ultimate fantasy Isaac never dared to dream about. A reversal of their roles.

An opportunity to give Colton a literal taste of his own medicine.

The rest of the week flew by in a haze of mundane tasks and monotonous days where Isaac's mind could only focus on one thing: the proposition. He couldn't believe he'd postponed his plan. And for what? A blowjob? A power move. Was it a power move if Colton offered it up? Isaac sucked plenty of dick, taking sheer satisfaction in bringing a guy off, maintaining control in a way he never did when servicing Colton. No, with Colton, he had held all the power. So what Colton offered was genuine surrender, and the thought made Isaac hard.

The thought was wrong, too. A bit twisted, which only made him more nervous, more excited, more curious about what would play out between them. He couldn't think of anything else other than Colton on his knees, sucking him off.

"Earth to motherfucking Izzy." Jazz snapped her fingers until Isaac blinked away the sordid images of Colton choking on his cock.

He let the bustling cacophony from the student center replace the fantastical gagging slurps he envisioned eliciting from Colton.

"What?" Isaac hissed.

"Boy, do not get an attitude with me when I just bought your rude behind a milkshake." Jazz slid over the melting chocolate shake and gave him her grumpiest side-eye.

He huffed. "Thank you."

"I am far too good to you." Jazz did an imaginary hair flip, running her nails along the fade of her buzzcut.

"Where's my milkshake?" Mina asked, joining the table.

"Somewhere out there in the yard." Jazz playfully pointed out to the windows of the dining hall. "I don't know. Bringing them boys and shit."

"And the girls." Mina wiggled her hips.

The GSA Club Representatives arranged their schedules so everyone could meet on Tuesdays and Thursdays for leadership lunches, which sounded fancy but was just an excuse to hang out and joke around.

With Isaac's mind lost on the proposition and Friday a day away, he could hardly focus on anything mentioned at the table.

"Where is your mind?" Jazz asked, nudging an absentminded Isaac with her foot.

"Huh?"

"She said…" Mina jumped in, singing a song from the Pixies and belting it loudly in Jazz's ear just to get under her skin.

Those two had the most ridiculously obvious chemistry, with drive-you-crazy passion written all over their faces and palpable flirtatious zingers every time they hung out. Which, to be clear, was almost a daily occurrence. It seemed the only people who didn't know Mina liked Jazz or Jazz liked Mina were Mina and Jazz.

Isaac didn't have the energy to watch the two of them bicker and beat around the quite literal bush instead of for once being direct about their feelings. He didn't have the energy because all of it went to the quandary on his mind.

"If someone wronged you and you had the opportunity for revenge, would you take it?"

"Hmmm." Jazz took a contemplative pose, strumming her shortly manicured nails against her chin. "That's a random question."

"Well?"

"Hell yeah," Mina said. "Fuck 'em up, I say."

"No, there's a lot to consider," Jazz interjected. "What did this person do to wrong me? What would my revenge be? What relationship did I have with the individual?"

"Oh, I like this game." Mina snatched a handful of fries. "Bitch stole my parking spot. My revenge would be slashing their tires. My relationship is it's that loud asshole on the third floor."

Her eyes locked onto Isaac, revealing how truly exacerbated she was by the noisy neighbors in her apartment complex. Isaac offered his sympathies in the form of sugary chocolate as he pushed his milkshake toward her.

"What if you could do the same thing to someone that they did to you?" Isaac asked, still seeking some type of guidance. No, he wanted validation. Acceptance, a green flag stating he wasn't a sadist and that his sadistic desires were okay.

"Hmmm," Jazz considered.

"What if the person in question suggested it?"

That made everyone at the table look a bit skeptical.

"If they suggested it, is it even revenge?" Mina smacked her lips as she sipped Isaac's abandoned milkshake.

"Depends on what they suggested," Jazz clarified. "Is it revenge or atonement?"

Oh, that made Isaac's mind spin in a thousand different directions on what could possibly be going through Colton's head at the moment.

"It's a lesser of two evils," he answered. "Maybe."

"Nope, you wanna go with the more evil option," Mina said. "Otherwise, it's not revenge. It's a compromise. Don't ever compromise with a bitch that crossed you. That's what I always say."

"You are so full of it," Jazz mocked. "I have literally watched you apologize to inanimate objects after bumping into them."

"Girl, my dresser hasn't done anything but support me." Mina sipped her drink. "Mind your business."

"So, hypothetically, revenge is the wrong choice?" Isaac asked.

"Yes," Jazz said. "Even if they suggested it."

"Yeah, never go with something someone suggested," Mina added. "Make it worse."

"Noooo." Jazz shook her head.

Isaac's eyes perked up at Mina's suggestion, awaiting clarification.

"If they recommended it, it's not revenge," Mina continued. "So, like, say someone stole from me, and they were all like, 'oh, you caught me, here's my hand for you to cut off.' Do you think I'm gonna play into that nonsense?"

"Why in the hell would anyone let you cut off their hand?"

"It's hypothetical, Jazz." Mina put her hand in her friend's face, then slapped her hand on the table, playing the role of the would-be thief. "So, they're like take my hand. It's yours. Revenge has been had."

Isaac watched as Mina switched roles, now playing herself holding an imaginary axe or what he assumed was an axe since she wielded it with two hands.

"Now, am I gonna play into their *hand* and take just their hand?" Mina waved her imaginary weapon back and forth as if to say 'no' and then chopped at the table, dramatically screaming as she pretended to lose her entire arm. "I'm gonna make it worse. Get my real revenge."

"You're a fucking monster." Jazz shook her head.

"Only if you cross me, Jazzy." Mina blew a kiss.

Jazz rolled her eyes and turned to Isaac. "So, you going to elaborate on this hypothetical revenge?"

"Philosophy class," Isaac answered. "Not mine. Suite mate, but it just got me thinking."

"You're so boring," Mina said. "I thought you had someone by the balls. I was about to ask for all the tea."

"Okay, if we're talking about philosophical debates, do I have some good ones…" Jazz's thunderous excitement brought everyone in at the table as she started the next hypothetical scenario.

While Mina and Jazz hadn't offered the most concrete advice Isaac needed, they had opened his eyes to the situation.

Jazz pointed out that this could actually be a form of atonement, so maybe by following through with the proposition, Isaac would make Colton a better person. He scoffed at that, unable to even delude himself with a lie that flimsy.

Mina's comment clung more closely to Isaac's thoughts, even after lunch. He went to his classes, then his room, and all he thought about was how to make the revenge real. If Colton offered up the proposition, willingly surrendered, what could Isaac do to take more control? More importantly, should he?

He needed to let go of this rage, to release his hatred. But he couldn't. Isaac's mind spun to the most wicked things, and he acknowledged that he wanted more out of this proposition. If he was going to tarnish what remnants of his soul he had by blackmailing Colton, he wanted the jock to feel as insignificant as he had all through junior year of high school. Through all of high school, really, even before his role as Colton's residential cocksucker began. If he was going to keep his winning hand to himself, he wanted to break Colton in other ways.

A new proposition formed in Isaac's thoughts, and before he knew it, he'd concocted the most delicious revenge, wicked in a sense even stretching the limits of his twisted imagination. But he didn't want Colton to agree to these terms. In fact, Isaac wanted this addendum to the original proposition to push Colton over the edge and force the jock to reject Isaac, force Colton to accept his impending expulsion. Well, possible expulsion. Isaac was still slightly convinced Colton's parents would just buy him out of the issue like he was certain they'd done last year.

But even if they did…Isaac wanted to break Colton in every way.

CHAPTER 07

COLTON

EVEN after the buzz of booze had worn off, Colton's anticipation for what came next hadn't. There was a mix of dread and excitement that bubbled inside him over the next few days as he awaited Isaac's text message.

Everything he searched online confirmed Isaac's threat. What Colton had done would be considered plagiarism and could lead to expulsion. Not trusting the internet and their many conflicting sources, Colton turned to the student handbook, the code of conduct forms they had folks sign every year, and sifted through them to find anything that'd corroborate Isaac's threat.

It did. The worst part was Colton learned this could technically be used against him even after he finished the course. Isaac could hold onto it until Colton graduated. According to the language in the handbook, proven plagiarism could even affect graduates, but he found that unlikely. Also, since he planned on going pro, he didn't need to worry about his degree coming into question. He just needed to stay in a school where he could and would be scouted for the league.

His phone buzzed with a call from his mom, who he didn't have the energy to talk with. Chances were she was calling to remind him about some party where he'd be paraded around over the holidays. This was exactly the type of thing his parents could make disappear. The right donation to the right person, and Colton wouldn't have to lift a finger in his defense.

But his parents weren't going to bail him out of anything since he picked the University of Clinton. They made that clear last year when he was drowning in problems, and they just stood by, waiting for him to screw up beyond repair. And yes, they'd always bail him out, but only on their terms. If he got expelled, his father would have him enrolled in a new college without missing a beat. But that would mean his father would pick the college, choose the pathway, pay for the degree, and set Colton on a journey to follow in the family footsteps exactly how his parents had always wanted, leaving no room for deviation.

That was why Colton worked so hard to maintain his sports scholarship. He had money, he had a trust fund, but his parents controlled the strings of Colton's cash flow until he turned twenty-five.

When Friday rolled around, Isaac texted Colton his dorm information. It was a little bizarre Isaac still lived in a dorm since he was in his third year. Colton had been forced to stay in a tiny dormitory his freshman year with all the other newbie baseball players, but when his second year rolled around, Colton made sure to get into a campus apartment with a few teammates.

Once he arrived at the dorm, he signed in on the guest clipboard, putting down a fake name since the student working at the desk wasn't paying attention. Colton would prefer there not be a paper trail to his cock sucking evening. Lining the wall near the elevators, Colton saw a collection of pictures naming the building RAs and expressing how happy and excited they all were to help everyone living there have their best dorm life experience. Well, everyone except for Isaac, who glared in his photo and clearly didn't give a fuck about the RA slogan.

Guess that explained why Isaac still lived in a dorm room. It was funny to Colton how active Isaac made himself on campus despite seemingly not caring about anyone or anything.

The time had finally arrived. Colton made his way to the elevator and took it up to the sixth floor, then knocked at Isaac's door.

He couldn't believe he was about to do this, about to suck Isaac's dick. No, it would be more than that. Colton realized Isaac would definitely use his mouth and throat the same way Colton had countless times before. Hell, he'd probably be even more brutal, all things considered. But Colton would let him. He'd allow this because, despite everything, a part of him hoped to make amends.

This wouldn't right things between them, Colton knew that logically, but an illogical part of Colton that still dreamed of undoing the past—time traveling to the worst mistake of his life—that part believed sucking dick could end this war between him and Isaac.

"You're here." Isaac ushered Colton into the room and immediately went to sit in his desk chair.

Colton expected Isaac to whip out his dick and demand Colton get to work, but instead, he typed away at his computer, seemingly disinterested in Colton's arrival. As Isaac remained aloof, Colton studied the sinister atmosphere of the dorm suite. Isaac's goth tastes extended to posters of metal bands, Halloween decorations strewn about, and oddly Funko Pop collectibles by the dozens. The main ones Colton recognized were the completed set of *The Nightmare Before Christmas* cast lined on the shelf above Isaac's desk. Colton liked that movie. And it was probably the only movie displayed in Isaac's room that he knew. The poster directly beside Isaac caught Colton's attention, a giant set of red lips with a bloody title: *The Rocky Horror Picture Show*. Weird. But everything about Isaac was a little weird.

"So, we doing this?" Colton asked, antsy and unable to handle any silence.

"Yeah." Isaac rocked his head side to side. "I need to clarify this arrangement first, though."

"Arrangement?" Colton quirked an eyebrow.

"Yeah, the whole one-and-done thing just doesn't sit right with me," Isaac explained with a wicked glint in his blue eyes. "You suggested I had a desire to take back a bit of my power, show you the other side of authority, control, dominance. All things I willingly let you do."

Colton stood silently, listening intently.

"I admit, there's some truth to that," Isaac continued, gesturing for Colton to take a seat on the edge of the bed. "The problem is a one-time blowjob doesn't really feel like I'm taking back much."

Colton's inquisitive look turned sour as he began to register this new proposition.

"If I'm gonna do this, I want the full experience," Isaac said. "I want you to give me everything I gave you and more."

Colton clamped his jaw at that, recalling all the ways he used Isaac, from long, grueling blowjobs to quick and brutal throat fucks.

"I want you whenever and however for the semester."

"The semester," Colton snapped. "Hell no, that's ridiculous."

"Why not?" Isaac shrugged. "I gave you nearly five months of service without hesitation."

"And you want the same." Colton's expression turned quizzical, almost considering this extended arrangement. But based on the sheer sadistic look from Isaac, he knew there was still more to be explained, more to push at Colton's comfort levels.

"Actually, I want so much more. When I say jump, you jump. When I say drop to your knees, you drop to your knees. When I say open your mouth and take this dick...well, you get the idea." Isaac smirked. "And I don't just wanna fuck your face. I want all of you."

"I'm not letting you fuck me in the ass," Colton growled.

"All right. Well, your choice and all that. But—pun intended—unfortunately, those are my only terms." Isaac stared at Colton with a harrowing, horrifying expression that twisted the fury out of Colton's face until all that remained was fear. "You will be mine, however and whenever I want. You will submit and surrender and satisfy."

"I can do that." Colton swallowed hard, choking on his own acceptance of the proposition. "With my mouth. Use me, use it, however and whenever you want."

"You're not getting it. Unsurprising, given your academic track record." Isaac's chuckle brought a small spark of Colton's anger back. "This isn't high school. I'm not you, some macho alpha prick, still figuring out my sexuality and the lengths I'll go to explore it. I know what I like. I like control. I like men. I like controlling men. I like using their mouths, their asses, their bodies. I like the quiver of a man when he can only take a few more strokes before he bursts, before he buckles, before he breaks beneath me."

Terror filled Colton's glossy green eyes, and he stared with a rapt expression, awed by Isaac's declaration. Isaac had always made himself smaller to serve Colton, and it was startling to realize there was this much aggression and drive for dominance buried within him. No, not buried. Swelling, growing with each angry breath Isaac took.

"I want you in every way, and I want you to accept me as the one in charge of your life for the remainder of the school year," Isaac said with a cheerful lilt to really drive in the statement. "If I'm gonna do this, I'm gonna do it right."

"I'm not a bitch." Colton wheezed, letting out all his rage in a heavy exhale like a dragon blowing flames. No, smoke. Because the fire inside Colton had died out, and based on Isaac's smirk, he'd seen the embers flickering.

"Hey, I get it." Isaac raised his hands, feigning surrender. "Your ass is worth more than your education. Totally valid choice."

Colton looked up with tears in his eyes. "You can't be serious."

"I am absolutely serious. If you want me to keep my evidence to myself, to let you cheat your way through yet another class, then I want you. I want you to feel the same way I felt."

"Powerless?"

"Drunk on serving someone else. Living and breathing for his needs, his pleasure, his cock," Isaac hissed, venomous hatred in the words he spat.

Colton recalled how much Isaac rearranged his days to tend to Colton's dick, sucking him off whenever the jock needed release.

First thing in the morning, missing his AP Chem class to help Colton relieve himself. After practice when he sucked Colton's sweaty dick before he'd shower up and head to a party with his friends. Late in the night when he'd sneak out of his house and meet Colton in the woods and let the jock hump his face while the back of his head slammed against a tree. Isaac had allowed Colton every opportunity to degrade him for his own pleasures. Hell, Colton knew back then Isaac would've eagerly bent over and taken the jock's dick in the ass just for a chance at love.

"Just say no already so we can be done with this," Isaac said with an almost convincing aloofness. Enough to fool anyone else, but not Colton.

"Fine. Let's get this done with."

"Perfect." Isaac swiveled his chair back to his computer.

"What are you doing?" Colton leapt to his feet.

"Getting this over with." Isaac shrugged. "Sending the emails. Duh."

"No." Colton's voice cracked. "I meant us. The arrangement. Just get this over with. Or started. Or started and over for tonight."

Isaac's jaw dropped. "Are you seriously agreeing to my outlandish terms? You'll let me use your mouth whenever I want? Let me fuck your throat until you can't breathe?"

Colton looked down and nodded.

"You'll be my personal cum bucket whenever I want?"

Colton's Adam's apple bulged as he swallowed profane words, and he silently nodded.

"You'll bend over and let me fuck that tight jock ass?"

Colton glowered, nostrils flaring. There it was. There was the line Colton didn't want to cross, the one Isaac had seemingly set specifically to force him to back down. Back out.

"You don't wanna do this, do you?" Colton asked.

"Fuck you? Hell yeah, I do."

"Then why are you trying to get me to reject it?"

"Because I'm not strong enough to," Isaac said with a breathy sigh. "You fucking threw me for a loop by offering your mouth. One and done wouldn't clear the board, wouldn't do anything except leave me wanting to use you more. So, I went with a real proposition, a twisted idea, a fantasy worth fulfilling. Something with the power of holding you in check for the semester."

"Then do that," Colton pleaded. "We can have that arrangement. You don't need the other stuff."

Isaac glared. "I do need the other stuff. I need to feel you buckle beneath me as I fuck all that confidence out of you. I need to feel your hole clamp down onto my cock as I pound away your pride and ego and your fucking arrogance. I need absolute control over you and your life. That is how I get my power back. That is how I win."

It became clear that Isaac wanted to break Colton, and he wanted Colton to go willingly into this arrangement or be the one to back out. Perhaps Isaac understood how deranged he sounded. What Colton had allowed to happen in high school was cruel beyond measure. But if Isaac did this, would he be any better than Colton?

"You're worried you'll be worse than me," Colton said. "That's why you want me to reject it."

"You never know if you've overplayed your hand until you set the card down." Isaac smirked. "Since we both know you're not about to take it in the ass, I think it's time we send that email."

Colton could reject the proposition the same way he'd rejected Isaac. He could put an end to this sordid rekindling of what-the-fuck-ever they were once upon a time.

"You wanna fuck me?" Colton pulled off his shirt and threw it to the ground. "Huh?"

Isaac's eyes widened as Colton kicked off his sneakers, unbuttoned his jeans, and pulled them down to his ankles before tossing them across the room with his foot.

"Then fuck me." Colton snarled, his fury sparked anew. "Fuck me right now."

Colton would surrender himself to Isaac. It would spare him from losing his future, and perhaps it would right what had gone wrong between him and Isaac. Colton didn't believe that part, but he yearned for it all the same.

CHAPTER 08

ISAAC

ISAAC couldn't flat-out reject the proposition. That was the point of pushing too far, too hard, and forcing Colton back out.

Even if every part of Isaac wanted to direct Colton to his knees and use him the same way he'd been used time and time again in high school. It took everything he had to let that little part of him die when pushing Colton beyond his comfort zone. The bastard was supposed to reject the arrangement, not strip off his clothes and demand to be fucked.

And sure, it was mostly bluster. Isaac could see that in Colton's shaky stance, completely unaware of what awaited him if he went down this path. Colton was supposed to accept whatever academic fallout would soon befall him, not accept the outlandish terms Isaac had set. It was the ultimate authoritative trip of his life, and Isaac couldn't deny the desire any longer. Not with a perfectly sculpted Colton standing before him, ready and willing to serve.

Colton stood in his tight red boxer briefs, his junk appearing so much bigger in the form-fitting fabric than Isaac recalled.

Completely unveiled from his outfit, Isaac found his eyes scanning every inch of Colton's perfect flesh. Unblemished tanned skin. Muscles everywhere, none too big, but so fucking firm. Colton took heavy, angry breaths which made his six-pack flex tightly, made his pecs swell and deflate in the most inviting manner. Christ, Isaac found himself lost in the curve of Colton's tight waist. How could a guy have such broad shoulders, such big biceps, such a wide chest, and still possess a waist so slim? Colton's thick muscular thighs only added to the subtle hourglass shape.

Isaac blushed, a bit frazzled at taking in Colton's body again, seeing how much he'd grown in the three years since they last interacted. Honestly, he was a bit embarrassed he'd intended to challenge Colton, hoping the first night would turn into a fistfight. Yes, Isaac was confident in his self-defense techniques, but seeing all the muscles underneath those clothes made him question his skills.

"It's just sex," Colton said firmly, but Isaac saw the struggle to maintain his composure. "I've had plenty of sex. It doesn't mean anything. You wanna fuck me, fine. No big deal."

Sure, he said it with conviction, but Isaac heard the crack in his voice, the nervousness of submission. As Colton slipped his hands under the elastic, Isaac watched it snag at the curve of Colton's firm bubble butt.

"Wait." Isaac raised his hands, and Colton paused, leaving his boxers on. "You're serious? You'll submit to me? Just like that?"

Isaac's mind sank into the abyss of his fantasies, lost to the idea of all the muscles that would bend and break to serve him.

"Just like that?" Colton scoffed. "It's either fuck you or fuck my future."

"To be clear, you won't be the one doing the fucking," Isaac said. "Ever."

Colton simply stared at Isaac.

"Don't get any ideas. You will be mine and mine alone." Isaac stood from his chair. "None of this fooling around on the side like high school. I shared your dick then; I won't be sharing it now."

"I thought you said I wouldn't be doing the fucking here."

"When I'm railing you," Isaac leaned in close and whispered into Colton's ear. "You'll fucking cum. You'll cum hard and beg for my dick to pound you even harder."

He savored the quiver his voice provoked from Colton. This was really happening. He was really going to do this. Colton was really going to do this. They were really about to move forward with the most deranged fantasy Isaac could even fathom. No, it was more fucked up than even his vengeful musings. It never would've crossed his mind that Colton would offer himself up, and now here Isaac was ready to pluck away the jock's dignity. He wanted to break Colton's masculine ego, his alpha standing, his cocky swagger, his entitled authority.

Isaac wanted to fuck Colton into submission, and that was exactly where the night was headed.

"Strip." Isaac gazed down at Colton's crotch as the jock obediently pulled down his boxers.

Colton was semi-erect already, and Isaac nearly ran his hand along the dick but resisted the desire. This wasn't about Colton or his satisfaction. For once in their sordid relationship, Isaac's pleasure was all that mattered.

Isaac unfastened his anime-themed belt buckle and yanked his belt off in a swift motion. The sharp snap startled Colton.

"Don't worry, baby," Isaac whispered, letting his hot breath hit Colton's ear. "We'll save the kink for later in the semester."

Colton's anxious expression made Isaac grin as he unzipped his pants and fished out his dick. It didn't take much to stroke himself fully hard since the fantasy of this moment had left him throbbing for most of the week. Even when he jerked himself dry every day, he found it impossible not to get a new boner the second he thought about Colton's lips on his dick.

"Fuck," Colton muttered, eyes practically bulging like some silly cartoon as he took in the sight of Isaac's dick.

It hadn't been something Colton showed much of an interest in in high school. Occasionally, he'd want Isaac to stroke himself while sucking Colton off, but he still only ever saw Isaac's dick through the mess of their sloppy blowjob sessions. Sometimes, Colton played with Isaac's ass, teasing his hole with his fingers, but not ready for penetration. Still, not the best angle to take in the full view of Isaac's cock.

And it was a massive cock. Nearly eight inches and a very thick circumference.

"How am I supposed to get that in my mouth?"

"You gotta big mouth, dude." Isaac ran his hand through Colton's short black hair. "It'll fit. I'll make it."

When Colton shook, Isaac took the opportunity to direct him to his knees with a forceful push on the top of his head. Colton didn't resist. He dropped to his knees and stared at the dick before him.

"You know what to do," Isaac insisted.

"I've never…" Colton stammered. "I mean, I've thought about it. But I haven't… It just seemed…gay."

"Yeah, that's what I always tell my girlfriends," Isaac said with a chuckle. "They're such homos out there, sucking their boyfriend's dicks."

"You know what I mean," Colton snapped.

"I don't, actually." Isaac shrugged. "I never struggled with hypermasculinity to compensate for my traditionally feminine desires. Guess having a big dick sort of made me secure in myself."

An absurd jab because Isaac had never been secure in himself a day in his life—too much wound-up anxiety coupled with constant existential crises—but he'd never worried about his perceived manhood. Not until Colton came around. Not until Colton broke him emotionally. The big dick comment was also excessive. It wasn't like Colton was inadequate at six inches. He just happened to be smaller than Isaac, and based on the way his eyes fixated on the veins of Isaac's longer, thicker throbbing dick, Colton's insecurity was definitely getting the better of him.

"What do you like from a blowjob?" Isaac asked. "Do that. Do something."

Colton nodded, then closed his eyes and opened his mouth wide. He leaned forward and took the head of Isaac's cock into his mouth. He nearly burst right that instant, feeling the absolute rush of so much pleasure that came from this simple act. It wasn't that Colton worked the nerves of his head, though he clearly tried by rotating his tongue. No. It was the power. The control which now fell to Isaac.

He let Colton work, his head slowly bobbing as he took in two to three more inches of Isaac's dick. The muffled gulps of effort aroused Isaac, heightening his hunger. Colton's jaw stretched wide as he continued taking a bit more of the dick, letting the head hit the roof of his mouth again and again. It was a lovely sensation mixed with a spectacular view. Isaac stood in euphoria as Colton's head moved back and forth.

Getting into the swing of things, Colton even tilted his head with a twist every few times, creating a rhythm with his mouth. It felt nice and kept Isaac hard as a fucking rock, but it wouldn't make him cum. Not now that he'd steadied his breathing and had gotten over the initial excitement of owning Colton's mouth.

"Look at you working so hard on my dick." Isaac stroked Colton's hair. "Use your hand."

Colton obeyed, gently running his hand up and down Isaac's shaft, even licking his palm to help make the tugs slick.

"Play with the head," Isaac instructed with a growl.

Colton did as he was asked, teasing the head and rotating his tongue round and round the nerves while he used his hand to stroke the rest of Isaac's massive dick. With his other hand, Colton moved the baggy shirt up some, as it hung low and practically draped around Isaac's dick. Isaac decided to offer assistance and raised his shirt up, tugging it over his head but leaving it wrapped around his shoulders. It fully exposed his pale, tat-tooed skin and the hair trailing from his crotch, a strip up his muscular stomach and spread across his chest.

The light chest hair wasn't very visible, not with the tattoo he'd gotten. While the flames lining Isaac's neck were always noticeable, the phoenix he'd gotten went mostly unseen. Very few ever saw Isaac nude or even shirtless. The majestic wings spread across Isaac's firm pecs—nowhere near Colton's level of fitness, but still, something notable. The bird's flames burned in several shades of yellow, orange, red, and blue.

Colton didn't seem to notice the awesome tattoo, not from his current vantage point. He kept working on his task, sucking Isaac off, while his eyes seemed a little lost on the only tattoo he could glimpse from his knees with his vision locked straight ahead as his head bobbed back and forth.

The tattoo of a razor-toothed smile that stretched from one side of Isaac's stomach to the next, tucked neatly below his belly button, gave Colton reason to pause. It was an eerie tattoo, something like the Cheshire Cat's smile but more shark-like. Or perhaps the shimmer of Isaac's belly button piercing threw Colton off, given his obsession with masculinity. Isaac couldn't decide, but with a hard thrust, he encouraged Colton to get back to work.

"You're doing so good." Isaac ran his hands through Colton's hair, taking pleasure in the soft strands before snatching a firm fistful of the black locks and pushing his head further down. "Come on. You got this."

Isaac groaned when his dick hit the back of Colton's throat.

"Ah, fuck." Isaac panted with delight as Colton gagged and gurgled. "Just like that. Hold it."

Isaac wrapped a hand under Colton's jaw and moved the other to the back of his head. With the solid grip he had over Colton, Isaac was able to further fuck Colton's face, keeping him in place all the while. Isaac became increasingly more aggressive with each thrust, lost in the ecstasy of ramming his cock in and out of Colton's throat.

Fuck, Colton's choking gasps as he held Isaac's dick deep in his throat brought such satisfaction. Keeping a firm hold on the jock's head, Isaac bucked his hips forward, trying to push the last few inches of his dick into his mouth.

Colton grabbed the belt loops of Isaac's baggy jeans and braced his hands against Isaac's thighs, doing his best to steady the chaotic rhythm that beat against his mouth and throat. It didn't lessen Isaac; in fact, it further encouraged him to fuck Colton's face harder.

"Stop trying to run from it, dude." Isaac stepped closer, eliminating the tiniest of gaps between himself and Colton, his pants practically wiping away the drool running down Colton's face. "That's it. That's it. Fucking take it. Take it just like that. Fuck yeah."

Isaac pushed Colton all the way to the base, holding him in place until Colton gagged and gasped and broke free for desperate breaths.

"Sorry, sorry." Colton wheezed, sucking in more air and wiping the tears filling his eyes. "Gimme a second."

Isaac didn't rush him, content to wait, enjoying the sight of Colton struggling so much. Each breath gave way to the sweat building on the brow of Colton's face. The tension in his strong muscles had a tired tremble; they'd do nothing to help the jock in this moment. Colton looked up to Isaac, teary-eyed stare begging for an end but ready to continue.

When Colton returned to his cock, the jock went slowly but somewhat directionless, almost as if he waited for Isaac's controlling grip once again. Isaac slapped his hands over Colton's head and rammed his cock further, happy the jock didn't resist. Colton even tilted his head upward, trying to make it easier for Isaac to push deeper.

"That's right, baby." Isaac thrust his hips, getting back into a steady flow like he had before the pause. "Choke on it. All of it. Now."

Colton's face turned red as his lips brushed against Isaac's brown pubes. Isaac held his head there, savoring each second before releasing Colton, who stole a few more breaths while stroking Isaac's cock and then slowly taking it back in. This pattern continued for a minute or so, Colton going to the base for a few seconds, slobbering on the cock, retreating, breathing, stroking, playing with the head, and repeating.

"Come on, Colt," Isaac growled. "Fucking take it. All the way. You're gonna remember this dick forever. You're gonna taste it in your mouth all winter break."

Colton struggled, trying his best from what Isaac could see but faltering. Filled with a primal urge of encouragement, Isaac smacked Colton's face. It wasn't very hard but enough to startle him as his eyes shot open wider.

"All the way, now." Isaac popped Colton again, a light pelt that made Colton work harder. Still, he pulled back instinctively, clearly controlled by his gag reflex when he needed to realize he was controlled by Isaac. With a third and fourth smack, Colton forced the cock further into his mouth. With the fifth and sixth, he held it there. The next few smacks were Isaac's way of expressing pride, similar to a pat on the back, but instead, he popped Colton's cheek. "Fucking take all of my dick, dude."

Colton gurgled his protests, coughing up spit and moaning miserably as he held Isaac's cock. It took everything he had not to retch. Isaac could tell as he looked down at Colton's watering eyes. He could tell from the jock's shaky hands squeezing Isaac's hips to hold himself in place. Every instinct in Colton's body appeared ready to lunge back and retreat from the cock pressing down on his throat, but he held himself still and even tried to push the last few inches in.

Isaac smirked at the poor attempt to deep-throat his massive dick.

"Good boy." Isaac wiped the stray tears from Colton's face and brought his gaze up to him. "I'll take it from here."

Colton had the most vulnerable and pleading expression as he stared up with his glossy green eyes.

"Just sit there and look pretty while I wreck you."

Isaac savored that expression as he fucked Colton's face, pulling his cock out far enough for the jock to steal a breath before ramming it all the way back in as far as he could. It took work, jackhammering his dick into Colton's mouth over and over as the jock's body wriggled and writhed while he remained as still as possible on his knees. Isaac gripped Colton's hair tightly, holding him in place as he face fucked him faster and harder and rougher.

Every time he found himself lost in an easy pace of pleasure, he recalled how many times Colton had brutally fucked his face until he came, never showing sympathy for Isaac's throat. He decided to do the same, pumping more aggressively, spiteful with a side of hatred which further fueled the throb in his dick.

Colton remained obedient, gagging and gurgling and choking on the few desperate breaths he managed between the drool that spilled down his jaw and pooled over the jock's bare thighs. The exhausted expression on Colton's face elicited more delight from Isaac. Every time he wanted to shoot his load, he turned Colton's head, changing his pace and altering the pleasurable feeling of the tight throat muscles just enough to keep from busting.

Isaac didn't want to release Colton from his first blowjob so suddenly. He wanted to savor every second, seconds he watched tick by on the superhero clock he had on the wall. The time was hours off, but it counted the minutes all the same.

After nearly fifteen minutes of reaming Colton's throat, abusing the tight muscles, and gagging the jock again and again, Isaac couldn't contain it.

"You fucking ready for this?" He bucked erratically, incapable of pushing all the way down Colton's throat.

Every time he tried, his body twitched, lost in the building spasms of climaxing. Isaac was on the verge of busting. He stifled his own whimpers of excitement as he kept humping Colton's face.

"Take it," Isaac hissed as his body convulsed, and he shot a jet of cum in the back of Colton's throat.

Oh, how he wanted to hold his dick there, keep the head snuggly in the back of Colton's mouth at the edge of his throat, but more importantly, he wanted Colton to taste him.

"Stick out your tongue," Isaac demanded as he pulled back his dick, shooting a second and third stream into Colton's mouth.

The third one hit Colton's tongue perfectly on the tip, and the jock didn't move, holding the load right there as Isaac jerked his own cock, tugging on the head to pour out the last white droplets. Pearls splattered on the pool of cum Colton held at the ready.

"Now, swallow."

Colton obeyed, gulping down the load and looking up at Isaac with his messy, spit-covered jaw.

He looked wrecked, and it was a beautiful sight. Isaac couldn't resist shoving his semi-erect dick back into Colton's mouth.

"Suck it dry." Isaac pushed it back and forth in Colton's mouth, savoring the jock work on his cock until it went soft, savoring the last little droplets of cum that escaped thanks to Colton's dedication.

"Goddamn, that was amazing." Isaac grinned. "Bet your ass is gonna feel a million times better."

Colton had this frightened bewilderment on his face that fed the beast of Isaac's depraved desires. He found himself lost to the lustful dominance he held over Colton in the same way he had lost himself to the lust of submission for Colton once upon a time.

CHAPTER 09

COLTON

COLTON'S throat ached. Despite doing his best to stretch his jaw, he couldn't seem to loosen the tension that pulsed with pain. It was harder than expected, more grueling than he ever realized, and while Isaac had been bigger in size and more brutal in his zealous excitement than Colton, he admittedly knew when it came to head, he enjoyed a sloppy blowjob. He just hadn't realized until this moment how much effort the other person had to put into it.

Isaac opened his window and sparked a cigarette.

"Um, should you be doing that?"

"No one cares when you're on the sixth floor." Isaac took a deep inhale. "Well, no one notices at the very least."

The most perplexing part of this whole warped arrangement—proposition—was how hard Colton found himself now. Thankfully, Isaac kept his attention mostly fixed on the window, where he exhaled huge drags of smoke. Still, Colton did his best to keep his boner to himself, pressing it between his thighs. It only added to the throb but in a somewhat uncomfortable manner, so Colton hoped now that Isaac was done fucking his face, the erection would fizzle out.

The hard-on itself didn't surprise Colton, so much so that Isaac elicited it. Yeah, he found Isaac attractive, enjoyed the time they'd spent together, but that had to do with Isaac's submissive nature. He'd never considered Isaac a very masculine guy, not feminine either, just sort of floating somewhere in between. Not that he did anything to help matters. He could've picked a different wardrobe, different style, avoided the nail polish and makeup, and maybe passed as a somewhat real guy. Well, a skinny guy, but still, something better than a goth twink boy.

All the same, Colton couldn't believe how much power and authority, and conviction spilled from Isaac's lips as he ordered Colton around, as he rammed his massive cock further and further down his throat. The way he manhandled him, used him, abused him. It made him miserable while also igniting some bizarre spark inside him. A craving for dominance he didn't believe existed.

Colton had always wanted to suck a dick. It was a curiosity he'd had since high school but one he created very clear measures and requirements about. He wanted someone stronger than him, someone on the cusp of queerness like him—no straight guys. There'd been a few last year, jerks like Leon who'd offered to shove their dicks down Colton's throat since he was a loud and proud flamer. Colton knew he'd never submit to someone like that, never allow someone to use his throat like some type of fleshlight, yet here he was, allowing Isaac to break him in for his own satisfaction.

Isaac didn't fit the cock sucking requirements. Not masculine enough. Too queer. He clearly hated Colton, same as the homophobes on his team who still hassled him about his bisexuality. Even so, there was something so primal about the way Isaac took hold of Colton, the way he forced Colton further down on his dick, the way he didn't relent.

Had he been like that in high school? Colton figured he got a little aggressive here or there, but not the same. Colton had face fucked people before but nothing to that degree. He never made someone continuously choke on their own spit, gag nonstop without a break, take it all the way to the base and hold there. And the slaps. Fuck, the way Isaac smacked Colton and demanded he hold his position. The whole thing fucked with Colton's mind.

"You look fucking wrecked," Isaac said, stubbing out his smoke. "You good?"

"Yeah," Colton softly replied, in part because his throat ached and in part because he found himself quietly humbled.

"Good to know," Isaac said. "Quick question. Are you clean?"

"I've been tested, um, but it's been a minute."

"Not that, but always a perk to know." Isaac nodded. "I'm recently tested and on PrEP, so that's something we shouldn't have to worry about."

Colton just stared.

"I meant more your ass."

"Huh?" Colton's jaw went slack at the accusation. "I wash my butt if that's what you're—"

Isaac laughed and shook his head. "No. I just mean that I sorta sprang this on ya, so you're not exactly as prepped as you could be. Not that it's required, though sometimes cleaner depending on the dude."

Colton blinked a few times in confusion.

"Do you have a rumbly belly?" Isaac asked, batting his eyes almost playfully.

"No. I'm fine there if that's what you mean." Colton waved a hand over his stomach and intestines and sort of pushed away the thought of Isaac's question.

"Cool. I mean, shit happens. But I wanted to check in since I'm about to rip you a new asshole. Thought it'd be generous to ask." Isaac walked toward his nightstand and pulled a bottle of lube from the drawer. "Go ahead and get on the bed."

Colton coughed. "Ugh, so we're doing this then?"

"Unless you had a change of heart."

This wasn't something Colton ever considered doing, ever considered giving up. Was it giving up? People got fucked all the time and loved it. But Colton couldn't imagine himself taking someone's dick, serving as a piece of meat to get someone off. Yet here he was, agreeing, committing, doing exactly that.

He told himself again and again it was because of what Isaac had on him. Colton didn't have a choice, not much of one anyway. Either Isaac would fuck Colton or fuck his life up. In any case, something Colton valued was going to be wrecked. He supposed if it was his hole, at least no one else had to know.

There would be no living down an expulsion, and his family would control his every waking choice if he screwed things up here.

"Hey, you listening?" Isaac snapped his fingers and gestured to the bed.

Carefully, Colton got up and wobbled a bit. He found himself more lightheaded from the face fucking than he initially realized.

"Lay back."

Colton obeyed, laying on the twin-sized bed with his knees propped up high and feet pushed close together and tucked under his butt. It was a poor shield, but he wanted something as he lay here completely nude before Isaac.

Isaac poured lube onto his index and middle finger, letting it slide down them as the goop glistened against his polished fingernails under the luminescent black lights.

"Spread your legs," Isaac ordered.

Colton had his legs pulled close, still hiding his erection.

"Now."

He grimaced and did as Isaac commanded, revealing his unrelenting boner as he parted his legs. Isaac didn't say a word about the erection, merely smirked.

"Ready?"

"For?"

"I'm gonna finger your ass for starters," Isaac said. "Probably toss a few toys in there, too."

"What?" Colton quirked a brow, finding the idea of Isaac sticking his fingers in him to be the most bizarre thing ever.

Including the fact he'd willingly agreed to let him shove other bigger parts inside him.

"Trust me, dude." Isaac brought his wet fingertips close to the ring of Colton's ass, and he jolted at the suddenness of the approach. "If you think it's scary having these fellas poking around, trust me when I say you'll be grateful."

"Just lube me up, whatever." Colton ground his teeth. "The sooner you fuck me, the sooner I can go."

"I don't know, sort of like the idea of dragging this out until the wee hours." Isaac teased Colton's hole, massaging the outside.

The sensation was unlike anything Colton had experienced. He quaked, nervous and excited and terrified, oh so fucking terrified. He didn't know if the fear came from the idea of getting fucked or the fear of liking it, craving it. Mostly, he didn't know if he wanted this. Colton did know he didn't want it from Isaac. It made his skin crawl, submitting to the guy he used on a regular basis, submitting to the guy he threatened and bullied and broke for years.

Part of him felt he owed Isaac this, that if he just sucked it up, quite literally, and let Isaac get his rocks off, it wouldn't be so bad. Another part believed full well that Isaac would make this excruciating, that he'd pour all the hate he had coiled inside him back into Colton.

When Isaac pushed his fingers inside Colton, he winced. It felt weird and uncomfortable, but not in a painful way, just an awkward sort of sensation. He knew that wouldn't last. He knew Isaac would hurt him soon enough, relish in the pain.

Colton had fucked enough asses to know the pleasure was minimal at best. It confused him why people enjoyed it, accepting some people were just built to please others, that was their role in life. Colton couldn't be one of those people. He had too much self-respect.

"Ooooooo," Colton moaned, sliding up the bed and away from Isaac's invasive fingers.

"Stop." Isaac glared. "Bring that ass right back here."

Colton swallowed his nervousness and lowered himself from the wall he was on the verge of scaling a second ago.

Isaac continued working his fingers inside Colton, lubing his hole, massaging him in a way that hit hard. It felt like nothing Colton had experienced. His cock throbbed harder each time Isaac pushed his fingers in deeper. It took everything Colton had to contain his groans of pleasure.

"Looks like someone is realizing their magic button."

Colton didn't respond, breathing heavily as his dick bounced from the faster push of Isaac's fingers and the subtle thrust of Colton's hips. He couldn't help himself. Part of him bucked so he could feel the sensation of fucking, even if all he did was fuck the air, and another part of him liked the way his ass pushed against the fingers inside him.

Isaac continued working his fingers inside Colton, the pain still there but hidden beneath the wave of pleasure. Colton closed his eyes, ignoring the sensations in his ass, focusing purely on the throb of his dick. If he pretended, pretended very well, he could almost imagine this feeling came from fucking. Him fucking someone. Anyone. Anyone but Isaac.

"You like that, don't you?" Isaac's voice slithered through Colton's ears, invading his imagination, and soon the silhouette that rode Colton's dick took on Isaac's form. "Such a tough guy on the verge of busting with a few fingers pressed to his prostate."

The pair moved in rhythm with each other, the imaginary Isaac grinding faster and harder the more the real Isaac worked his fingers inside Colton, the more he talked dirty to Colton, the more Isaac invaded his fantasy.

"Open your eyes."

Reluctantly, Colton obeyed, staring into Isaac's icy gaze. He clearly wanted to keep Colton in check; he must've wanted to ensure Colton understood where his pleasure came from, how it came to be, who made him feel this ready to erupt. If only Isaac understood that Colton couldn't escape Isaac even in his musings. Not right now. Not with his fingers poking faster and harder, stretching his tight hole and finding the perfect spot.

"Fuuuuuuuu…" Colton grabbed the comforter on either side, squeezing the mattress until his knuckles burned white.

His hips bucked erratically, and he shot a load of cum across his stomach and chest. Long pearl strands fired off as he moaned and convulsed and clung to the orgasm. Fuck, what an amazing feeling.

"If you think that load felt good, the one I'm about to fuck outta you with this dick is gonna be an orgasm you chase for the rest of your life, little pitcher." Isaac had this chaotic grin.

In an instance, the euphoric pleasure that came from release washed away, immediately replaced by shame.

Colton lay there, taking shaky breaths, while Isaac got up and walked toward his dresser, where a folded towel sat.

"You mind handing that to me?" Colton asked.

"I do." Isaac continued rifling through his drawer.

"Seriously?"

"Yeah, I want you covered in cum. Mine. Yours." Isaac turned and smirked. "It suits you well, little pitcher."

Colton glared, and Isaac returned to his unhelpful task. Instead of grabbing the towel, Isaac dug through a drawer and pulled out a large blue dildo.

"What're you doing?"

"You're gonna wanna get a little more prepared—trust me." Isaac plopped back onto the bed and lubed up his toy. "I had trouble slipping fingers inside you, and I don't feel like spending ten minutes trying to wedge my dick head past your tight defenses."

Colton grimaced.

"What? That's like a sports pun." Isaac waved the blue dildo, pointing it at Colton. "You're sportsy, right, little pitcher?"

"Don't call me that," Colton snapped.

"Not an accurate name, anyway." Isaac's eyes looked down.

"Ha, you're so fucking funny." Colton's face burned.

"What?" Isaac asked as he slowly pushed the dildo inside of Colton.

Now, his face burned for another reason. Fuck, it hurt more than Isaac's fingers, hurt more now that he'd already cum.

"You think I haven't heard all the catcher jokes from my team, from other assholes, from—" Colton moaned uncontrollably as the ridges of the dildo hit in the most sensational way, leaving him breathless.

He furrowed his brow, forcing rage to steady his composure. It angered him how quickly his body betrayed him in front of Isaac.

"I wasn't making a catcher joke." Isaac gripped Colton's semi-erect dick with his already lubed hand. "I was just recalling how big of a pitcher you really were, so little pitcher seems inaccurate."

Colton stifled a moan, locking his eyes onto Isaac's gentle gaze. A compliment. He hadn't expected that, not from Isaac, not ever. Not unless the compliment was meant to belittle or degrade him.

"Are you mocking me?" Colton asked, shuddering as Isaac continued working. "I'm not, I'm not... I don't always catch the insult, but I know when someone is... FUCK!"

Colton lay back, unable to finish his thought as Isaac got into a good rhythm of shoving the dildo in and out of his hole while simultaneously stroking Colton hard again. It shocked him how well Isaac moved his hands; they synchronized perfectly with each other.

"If I were mocking you, I'd ensure you caught the joke." Isaac shifted his position, sitting on his knees as he continued pumping the dildo inside Colton. "I have no reason to tease you, not when I have you."

Colton begrudgingly accepted that answer. Isaac slipped the dildo out of Colton's ass and set the slimy toy on the nightstand.

"Speaking of which...let's get you in position." Isaac gripped Colton's hips and flipped him over. "Ass up, boy."

Isaac's hands squeezed and pulled and positioned Colton, which he abided by. Colton spread his legs some, then pushed them together ever so. He raised his ass, then lowered it, then lifted it as he arched his back. Isaac knocked his knuckles against Colton's lower back repeatedly. Colton kept trying to arch more but couldn't bend to Isaac's satisfaction. Finally, Isaac slammed his hands into the small of Colton's back and forced the arch he wanted.

Colton yelped at the suddenness and found his face shoved into a pillow when Isaac slammed a hand to the back of the jock's head.

"Face down." Isaac's other hand traveled up Colton's back, making his spine quiver, and rested on Colton's shoulder. "If you need to scream into the pillow, that's okay."

Fuck. Fuck.

"Wait, what?" Colton turned before having his head half-shoved into the pillow again.

"First times can be rough," Isaac explained, which Colton already understood. "If it hurts, bite the pillow. I won't judge you."

That almost seemed considerate. Almost. The wicked smirk spreading on Isaac's face said otherwise, though.

"I'll just fuck you."

"Not hard. Not too hard," Colton clarified.

He knew what he signed up for, what he'd agreed to, and he expected some roughness. After all, if he fucked someone, he couldn't expect to blow his load going at a snail's pace, but still. He didn't know if his ass could handle a full fucking. Especially not with someone like Isaac, with Isaac's dick.

Isaac slipped off the bed and finally unbuttoned his jeans before letting them fall to the floor. His boxers were those big plaid kind, and they didn't really fit Isaac's look since everything about him held something gothy or connected to anime, games, or media in some way. Colton didn't know what he expected, maybe rainbow unicorns or cartoon faces. He certainly expected something more form-fitting, like Colton's tight boxer briefs. Isaac slipped the big boxers off in a quick, fluid motion.

Now that he stood mostly in the nude—aside from the shirt he still wore tugged behind his head and wrapped at his shoulders—he seemed so much skinnier again. Isaac had always had a slender build, but the toned muscles were a new look. The tattoos across his body, from an animated fight scene on his right thigh to some fat cartoon guy in glasses and green pants wincing as he squeezed his knee in pain, ironically tattooed on Isaac's left knee. He seemed to have lots of random stuff inked onto his legs, sinister skulls and cute animated stuff.

"How many tattoos do you have?" Colton asked, lost on the image of Isaac standing naked and hard before him.

"Not really sure." Isaac scanned his own skin, mouthing numbers and lightly smacking spots with tattoos. "Some probably count as bigger pieces, so, like, twenty-ish, maybe. Probably. I don't know, blame gay math or something."

Colton scoffed. "That's not a thing."

"It most certainly is," Isaac said, seemingly genuine and almost like the animosity between the pair had disappeared. "You're either a silly twink who can't add or Sir Isaac Newton. There's no in-between."

"Who?"

"Gay nerd. Dead now."

"Oh, I'm sorry."

"I didn't know the guy," Isaac huffed. "He's been dead for hundreds of years."

"Oh." Colton tightened his lips to bite back his next question because he often found it perplexing there were gay people in history. Lots of them, according to the GSA meetings he'd attended. Lots of bi people, especially.

The curiosity made him shift onto his side, eager for more conversation. It had this way of assuaging him, easing Colton into accepting this new position he'd found himself in or the new position he was about to find himself in. He fully took in Isaac, studying the guy about to fuck him, the guy he'd dreamed about fucking, the guy he'd wanted to kiss once upon a time. He'd never feel his lips now. Not ever since Isaac only intended on hate fucking him, a grudge railing didn't come with gentle explorations or soft embraces.

"All right, back in bitch position." Isaac's piercing blue eyes had this venomous stare as he approached.

His hands roughly adjusted Colton again until his face was shoved down onto the mattress and his ass was raised high.

"Christ, did you shave before coming here?" Isaac asked, spreading Colton's cheeks and seemingly examining his hole.

"No," Colton said with resentment.

He'd always been smoother, with no chest or back hair and only mild fuzz on his legs and forearms.

"Lucky me." Isaac spit onto Colton's exposed hole and rubbed his finger around the outer rim. "Just a bit right here, but otherwise, you're smooth. Seriously, check out these cheeks."

Isaac squeezed Colton's butt before sliding a hand up the jock's back and pushing him into a deeper arch. When he reached Colton's nape, he grabbed him firmly and locked him in place while slapping Colton's ass with his other hand.

Colton yelped at the suddenness.

"Save your voice. You're gonna need it." Isaac pressed his dick against the entrance of Colton's hole. "I'm about to fucking ruin you."

With that, Isaac unceremoniously shoved his dick inside Colton. It burned in a way Colton had never experienced, a throbbing tear that spread in waves. Isaac continued bucking his hips forward, taking tiny thrusts that splintered Colton until he shouted.

"Ow." Colton gasped. "Ow. Ow. Please."

"Pillow," Isaac said with a heavy grunt and a hard thrust. "Bite down."

Colton leaned forward and buried his face as Isaac rammed his way into Colton's tight virgin ass. It hurt so much, each push unyielding. Even as Isaac worked slowly, his dick ripped Colton asunder, breaking him with each nudge of his massive cock.

"All right," Isaac said, lightly dragging his nails up and down Colton's spine. It was a bizarrely comforting sensation, though the relaxation might've had to do with the fact Isaac finally stopped shoving his dick back and forth. "We're finally inside."

"W-what?" Colton nearly yelped again.

"Fuck, you're tight, dude." Isaac smacked Colton's ass. "But I chiseled my way inside."

Isaac laughed a bit to himself, palming Colton's cheeks and clearly enjoying the jock's firm glutes as he pushed his dick just a bit more inside.

"Aaaargh." Colton groaned into the pillow before turning back just enough to see Isaac in the corner of his vision. "That was just you trying to get your dick in?"

"It's a big dick," Isaac said like he deserved credit, and maybe he did. "I'm gonna let it settle inside, let your hole learn to handle the girth."

"Thank you, thank you, thank you," Colton muttered softly as he eased his breathing.

"Yep...and then I'm gonna plow you."

Colton gulped at that comment.

"But don't worry, I'm sure it won't be enough to break an alphahole stud like you." Isaac's menacing smirk frightened Colton, so he turned back and buried his face in the pillow as he awaited what came next. "I'm sure your alpha hole will be just fine."

Once Isaac seemed confident that Colton's hole had adjusted, he moved up ever so, putting more weight onto Colton's body. He didn't believe Isaac could feel so heavy pressed down on him, but he believed he was pinned beneath a much larger man. Isaac leaned forward, pressing his chest to Colton's back as he bucked and worked his way in deeper. Colton gritted his teeth. Isaac's excited breaths hit the back of Colton's ear, and he lay completely still as the man pumped into him harder.

Despite having his hole fingered and toyed with, the instant Isaac shoved his cock further in, a hot, unbearable pain spread throughout Colton's body. He wanted to scream at the sharp sensation forcing itself further inside him. He wanted to cry. He wanted to do something, but his voice went hoarse, and nothing came out.

He silently gasped as Isaac pounded away at his rear, tearing into Colton with his dick. Christ, it was unlike anything Colton had experienced. Hell, he'd been hit across the back with a flying baseball bat before, and that felt like a fucking spa day compared to this actual fucking. How could someone enjoy this?

Well, clearly, the top could. Isaac's hands ran over Colton's skin, feeling up his taut muscles while he worked his way in and out of Colton's ass. The jock tensed the more Isaac plowed into him, and the harder he fucked, the more Colton's body resisted.

"Stop clenching," Isaac said, holding Colton's hips and ramming himself deeper into Colton's hole. "You're just gonna make it hurt more."

He tried to stop resisting, to accept Isaac's cock, but he couldn't help himself. His body flinched at the intrusion, fought back of its own accord; his ass clamped down like it'd somehow prevent this. The way Isaac grunted, the pleased hum of his moans as he thrust harder into Colton, said clearly that the tight resistance didn't bother him. It must've felt even better on his massive cock, a cock currently wreaking havoc on Colton's insides, rearranging them to make room for each added inch.

"Please, slow down." Colton whimpered, biting the pillow in hopes it'd hide his teary-eyed begging.

"Relax." Isaac stopped thrusting and ran his hands gently over Colton's back, massaging his tensed muscles. "Relax your hole, spread your legs a little wider, and stop curving up your spine."

With that, Isaac shoved his hands onto Colton and forced him back into an arch he hadn't realized he'd lost. Surrendering to Isaac's suggestion, Colton did his best to relax his hole, and he opened his legs wider. It felt like he was doing the splits on the bed, but the position helped accommodate Isaac, who moved in closer and pushed his cock further.

"Oooooooo, argh, fuck." Colton scrunched his face, willing himself to remain calm while Isaac buried himself deeper.

Now that Colton had stopped resisting, Isaac's dick eased into the loosened hole without as much piercing pain. Isaac grabbed a fistful of Colton's hair and yanked his head back, grunting in unison with the panting groans that escaped the jock's lips. He couldn't help himself, couldn't quiet himself. He lay there, sprawled out like a damn ragdoll, as Isaac railed him again and again, leaving Colton gasping and drooling.

Isaac's dick was unrelenting, and his aggression seemed to only grow more with each thrust, each passing minute. He shoved Colton's face into the pillow and picked up a faster pace, jabbing Colton's insides with his cock as their skin slapped. Each stroke held hate, taking on more brutality. It didn't seem to matter that Colton had relaxed his body, surrendered himself to Isaac. The intensity kept climbing higher until Colton couldn't breathe, couldn't keep up.

He turned his head, still enduring the firm grip of Isaac's hand, pressing his face into the pillow, but positioned himself just enough to lay there and take in tired, heavy breaths. It didn't help Isaac had already shot a load down Colton's throat. Now that he'd busted once, he'd last longer for sure. At least that was Colton's own personal experience. He prayed that Isaac would cum quickly. Each muffled whimper as he took Isaac's dick came with a hope the man would finish.

He watched the clock, vision hazy and delirious as Isaac kept fucking him until finally, he had to speak, had to beg, to cry, to admit he couldn't continue.

"Please, stop," Colton pleaded. "It hurts. It hurts too much."

He prepared a thousand more things to say, to offer, to express, but found himself lost to the agony of taking Isaac's cock. It was a futile request, one Colton knew would go unanswered. He'd offered himself up to Isaac, knowing full well what that entailed, but he hoped at the very least Isaac would have pity on the man and slow his pace, slow down just enough for Colton to catch his breath, to wipe away the tears welling in his eyes, to recover from the sheer intensity of getting fucked with so much hatred.

Surprisingly, before Colton could continue begging for a reprieve, Isaac had already slipped his dick out of him, letting the slick beast of a thing rest on an angle against Colton's ass cheeks. Isaac took a few slow breaths, seeming to calm himself, and he crawled off Colton entirely, freeing him from the pressing weight and brutal pumps.

"You stopped?" Colton rolled onto his side, taking in Isaac, who walked to the opposite side of the room and lit a smoke.

"You need a break, so we're taking one."

"Really?" Colton's expression turned skeptical. "Just like that?"

"I might own you in this arrangement, but consent is still a thing." Isaac chuckled, making the smoke waft from his mouth in big, breathy puffs. "A paradoxical statement in itself."

"A what?"

"It's just weird," Isaac answered. "I'm weird. Even by my very curved standards of what constitutes as weird, I know how fucked in the head I am."

"That so?"

"I hate you with every fiber of my being," Isaac said calmly and bluntly, like mentioning the weather. No malice in the words, just a fact. "I don't care how you feel right now. I like the twisted emotional toll this is having, the crisis of your ego, the lost identity, the pride diminished."

"I think you're giving me too much credit." Colton scrunched his face, lost a bit on the complexity of Isaac's ramble.

90

"The point is, I'm not concerned about your feelings." Isaac blew out smoke. "You're miserable? Good. Feeling degraded? Yes. Realizing you're worthless? Fuck yeah, lemme stack onto that feeling."

Colton definitely agreed with the sentiment, believing Isaac would only ever despise him.

"But all the same, I can't bring myself to actually make you suffer, suffer like…" Isaac shook his head dismissively. "No, not like I did. You could never feel that pain. After all, I walked into that arrangement willingly like a stupid fucking moron dumbass lovestruck teen bitch boy."

"I'm here willingly."

"Are you, though?" Isaac rolled his eyes, perhaps a bit lost in the sordid proposition. "Look, deal or not, consent still matters to me. Which is fuck-all weird since I basically said screw your choices and delivered the most deranged I'm-gonna-fuck-you either way ultimatum."

"Actually, technically, I made the deal." Colton sat up at that. "I mean, initially."

"Minus the screwing part."

"Just my face." Colton shrugged.

Isaac snorted at that, and for the blink of a few seconds, Colton believed they were having a moment. He believed they'd turned back the clock on all the things that ever went wrong between them.

"If it's too much, just say something. I'll stop. We'll stop. We won't do this." Isaac had this lost gaze, this absent look, a stare off with the wall.

"I'll be fine," Colton said, trying to steal Isaac's attention.

He appreciated the break, oh how his body needed it, and he found himself lost on the empathy that came from Isaac in waves, but he suspected the lust of piledriving Colton carried this compassion. Colton worried the sentiment would fade once his erection did, once his guilt dissipated. He couldn't chance Isaac moving forward with his blackmail.

"I'm ready." Colton rolled back onto his stomach and positioned himself, hoping to finish the night quickly.

"Well, I'm not, so relax, dude." Isaac tossed his smoke out the window. "Rest up and chill."

When Isaac returned to the bed, the pair rested together for a while in silence. Colton wanted to speak, to say something, anything to break the quiet, but Isaac seemed content to stare off into nothingness. More than anything, Colton wanted Isaac to be happy since his life seemed to hinge on the whims of Isaac's mood.

"You ready?" Isaac finally turned his gaze onto Colton, who nodded. "Good. Get me hard again."

In the few minutes since pausing, Isaac's erection had almost disappeared altogether. He retrieved the lube and squirted some onto his flaccid cock. Colton went to stroke him hard again.

"Mouth, please."

Reluctantly, Colton leaned forward and sucked on Isaac's cock. It didn't escape him how Isaac's cock had just been inside him, which gave Colton a strong taste of his own ass as he worked to get the guy hard again. He expected some type of taste from the lube—or perhaps hoped, anyway—but aside from the goop added to the saliva in his mouth, it didn't carry much flavor.

Thankfully, Isaac was rock-hard again quite quickly, and Colton pulled away to lay back on his stomach.

"Roll over." Isaac nudged Colton until he moved onto his back. "Grab your legs."

Isaac lifted Colton's legs and slipped in between them as Colton wrapped his hands around the back of his lower thighs. Isaac pushed down on Colton's legs, forcing his feet to touch the wall and practically twisting his body until the jock's ass was high in the air and his head was pressed beneath the weight of both their bodies.

"I wanna see that face while I fuck you."

Colton gulped, watching Isaac's cock slowly slide inside him. It seemed like the perfect vantage point for Isaac. He could watch Colton's expression contort with each thrust, and Colton would have to endure the visual of Isaac's cock ramming him again and again.

"Remember, I own you, own this ass." Isaac smirked as he thrust his hips, getting into a slow rhythm. "And I don't break my things."

Colton winced, partly from the returning pain and partly from the degrading commentary. He felt valued and worthless all in one statement.

"If it's too much, say something." Isaac rutted deeper into Colton. "I can take as many breaks as you need. By the end of the night, your hole will learn its place."

Colton nodded and turned his head.

Isaac kept a steady pace, easing his cock into Colton's hole, allowing him to adjust once again. "Eyes on me, bitch."

Colton obeyed, perplexed by how validated and simultaneously disregarded he felt.

Isaac's expression turned more and more aggressive as time passed. Soon, he bucked harder into Colton. The same rage he'd unleashed before came back just as powerful as he pumped, hips smacking Colton's thighs. Slapping skin served as the drumbeat to the vocals of Isaac's angry grunts and Colton's exhausted groans.

It started to hurt again, hurt so much Colton pressed a hand to Isaac's hip, hoping to ease his pace. Since he'd released one of his propped legs, Isaac took that as his opportunity to grab ahold of Colton's free thigh and push his leg further back, bringing the knee almost to Colton's head as he rammed harder into him. Isaac had begun jackhammering Colton, finding a brutal rhythm that Colton gritted his teeth through, stifling his screams until they transformed into moans.

"Fuuuuck," Colton bellowed.

Isaac had hit the spot again, turning the pain into pleasure. It still hurt. Fuck, did it hurt, but now there was this pressure of ecstasy that built with each thrust of Isaac's hips. Colton found his hand sliding from the front of Isaac's hip to the side, almost cupping the top of his ass as he encouraged the railing.

Isaac's blue eyes seemed to sparkle, holding an illusion of gentle light. Whether in contrast with his menacing expression or the dark eyeshadow and eyeliner, it made his baby blues pop and pulled Colton's focus. He locked his gaze onto Isaac, their bodies pressing closer together with each thrust, their embrace tightening as Colton felt himself closer and closer to climaxing.

Something about Isaac's lips called to Colton in that moment, perhaps the panting breaths they shared. The more Isaac worked his way in and out of Colton, the closer his face got, the closer his lips got, and while Colton hadn't kissed a guy yet, hadn't shared that experience like so many others tonight, he believed this was one thing he'd gladly give to Isaac. He'd wanted to taste the other boy's mouth since they were in high school.

Colton quivered in anticipation as Isaac's lips nearly brushed against his own. Isaac leaned back just enough to stop himself, then slapped his free hand over Colton's mouth, railing him harder and eliciting a pained groan, which the hand muffled.

When the moment passed, Isaac freed his hand from Colton's mouth and continued railing the jock deeper into the mattress.

"I think, I think…" Colton grunted, miserably blissful, lost in the sex.

He looked down at his cock, which flopped around only half-erect. It didn't make any sense. Colton thought he might burst any second, one more thrust inside him could very well make him explode, yet his cock didn't seem nearly as excited as the rest of his body, as excited as it'd been all night.

"I'm gonna…ffffff…" Colton bit his lower lip, stifling a howl of pleasure as Isaac's dick worked him over in ways he never knew possible, and he realized he didn't need to be hard to feel the intensity of a true orgasm.

Colton had made partners cum through anal, but that required their assistance. His partners had to either finger or jerk themselves while he fucked them, and even then, in some cases, they didn't cum until after the fact. He'd never felt so incompetent in his life, realizing how powerful his strokes should've been, could've been, but as he continued taking Isaac's cock, feeling his orgasm build bigger with each breath, he embraced it.

Warmth filled his tightening balls, and suddenly, a wave of pressure erupted. It sent heat washing over his skin. Colton cried out in pleasure, dropping his hands to the mattress and gripping the blanket like it'd somehow steady his convulsions.

Cum shot from his cock again and again, pooling on his stomach and spraying across his chest. One thread even reached his face, and Colton merely moaned in response, continuing to take Isaac's dick.

Isaac bent Colton's leg and turned him onto his side so he could hump him from a different angle. "You fucking love it, don't you?"

Colton didn't reply, too tired and satisfied to find the words. Isaac rammed harder, eliciting a pained wince from Colton, but he took the dicking, wondering if it would extend his second orgasm of the night. He couldn't fathom possibly having any more cum inside him, not after that bucket that poured out.

Isaac growled, clawing at Colton's thigh, his ass, slapping him with his hips as he took erratic and wild thrusts. "Fucking take it."

With that, Isaac came, shooting his load deep inside Colton and thrusting a bit to cling to the sensation. He pulled his cock back so only the head remained wedged inside Colton, pulsating and firing another jet of cum before he pulled out entirely and let the last spurts splat against Colton's bare ass.

After a few seconds, Isaac shoved himself back inside Colton, grunting with haggard breaths as he buried his twitching cock. Colton lay there, feeling Isaac's ferocity diminish and his cock shrink. Each of them took heavy, panting breaths. Isaac passed out awkwardly atop Colton's contorted frame as they clung together with their sticky, sweaty bodies. He kept his flaccid dick inside of Colton for a moment before finally slipping out of him and rubbing the head against the crack of Colton's ass.

"It's late," Isaac said. "You can sleep here, then head out in the morning."

"No, it's okay." Colton wheezed. "I should be getting back to my place."

"That wasn't an offer; it was an order," Isaac said quite matter-of-factly. "You do recall agreeing to my whims, correct?"

Colton nodded.

"Good." Isaac had this cocky authoritative smirk which infuriated and intrigued Colton. "My whims suggest I'd rather you not roam campus at two in the morning."

Fuck. Had it already gotten so late? Colton looked at the clock to see it had actually gotten a bit later, being a quarter after two.

"Do you have a spare toothbrush or something?"

"I could shoot another load in your mouth," Isaac said. "Everyone knows cum has a bleaching effect."

Colton scowled, which provoked a minxy smirk from Isaac, who played with his lip ring as he stared at the grumpy jock.

"Kidding. Geez. My brush is the pink one; you're more than welcome to use it." Isaac pointed to the door, obviously gesturing to the common room bathroom shared by the dorm suite.

"Seriously?"

"Pink's hot." Isaac grinned. "Don't be a hater."

"You want me to use your toothbrush?"

"Dude, you just swallowed my dick and my load. I think you can handle my teeffy germs."

Colton stepped off the bed and went to retrieve his clothes.

"No need." Isaac waved him off. "Roommates left early, so the suite is silent. Go on."

Colton still hesitated. It wasn't like he hadn't strutted around a dorm room in the nude before, but there was something significantly different about walking around boldly after fucking someone and walking around after being fucked. Being conquered. That was what it felt like, and it seemed Isaac had the strut of someone riding a victorious wave.

"Fine, I'll go first." Isaac went to the bathroom, completely naked, and stepped with a swagger.

Isaac had two tattoos on his backside. The first was a set of bloody stitches on his back beneath his shoulder blades, which looked like they closed up matching wounds. They were placed in such a way that it almost seemed like the stitched injuries sealed a set of fallen wings, or the spot wings would be located on an angel. Well, a demon in Isaac's case. The second tattoo was the word TRAMP written on his lower back in a bold, stamp-like font.

"You have a literal tramp stamp," Colton said with a snicker as Isaac strutted back toward the room, taking his time in the empty common area space.

"Lost a bet, but it's pretty funny." Isaac smirked. "Alas, it goes unused since I don't let anyone rail my ass like some fellas I know and shoot their shots for target practice."

Colton glowered, rolling his eyes. Once Isaac stepped back into the room, Colton moved through the common area, sweaty and tired, and rushing across the living room space to reach the bathroom like he was being chased by the monster under the bed. But there was no monster under the bed, merely in it. Isaac.

As he stepped into the bathroom, Colton felt the cum dripping down his crack and the inside of his thigh. He grabbed a towel, not caring whose it was, and wiped the cum from his chest, stomach, ass, thighs, and everywhere he could think except for the loads deep inside him.

Colton went to the restroom, an awkward affair, and cleaned up a bit before brushing his teeth and finally examining himself. His hair was disheveled, his face was washed out, but otherwise, he appeared completely normal, completely himself. He expected to look different. He certainly felt different.

After taking more time than he needed, Colton returned to Isaac's room and joined him in the bed. Isaac lay sprawled out on the twin bed while Colton curled up in a tight ball, taking up as little space as possible. He felt so much smaller now, lost in his thoughts. He lay awake while Isaac seemed to doze off almost immediately.

He had a light snore, not something he used to have. Not from what Colton recalled when they were younger and used to have sleepovers. Then he thought about the number of times Isaac ended up with a busted nose, someone reminding him of his place when he got mouthy at school. Maybe it got broken one too many times, and that caused the wispy noise. Either that or Isaac was faking as a way to annoy Colton after already pounding the fuck out of him.

When Isaac rolled over and pressed his naked body against Colton's, he nearly jumped. The startled flinch didn't rouse Isaac, and he continued moving in closer for a tighter embrace, sleep-cuddling with Colton. He pressed his chest against the jock's tired back, wrapped a leg over the jock's aching thigh muscles, and rested his crotch against the jock's worn-out ass.

Colton tried to wriggle loose but found Isaac's squeeze only tightened as he grumbled incoherent mutterings. Somehow, even unconscious, Isaac had learned how to issue commands that Colton found himself obeying.

Colton didn't spoon. He occasionally cuddled. But he certainly didn't make himself the little spoon who got cuddled. Despite the humbling factor, it did feel nice. Maybe it only felt nice because the fucking had finally finished.

Geez, he couldn't get that orgasm out of his head, the sheer volume that shot out of him, the way his body ached and begged for more even after Isaac's cock had pounded out the last drops from Colton's. And when he continued, when he kept thrusting into Colton's sore hole, part of him wanted Isaac to finish, and another part wanted him to keep going, keep fucking him until he climaxed for a third time.

Colton ignored all the thoughts, the incredibly confusing and fucked up thoughts swimming through his mind, and tried to fall asleep in Isaac's arms.

CHAPTER 10
ISAAC

ISAAC awoke at five in the morning, incredibly hot from being tangled in the blankets and Colton's body. When had he snuggled up to him? It didn't matter. Isaac shoved off and moved to the other side of the bed, nearly rolling off to escape the comforting embrace.

Isaac glared at Colton as he slept, thinking back to last night, how it felt, how he felt, how Colton's body trembled in his grasp, and he took in all of Isaac. He'd almost kissed Colton last night. Christ, how he craved Colton's lips, his soft pillowy lips. They were perfect for Isaac's cock, which should've been enough, but when he moaned from the sheer ecstasy of Isaac's powerful thrusts, Isaac wanted to taste the mix of pleasure and pain that spilled from Colton's voice.

That couldn't be, though. Isaac buried the desire, hoping it hadn't been the root of his morning wood. After an hour of sitting silently with an unyielding erection, he shook Colton's shoulder.

"You up?"

Colton huddled tighter under the covers, squeezing the life out of the blanket.

"Come on." Isaac playfully nudged Colton's lower back, poking him with his finger in a very suggestive manner. "I'm up. A part of me is up, up, and ready to go."

"Uuuuuuggh." Colton rolled over to face Isaac, a groggy glare on his face which only further enticed Isaac. "My ass still hurts."

"It'll be fine," Isaac said. "You just gotta give it a few days to bounce back. It's actually a shame you're leaving for winter break because now I'm gonna have to break that ass in all over again. Think of last night as a preview for the semester."

Colton groaned and tossed off the covers. Isaac stopped Colton mid-motion, as the jock started to roll over and accept his fate. Fuck, Isaac could live on this high for the rest of his life.

"Relax." Isaac stroked Colton's hair. "You're more than just a hole to me."

The bewildered expression on Colton's face carried an intoxicating allure as he studied Isaac, searching for the sincerity, for the goth's genuine attitude. Isaac let the comment linger for a few more seconds as the shock faded, and Colton nearly smiled.

"You're also a mouth." Isaac smirked, grabbing a fistful of Colton's hair and yanking his head back. It exposed his neck entirely, making his prominent Adam's apple bulge. "How about you lay back and let me fuck that throat?"

Colton frowned, then followed Isaac's hand as he shoved him further down the bed. He lay on his back with his face lined up a few inches above Isaac's hard cock, a beast of a thing barely contained by the big boxers Isaac wore. He didn't even slip them down, instead merely sliding his cock through the open slit in the front.

"Don't worry, I'll be quick." Isaac pressed the head of his cock to Colton's lips, savoring the expression, the gratification he'd soon receive.

"How quick?" Colton asked.

The idea of fucking Colton's face for hours held a satisfying urge, but the idea of using the jock's throat for a quick pump and dump for his morning wood load held even more appeal.

"Remember our morning rendezvous?" Isaac studied Colton's eyes, the realization of every morning meeting they had junior year.

Colton would wait in his car. Isaac would have to walk the length of the student parking lot because Colton wanted to ensure they had privacy. If he really wanted privacy, they'd have hooked up at Isaac's place or Colton's home, but that would require the jock to let people know he hung out with Isaac. Absolutely not.

Isaac's mind wandered to every quick and sloppy morning blowjob he gave where Colton slammed Isaac's head down and rammed his dick as deep into Isaac's throat as possible until he pumped a load out. He used to use Isaac well past his limits. Even when Isaac would explain it was too much for him to handle, Colton would promise to take it easier next time, but then he'd ream Isaac out all over again until his throat was sore, voice was hoarse, and tongue was coated in cum.

Letting the memories fade, Isaac positioned himself onto Colton as his expression stirred, possibly recalling their morning hangouts too.

Isaac straddled Colton's chest, letting his cock rest against the jock's puckered lips. Fuck, it was the perfect sight. The way Colton played with the head of Isaac's cock made him throb harder, the way Colton looked beneath him, made Isaac's body burn with a primal desire. He had Colton—he had the fantasy, the power, the authority he craved.

Yet as Colton worked on Isaac's cock as best he could from this pinned angle, Isaac found himself wanting more. Last night, he'd come close to kissing Colton. Isaac loved pressing his lips to another person's, feeling the smack of an embrace. Hell, get a few drinks in him, and he even made out with his girlfriends because, quite frankly, they had some of the most fun lips.

Kissing Colton wasn't on the agenda, though. The urge had struck last night when he fucked him, when Colton whimpered and took Isaac's cock obediently. He seemed so perfect in the moment, and Isaac wanted to taste that perfection. He wanted to swallow Colton's voice, taste all of him. But kissing came with feelings, with passion, with lust. Isaac kissed his boyfriends and his hookups in equal measure, but Colton wasn't either. Colton was here to serve; Colton was here to learn. Colton was meant to feel as worthless as Isaac had felt when they were together in high school. Kissing him now would only complicate and confuse matters.

"Open your mouth," Isaac ordered.

Colton stretched his jaw as wide as he could and braced his hands at Isaac's hips.

"Keep those at your sides." Isaac glared, bringing his dick away from Colton's mouth for a moment. It allowed him a wonderful view of those beautiful pouty lips. They were kissable and fuckable, but Isaac only intended to use them for one purpose.

Colton put his hands at his sides, even going a step above and pushing them under his back, subsequently pinning them so he wouldn't be tempted. This would make Isaac's morning face fuck even easier.

"You ready for this dick?"

When Colton went to answer, Isaac rammed his cock right into the jock's mouth. The immediate struggle from the suddenness sent a primal heat through him. He rocked his hips back and forth, pounding against Colton's face and stuffing his dick deeper into Colton's tight throat.

Isaac got into a quick rhythm with Colton lying back on the bed. While Isaac forced his cock further into Colton's throat, he noticed Colton's legs kick a few times, his only sign of resistance as his gag reflex had nowhere to run from this angle.

Gravity and Isaac's position helped get his cock all the way down Colton's throat, where he went to work reaming it. The pleasure that came from shoving in and out as Colton gagged and gurgled and choked on copious amounts of spit that soon spilled from his mouth ignited a fiery passion inside Isaac. He could spend all day fucking Colton's face, breaking in his throat to make it perfect, but he'd promised to be quick.

Isaac humped Colton's face, savoring the sensation and groaning. His balls slapped against Colton's chin, barely contained by the fabric of Isaac's boxers. Part of him wanted to slip off his underwear, really let his balls smack Colton's face as he fucked his mouth, but that would require him pulling his cock out of Colton's mouth. A seemingly impossible task now that Isaac had gotten into a perfect rhythm, feeling a warmth spread throughout his body as his dick pulsed more and more with each pump.

The weight of his body and the fast thrust of his hips made Colton's eyes tear up, and Isaac loved the sight of those glossy green gems. They were locked on Isaac's aggressive expression, one he let consume him as the primal need to own Colton consumed him.

"Yeah, baby." Isaac rammed harder into the tight muscles of Colton's throat. "You ready for this?"

Colton gurgled and continued taking Isaac's cock.

"Answer me," Isaac demanded, shoving his cock all the way to the base and holding it there.

Colton squirmed and writhed beneath Isaac, gasping on the fabric of the boxers and choking on the finely trimmed pubes. He couldn't hold Isaac's cock for much longer, but the angry goth didn't let up.

"Answer me." Isaac smacked Colton's head and then tugged his hair. "Tell me how much you want my cum."

"Uuuuuhhhhmmmm," Colton barely managed.

The sheer satisfaction of watching him struggle to be so obedient sent a rush of pleasure through Isaac.

"Take my load," Isaac said, pulling his cock back but keeping the head in Colton's mouth. He stroked himself a few times, using the spit on his slick dick. "You want this cum, don't you?"

Colton continued sucking on the head of Isaac's cock, taking frantic, gasping breaths as he worked hard.

"Open your mouth, bitch." Isaac growled, and Colton obeyed. "Tongue out."

The instant Colton stuck his tongue out, the sight sent Isaac over the edge, and he shot three powerful jets of cum into Colton's beautiful used mouth.

"Swallow it," Isaac panted with a fiery command, and again, Colton obeyed.

The exhausted look on his face, coupled with the loud gulp as he ate Isaac's cum sent a whole new rush through Isaac as he continued stroking himself.

He twitched and released his fourth and final shot; it missed Colton's mouth, but the landing was somehow even better. It splattered in the corner of his eye, which made the jock hold them both closed. Isaac took his cock and rubbed it against Colton's face, pressing the head against Colton's eye and smearing the cum down the jock's cheek.

"You are a fucking sight to behold." Isaac slipped off Colton's chest and let the jock lay there, taking heavy breaths now that he finally could.

"Can you get me a towel or something?"

"In a minute." Isaac sparked a smoke and made Colton lay on the bed, with his flushed face covered in spit and cum.

After his smoke, Isaac retrieved a towel and gently wiped down Colton's face. Isaac sat close to Colton, too close. When the jock opened his eyes, he had this vexing expression of gratitude.

"You should get going," Isaac said before Colton could speak, before he could utter a pointless 'thank you' as if Isaac deserved such things. "It's a long drive to Straight Arrow."

"Yeah." Colton nodded.

"Have fun with your time off." Isaac's cocky expression inferred he meant with classes and having his new submissive role in life.

"Are you going to be in town?" Colton asked, a softness to his voice. "Pretty sure our old haunts are still discreet if you wanna—"

"I have no intention of ever stepping foot in that town again," Isaac interjected. "I set fire to all those bridges the day I graduated."

"Of course." Colton cast his gaze down, studying Isaac's shaky leg. "If you need me to do anything or come back—"

"Relax." Isaac pressed a hand to Colton's shoulder. "Enjoy your break. We'll have plenty of time once the spring semester kicks off."

"What is this exactly?" There was a soft curiosity in Colton's eyes.

Isaac had seen it last night, too. He'd railed Colton so hard he must've fucked some feelings into the jock. That position of vulnerability, coupled with their sordid history, was doing Colton no favors when it came to seeing this for what it was. It wasn't doing Isaac any favors either. Looking at the tiny tremble in Colton's lower lip, Isaac lost himself in Colton's pleading gaze. Fuck, Isaac wanted to kiss him, to taste him, to say 'fuck it' to the arrangement they had and try to give this a real shot. His younger self stalked from the shadows of his mind, reminding Isaac how much he'd always wanted to be with Colton, to really be with him, to hug him and hold him and love him. To be equals together. To be intimate together.

But Isaac couldn't have that. He'd used Colton last night, and there was no undoing the malice in his actions, no sating the hate that had seeped into his heart, no altering the wicked manipulation to get Colton in his bed.

"This is an arrangement where I fuck you and use you, and when I'm bored, I'll release you." Isaac stared at the stark realization crumbling Colton's calm demeanor.

"Right, duh." Colton quickly nodded. "It's just like high school."

"Exactly." Isaac squeezed Colton's shoulder tighter. "Except you're the one taking it now."

"Every which way." Colton gave a weak laugh. "I should get going."

"Be safe." Isaac cringed at his well wishes and turned away before Colton could look at him.

Isaac waited until Colton left before returning to his bed, where he faceplanted onto the mattress and lay there until the sun went down. The anxiety of this whole arrangement sent his mind spiraling in a million different directions.

Thankfully, campus was damn near empty over winter break, and Isaac planned on using those long, lonely days to reflect on what he'd done, what he planned to continue doing, and most importantly, what he couldn't allow to happen. Isaac wouldn't let old feelings fester, he wouldn't let Colton's golden boy charm worm its way into his heart. He wouldn't pine for the jock who'd already shattered his very being.

This was purely sex. Revenge. A twisted delight to get his rocks off and knock Colton down a peg. Several pegs.

Still, as he lay in bed, consumed by his thoughts, he found himself longing for the kiss he kept avoiding. Isaac stroked himself hard at the idea of kissing Colton. His fantasies shifted from forcing the jock to his knees, forcing him on all fours, to turning into something soft and sweet. Rough sex danced at the edge of his fantasy as he jerked himself faster, but sweet kisses filled the images in his head, kind words, happy smiles, and suddenly Isaac was cumming harder than he had last night.

"Fucking hell," Isaac huffed.

It seemed even with Colton giving Isaac everything he wanted, he couldn't be happy.

CHAPTER 11
COLTON

IN the days that followed his trip home, Colton had this hollowed-out sensation wherever he went. It wasn't just the fact his ass still ached from Isaac's cock, or how he could still taste the cum in the back of his throat. A phantom flavor lingering no matter how many Christmas cookies he scarfed down to avoid conversation with family. It was a yearning that swelled deep inside him; with every breath came flashes of Isaac's face, Isaac's hands raking over Colton's muscular body, Isaac's heavy grunts as he railed into Colton, Isaac's soft expression when his lips lingered close to Colton's mouth.

Every thought Colton had was of Isaac. This was what Isaac had wanted—Colton to lust for him the same way he'd lusted for Colton. There was so much about this arrangement he loathed, yet so much he couldn't help but ponder with each passing second lost in a daze.

"You've been awfully quiet." Colton's mother sauntered toward the corner where Colton had holed up. "You feeling okay?"

He nodded, then grabbed another cookie. Normally, he hated the quiet, loathed awkward silence and fed off the energy of idle chitchat. But his mind was lost on the arrangement he'd made with Isaac, on the pain still thrumming softly inside him, on the circumstances that led him down this path, and how he desperately wanted to discuss this with someone.

BEND HIM BREAK HIM

Not Isaac holding blackmail over him, not the fact he'd bent over and been railed out rough by Isaac's cock. No, those were things he'd keep secret forever if possible. The warped feelings that fluttered in his chest gave him pause, the recollection of the intense pleasure that came with the excruciating pain still radiated inside him.

No matter what he did, Colton could think of little else other than how Isaac made him cum. Not once, but twice. All with his touch, with his dominance, with his aggression and hate and authority all wrapped into a fuck that Colton couldn't get out of his head.

His insides twisted in on themselves as he thought about reliving that carnal experience. What else would Isaac do to him? Would it be more of the same? Would things escalate? In the beginning, when Colton sought out Isaac for oral, he wasn't nearly as rough on the teen goth's throat, but by the second month, he was face fucking him so brutally it made Isaac's rough demands seem almost considerate.

Colton couldn't get the reversal of fortunes out of his head, the way he'd still clung to feelings and desperate pining for Isaac even after everything that broke between them. But the idea of submitting, of regularly being bottomed out for Isaac's entertainment, made it impossible for Colton to focus on the vacation.

"Are you even listening to me, sweetie?"

Colton nodded, doing his best to smile at whatever tangent his mother had been going on about. Given the crease in her brow and the side eye she shot in the direction of the party, there was someone in attendance who'd offended her and would soon receive her ire.

"Is it school?" his mother asked, genuine concern showing on her face.

His mother wasn't nearly as bitter at Colton for following his heart as his father was, but she didn't defend his actions either. Colton made the error of going out independently, so if he floundered in college, his family would be there to remind him they told him so.

"Do you want to talk about it?" she asked, likely trying to gauge how his academic probation was going since Colton had stopped sharing details about school after his father mocked his freshman failings. Now, his folks

108

fished for information, and Colton did his damnedest to ignore the bait. "Are you struggling with your grades again? From what I hear, the campus has some wonderful tutors."

"Grades are fine," Colton said. "Aced everything."

Okay, not true, but he did maintain a B average his semester, which was almost worth bragging about.

When he spotted his father from across the room, Colton sighed. He was making his rounds quickly as he came to join Colton and his mother, which could only mean they planned on grilling him for more details. They wanted to know everything about his college experience, except how he was enjoying things, fitting in, coping with independence, his performance in baseball, or a multitude of other questions that leaned toward support.

"Colton." His father slapped his shoulder and rattled a little life back into Colton's weary disposition. "Join me. There's a few people I want to introduce you to."

Ah, fuck. Based on the layout, there were no board members or alumni or bullshit donors to any of the Ivy Leagues Colton's father continued trying to pressure him into attending. That meant the holidays had been reserved for romance instead.

The most grueling part of coming back home. Since being outed, Colton's parents had taken a strong interest in his love life, something they never did in high school. It was funny how many women they casually tried to arrange with him, reminding him how much they supported his bisexuality and that, as a bisexual, he should enjoy these beautiful, educated young women.

They were the furthest thing from subtle. Normally, he'd eagerly chase the skirts, but having his parents pick out his dates only made Colton want guys more. Anything to piss them off and have a good time.

Colton's parents had taken a strong stance on tolerating his predilections to whatever phase he was going through so long as he eventually leaned down the correct path. His mother blamed the media, and his father blamed the liberal college Colton picked. If either of them realized he'd first longed for cock while attending a prestigious conservative prep school, their heads would probably explode. A tempting idea to test, but that would involve having an honest conversation with his parents, something Colton had never done in all his life. Not that he could recall. Perhaps as a little kid, but even then, his mother was going through her European travel phase, and his father always believed children were best to be seen and never heard.

Colton shook away the curiosities and the annoyance about the random women scattered throughout the party. Part of him considered sneaking off and flirting with a potential suitor. Hell, part of him considered downloading an app to see if there was a discreet, unsuitable companion for the evening. But he buried those thoughts as quickly as they came.

Isaac's commands rang loudly in Colton's mind. Isaac's demands of ownership, of exclusivity, struck a chord that held Colton in check. He didn't want to assert himself with another person, especially someone his parents picked out. And he didn't want to explore the curiosities he'd allowed Isaac to perform with another man.

So, Colton abandoned the party early and went to his room, where he stroked himself hard until he could relive the best orgasm of his life.

Nothing he did kept his attention, mind unable to focus on porn of any kind, thoughts to fantasies that once brought him exhilaration now fizzled out along with his erection. No. The only thing that kept him throbbing was thinking back to the night he feared repeating. The night he feared might not come again. Isaac had stayed true to his word, allowing Colton to enjoy the break without his presence, but now it felt more like a punishment. Fitting, since Isaac wanted Colton to suffer.

As the days pressed on and the holiday engagement remained an exhausting ordeal of smiling faces with cutting comments, Colton came up with an excuse to leave early. A break with his family was more work than it was worth, so he blamed baseball practice and headed back to campus. His parents grumbled that he had to leave right after New Years, but he needed a few days of quiet to clear his head. It helped that his folks didn't know the first thing about Colton's baseball schedule since they'd never shown an interest in any of the sports he played.

The campus was mostly abandoned. Even the parking lot for the apartments in the back of the school grounds was left barren. A few cars were scattered about, but Colton figured most of them had just left their vehicle and taken a flight home instead.

When he stepped into his apartment, the living room and kitchen were trashed with empty liquor bottles, wrapping paper, and a bunch of holiday bullshit that intended a terribly themed Christmas college party. Definitely not Tim's scene since he didn't celebrate and also cleaned up after his parties. Colton's other roommate, Devon, was usually better, but since he started hanging with Leon, he'd gotten sloppy on and off the field. This was probably some petty advice from Leon to leave the mess as a way to fuck with Colton. He shook away the thought, as if he'd ever care about a mess, and didn't want to be so petulant that he assumed everything revolved around him.

Colton had intended to hide out during the rest of the break, but he told himself that Isaac might notice his Mercedes had returned to campus and be cross if he didn't reach out.

That was the flimsy excuse Colton fed himself as he texted Isaac. His chest tightened, and his heart skipped a beat when the three floating dots bubbled on his phone. They started, then stopped, then started again, and Colton held his breath the entire time he awaited Isaac's impending command.

> Isaac: K.

Seriously? Colton furrowed his brow. He didn't expect enthusiasm but figured the young dom would demand his presence.

> Colton: Thought you'd wanna know since you know...

> Isaac: Come over tomorrow.

> Colton: Surprised you don't want me to *come* now.

He debated adding an emoji but decided against it. The play on words made him giggle. Colton wasn't the best at innuendos, so when he thought of one, a bit of immature pride filled him. It wasn't much, but that little joke helped lighten the mood between them, at least for Colton, anyway.

He waited half the night, expecting Isaac to send some type of follow-up message or perhaps a horny late-night change of heart on Colton's offer to come over. After two hours of being left on read, Colton told himself when Isaac sent the desperate message looking to get off, he'd ignore the text and let the dickhead suffer. All the same, he remained glued to his phone, awaiting a message that never came until he finally passed out late in the night.

The next day, he got ready as best he could, trying to look good. Why was he wasting his time trying to look good? Isaac wouldn't care, and if he did, he wouldn't show it. Still, Colton spent extra time cleaning himself, used his favorite colognes, put more effort and product in his hair than usual, and changed outfits about five times before settling on a combo of the first and third attempts.

The walk across campus was quiet. Between the eerie silence and the crisp, cold air of January, Colton found himself more alert than usual. He enjoyed the emptiness of campus and hoped he'd have a bit of time to wander and roam over the next few days before the bustle of thousands stampeding to and from started up again.

When Colton arrived at Isaac's dorm, the grumpy goth greeted him with a surly frown.

"You're late."

"Traffic." Colton shrugged, to which Isaac merely rolled his eyes and yawned.

Isaac appeared to have put in the opposite amount of effort into his attire, wearing an oversized hoodie that had been slashed to rip a jagged V cut neckline in front and shredded to cutoff like a crop top. It exposed Isaac's pale, muscular stomach. The sparkle of his belly piercing and the detail of the twisted shark tooth smile tattooed on his lower stomach both drew Colton's gaze. The slight ab muscles poking out kept Colton's attention. While Isaac didn't have nearly the same level of muscles as Colton, he did have a tight, firm form.

Isaac also wore a baggy pair of cartoon pajama pants, which hung low, exposing his flannel boxers. They were bulky but still accentuated his butt. For such a slender guy, Isaac had more of an ass than Colton remembered. Not that he'd get to experience it, but his immediate thoughts did wander, especially since he knew where the day was leading.

"So, what's on the agenda?" Colton asked, unable to bear silence for more than a minute, unlike Isaac, who would seemingly say nothing. "I mean, I've got an idea."

"Don't do that," Isaac said, closing the door behind Colton and directing him toward the desk instead of the bed.

"Don't do what?"

"Don't have ideas or assumptions."

"'Cause it'll make an ass out of both of us?" Colton feigned a smile. "Here, I thought you wanted to make an ass out of me."

"I'm not fucking you today," Isaac said quite bluntly as he sat in a chair at his office desk and ushered Colton into the second seat.

"You know I got all shower fresh, even ate light considering." Colton gestured, wanting some validation for his efforts.

"And this is why I say don't make assumptions," Isaac said. "Ask me for clarification, for instructions, but don't waste your breath trying to gauge my thoughts."

Colton huffed, giving Isaac a cold stare. Isaac returned the look, then cocked his head with a curious expression. He studied Colton's body with unblinking eyes, which made the jock fold his arms over his chest as if that'd somehow hide him from Isaac's intrusive gaze.

"You wanted to get fucked."

"No." Colton scoffed with as much bluster as he could manage. "I don't wanna get fucked. I was just ready for it is all. Which you should be grateful for. Show some fucking gratitude. I'm playing the part you want me to."

"Uh-huh." Isaac's face had this aloof, unconvinced quality. "You want my dick."

Colton clenched his fists, stood tall, stood proud, like he hoped the sheer force in his stance could disprove Isaac's belief.

"Makes it even better to deny my cock for the evening." Isaac chuckled, his bored face transforming into a minxy grin. "Don't worry. We'll be screwing again soon enough. Just gotta set up a fuck fest routine for my cock hungry muscle bottom."

Colton snarled at that, almost tempted to snatch Isaac by the collar. As he moved, he saw Isaac's foot press against the corner of the desk like he was bracing himself and ready for any potential outburst. That made Colton's anger dissipate, made the shame of Isaac's mockery fizzle out, only to be replaced by a different type of guilt. Isaac's immediate defenses, his paranoid processes, his ruthless tactics. They all came to be because Colton broke him, allowed him to be beaten and bullied and belittled to such a degree, it nearly killed Isaac.

"Then why am I here if you don't wanna fuck me?" Colton didn't note the offended pitch in his voice until after he'd asked his question.

Why was he offended? He should be grateful. Last time Isaac piledrived his ass, Colton nearly broke down in tears. Still, he couldn't stop thinking about that orgasm. He'd jerked off every day over winter break, sometimes twice a day, and he couldn't relive that experience, that explosive release.

"You're here because I demanded it." Isaac yanked Colton by the collar of his shirt, pulling him closer so his breath hit the back of Colton's ear and sent goosebumps trailing down his spine. "Sit."

Colton obeyed, and Isaac released his grip.

"We need to set up some ground rules moving into the start of the semester."

"You call, I come over, you cum." Colton shrugged. "Seems pretty self-explanatory."

"Well, well, well, looks like you can be taught." Isaac trailed his fingers along Colton's leg, teasing him or taunting him. Colton couldn't determine which, and it was maddening. "There might be a good boy in you, after all."

Colton quivered as Isaac's touch ran further up his thigh, fingertips grazing the stiff bulge in his jeans. An erection he hadn't expected but one that'd followed him since he left his campus apartment.

"Are you a good boy, Colt?" Isaac asked. His words slinked through the air, adding to the hot and bothered arousal that wouldn't be sated tonight. At least according to Isaac and his lack of a mood.

"I'm a very good boy." Colton moved forward, adding the same sultry flair to tease, to test, to tantalize.

The look in Isaac's eyes came with a hunger—the same one he had beneath the anger and hatred, the same yearning as he fucked Colton.

"That so," Isaac leaned closer, sliding his firm hand up Colton's abs, then resting on his chest. "Then be a good boy and sit back and be quiet."

With that, Isaac shoved Colton and turned his attention to the laptop like they hadn't just had a moment. Apparently, they hadn't. Another way for Isaac to toy with Colton's mind, and he imagined most of the semester would go this way.

Colton didn't respond, simply obeyed. Ultimately, he knew if Isaac said jump, he would. There was something freeing and frightening about giving over control to Isaac. Every second was like navigating how much shame he could endure while also opening him up to a level of comfort he'd never known. Colton wished Isaac didn't hate him so much, wished there was something more to this arrangement. He wondered if Isaac felt this way when Colton used him for a daily release. He wondered if this tension and trepidation crawling over his skin would change over the next five months. Would it lessen? Would it get worse? Would he be lost to the lust by the end of the semester?

"Put in your student ID." Isaac slid his laptop toward Colton.

"Why?"

"So, I can see your schedule."

"Oh, I can pull it faster." Colton retrieved his phone.

"Did I ask that?" Isaac glared. "You need to learn to listen. I didn't say pull up your schedule. What did I say?"

Colton swallowed nervously.

"What did I tell you to do?"

Colton averted his gaze, looking at the floor. "To put in my student ID."

"Then what should you be doing?"

Without further prompting, Colton typed in his information and pulled up his student dashboard so Isaac could review his schedule. This was what ruined the tension between them. Isaac's disgust, which always seemed to rear its ugly head between their moments. It'd happened since Colton came to Clinton University. It'd happened since this arrangement began. And it seemed no matter how Colton behaved, Isaac's attitude wouldn't change.

"Yeah, we're gonna have to flip some of this around."

"Wait, what?" A wave of nervousness washed over Colton. "You can't just change my schedule. It's important I follow a strict—"

"Yeah, yeah, yeah." Isaac lifted the student handbook tucked within a stack of other books. "I reviewed all the academic probationary bullshit. They're such cucks about their requirements to get off."

"Huh?"

"Get off probation." Isaac winked. "I'm just gonna rearrange some stuff so our schedules overlap a bit better. Plus, you have all this open and wasted time in the afternoons and evenings."

"Baseball practice. I need that time."

Isaac sucked his teeth. "Okay. Write down your times and stuff and whatever. Games. Things. Practice. Yada yada."

Colton scribbled practice times. "Games vary, but I can pull up the schedule. I have an early one on my phone."

"Text it to me." Isaac tinkered with Colton's classes, dropping two of them immediately.

"Shouldn't you make sure another class is available before dropping one?" Colton asked, his stomach twisting in knots. "If I'm not registered as full-time, I'll be in violation of my probation."

"You don't say?" Isaac waved the student handbook before chucking it behind his head and onto the floor. "I'm saving your ass, if you'll let me."

Only so he could fuck it; Colton scoffed at the snappy comeback he kept to himself.

"You had econ with Bates, who is an absolute hard ass who hates anyone daring to take his general ed requirement and not treating econ like the most valuable course in the universe." Isaac made a jerking motion with his hand. "He's a sad old man who likes to stroke his ego daily and punish anyone not ready for a metaphoric facial where he expresses his genius."

"I only understood about half of that." Colton scrunched his face. "Does he, like, sleep with students?"

"Gross and no." Isaac shuddered dramatically. "Just know he's a dick who likes to abuse his authority over people."

"I couldn't imagine having to deal with someone like that." Colton glowered at Isaac until the goth broke out into a mischievous grin.

"Point is your professors are always informed of your probation status, and someone like Bates would probably make your life hell just to see you squirm."

Colton was surprised. Isaac switched him to a nicer professor but at an earlier time of day. Colton didn't like the idea of getting up at 8 AM three days a week, but he did like that the new professor apparently graded heavily on participation, which meant just showing up and nodding. That was something Colton could definitely do.

"Why are you working so hard to make my schedule better?"

"So, you don't fail out." Isaac shrugged as if it were the most obvious thing in the world.

Colton knew their arrangement and what he agreed to, but that was only so Isaac wouldn't out his plagiarism, his cheating. Nothing about what they discussed involved Isaac going out of his way to ensure Colton passed his classes.

"Why do you care?"

"If you fail your probation, I don't get to fuck you anymore," Isaac said with a wicked grin. "I'm digging the cheap and easy lay. I'd have to hop back on those hell apps to get off if you stopped getting me off."

Colton scoffed and let Isaac work. It was a lie. An obvious lie that even Colton caught. Even if he failed his courses, the disciplinary committee only checked his grades at the end of each semester. Isaac's arrangement went until the end of the semester, so the timeline of his concern didn't add up.

"Thank you," Colton said.

"Whatever. Just try not to fail these easy courses."

It seemed Isaac had info on all the professors worth taking or avoiding and did his best to set the jock up with the best of the best for a light spring semester.

"All righty." Isaac clapped his hands and went to retrieve a notebook and highlighters. "Time for some arts and crafts."

"Seriously?"

"No." Isaac chuckled. "But I do enjoy a color-coded schedule."

Soon, Isaac was writing out times and days when Colton and him could hang out. He'd taken into account Colton's classes, practices, and studying time—which Colton wouldn't use. Still, watching Isaac work so meticulously to set up a schedule, to rearrange his classes so he'd actually be successful, to carve out "SOLO" time every single day so Colton's every waking minute wasn't spent on school, baseball, or serving Isaac. There'd still be time for peace. Extra time since he'd take those chunks of studying sessions for games or something fun.

An impulse rattled inside of Colton, one that'd struck him many times before, but he'd always managed to quell it. He always managed to push down the desire with logic and fear, to wait for the right time in the right situation with the right guy. That'd never happen. The only guy in his foreseeable future was Isaac, the only person, and while he might hate Colton, he'd already shown him more compassion than Colton felt worthy of. He took an interest in Colton's wellbeing.

It was enough to make him hunger.

Without thinking, without hesitation, without warning, Colton leaned over and kissed Isaac on the lips. Much to his surprise, Isaac didn't pull back. There was shock in his eyes, and his shoulders tensed from what Colton could see, but his mouth accepted Colton's tongue.

Such a bizarre feeling. He'd kissed lots of girls but never a guy. Colton expected the sensations to strike differently, and to some extent, they did. Isaac brought out more enthusiasm from Colton. He found himself lost in the goth boy's mouth. The piercings added something, too. The lip ring was little more than a decoration, but the tongue piercing—oh, that added a spark every time Isaac lapped at Colton. He'd run the metallic bar along Colton's tongue, leading the kiss. It was intoxicating, hypnotizing.

Their lips smacked and Colton let himself fall into the kiss, leaning closer to Isaac and savoring the taste of his mouth as he ran his tongue over Isaac's.

"What are you doing?" Isaac pressed his forehead against Colton's, forcing their lips apart.

Colton panted, hungry for Isaac's mouth. "Just saying thank you, I guess."

"That isn't how people say thank you."

"You're obviously not being thanked by the right people." Colton turned his head ever so to go in for another kiss.

Isaac pulled away and moved from his chair to go stand in the center of the tiny dorm room.

"You don't make the rules here, make the moves, make anything happen that I don't want." The edge in Isaac's voice roused the same tension that'd settled inside Colton over break.

He liked Isaac's aggression, his anger. While he hated the way Isaac's rage twisted into hatred for Colton, he did find it somehow alluring how Isaac could pour that malice into Colton and create a spark of... Colton didn't know what exactly. But he liked the feeling. There was something fiery and primitive about it, and while it frightened him, he wanted to dive deeper into the experience. After all, he didn't have much say in things, so he allowed himself to be taken in by the currents of Isaac's authority.

"I know you're in charge. And I'll abide by whatever you want. You can see that, right?" Colton rose from his seat and approached Isaac, cautious in his steps even though Isaac was a force of power. "But I can't get our night out of my head. It's not what I expected, what I ever thought I wanted, but there's something about this. About us."

"There is no us."

"Yes, there is." Colton ran his hands through his hair, searching for the right words, but only left with a feeling. "It's wrong in this right kind of way, and it's reminded me of what we had but also what we never had."

Isaac's anger faded for a moment, replaced by curiosity, perhaps the same insecure musings that'd haunted Colton over winter break. Surely, he'd felt the spark between them again after so much time apart, so much hate, so much wrongdoing.

"I want to explore these lost feelings, the missed opportunity between us."

"There was no missed opportunity," Isaac snapped. "There was only you destroying what we had, what we could've had. Now, we have nothing."

"We have this." Colton grazed his knuckles along Isaac's forearms, gentle yet eager. "Let's explore what we never had the chance to before."

"Fine. But don't get any ideas." Isaac kissed Colton again, this time leading their mouths. "You're just a mouth, a hole, a body for me to use and explore."

"Of course." Colton pressed up against Isaac, letting his sculpted muscles push them back toward the bed.

"Don't confuse this with something it isn't." Isaac wrapped a hand around the back of Colton's neck and held him in place. "You mean nothing to me."

"You keep saying that. Yet you've gone out of your way to help me be more successful. You've also—"

"If you fail, I lose my fuck toy," Isaac growled, tilting Colton's head and running his teeth along the jock's neck. "Your success is merely for my benefit. Nothing more."

"Of course." Colton shuddered at the way Isaac's tongue licked from his collarbone up to his jawline.

In an instant, Isaac threw Colton down onto the bed and fell atop him, their bodies lost in a grind guided by their kisses.

Both boys had wanted to kiss for years now. Colton had seen Isaac's desperate yearning to press lips since the first blowjob, and now, they were locked in a passionate make-out session. Colton did let this confuse him, buying into the illusion and deluding himself with the notion that this somehow brought them closer. It brought them closer than any apology ever would, more than any sex.

Colton lost himself in Isaac's rough hands that caressed his body, pushing him back onto the bed so the angry goth could have his way with Colton's mouth. Every part of him tensed in anticipation of Isaac ripping off his clothes, to slap him mid-kiss, to flip him over and ram his cock into Colton's hole.

Isaac didn't do any of that, though. He just kissed Colton while grinding against him. When Colton grinded back, the two panted between kisses.

CHAPTER 12
ISAAC

ISAAC had gone into this arrangement expecting to play head games with Colton. Instead, he found himself avoiding the irksome jock since their make-out session at the end of winter break. It was a busy first week of classes, anyway. Plus, Colton needed to adjust to his schedule. Not that Isaac should care. He didn't. It was a convenience factor only.

> Colton: You look bored outta ur fucking mind.

Isaac glared up at Colton, who sat in the same seat as last semester, with the same group of jocks and the same bored expression as the lecture went in one ear and out the other. He and his friends chatted during the lecture, quietly for a change, but still absurd.

> Isaac: You should be paying attention.

> Colton: I'll just ask the TA for the answers after class.

> Isaac: There's no answer key to an essay!

Colton: Learning something new already.

When he looked up again, Colton had this cocky smoldering expression that matched the flirty emoji he sent next. It was infuriating.

Colton: You can sum up everything I missed. Unless you plan on dodging me again.

Isaac: I was letting you get settled with your schedule.

Which was true since Colton had started classes and baseball training—not that he or his teammates paid much attention in class. Or any class, Isaac wagered.

However, since Colton wanted to get frisky and flirty and frustrate Isaac, he decided to put an end to his considerations and remind Colton of the purpose behind their arrangement.

Professor Howard wrapped up her lecture and dismissed the class before heading out quicker than the students so she could take advantage of her lunch break. Isaac didn't need to rush, and he didn't want to. According to his schedule, this was the perfect time to speak with Colton.

"Hey, Colton, hang back for a bit."

Colton and his team paused. Colton was likely waiting for a reason—a plausible reason—he needed to hang back, and the teammates simply seemed curious why some prick TA was hassling one of them.

"Damn, man, those queer kids still riding your dick? He's not a mascot, you know?" Leon side-eyed Isaac with a playful smile but a menacing gaze. One Isaac had become quite familiar with in high school.

He gulped, only catching himself after the long-forgotten habit. A little action that used to help him swallow his words and hide his fear when bullies approached, which was a daily occurrence. Isaac knew what would happen next. Colton would save face like he'd always done when Isaac was stupid enough to talk to him in public. Colton would likely say something insulting, offensive, and degrading. The only difference between then and now was at least Isaac could scold Colton for his behavior when they were alone. Which clearly wouldn't be now, based on Colton's wide-eyed stare.

"I'll catch up with you," Colton said, waving off Leon and the other players. "Like everyone else, GSA loves a star pitcher."

Leon lingered a bit longer than the others, eyeing Colton as if he were evaluating him—the sincerity in his jovial voice, the free nature of his body language. Isaac's anxiousness quickly twisted back to anger the longer Leon looked Colton over.

"You say star like you're the only one on the team." Leon grinned, phony and twitchy to fight back a frown. "I'm a great pitcher, too. Though, not the kind this lot's looking for."

Leon nodded at Isaac, who bared his teeth in response. Colton merely laughed off the joke, adding his own gay baseball humor onto Leon's cutting comment.

When Leon finally left and the rest of the class cleared out, Isaac led Colton out into the empty hallway for a private discussion.

"Why do you always do that?" Isaac snapped.

"Do what?"

"Play pretend when someone's insulting you. Right to your face, in fact."

"Because unlike you, I learned a long time ago that life's a lot easier if you don't make everyone an enemy."

"And unlike you, I learned life's a lot easier if you stop treating enemies like friends." Isaac glowered. "That douchebag pitcher needs his teeth knocked out."

"Leon's an acquired taste for sure." Colton sighed. "But he's got it out for me, and it's better to play along than start an outright feud."

Colton explained the complications he dealt with as Isaac led him down the hallway. He revealed how his seemingly starlit spot on the baseball team was quite precarious, given his disciplinary issues, struggling grades, and homophobic teammates who bucked against his position. Sure, many supported him, but it only took a few complaints to make waves. Leon led the tug-of-war for starting pitcher, for star player, for everyone's favorite MVP.

Isaac lost focus while listening to the explanations, almost forgetting where he intended to lead Colton until they reached a four-way intersection near some elevators.

"Now you see why essays and assignments aren't at the top of my to-do list." Colton wiggled his eyebrows, being cute, which didn't work on Isaac.

"Maybe if you spent more time studying, you'd have a better solution to deal with your enemies."

"Ooooooh." Colton smirked. "Is that why you're so crafty with your punishments?"

"You wanna see punishment?" Isaac stepped closer, removing any distance between him and Colton.

The near embrace almost made Colton fall back against the wall. He might be out, but he didn't do PDA with guys, especially guys like Isaac.

"Meet me in the bathroom, last stall."

"What?"

"I need some relief, and honestly, you need a lesson on what happens when you run your mouth during class."

"Here?" Colton shook his head to protest.

"You think I'm gonna drag you back to my dorm room every time I wanna plow you?" Isaac's icy blue eyes locked onto Colton. "Did you take me back to your place every time I sucked your dick?"

"No, I never brought you…" Colton paused, frantically checking over his shoulder for anyone approaching, but there was no one around—Isaac knew that much at this time of day. "This isn't high school. We can't just mess around behind the bleachers or in an empty locker room or my car."

"Why not?" Isaac pressed himself against Colton, relishing the heavy beat of the nervous jock's heart. "From what I've gathered, alpha stud baseball star fucks around wherever he feels like swinging his bat."

"That's different."

"How so?" Isaac batted his eyes, tempting Colton to confirm his apprehension for public play. "Please explain how me fucking your throat in the bathroom is different from you getting sucked off in a locker room."

"Well, for starters, you already know I have an issue with public indecency." Colton huffed. "The rumors are true. I got caught getting a blowjob, and it nearly ruined me. You know, you can get arrested for that kind of stuff."

Isaac tsked. "Not if we're careful."

Colton's Adam's apple bulged as he swallowed hard.

"Come on." Isaac led the way, knowing Colton would linger and check the halls a dozen times over before meeting him in the bathroom.

Standing in the last stall of the empty bathroom, Isaac unfastened his belt. Colton trembled a bit when he stepped inside, looking over his shoulder at the sliver of visibility around the stall door. Barely an inch of space, and given the lack of lighting at the far end of the bathroom, the two of them stood in mostly darkness with minimal lighting reaching them.

"Relax." Isaac patted Colton's shoulder and guided him to his knees where he wanted the jock.

Colton gulped, then reached out to quickly whip out Isaac's cock. Isaac grinned, more entertained than pleasured once Colton got to work on sucking his cock. The trepidation oozing off Colton was a familiar one. The jock had stood in a bathroom stall with his dick out at least two dozen times for Isaac to polish his knob during the school day, but this was a first for him. Here Colton was, on his knees, bobbing his head, and using every new trick he'd acquired to get Isaac off.

It was a quick and sloppy blowjob involving lots of hand work on Colton's part since he had trouble taking in all of Isaac's massive dick. Isaac contributed this to Colton's anxiety, recalling how his nervousness in the beginning had played a role in the quality of his own performance. In the woods, Isaac could swallow Colton's cock to the base. But when he slipped into a bathroom or the boy's locker room after practice, he'd gag halfway down.

From this angle, in this location, Isaac didn't want to attempt ramming his cock too deep, too fast. Colton would choke for sure, and without the bed to hold him in place... Well, Isaac imagined more work on his part.

"You're doing great." Isaac ran his fingers through Colton's hair, gentle and encouraging and helping to push his head down just a bit further every time.

Colton's face turned red as he worked harder, focusing purely on the task of bringing Isaac off. That determination more than the act itself brought Isaac closer and closer.

"Let me take over." Isaac wrapped his hands around the sides of Colton's head, practically gripping the jock's ears.

Colton didn't respond but gave an understanding look up. He dropped his hand that had been working the base of Isaac's dick.

With full control, Isaac slammed his dick in and out of Colton's mouth. Only the first half, but damn did it feel great to slide against the roof of Colton's mouth before hitting the back of his throat for just a second or two. The jock gagged, drooling immediately from the rough thrusts. His eyes scanned the door, anxious his noise would draw in an audience.

The tremble in Colton's body only worked to further entice Isaac. He could savor this experience all day, edge himself on Colton's tight throat muscles and keep this going. Instead, he plunged his cock as far back as possible, holding a relenting Colton's head in place until his dick pulsed. Isaac sucked his teeth to hold back the shiver of delight. He pulled his cock out of Colton's mouth and gave it a few quick tugs before it twitched, and he shot his load all over Colton's face.

"Rude."

"Rude would be making you wear it." Isaac rubbed two of his fingers and brought the sticky mess to Colton's lips. "Taste it."

Colton sucked on the salty load, licking Isaac's fingers clean until he removed them and collected a bit more of the cum dripping down Colton's face. This continued until Colton had swallowed all of Isaac.

Afterward, Isaac unlatched the stall door and allowed Colton to stand and exit first, even waiting while he rinsed his face. His cheeks were flushed, and his eyes were watery, but he seemed content enough to leave the bathroom.

Isaac lingered for a moment, contemplating, and then stepped outside to find Colton patiently waiting right outside in the empty hallway.

"I know your teammate was being a prick," Isaac said, adjusting his slacks, "but it would be good to see you at GSA again."

"It's not in my schedule."

"There's room to fit it in." Isaac leaned over, lips almost meeting Colton's. "You'll be hearing me say that a lot this semester."

Colton blushed, scanning the empty halls like someone would miraculously appear.

"Seriously, the others would love having you there, and it might help the club overall."

"Is that an order?"

"Does it need to be?" Isaac quirked a brow. "We both know you only avoided attending because of me."

"Not just you." Colton's shoulders raised nervously. "Mostly you. But also maybe an awkward hookup."

"Damn. You fucked Mina?" Isaac smirked as he led them outside the English building so he could have a smoke. "I knew she had a thing for you, but wow."

"Wait. What? No. A different member." Colton anxiously followed behind Isaac.

"William?"

Colton's lips twisted into a grimace.

Isaac snorted. "Not a big deal. I've fucked William. Just about everyone has. It's a rite of passage or an easy late night. Or both."

Colton remained quiet for a long minute, lost in thought more than the revelation of Isaac's hookup. "You know the tape I mentioned?"

Isaac didn't reply, merely stared and did his best to hide the curiosity brimming inside him.

"I was sort of occasionally messing around with William." Colton grimaced. "Then that reporter caught us—which I didn't know at the time."

"Because you were busy getting head?" Isaac asked, flicking his lighter.

Colton coughed, clearly uncomfortable with the topic, not at the spark of Isaac's cigarette. "They threatened to leak the video unless I gave them an exposé, and I was climbing the walls, freaking out over what to do."

"I bet." Isaac ground his teeth, wondering what kind of fucking person would make that threat.

"I didn't know which would be worse for my family to see—an exposé or amateur porn." Colton sulked. "Then there was the baseball team. Being queer seemed impossible back then—and it's not easy now, but it's bearable. But if the video had leaked? Yikes. They'd have cut me for sure."

"Cheap pornos are embarrassing but not the end of the world."

"I signed a morality clause," Colton said. "Pretty sure fucking some dude's face on camera violates that."

"That sucks," Isaac said. "Pun not intended but obviously hilarious."

"Yeah," Colton sighed. "Point is, it's just awkward because Will freaked out about the video, and I told him I'd take care of it, which I did, but then it was such a whirlwind of news and reporters and social media and campus and the disciplinary board because of grades and baseball season and... Well, you kind of sort of know the rest."

Isaac gave a stoic stare of acknowledgement.

"Then I ghosted him, which makes going to meetings awkward since he, like, runs them with you."

"William doesn't run shit," Isaac scoffed. "And he was upset about the video?"

Colton nodded.

That was perplexing since Isaac knew William had dabbled in webcam fandom pages and never seemed shy about showing off in front of a camera or audience of any kind. Most importantly, William never shied away from divulging his many illustrious hookups. At least not with his inner circle of his five-hundred or so most trusted confidants. In other words, William had a big mouth in more ways than one. It was unlike him to at least not brag about a hottie hookup. He'd named dropped several closeted guys to the GSA team already. Surely, Colton wasn't special. Isaac had a sinking suspicion and a building anger.

"Don't worry about William," Isaac said. He took a deep drag. "He's no doubt focused on his next conquest."

"Okay."

"Attend the meetings," Isaac said. "You fit in really well, and it seemed like you enjoyed it."

"I did," Colton blurted. "I do. In a casual, chill way."

"Yeah, whatever. It's good for you, good for the group," Isaac said, tossing his smoke unfinished. "Just don't chat me up too much during them. As far as everyone's concerned, I still hate you."

"Wait." Colton cocked his head. "So does that mean you don't actually hate me?"

"I don't hate pumping a load in you, but that's really about it." Isaac stuffed his hands into his pockets and shrugged.

"Oh…okay." Colton nodded with this arrogant glint in his eyes, like he hadn't just been in a bathroom stall on his knees and choking on Isaac's cock. "Anyway, I'm gonna grab lunch before practice if you wanted—"

"Good luck," Isaac interjected, not wanting an invitation.

"With eating?" Colton made a face. An annoyingly cute face.

"With baseball stuff." Isaac raised a hand in mock cheer enthusiasm. "Go, Munching Beavers rah-rah!"

"It's Batting Beavers," Colton said, correcting the most absurd mascot Clinton University could've chosen in Isaac's mind. "And it's just practice."

"Well, whatever. Just hit balls or something. Swing your bat better than everyone else."

"You don't know a damn thing about baseball, do you?"

"Go away."

With that, Isaac nudged Colton and parted ways with the captivating jock who continued vexing him in new and irritating ways. Right now, Isaac wanted to look into this outing ordeal connected to William.

CHAPTER 13
COLTON

COLTON found his way to the GSA meeting, sitting alone for the time being but leaving room for Isaac to join him. Or so he'd thought. In a matter of minutes, several members grouped up by his part of the table. Mina sat on his left, Carlos on his right, and a whole slew of people who seemed to take up Colton's side of the room, leaving the other half of the outstretched tables mostly abandoned.

"Okay," Mina asked, gesturing with her hands excitedly. "When are we doing another Rocky Horror live show?"

"Not sure when the Amp is putting on another show," Carlos said. "They used to do it monthly, but now it's more of a seasonal whenever thing."

"Well, shit." Mina made a sour face. "Let's have our own Rocky Horror."

"Only if you convince Isaac to be Frank again."

"Not in a million years," Mina said with a high-pitched laugh.

Small talk was Colton's favorite thing, so he leaned in to join the chat. There was no pressure because it didn't really matter. He didn't have to worry about blundering up details or misquoting information or caring if the other person was engaged. It was just to pass the time and hopefully have a few laughs while waiting for the meeting to start.

Isaac barged into the GSA meeting with a bloody-faced William in tow. The pair beelined from the door to the front, where Jazz set up the podium so fast that barely anyone had a chance to absorb the sight.

"We need to talk in private," Isaac said matter-of-factly as he helped William take a seat in a nearby chair.

Colton didn't know what to make of the sight. He blinked a few times, half convinced he was seeing things, but the longer he stared, the more it sank in. Blood gushed down William's face from his nose, where he kept pressure applied with one hand. His other hand remained cradled close to his chest, fingers twisted with a faint black and blue discoloration. Colton winced at that, recalling the time he'd broken his finger during a game. Longest recovery of his life, each day waiting and wondering if he'd play as well as he had before.

"Again, we need the room," Isaac said with a sharp tone.

His scowl sent people scampering for the door, but Colton wanted to wait, to understand what was happening. Instead, he stood and joined the wave of GSA members moving to the door.

Everyone obeyed Isaac's request and cleared out of the meeting room, ushered away by Carlos and Mina, who urgently directed GSA members to the door before closing it behind them. Not that it did any good. Each meeting room was equipped with large windows allowing a full view inside so long as the blinds remained open, which they had been.

"Bet he messed around with one of those DL jocks again," someone whispered.

"My money's on some townie fuckboy douchebag," another member added.

It didn't take long for the gossip about William's taste in men resulting in a violent outburst. The lack of tact from onlookers coupled with his genuine concern for Will twisted Colton's stomach in knots. He knew people were crude and unfeeling when idly discussing the misfortune of others, especially since he'd been on the other end quite a lot since entering college. Still, the timing of these injuries seemed rather suspicious to Colton. He quietly watched alongside the others, ignoring the rumor mill as so-called friends and allies brought up Will's history of hookups to explain away the obvious danger he'd put himself in that led to ruining tonight's GSA meeting.

Jazz immediately went to work, tending to William's injuries. She sat him in a chair and carefully examined his face. Colton recalled her mentioning something in the medical field for her major. It wasn't doctor or nurse. Nothing so simple. She'd used a fancy term, some weird, specialized position, but it must've included a basic understanding of handling bloody noses. That or maybe Jazz just had first-aid training.

Isaac said something, something no one watching from outside could hear, but Colton shivered at the snarled expression on Isaac's face, almost hearing the hiss of anger in the goth's voice.

The words must've been as venomous as Colton imagined because Jazz immediately stopped what she was doing. She took a step back, the look on her face skeptical and sickened. William dropped his head in what Colton could only imagine was shame. Shame for the immediate disgust that swept across each member's face.

Still, Jazz clamped her jaw and fought back a desire to speak while she returned to working on William.

Mina eventually came over and shut the blinds. Not that that stopped anyone from trying to steal tiny glances through the sliver of space between the shades or press their ears to the glass to listen in on the conversation. A conversation that'd turned into a screaming match between Jazz and no one else. She fumed, speaking at the top of her lungs.

"How could you?" she'd shouted at least four times. "What kind of person? Why? And you think that's okay? What if it'd been you? You think that justifies it? It's sick. This is not the type of behavior we're here for! This isn't community!"

Whatever William's responses were, they didn't satisfy Jazz. She continued berating him, repeating her questions a dozen times over while likely still tending to his injuries.

Colton wasn't a paranoid person. He wasn't the type of guy to connect random dots and create a pattern. Mysteries often eluded him simply because he didn't care about the so-called intrigue. If there were answers to be had, they'd present themselves eventually, otherwise Colton easily ignored them.

But nothing about this was vague. Even Colton pieced together the bizarre coincidence, and he didn't like the results his paranoid thoughts came up with.

He told Isaac about William, about how they'd hooked up, about how it might be awkward to attend GSA given that fact. And suddenly, William showed up to the next meeting with a bloody nose and blackish-blue gnarled fingers. Isaac had declared it would be fine to attend meetings, that William wouldn't be a problem. Had that been a lie? Had this been the result of Isaac securing awkward free club attendance?

Heat spread across Colton's face and chest. If Isaac brought it up to William, did that mean he mentioned their arrangement? Surely not. Isaac wanted to keep that a secret more than Colton, right? Still, he panicked over the paranoid thoughts bubbling in his head like his brain was a stew boiling over with sizzling ideas he couldn't squash or predict or handle. It was a bizarre feeling he'd never truly experienced before, drawing the worst-case scenario with each sharp breath he took.

Unable to remain idle much longer, Colton texted Isaac for clarification. No response. Not shocking since it sounded like lots of yelling was going on behind closed doors—and windows. Colton sent another text.

He waited five more minutes before sending a third. As much as he didn't want to appear needy, he craved answers far more. Besides, it was Isaac. He'd be thrilled to see Colton desperate for answers. Maybe that was all this was. Some ruse meant to spike anxiety into Colton as part of some sick joke by Isaac.

No. Colton shook away the thought. Even that seemed too unlikely a stretch for his delusional fears.

"I'm heading out," a GSA member said with a languished sigh.

The crowd of members clustered outside the meeting room began to thin over the next ten minutes. Soon, only half remained, waiting with bated breath and curious eyes. They wanted answers as much as Colton, but he suspected none of them relied on the answers. While they wanted to understand the strange events that unraveled before them to satiate their curiosity, Colton craved the answers to quell the paranoid beast swelling inside him. It was ferocious and unlike anything he'd endured. He didn't like worrying for the sake of worrying.

Colton went to send another text but paused when three dancing dots bounced in his chat box. Isaac was responding. Well, possibly. A blink later, and the dots had vanished. Then they started up again, only to stop once more. They started, then stopped, then started, then stopped, and Colton wondered if he was about to get an essay in response to his inquiries.

Isaac: Relax. Swing by my place tomorrow.

Seriously. After all that waiting, that dread, Isaac had only sent some cavalier reply not even acknowledging Colton's concerns. Valid concerns. They were valid, right? Colton began to wonder if he was working this all up in his head, if he needed to worry. What he needed to worry about. Who cared if people knew he hooked up with William. No, that wasn't the fear. It was more to do with the fact Isaac might've tipped his hand about their arrangement in the process. The idea sent a jolt of excitement through Colton, superseding the fear rooted inside him.

Isaac: I'll explain everything. But I can tell you now that it's nothing you have to worry about.

Okay, that part eased the tension building inside Colton, allowing him to take an actual calm breath.

Isaac: You don't have anything to worry about ever.

Colton chuckled to himself. The absurdity of that statement… It sent a rush through him. Isaac couldn't simply wash away every worry ever—especially since he was often the cause of Colton's confusion—but the mere idea he would make the valiant effort sparked a curiosity in Colton.

There were so many feelings knotting him and Isaac together in this warped connection that he fixated on that until it superseded the worry that gnawed at him. He left the building with more questions than answers but a bit lighter all the same.

CHAPTER 14
ISAAC

ISAAC anxiously awaited Colton's arrival, chain-smoking while his mind whirled around everything that'd happened over the last few days. There was so much he wanted to say, to share, to get off his chest. When Colton had explained his outing ordeal, it didn't sit well with Isaac, so he approached William for clarification on his concerns. Isaac hadn't expected to punch William. He hadn't expected to break his nose, to dislocate two of his fingers, to threaten him from an inch of his life.

But he also hadn't expected William to do something so malicious for no other reason than a chance at his own entertainment. It was the laugh he'd given when Isaac confronted him.

"You hate the guy. I mean, you hate everyone, but seriously, what's it fucking matter?" William playfully slapped Isaac on the back—his biggest mistake during their encounter. "He's better out of the closet, anyway."

Isaac knew William had a history of outing folks, unintentionally and well-timed coincidences, according to their mutual friend Carlos. Although the other GSA member didn't consider William much of a friend. Carlos often gave people the benefit of the doubt, so when he aired on the side of caution around William, Isaac knew to keep a careful distance. The only problem was that Isaac never considered William a personal threat or issue since he wasn't in the closet and didn't have any closeted friends. He still didn't. Colton wasn't a friend. Still, the knowledge of William's actions didn't sit well with Isaac.

"He's happy." William had tightened his grip on Isaac's shoulder, nearly setting him off right then. "The world hasn't turned upside down on itself, and we have a queer athlete to act as a beacon or icon or role model. Or just a model. Seriously, dude is fine as hell, and when I tell you he's got a nice package, Izzy, you've got no idea."

It was then that Isaac had to set the tone of their conversation. He twisted those fingers still touching him, tempted to break them, but he still had more questions, more things to account for.

When William had satisfied Isaac's curiosity, he contemplated giving his theater friend a chance to discreetly and quietly fade away from the GSA before Isaac made it his mission to destroy him. But if Will walked away unscathed, not only would he learn nothing from his errors, but others would never suspect him of foul play in the future. The rumor mill Carlos clung to would continue to grow, but that'd be all.

The worst part of this whole nightmare was the gnawing guilt that clawed its way inside Isaac and hollowed him out. Not for William. In a matter of days, he'd forget Will ever existed, releasing that friendship to the ether as gently as he had his love for his family. Severing ties never came hard for Isaac. He preferred to be alone; it left less risk of being hurt.

No, the pain and guilt gutting him again and again had to do with Colton. Not the outing itself, an old wound for sure, but still there were events Isaac had orchestrated to put Colton in his place. Now, his reasons began to blur as Isaac considered the lengths William had gone to for his own agenda. What was Isaac's agenda? Justification?

A sudden knock at his door roused Isaac from his spot. Tossing the cigarette, Isaac shook loose his nerves and went to let Colton inside.

Colton stood there, too dressed up for a conversation. "You look extra frumpy."

"Thanks?" Isaac hissed, closing the door behind them.

"Just saying, you put in like zero effort when you could actually rock some good looks."

Isaac didn't respond.

"Okay, small talk is dead." Colton clapped his hands. "Care to tell me what the hell happened with William?"

Isaac was certain the other members of GSA were climbing the walls awaiting answers—answers Jazz was currently finding the right words for. Isaac didn't do the right words; he didn't do the right anything. It was his leftie claim to fame. He merely acted when the impulse struck. While waiting for Jazz's thoughtful reflection would probably be best for Colton in the long run, Isaac believed he deserved the truth now, unfiltered, especially since it connected so deeply to the jock.

"I spoke with Will about my suspicions surrounding your outing."

"Suspicions?" Colton quirked a brow.

"William isn't the discreet type. And this isn't the first time I've suspected him of having a hand in someone's coming out story." Isaac explained his theory. "I got him to admit he was the reason you were recorded, outed."

Shock filled Colton's face, his stance turned shaky, and he nearly stumbled backward. Isaac swept in faster than he realized, faster than he should have, but it was too late. One hand was already wrapped around Colton's waist and pressed to the small of his back while the other gripped his shoulder.

"It's a lot, I know," Isaac said, keeping his grip firm until Colton's breathing eased. "I had this sinking feeling when you shared your story with me."

"You just came up and asked about me?" There was a tremble in Colton's voice.

"No." Isaac gritted his teeth, ashamed of how he'd prioritized keeping his arrangement with Colton a secret, which clearly meant he was no better than William or anyone else Isaac despised for a lack of morals. "I addressed my concerns about a few rumors, rumors which tied in well when adding yours to the list. Like I said, this isn't the first time Will has been suspected of having a hand in someone's coming out story."

"Was it all a con from the start?"

"No," Isaac lied because he hadn't asked William for that clarity, but he knew his friend was more opportunistic than calculating. "I think because your hookups were recurring, he just saw a way to have fun and exploit someone else in the process."

"Fuck." Colton ran his hands through his hair, a gesture Isaac noticed him do when nervous and trying to think more clearly. "You know, I always assumed this was my fault. My bad luck and reckless behavior catching up to me, leading to my big scandal."

"You don't have to worry about William anymore." Isaac grimaced as if William were the worst of Colton's problems. William's actions were reprehensible, but his grievances were old news, no longer a wound that pained Colton. "He's gonna step away from GSA for a while. He wants to focus on his theater credits."

"He just chose to step away?"

"Carlos might've noted a few other instances where he also heard rumors." Isaac let Colton absorb that comment. He didn't need to further elaborate how Colton wasn't the first, merely the biggest fish in William's sordid history. "Jazz is a very accepting person, very open-minded and forgiving, but she won't allow someone on the GSA committee who had a hand in outing people, in taking away that choice from them."

"Like a morality clause." Colton nodded. "I have one of those in my contract."

"Not exactly." Isaac shrugged. "There's official ways to remove someone from their role as a club officer, but between Jazz laying down the formalities of officially bringing up sanctions to Mina threatening to break his nose a second time and Carlos reminding folks that he'd picked IT cybersecurity for a reason—so whatever dirty secrets William still had, might not remain so secret."

"Yikes." Colton made a playful face of fright, which quickly dissolved into genuine concern. "So, everyone's gonna know he outed me?"

"Maybe. Folks will likely just speculate. Like I said, Carlos mentioned others. Quite a few, apparently." Isaac shrugged. "Members will know William had a hand in outing guys on campus or outing members to their families accidentally before they were ready."

Colton's eyes went wide at that. It wasn't like his family didn't already know his sexuality, but Isaac imagined it was still a difficult topic to broach.

"I can't believe you exposed him, connected those dots."

"Studying people is what I do," Isaac said, thinking about how his paranoid mind always tried to imagine the worst-case scenario in every possible situation so he could prepare for the inevitable painful outcome and brace himself. It'd served him well and helped him avoid awful fates since his incident junior year. "Part of me considered keeping it quiet, threatening to expose him, in exchange for the tapes, but he claimed not to have access to them."

And Isaac knew that was the truth, considering the private and brutal beating he unleashed, threatening with all sincerity to do so much worse to William unless he convinced Isaac he wasn't lying.

"You do blackmail like no one else." Colton chuckled, more amazed than frightened.

That gutted Isaac. He couldn't stop seeing himself as any different from this reporter, hungry for a story, or William, who enjoyed the rush of puppeteering people's lives. But he buried that feeling like he buried every feeling that struck when nearby Colton.

"Since William was a dead end on your outing, I looked up the name of the reporter who did your first story." Isaac scoffed. "You realize, you have like a thousand coming out articles."

"Only a thousand? That's a bit disappointing." Colton shot Isaac a weak smile. "You should check out how many reaction posts there were."

"Just know, I'll get back the tapes and ensure—"

"Don't. There's no need." Colton was too calm about the situation, likely still not fully registering exactly how manipulated by the situation he'd been. "He never planned on releasing the tapes. Just wanted the exposé on my coming out story."

"You don't know that."

"I do. Once he had my story, he gave me the copies, and I burned them."

"You're sure he doesn't have others?"

"If he does, he's made no move with them after months." Colton shrugged. "Releasing a vid like that after we won The College World Series would've been a huge blow to my career."

"Pun intended."

"Huh?" Colton stared, either not realizing the humor in the comment or registering what a pun was. "Besides, it's not like he could post the tape on his news site. They're all professional and shit. It would've just been leaked online. No profit for the guy."

"People can still be vindictive for the sake of hurting someone else."

"I think that chapter of my life is done." Colton sighed. "Now, the fall-out to it? That's like a whole textbook."

Isaac dropped the tape and let Colton convince him there was nothing more to be done about it. However, he made a mental note to double-check with the reporter by having a conversation in the same vein as his chitchat with William's face.

A realization struck Isaac, and the guilt for his own actions began to eat away at him. William convinced himself what he did to Colton was acceptable because he was a closeted jerk. The reporter probably convinced himself it was acceptable because he'd transform Colton into a queer role model for athletes. And what had Isaac done to convince himself that blackmailing Colton was acceptable?

"Fucking A." Isaac rushed over to his laptop and logged into the system, searching his files, his backups, and his professor's cloud storage.

"What're you doing?"

"The right thing too little and too late." Isaac deleted his leverage. "Your essay is gone."

"What?" Colton seemed taken aback.

"I removed it from Howard's cloud saves; it's a mess of ten years' worth of papers from countless courses. No one's gonna go looking for some silly old final." Isaac stood from his seat and rushed to the other side of the room. "I also wiped out my backups, my email drafts, and everything on my computer."

He tossed Colton a flash drive, then unlocked a metal box tucked under his bed. Inside were a handful of things he missed from his old life, gifts and mementos, other things he was too weak to let go of but refused to see as a daily reminder to the family he cut ties with. Folded among the mess was Colton's essay.

Isaac kicked the box back under the bed, lit a cigarette, and stood close to the window. Using his lighter, he ignited the printed essay.

"What the hell, Isaac?"

"Don't worry. Not gonna set off any alarms." Especially since Isaac had learned to discreetly tamper with the smoke detectors in his room years ago.

Isaac dropped the essay in a nearby metal trash bin, letting it burn to ash along with the tissues and other junk already in the small can.

"You're free."

"Wait, what?"

"You're literally holding the only evidence of your cheating essay." Isaac gestured to the flash drive. "Break it. Burn it. Whatever. We're done."

"The semester's just beginning."

"I know. And I can't undo what I've already done, but I can give you back something." Isaac took deep drags off his cigarette, hoping the nauseous feeling came from too many quick inhales and not the festering guilt clawing at him. "If you want to keep attending GSA, I can drop the club. You seem to like it. And first thing Monday, I'm gonna tell Howard I need my TA courses swapped. I'd leave campus altogether, but that's not really possible right now."

"What are you going on about?"

"You won't have to see me." Isaac's heart hammered in his chest; each beat a heavy acknowledgment of what he'd done. What he craved. What he'd continue to do if William hadn't unknowingly held up a mirror to Isaac's face, showing him how much of a monster he was too.

"I don't want you disappearing—that wasn't the arrangement."

"We don't have an arrangement anymore." Isaac stubbed out his cigarette. "You're free."

"No." Colton's voice went low, gravellier than usual. "You don't disappear on me again."

Again. Damn, that hit Isaac hard. Not that he'd chosen to vanish, but Colton's actions, his role in something so devastating, left Isaac broken and needing to hide. Those horrors seemed so far away now, not forgotten. If Isaac closed his eyes for too long, he'd feel every hit from the jocks as crisply as he did the day they cornered him in the custodian's closet. The shame and embarrassment burned inside him, as fresh and mortifying as the day they swung open the door, chased him in the halls, took pictures of him for all to see.

"This was stupid and fucked up and wrong and twisted and—"

"And I don't want it to stop." Colton grabbed Isaac's head, wrapping his hands on either side and forcing their eye contact. There was a desperate hunger in Colton's green eyes, a longing in his expression, and a tremble in his body.

Isaac craved him, craved this, but he knew this path led to Hell.

"Just because I don't have a hand to use against you doesn't change things." Isaac wheezed, fighting back his shaky words to appear strong. The idea of being vulnerable around Colton was more frightening than a thousand memories of abuse and harassment and bullying. "I will still be in charge. I will still be the priority. You will only be here to serve."

"I know."

Isaac didn't know if he'd unlocked some curious hungry sub hidden beneath the masculine ego Colton wore all day or if the jock still clung to the guilt of his actions in high school and used this as a tool to apologize.

It didn't matter; Isaac wouldn't let it matter. Ever.

"I'll fuck you," Isaac said, leaning closer so his lips nearly pressed to Colton's. "I'll use you, keep bending you over to my satisfaction."

Colton's hands fell away, and he shivered as Isaac's teeth grazed his neck. The quiver in Colton sent a spark of desire through Isaac.

"But you need to understand, I will never forgive you." Isaac bit down on Colton's neck and ran his hands over the jock's strong muscles. "I will never acknowledge you as anything more than someone for me to fuck and use."

"I understand." Colton trembled, taking desperately shallow breaths to keep himself calm.

"Are you okay being meaningless to me? Serving me? Existing only for my pleasure?"

"Yes," Colton said with a breathy whisper.

That was all Isaac needed. He spun Colton around, yanked his pants down, and shoved him onto the mattress. Staring at his beautiful bare ass, Isaac palmed at his firm glutes, rubbing his hands down around Colton's thighs but keeping the pants where they were. He rather enjoyed how confined they kept Colton.

It took everything Isaac had to pause and retrieve a bottle of lube before pulling his own pants down, but he managed, and Colton remained obediently bent over the bed on his hands with his ass exposed.

Isaac slapped his cock between Colton's cheeks, grinding up and down, savoring the skin-to-skin touch, the warmth of Colton's ass. When he pressed the head against Colton's hole, he stifled a startled moan.

Instead of pushing in with a sudden and painful thrust, Isaac lubed his dick and Colton's ass, rubbing his cock up and down the crack. He enjoyed the easy gratification of stroking his cock between Colton's cheeks without entering him, teasing the jock, making him yearn for the return of such a brutal fuck.

"I'm ready." Colton's hands gripped the comforter of the bed, and he did his best to arch more.

"This isn't about you, little pitcher." Isaac smirked at the growl that brought out of Colton.

After grinding against Colton's cheeks until his dick pulsed, Isaac finally thrust into the tight jock's ass. He shoved in as deep as he could with a powerful grunt, not taking his time to push the inches in a bit at a time as he had their first night. Colton screamed, stifling the noise with a terrible groan as he buried his face into the mattress.

"Relax." Isaac gently scratched Colton's back, trailing his fingers up each column in a soothing manner. He worked his way up to Colton's shoulders and all the way to the dimples on the small of Colton's back. "This is what you wanted."

Colton lifted his head, taking heavy, forced breaths through his nose as he ground his teeth. Every muscle of his body flexed tight, inviting Isaac to wrap around him even more. Isaac wanted to feel Colton quiver and surrender to the pain, to the pleasure, to the man in charge of him. Submit to Isaac.

Oh, how the flexed muscles across Colton's back aroused Isaac even more as he calmed his stressed sub, eliciting more rushed thrusts as he found a new home for his cock.

Colton dropped his head again, grunting loudly with each slap of skin from Isaac's rough pounding at the jock's rear.

"Don't." Isaac yanked his hair. "I wanna hear everything."

Isaac railed Colton, fast, brutal pumps from tip to base, finding an ecstatic rhythm that brought him close to climaxing almost immediately. He leaned forward, placing his knees on the bed and saddling on top of Colton as he pushed the jock's back further down into an arch. With his weight pressing down on Colton, he adjusted his pace, taking shorter, quicker thrusts.

"Lift your ass," Isaac demanded, watching Colton struggle to reposition.

It didn't help Colton was still constrained by his pants and now had the full weight of Isaac pressing down on him as he pushed in deeper, still thrusting while Colton obeyed. Colton's face became muffled again as he worked, adjusting his body so Isaac could ram him at an almost ninety-degree angle.

Colton panted, unable to breathe and turning his head to the side. There was a beauty in his exhausted face that Isaac wanted to savor forever, but each second he stared made him that much closer to cumming. The whimpers escaping Colton's lips as he took the railing brought Isaac to the edge of his climax, forcing him to change his pace yet again. He needed to change his position but fuck, it felt so good straddling Colton's ass and riding him.

With one hand pressed to the back of Colton's neck, Isaac held him in place. With his other hand, Isaac began smacking Colton's ass cheek.

The suddenness sparked a yelp from Colton, which was quickly replaced by a muffled groan as he let his face sink back into the mattress.

"Mmmfffmm."

"Lift your head," Isaac said with a loud smack.

Colton moaned as he obeyed, hair and expression equally disheveled from constantly retreating to the blanket.

Isaac slapped Colton's ass harder, rhythmically syncing his thrusts so every third pump, he could hammer his hand down against Colton's cheek.

Lubing up his hand, Isaac reached around, sliding his slick fingers between the bed and Colton's hip. Colton's cock was rock-hard and throbbing. Between the fine fabric of the comforter and Isaac's aggressive pounding, Colton's dick leaked precum, twitching.

Isaac gripped Colton's cock and let it slide in between his fisted hand. The moans Colton unleashed were euphoric, nearly making Isaac cum right then and there, but he wanted to ensure Colton finished first. He owed Colton that much. Maybe he didn't owe Colton anything. Maybe the only thing these two men owed each other was a promise to walk away and never look back. But Colton didn't want that. He wanted to surrender to Isaac. He wanted to give him control; he wanted to be obedient.

"You like this?" Isaac bit Colton's ear as he continued stroking the man, fucking him with pent-up passion and fury that intertangled in the most bizarre way. "Answer me."

"Yes." Colton moaned through gritted teeth, barely capable of speaking.

"Prove it." Isaac licked Colton's neck, kissing him from his nape to his jawline. "Cum for me. Cum now."

Colton groaned, desperate and pleading as he continued taking Isaac's cock, his own so close Isaac could feel it each time he rubbed. Changing his approach, Isaac grabbed the head of Colton's dick, letting his lubed palm press against the most sensitive nerves and massage the tip with the illusion of a warm mouth.

The way Colton bucked forward, pulling his ass away from Isaac's cock so he could ram his dick into Isaac's hand, brought a snarl of satisfaction from the assertive goth. He jerked Colton's dick faster, steadying the pace of his strokes to Colton's panting pleasure.

"Aaaaaagh." Colton came hard, his body convulsing beneath Isaac, which only brought Isaac closer to the precipice of release.

"Look at me." Isaac snatched a fistful of Colton's sweaty black hair and locked his eyes on the moaning man beneath him.

Colton's sparkling green eyes rolled back, lost to the pleasure, and Isaac moved in to kiss him. He wanted to taste the sound of Colton's orgasm. Every time Colton moaned, Isaac slammed into him again, extending the groans that came with Colton's release. Isaac did all the work for this kiss, using his tongue to guide Colton's, using his lips to swallow Colton's voice, using his hand to hold Colton's head upright.

Soon, the blanket and Isaac's hand were covered in the warm spatter of Colton's load.

Isaac wiped his messy hand on the blanket before lifting and adjusting Colton's limp body like a ragdoll. "You ready for me? Ready to take me? All of me?"

Colton panted with a euphoric expression and a weak nod. That face, glossed over in ecstasy, quickly crumbled away once Isaac began piledriving into Colton as quickly as he could. Colton gripped the sheets, biting them too, and Isaac allowed it. Part of him—a primal, hungry part—wanted to yank his hair back and hear every shout that escaped Colton's lips, but another part of him understood that after cumming this must've been more painful than pleasureful, so Isaac focused his brutal strokes to achieve his climax.

It helped when Colton clenched inadvertently and moaned with a breathy whimper at the end.

"Fucking take it!" Isaac slapped his hands over Colton's ass, clawing more than palming the cheeks.

His muscles tensed, and everything in his body erupted as he shot his seed deep inside Colton. Isaac wanted to pass out on top of Colton and just lay there, comfortable after conquering the jock's ass once again.

Instead, he pulled out, keeping a hand pressed to spread Colton's cheeks as he watched a few drops of cum spill from his hole and drip down Colton's taint and balls.

"I'll get a towel for your ass, but you're gonna have to actually clean my blanket."

"Seriously?" Colton scoffed, wiping the beads of sweat from his brow. "I barely do my own laundry. Not happening, man."

"You said you'd still obey my every whim." Isaac brushed his knuckles along Colton's face. "That extends to more than the bedroom. You behave in every way, or this doesn't work."

Colton stared silently for a minute. The longest, most intense minute of Isaac's life. He'd overstepped, overreached. But maybe that was for the best. This whole arrangement, even without the pressing threat of blackmail, was totally and utterly fucked up.

"Okay," Colton finally agreed.

"Okay?" Isaac's eyes widened, a bit surprised. "What?"

"Okay, sir," Colton immediately followed, confusing Isaac's bewilderment for a demand of authority and obedience.

Colton's face had turned red from the pounding and possibly the little shame that came with submitting himself layer by layer.

Fuck, how Isaac loved the sound of that.

"Come here." Isaac held a towel and patted Colton's sweaty body, enjoying the sight of his tired muscles; then he directed Colton to the front of the bed as they stripped off the comforter, and Isaac retrieved another lighter blanket. "We'll deal with it tomorrow. For now, let's just sleep."

"I do actually have a busy day tomorrow, so I can't—"

"I know your schedule," Isaac said, reminding the jock how hard he'd worked to organize it based on an arrangement that did and didn't exist any longer. His very own Schroeder's Cat scenario but with Colton's ass and mouth and body and emotions.

The emotions were the most difficult part for Isaac to comprehend in this variable of destructive choices. Isaac did his best to pretend they didn't exist so the pair could just enjoy each other's bodies without baggage.

"Come on." Isaac slipped into the bed. "You need to sleep if you're gonna do well in your first game or whatever."

"Opening game, start of the season." Colton chuckled as he hopped into the bed. "Not my first game."

"Not your first time pitching?" Isaac teased.

"Ha! Just because I haven't pitched with you doesn't mean I haven't pitched."

"Guess I'll see how your reputation holds up," Isaac said. "Well, with the baseball pitching, at the very least."

"Wait, what?"

"GSA is talking about making it a group thing, whatever." Isaac huffed, dramatic and unnecessary, but it was too late to undo his behavior, so he leaned into the whiny reaction. "Get some sleep and prepare for the imminent gay invasion about to puke rainbows all over your bases and stuff."

He expected a frown to fill Colton's face, a sign this was an intrusive overstep and something to encourage Isaac to ruin the GSA's game spirit plans for tomorrow. Colton didn't frown, though. Instead, he released a breathy chuckle as his eyes glazed over with the possibilities, and then he smiled. Oh, how he smiled. It was as big and bright and carefree as the one he'd arrived with tonight. The same smile Isaac had studied for years, analyzing the layers of genuine joy to the many facades Colton would put up. Isaac liked how captivating and charming Colton's smiles could be when he basked in the simple things that made him happy.

Without a retort or final word, Colton rolled over and went to sleep, leaving Isaac awake with his thoughts. His fingers nearly brushed against Colton's back when he hesitated. It'd be so easy to slide over and cuddle. Maybe even blame it on a restless sleeping body and a tiny twin bed. Isaac longed to touch Colton again, to hold him, to kiss him, to talk with him all night.

CHAPTER 15
COLTON

COLTON lost himself to the opening game of the season. When he pitched, the world and all the problems fell away. Family who didn't support his goals. Gone. Family who didn't acknowledge his identity. Gone. The uncomfortable truth surrounding his outing. Gone. Difficult classes. Struggling academics. Hot goth guys. Gone. Gone. Gone. All in all, Colton let it all vanish when he stepped onto the field. All except for players who still resented him as the starting pitcher.

Teammates who created conflict were really the only thing locked in Colton's head during a game because their arrogance or showboating or plain indifference usually cost the rest of the team. He didn't have the energy or desire to rally the players who hated him for something he couldn't control, so he focused his efforts of morale on the teammates who didn't judge, who still respected Colton, and who played with all their hearts even if they were up by eight.

During the seventh-inning stretch, Colton took the time to stretch and search the stands. He'd long since given up on finding his family in the stands, but it didn't take long to spot the GSA members sitting close to the railing and taking up a few rows. He scanned the group of nearly twenty members who'd shown up, which was close to half of the overall members.

Lots of them were holding signs for the Batting Beavers or for Player 33, which was Colton's number. His heart skipped a beat when he spotted Isaac sitting squarely between Jazz and Carlos, almost unnoticed. Isaac didn't care about the no-smoking policy or Carlos' exaggerated coughs. He simply sat hunched on the bleachers with his gaze locked onto Colton.

Colton pretended not to care, keeping his expression calm as he waved to his cheering audience. It took all his strength not to jump up and down. Colton had tons of fans, friends, and loyal teammates, but he'd never had people genuinely go out of their way to see him play. In high school, it was usually just school spirit that brought folks out, people who rooted for Colton even though they didn't know him. It was nice having people who saw Colton for who he really was, accepted that, and came to support him.

"Wooooo!" Jazz shouted, leading the GSA into a ridiculous cheer.

Okay, the calm demeanor he kept definitely broke as Mina led moves the GSA members couldn't sync up with for the life of them, making the routine a terrible mess. Still, it was way more fun to watch than the half-time performance or the fawning cleat chasers who didn't so much like Colton as they did his standing, popularity, and, honestly, any boy wearing baseball gear.

As Colton lingered close to the stands, he noticed Isaac didn't have on his usual heavy black eye makeup. Instead, he wore the school colors for his eyeshadow, and it matched everyone else on the GSA team who also sported Colton's player number on their cheeks.

A warm buzz hit, and Colton casually wandered in the direction where his friends were lined up, a bit more excited than he expected but hopeful to make some idle chitchat during the break.

Unfortunately, Leon took the opportunity to speed walk in Colton's direction, preventing him from casually striking up a conversation with the GSA.

"Looks like you got yourself some queer groupies." Leon slapped Colton's back, intentionally too hard but smiling all playful and phony as per usual. "They're all rawr rawr something something blah blah for you."

Colton ground his teeth, fighting back an angry expression, but he knew his eyes shot daggers. He knew because of the glint of satisfaction in Leon's gaze. He was provoking a rise out of Colton and taking pure sadistic joy in it.

His roommates, Tim and Devon, stood halfway across the field, talking to each other, but their eyes pressed onto Colton and Leon. Chances were, they were both looking for an excuse to mosey on over to offer backup. Tim always managed to shut Leon down quickly and Devon successfully warped Leon's words, painting them as friendly instead of fucked up.

"You think any of 'em actually know how the game is played?" Leon asked loudly, drawing the GSA's attention and definitely hoping to make them squirm as he went to work cutting down Colton.

It was something Colton had experienced in the locker rooms before, Leon saying something spiteful to get a rise out of players who weren't bothered by Colton's sexuality while feeding into the discomfort of those who did have a problem with it. Now, he sought to pour his venomous feelings for Colton out on the GSA members, who would probably never attend another game under the assumption that everyone on the baseball team was like this. They weren't. Most players were fine.

It was Leon who fanned the flames of hate—more for his craving to be the starting pitcher and less because of any actual homophobia. Not that it was an excuse in Colton's eyes, but he wondered what tricks Leon would've resorted to if he didn't have Colton's bisexuality to use against him.

"Any of y'all actually know what's going on?" Leon gestured to the field, the scoreboard, and the dugouts. "Or you just looking for a reason to get all dolled up and play cheerleaders?"

Leon laughed loudly, forcing it at first but then getting into a real obnoxious rhythm of taunting the queer crowd.

"And what the fuck do you know about baseball?" Isaac leaned over the railing, ready to lunge from above and tackle Leon.

He had wild eyes, like a deranged tiger on the prowl...or what Colton would assume a large cat about to pounce looked like. It startled the laughter out of Leon's lungs.

"Yeah, punk ass." Mina lounged on the railing beside Isaac, tapping her nails to draw Leon's attention. "You've been sitting side-bitch all night long."

"That's not true," Jazz interjected, wedging herself between an angry Isaac and an enraged Mina. "He was lucky enough to get off the bench long enough to strike out at the plate both times his coach called him in, which was considerate since it helped remove the strong lead their team had and afforded the opposition an opportunity at a solid comeback."

The wave of embarrassment that struck Leon's face left him and Colton speechless, all while Jazz continued listing off player stats like she had the entire college MLB roster memorized. Then, she took her seat, inviting Isaac and Mina to retake their vicious positions.

"For someone who regularly professes his macho bullshit with pathetic posturing, you've had your ass pressed to hard wood all night." Isaac nodded to the bench in the dugout where Leon had desperately waited to sub in for Colton. "Maybe if you scream daddy to the dugout, you'll get to pitch, bitch."

"The only pitching I've seen him do is pitching a tent with an envy boner as the rest of the team scores," Mina added.

Isaac and Mina continued hurling more insults at Leon until his face turned beat red and he seethed through gritted teeth, unable to find a comeback or time for one during the onslaught. When one of Leon's lackies came to interject, Mina shut his ass down with a comment on his inability to land her a homerun when they hooked up. She might not have known much about the sport, but her analogy on his weak batting and premature swing leading to a quick completion and her lack of even reaching a base got a lot of the crowd's attention.

By the time the game had resumed, Colton found himself on a new kind of high. He had the support of the GSA, who would shut down any members of his baseball team that didn't support him. Those who did were met with cheers, while those who didn't faced the wrath of Pride.

While this certainly wasn't his best game, and eventually, he had to sub out for Leon, Colton loved how the evening went. Leon's balk pitches were called early on, his confidence was shaken, and he ended up helping the other team land more scores than strikes.

It afforded Colton a chance to return to his role and help the team finish barely ahead by the time the game was called.

Everything in Colton's life was so hard to control, but something about handing over the reins to Isaac lessened the weight constantly on his chest, his shoulders, and his back. The pressure of failing the world, faltering after so many years of hard work, fumbling his biggest dream... All of that washed away when he submitted to Isaac. It gave him a sense of freedom while simultaneously stripping him of his choices. He savored every whim from the angry goth who claimed he felt nothing for Colton.

He must've felt something. The way he fucked Colton with such hate and care... That required feeling in both extremes. And the way he kissed Colton, even when he thought the jock had dozed off. His lips were soft in the middle of the night as he kissed the crook of Colton's neck before he snuck in to snuggle again. Isaac could pretend he didn't care, and he likely was still mad and hurt from the past, but Colton knew the truth. He believed they'd repaired something. He'd keep it to himself; he'd serve at the altar of Isaac and work to rebuild what he broke so long ago.

Colton quickly got into the swing of things—pleasing Isaac, balancing his schedule, baseball games, and GSA events. Leon and the other players had even stopped hassling him, finding the new queer squad members lining up and biting back every time someone caught wind of certain closed-minded jocks being dicks. They'd harass Leon during practices, in classes—hell, sometimes, someone would even walk over to him during team lunches. Colton let it be. Just like he couldn't control Leon and his homophobic beliefs, he couldn't very well control the GSA members who lashed out in response.

Colton was convinced Isaac had a hand in it, instigating Pride students and reminding folks this wasn't some conservative stomping ground. The University of CLIT was queer, feminist, and fucking liberal as hell. But whenever he brought it up, Isaac simply stared at him, taking long, slow blinks like a wicked cat with a million secrets. Isaac did a lot of tiny things to help Colton over the next two months.

He started leaving study notes in Colton's textbooks. He added hyperlinks to Colton's papers, forcing him to look into the attached articles and find useful information that inevitably made his essays better. He even tricked Colton into attending a math tutoring session by convincing the jock they were going to fuck in the library. Thank God Colton hadn't unfastened his pants before walking into the study room Isaac had reserved. That would've been awkward dropping his slacks in front of a room of folks.

Isaac had also started leaving Colton healthy snacks, prepping meal days for him to assist with his diet. It helped since he had to balance fitness for baseball and something digestive for bottoming on a regular basis. There was an awkwardness Colton clung to when discussing his bathroom needs, but Isaac was very nonchalant about the whole thing, simply there for Colton and his ass whenever it was ready for Isaac to take.

Everything since they got together had been the dream experience Colton had always wanted with college. Even the awkwardness, the bizarreness, the uncomfortable manner that brought them together held this dreamy nature in Colton's mind. He had everything he wanted: success on the field, success in classes, success in the bedroom. It was an unexpected success since he never considered subbing before this arrangement. And now, he couldn't imagine anything else. He couldn't imagine not having Isaac dictate his days, plan out his schedule, help sort out his conflicts.

The only issue came with the fact that he'd found the perfect guy to date who didn't want to date him, to acknowledge they were anything other than physical. Even these gestures were just a way for Isaac to exert control, which Colton liked. Wanted. Needed. Craved. More than that, he wanted to show off Isaac, to share what they had, and maybe scare a few people with his intimidating goth boyfriend.

Every minute of every day was planned out with something adventurous, even in a tiny way. Colton would have lunch with the GSA members, then slip off to the student parking lot, where he'd trail behind Isaac, following him to his beat-up, old station wagon. The pair pretended not to be in company until Colton could discreetly get in the back seat. The fear of getting caught always aroused and frightened Colton, but Isaac would find the perfect parking spot to pound out Colton's ass between classes or ream his throat raw.

Oral after his Composition II course became standard practice. By the end of the first month, Colton had become a pro at swallowing Isaac's massive dick. Sure, he still gagged and choked, but not nearly as much, and always in just the right way to get Isaac off in under ten minutes. Under five on good days.

Though, Colton did notice Isaac came quicker when they were in public—whereas when he'd head over to Isaac's dorm room, the grumpy goth would drag out his fucks. Whether using Colton's mouth or ass for the night, he'd always edge himself close and keep going, savoring the satisfaction of pumping into Colton until the jock's body quivered. Colton became raw with his emotions, with the pleasure and pain that came with pleasing Isaac because that often brought the dom to climax.

Isaac always found new ways to spend time with Colton, which he loved. When the goth boy started showing up to the campus gym, Colton nearly burst into laughter. The first day he came, he was in hot pink jogging shorts exposing his pale tattooed thighs, knee-high anime socks, and an oversized hoodie with some death metal band image.

"You're gonna need something different unless you want everyone staring at you," Colton said discreetly during a well-timed water break where he and Isaac could linger close to each other. "Staring at us."

Colton wanted to drop the act and workout with Isaac, but the rest of the GSA wasn't at the gym, and Isaac still preferred the group dynamic as a public buffer for their interactions. Not that he ever interacted with Colton when the others were around, merely stayed silent and kept close.

Here at the gym, though, a lot of athletes were in attendance, some from Colton's baseball team or, at the very least, friends with them.

"No one's staring at me." Isaac glanced around, leading Colton's gaze where he noted how people actively avoided looking too long at Isaac.

They might steal a look and snicker at Isaac's silly outfits which he continued wearing every time he worked out nearby, but no one wanted to be caught gawking at the pasty goth guy wearing weird clothes. It seemed Isaac had the perfect camouflage.

Though Isaac and Colton had very different workout routines, Colton did ensure he always timed his cardio alongside Isaac's. And while Isaac never looked his way, never acknowledged his close proximity, he always picked a machine where either side was empty so Colton could always slip in and run beside him, bike next to him, or walk up a mountain of steps miserably with him.

"You're in a lot better shape than you look," Colton wheezed after finishing his cardio.

Despite being a smoker, Isaac didn't take nearly as many heavy breaths. And while his frame was slender and his muscles weren't nearly as big as Colton's, Isaac had a firm, solid build. His biceps were well-defined, and his leg muscles put Colton to shame. His abs even poked out a bit, less definition than Colton's but there all the same.

"Everyone looks at me and sees a sassy twink." Isaac grinned. "But I'm more of a sadistic twunk."

Colton snorted at that, then resumed the rest of his workout.

And like most things the pair did in public, when all was said and done, they'd make their way to the locker room and find the last shower stall. Sometimes, they'd linger for a few minutes until it cleared out a bit, but often, someone would be blasting music while they cleaned up. If not, Isaac would turn on heavy metal and rage fuck Colton while they washed up.

Beneath the music, Colton only ever heard his own muffled groans, Isaac's aggressive grunts, the slap of wet skin, and the squeak of their shower shoes. Getting fucked against a tile wall always seemed so much hotter in Colton's mind, and for Isaac, it must've been something exciting. He always ravished Colton a bit more assertively in the showers, slamming into Colton with no reservations and running his soapy hands up and down Colton's tired muscles. But Colton found it exhausting to stand hunched over, spreading his cheeks as he was railed against the wall, all while stifling his voice until Isaac got off.

Colton only climaxed about half the time in the showers, but he didn't push to finish either, usually telling Isaac he had so they could hurry up and actually clean off. Isaac was a stickler about bringing Colton off, either with a brutal fuck or a gentle hand tug. Sometimes when Isaac would lube up his hand and stroke Colton to completion, he'd close his eyes and envision all the times Isaac had blown him. He missed Isaac's mouth, missed the devotion he spent sucking Colton off, but he'd learned to take pleasure in this new dynamic, finding the role of serving Isaac mostly intoxicating. Even if his dick still throbbed with an ache for dominance, still craved to ram its way into a tight hole and fuck and fuck until Colton had been fully pleased. That wouldn't happen between him and Isaac, though, so Colton put it out of his thoughts, rarely entertaining the fantasy.

"Still coming to game night?" Isaac had asked as he changed beside Colton in the empty locker room. It was the only reason he spoke. If even one person was in there—someone either knew or not—Isaac would be on the opposite side getting dressed.

"Yeah," Colton answered, knowing this was not one of the GSA game nights that he kind of enjoyed. They played ridiculous board games while making terrible cocktails, but it always turned into a silly event that Colton enjoyed much more than the noisy frat parties he'd grown tired of attending.

When Colton got to his apartment, he rushed to get ready.

"Whoa, whoa, whoa," Tim intercepted Colton before he reached his room. "Where ya heading, dude?"

"Out." Colton shrugged and half-smiled.

"Care if I tag along?"

"Uh, um, I'm sort of a guest of a guest." Colton's smile twisted into a frown. "I can text 'em about it. Not sure the situation."

"I fucking knew it." Tim slapped Colton's back and laughed. "Who are you banging?"

"What?" Colton croaked.

Devon rustled in the kitchen, clearly curious by Tim's comment and probably ready to report back to Leon with any findings. Fuck, how Colton hated that friendship. If it were just Tim, then maybe he could share the information. No. No, he really couldn't. Isaac and Colton agreed on discretion. That meant he couldn't even tell Tim. Even if he believed his friend, his roommate, his teammate could and would keep the secret.

"It's not like that."

"Oh, then it's definitely like that." Tim grinded against the air. "Just tell me it's DL because of commitment issues and not their relationship status."

Colton quirked a brow.

"Don't fuck a bitch with a boyfriend. Or with a girlfriend." Tim winked. "It never ends well, and then suddenly, you're the asshole for breaking up a couple. Like, I can't help it if I lay down better pipe."

Tim didn't ask if Colton was bedding a guy or a girl or anyone else, but he didn't make any assumption either way. And Colton knew that Tim truly didn't care.

"Maybe your pipe doesn't matter," Devon said sharply. "Maybe you just don't fuck someone in a relationship."

"You're still salty over Trish?" Tim tsked. "Probably cause you're busy licking Brandon's nuts. You can tell him the same thing I did—I didn't know they were together until we were already a thing."

"Yet you kept going," Devon hissed.

Tim turned his attention to Devon, and the two unpacked the entire argument from last year's drama. The biggest flaw and strength about Devon came from his conviction to take sides. Last year, he didn't care about Tim hooking up with some random girl dating a wrestler. But when he suddenly became friends with the guy—after his bestie, Leon, introduced them—Devon became devoted to judging Tim at every turn. Colton mostly hoped that Devon would move out when the year ended and just become a full-time cuck for Leon since he pretty much worshipped the prick already.

Since Devon had his lecturing face on and Tim responded to every comment with lewd quips about his dick, Colton took the opportunity to slip away unnoticed and head out without further discussion on who he may or may not be spending all his time with lately.

Colton got dressed up—like he usually did, looking his best, smelling his best, prepping his best—but he didn't expect sex. If Isaac intended on fucking him, he would've said so before inviting Colton. It was something the jock learned early on in their arrangement, never assume something from Isaac because if you pivot left, he'd just weave right.

Still, when he arrived at Isaac's and found him in his office chair with a headset on for a game that didn't even have multi-player add-ons, he was perplexed.

"Where's the other controller?" Colton plopped onto the bed, studying the dresser used as an entertainment center for the television and console.

"Gaming night is less a reward and more a punishment." Isaac waved a single controller.

"Punishment? For what?"

"For being a naughty boy."

Colton chuckled, laughing harder until Isaac's glare didn't relent.

"Seriously?"

"Seriously," Isaac continued. "You'll be playing a supporting role since you've been using your solo study time to game behind my back, despite already providing you plenty of goofing around time in your schedule."

"How'd you know?"

"I know everything. I'm a god, a demon, a psycho stalker." Isaac shrugged. "You decide."

"Studying is so boring, and I'm passing without the daily sessions."

"With Cs," Isaac hissed. "You could easily have As or Bs. But no, you wanna play some shoot 'em up game, so I'm gonna see what all the fuss is about while you help support my efforts."

"So, what is my punishment, oh great Isaac?"

"For starters, losing the attitude and gaining some humility." Isaac spread his legs, directing Colton to meet him.

Motherfucker. Isaac was using a fantasy of Colton's against him. He'd mentioned on more than one occasion about having Isaac come over to help him cum when he was playing online. The only reason he'd never done so was because that meant he had to actually let Isaac into his home, which his paranoid closeted mind still held a lot of reservations about.

"So, I'm just gonna suck you while you play?"

"Pretty much." Isaac stroked Colton's face. "If you do a good job, I might not remove your gaming time currently scheduled."

"Wait, what?"

"Oh, I obviously have to update your schedule since you don't believe in studying." Isaac shrugged. "Another problem for another day, little pitcher."

Colton quivered, hiding the eagerness because as much as this turned him on, it also really pissed him off. But in the hottest way, which only further frustrated Colton.

When he first took Isaac's dick into his mouth, he did so reluctantly. Colton practically frowned as he bobbed his head up and down until he realized the hand he'd been dealt. Quite literally, in fact.

"Someone's happy," Isaac moaned at the changed enthusiasm from Colton.

Realizing the advantage he had and the opportunity he'd been given, Colton worked harder on Isaac's cock, gripping his hips to keep Isaac seated in his chair and barely able to buck. Not that he made much effort with his attention split on the blowjob and the game.

With his hands busy, Isaac had to give full control to Colton. It wasn't much, but Isaac preferred to control every aspect of their relationship. Even though this was a punishment for breaking Isaac's tedious rules, he still gave Colton a reward. And Isaac didn't show offense to Colton's devious edging when Isaac was in the midst of combat or the deep-throating efforts when Isaac was about to take aim at a target.

"Fuck," he muttered. "Goddamn, you're an eager boy."

The praise continued, and even though Isaac died more times than he could count, he clearly enjoyed his time with the game and Colton's technique. Colton took satisfaction in controlling the pace of Isaac's arousal, bringing him close before taking away his climax.

MN BENNET

Colton had spent so much time swept up in Isaac's schedule, routine, and servitude that he hadn't even realized the lack of animosity on the field. Some time ago, the players who backed Leon drifted from the ruthless pitcher who sought to steal Colton's spotlight. Now, Leon merely glared from the benches with only Devon, eagerly awaiting any opportunity the coach would offer him. In the past, Colton would've asked for a sub after the seventh inning out of pity and hope not to cause more waves with Leon.

Now, he felt too powerful to step aside, too confident to serve someone else's ego, which was ironic since that take-charge strength he found on the field came from surrendering all authority in the bedroom. Okay, in literally any location where Isaac sought to plunge his cock inside of Colton.

This was likely his best game to date. Sure, it wasn't a championship, and they were all but guaranteed victory before stepping onto the field, but Colton threw more strikes than every game this season. His batting landed a homerun. His team brought it together from start to finish without one argument, without one shady misstep, without anyone fighting for glory over each other. The part that made the game better than any other he'd played was the cheer squad of friends from the GSA, accompanied by a reluctant Isaac who appeared bored yet studied every play.

After the game, Colton lingered on the field instead of going to the locker room. Isaac had requested he wait, so Colton did so obediently, even if every second he remained in the dugout sent a shiver of anxiety through him.

There was only one reason Isaac would ask Colton to stay, only one thing Isaac wanted from him here on the baseball field. While Colton would offer himself, it did feel like he was pressing his luck here of all places.

"You were amazing," Isaac said, appearing from out of nowhere after everyone else had vanished and the evening sky started to take hold.

The sun had faded like it waited for Isaac's command, too.

"Thank you."

Colton took in Isaac's sportsy getup for this game. The GSA still rocked Colton's player number, and Isaac's untattooed arm had the phrase #PitcherStrong with a rainbow beside it which Jazz declared she'd make a trending

163

hashtag before the year ended. Colton didn't need any more viral sensations right now. And while they came to support Colton, the GSA hadn't done their eyeshadow in school colors for this game. Instead, they'd gone full-blown Pride with their makeup; Isaac wore rainbow eyeshadow on his left eye and a trans flag-colored eyeshadow on his right eye.

"What's with the eyes?"

"Fuck all if I know. Jazz being Jazzy." Isaac pointed to the rainbow on his left eye. "There's more than one way to live the *right* life."

"Because it's on your left eye?" Colton nodded.

"Yeah, but then her other motto sort of undercuts the first message." Isaac pointed to the trans flag colors on his right eye. "Living your truth is the *right* choice."

"It's cute." Colton shrugged. "Maybe cuter without the play on words."

"Agreed." Isaac huffed, tugging on the straps of his suspenders which held up his baggy Tripp pants and accentuated his exposed stomach in the crop top long-sleeved shirt he wore.

Isaac always picked the most dramatic clothes, which Colton envied. He wished he could be so bold, dress so provocatively. If he wanted to show off skin, the best he could do was go shirtless to the gym or on a run. Maybe he could pull off short shorts in the right conditions. But he felt weird being so free in his style, unlike Isaac, who dressed like a slutty grim reaper most days.

"Three guesses on why you're slowly leading us off the field and toward the dugout." Colton pursed his lips a little, suggestive and flirty and all but saying he was okay with it. Albeit a bit nervous. Okay, a lot nervous.

"What could I possibly want, little pitcher?" Isaac grinned. "Well, not-so-little pitcher."

Colton rolled his eyes as he led Isaac through the opening in the fence and into the dugout.

"I think what I want is to see that winning pitcher in action." Isaac's grin widened, and Colton's thoughts twisted into all kinds of bizarre fantasies. "I wanna see that take charge attitude you unleash on the field."

Isaac bit his lower lip, playing with his piercing and teasing Colton with an unreadable expression. There was no way Isaac was suggesting what Colton thought, what he never dreamed of wondering, what he'd given up considering in their relationship. Well, relationship wasn't the right word. Colton suspected there wasn't a correct word, not one he liked.

Honestly, Colton had stopped wanting to top, to take charge, to assert himself. This new submission kept him enticed more and more, and while the idea of railing Isaac did cross his mind on the rare occasion, it was a fleeting fantasy.

"What're you getting at?"

Isaac slipped out a bottle of lube from a side pocket just above his knee. "This is your field; you're in charge. I want you to take charge right here, right now."

"So, I'm on top then?"

"In a manner of speaking." Isaac sat on the bench, sliding his pants down and exposing his semi-hard cock.

Colton knelt and went to spread Isaac's legs.

"Don't." Isaac poured the lube on his dick and began stroking himself hard. "Today's less about serving my needs and more about showing me yours."

Colton didn't know what to say, how to respond.

"Why?"

"You don't ask why," Isaac said with a demand in his voice. "It's my desires you obey, and right now what I want is to see you commanding the evening."

Colton swallowed hard, watching Isaac ready himself until his own dick began to throb at the sight of Isaac's hard erection.

"Use my cock to get off," Isaac growled. "I wanna see what makes you cum."

That was so much pressure. Colton knew what he liked, and what he liked was the surrender, the patient wait of Isaac finding the right rhythm, the right pace, the right spot to fuck an orgasm out of Colton. The idea of taking Isaac's dick but leading seemed off from how their arrangement worked.

Although, it wasn't all that long ago when Colton controlled the oral he offered. Maybe that was why Isaac was allowing this, experimenting with layers of control given to Colton. No matter the reason, Colton accepted it and slipped out of his shoes and pants.

"Keep the top on." Isaac didn't elaborate on the shirt or hat, but Colton suspected he meant both. "The uniform is fucking sexy."

He went to take off his socks until Isaac's free hand grabbed Colton and guided him closer, so he kept the socks on as he slowly straddled Isaac's dick. Isaac massaged Colton's hole, generously applying lube before aligning his dick for Colton's ease. He didn't slide into the jock, leaving that moment to Colton.

"Mmmmmmhhhhm." Colton squeezed Isaac's shoulders, shuddering as he took in the cock. It couldn't have been more than half, but at this new angle, he found it so much harder to push all the way to the base. His body wanted to retreat. The pressure on his ass, coupled with the discomfort of his knees spread on the bench, didn't alleviate the want to stop.

It was awkward keeping Isaac's dick where it was, but he didn't want to take anymore yet. Thankfully, he didn't have to. Isaac made no efforts to slam the rest of his cock into Colton. He didn't even buck or thrust to control the motion of their bodies. Instead, he kept his hands wrapped at Colton's waist with a stillness that indicated they were merely there for Colton's balance and nothing more.

Slowly, the jock thrusted on top of Isaac, letting the dick stay where it was but allowing his hole to adjust to this new position. Inch by inch, he took more into himself, but when he slid too far too fast, Colton pulled up and let the entire thing fall out of him.

"Sorry."

"Don't be." Isaac had an unblinking stare, patiently awaiting Colton's next move.

It took some adjustments, but Colton finally got into the swing of riding Isaac's dick, taking it faster and harder but at his discretion. That made it challenging for him, still awaiting the rush that came with Isaac slamming into him with a primal need and taking what he craved. Colton surrendered that fantasy and worked on a new one. A fantasy that required his command over the ebb and flow.

Once he found his spot, the perfect push of pressure, Colton convulsed and let out a small yip. Despite biting his lip, he hadn't stifled the noise, and the wicked smirk on Isaac's face suggested as much.

Colton grabbed Isaac's crop top and held it like the reins of a horse, riding faster and faster, focused purely on hitting the sweet spot inside him with each stroke. In a matter of minutes, his rock-hard cock twitched uncontrollably and splattered a hot, sticky mess all over Isaac.

"Sorry about that." Colton panted, lost in the rush.

"Don't be." Isaac kissed Colton, swallowing his exhausted panting voice. When the last of Colton's shaky breaths eased, and the lingering convulsions ended from climaxing and the cool night weather, Isaac gently pushed the jock off him.

"What're you doing?"

"You came."

"Finish." Colton squeezed Isaac's shoulders and tightened the grip of his legs around Isaac's hips, unrelenting. "You said I was in charge tonight, so I'm taking charge."

"You look good on top." Isaac smiled, cute and sweet and devious as his hands tightened around Colton's waist. "You ready for me to finish? Really finish?"

Colton nodded and braced himself for Isaac's sudden thrusts. There was no slow start, no easy flow, just quick and powerful strokes as Isaac bucked upward into Colton, pushing the jock down onto his dick and holding him in place with a powerful hug until he came.

Isaac leaned into Colton, groaning. His dick had slipped out, but he continued his erratic thrusts, sliding his cock against the crack of Colton's ass. The two took heavy breaths until they were capable of composing themselves and leaving the baseball field.

CHAPTER 16
ISAAC

ISAAC had begun to lose himself in the routine he had established for Colton. Their days spent together were supposed to be compensation for his time lost lurking in the shadows for Colton's convenience, supposed to be an acknowledgment of the control he surrendered, supposed to be some warped revenge, but Colton liked the authority used on him, and Issac liked how much Colton enjoyed submitting.

Their arrangement was no longer held in check by Isaac's devious actions, though part of him clung to the fact none of this would've happened without his hatred. A hate he still couldn't let go of when he spent time with Colton. It didn't burn quite as hot, but he found himself too paranoid, too bitter, too Isaac to simply release the past and take pleasure in the now.

"Looks like we're gonna have to wrap this up," Colton said quite mischievously as he pulled Isaac from his stirring thoughts. "I know it's important to study. Lesson learned. I can't wait until the next one."

Since Colton couldn't handle independent study sessions, Isaac took it upon himself to assist with the occasional tutoring. Colton wasn't stupid, but he definitely leaned into that mentality and allowed himself to flounder. That irked Isaac to no end.

"We're not finished." Isaac pointed to the chapters Colton had left to review, the equations he hadn't even begun, and then opened his blank Word document to show Colton still hadn't created a thesis statement. "You don't even know your topic yet, which you need in order to pick out your sources."

"It'll be fine. I'll just wing it. That usually works."

"I've read your winging it papers; they suck."

"The best guys do," Colton said with extra sass.

He hadn't gotten to the point of public pride about his sexual exploits, which meant Isaac had to endure an extra layer of bravado when they were alone. After all, Colton only had Isaac to brag to about his dick-sucking skills, among his many other newly acquired talents.

"Look, I know you wanted an updated schedule, and I'm not complaining…much." Colton swiveled in the office chair, rocking a bit until his knee pressed between Isaac's legs. "But, per *your* schedule, we should be moving on to other things."

Isaac had added two days of tutoring in his dorm room, which coincided with time they could then use for screwing. It was convenient to schedule them back-to-back since they'd already be in Isaac's room.

"I don't need to schedule sex," Isaac said, pushing Colton's leg away and turning him back to the desk.

"Yet you're the one who did." Colton huffed, pissy because he'd grown accustomed to getting his way when it came to intimacy. Sure, he submitted to Isaac's whims, but as the slack of his emotional collar loosened, Isaac gave Colton more and more control, more voice during their hookups.

And yes, Isaac still had sex on the busy schedule he'd concocted for Colton, but it was more a reminder. So much of his time was spent on the mundane day-to-day tasks with Colton that sometimes, Isaac almost lost himself to the idea of an actual relationship, which this most certainly was not.

"Look, I can screw you whenever I want, whenever is convenient for me and my cock," Isaac hissed with a deep breathy voice on the back of Colton's ear.

The quiver it provoked sent a rush of heat spiraling through Isaac.

"But I can't fuck you if you fail out by midterms, so get your ass in gear and take these study sessions seriously."

Colton groaned, dramatic and whiny and slightly similar to how he'd act in high school when butting heads with the rare teacher who challenged the academic slack offered to the athletes of the school.

"So, nothing's happening today?"

Isaac took long, slow blinks, staring at Colton's irritated expression.

"Not a damn thing?"

"Something's gonna happen."

"Oh?" Colton twirled his pencil. "Do tell."

"Well, if you work hard and diligently," Isaac dragged out the words slowly, letting Colton's imagination fill in the pieces.

The green in Colton's eyes shimmered as he possibly predicted that, with solid effort, he could still end his evening getting off.

"By showing how dedicated you are..." Isaac whispered, knowing his breathy words on the back of Colton's ears only further tantalized and teased him. "Then today, what will happen is that you'll learn something."

"Learn you're a boring tease."

"What? You said nothing was happening right now." Isaac tapped the textbook. "We've got lots of stuff going on right now."

Colton dropped his head onto the textbook and lay there unmoving, just pouting until he realized Isaac didn't care. With his tantrum slightly curbed, Colton returned to his assignments and pestered Isaac every five minutes with a question. Even with things he already comprehended. Isaac was certain this was Colton's bratty behavior showing. Perhaps too much leeway from Isaac as of late, or maybe a test to see if he could rouse Isaac into teaching him manners instead of coursework. In either case, Isaac would reprimand Colton later.

CHAPTER 17
COLTON

ISAAC only teased Colton about his studies for another day or so before they resumed their regular routine. The swift and brutal thrusts made Colton cum unlike anything else. In fact, the few days off and Colton's patience had paid off brilliantly.

When Isaac slammed into him, it didn't take much for Colton to throb, having refrained from jerking since it no longer offered the same level of release but instead a pale imitation. Isaac, as always, took his time when fucking Colton in the privacy of the dorm room suite. Some twisted song by a creepy band called Nine Inch Nails played on a loop, encouraging the primal pace of Isaac's hips as he rammed Colton.

The chorus of the song Closer fueled Isaac's need to fuck Colton like an animal, use him and breed him, and pound him deep into the mattress. Even without touching his cock, Colton came, squirming beneath Isaac with a hungry need for more. And Isaac delivered until he finally buckled himself, depositing his seed deep inside Colton and gingerly stroking the jock's damp hair as he gave him sweet kisses along his neck before reaching his lips.

Once they'd finished, Isaac collapsed on top of Colton, letting the full weight of his body pin him. For such a small guy, Isaac kept Colton confined. Colton focused on the warmth of Isaac's skin, the firm touch of his arms and legs wrapped around Colton's arm, and not the pool of cum splattered on the blanket beneath him. The pair lay motionless on the bed for close to an hour with Isaac's soft dick still inside of Colton. It was something Isaac referred to as cock warming, and he'd done it off and on with Colton as a way to help his ass adjust to the regular intrusion of such a big dick.

"I'm thirsty," Colton finally said.

"Should've swallowed my load when you had the chance."

"Isaac," Colton whined, which provoked an immediate response.

The domineering goth grumbled, gently shifting himself off Colton. There was a small pop as his slick dick slipped out of Colton, and then he kissed the jock on the back of the neck before rolling off the bed. He quickly retrieved a bottle of water from his mini fridge and some flavor packets in case Colton craved the flavor.

That made Colton smile as he rolled onto his side and took the water. He didn't need or want the packets, but he liked the small gesture. He liked all of Isaac's thoughtful gestures, even if he never elaborated on their purpose or acknowledged them as anything more than a simple whim he had. Isaac refused to take a thank you, refused anything kind most days.

Explaining himself was never Isaac's strong suit, but Colton yearned for conversation almost as much as he craved Isaac's body. A body covered in tattoos, which were fully exposed as Isaac stood naked by the bed. He waited for Colton to finish gulping down the water before tumbling back onto the mattress.

"What's the deal with the tattoos?" Colton asked, curious and hopeful this might be the sort of thing to encourage Isaac to explain something about himself.

"I get bored and don't suffer from indecisive decisions."

"There's more to it than that."

"It's also proof I don't have self-control and should never be trusted with money."

Colton nudged Isaac, glowering.

"I also like the pretty colors." Isaac batted his long lashes, proving to be as reluctant as ever.

Colton changed tactics, aiming for a pleading expression, which only managed to force Isaac to turn his gaze elsewhere. A small opening which Colton would exploit.

"Come on." Colton tapped the black rose flower on Isaac's forearm. "What's this one? It's more than just rainbows."

He traced his fingers along the stem of the rose, then grazed each scattered petal that was colored in with a different queer flag from gay men to lesbians, to trans people, to bi folks, and so many other identities that Colton had never heard of until regularly attending GSA meetings.

"The rose is me," Isaac said, ignoring the petals and running his hand along the barbed wire tattoo on his wrist.

It did a lot to cover the scars, unlike his other wrist, which showed the full attempt he'd made after his attack in the custodian's closet. The pain he struggled with all by himself, the pain he rarely acknowledged, not once since the night he first erupted at Colton about his suffering. Colton swallowed hard, filled with guilt and remorse and a million apologies he didn't think he was worthy of uttering.

"The barbed wire was a reminder that holding onto people who don't want you is painful." Isaac frowned. "Too painful."

Colton read the text—'Learn to Thrive Without the Roots'—which was etched within the barbwire tattoo. Isaac never spoke of his family, never spoke of their hometown, pretending the entirety of it never existed as far as he was concerned.

"So, you just wanted a reminder it's safer to cut yourself off?"

"A reminder it's not a death sentence to cut yourself loose from someone or something." Isaac's blue eyes glossed over for a moment, then he grinned. It was wicked and forced, but Colton smiled back all the same. "The queer shit came later. Jazz found me in our Freshman Seminar class and dragged me to GSA with her, basically holding me hostage until Stockholm kicked in."

Colton snorted.

"Now, I'm a willing participant in the gay agenda. Damn lesbians."

That brought a genuine smile out of Isaac. How it comforted Colton to know he found such a wonderful community after escaping their hometown. Colton was grateful for that, grateful that Isaac invited him into this world, allowing him to grow with the GSA members.

"Okay, and the phoenix." Colton tapped Isaac's chest, mainly looking for a reason to feel the muscles.

They weren't massive pecs like Colton's, but Isaac had a nice build, not that he saw it that way. Whenever Colton would caress Isaac's body, he'd clam up, then usually toss Colton into a new position and rail him harder. Now, though, he just accepted Colton's gentle touch.

"Pretty obvious. I'm a flamer, so…" Isaac pursed his lips teasingly while Colton rolled his eyes. "Okay, but seriously, it's just a reminder of rebirth and coming back stronger."

"Kind of like the butterfly." Colton nodded to Isaac's hand.

He didn't need an explanation of the phrase D E A D S O U L across his knuckles or the smiley face on one thumb and frowny face on the other. But the butterfly seemed so bright and cheery compared to so many other tattoos.

"Not rebirth." Isaac traced his finger over the butterfly's wings. "Second chances. It's important everyone gets one."

"Thank you," Colton said, unable to hold it back.

"For what?"

"For my second chance."

"This." Isaac pointed back and forth between them. "This isn't a second chance."

"It kind of is," Colton scoffed because Isaac was always so damn reluctant to see this arrangement as anything more than sex, no matter how much of himself Colton continued to offer to Isaac.

He'd gladly give him more if he had it. If only Isaac would tell him what he wanted, Colton would do it. He'd make it happen, offer Isaac the world.

"You had your second chance."

Isaac didn't need to elaborate any further. Colton's second chance had come when they first started hooking up, when Isaac looked past the years of bullying and saw the frightened guy in the closet desperate to explain his needs. Colton realized now that he'd ruined his second chance and that Isaac was too closed off to offer a third.

"I know I'm a dramatic bitch," Isaac said, lifting the mood. "But they aren't all pretentious pieces with deep meanings."

Isaac gestured to his legs, covered in random cute or silly tattoos. Then he slapped his belly and poked the shark-toothed smile stretched from one end of his stomach to the other.

"I think my favorite rando tattoo you have is the tramp stamp." Colton giggled.

Isaac plopped forward, lying on his stomach so Colton could see the word TRAMP was boldly written on Isaac's lower back. The literal tramp stamp always made him smirk.

"You said it was a bet."

"Yes, and I'm not telling you anymore other than the fact that Mina is vile."

"I'll just ask her."

"Oh, she'll never say." Isaac gave a menacing expression, wicked with a glint of humor. "I've got way too much dirt on her."

"Well, I like them all." Colton kissed the tattoos on Isaac's back, the stitched-up wounds that represented missing wings. "They're super artistic."

"Yeah, the art aspect does make me happy."

"You like to draw, don't you?" Colton asked, continuing to kiss Isaac's shoulders. "Any of these yours? Like your drawings?"

"That's a big ass no on both fronts," Isaac said with a strained laugh, his blue eyes lost for a moment, possibly on Colton's question.

It hit Colton how Isaac had liked to draw a lot when they were younger. Almost all day in every class when they were in middle school, but then by the time they were freshman, he practiced less and less. By the time Isaac was a junior, he'd thrown away all his sketchbooks. Colton realized that was because of him, because of the other guys who made Isaac miserable any time he pursued anything of interest.

Colton struggled to find the right thing to say with Isaac most of the time, the right thing to do. He always felt like he ruined their arrangement by talking.

"Keep doing that," Isaac said with a soft growl.

Colton continued kissing Isaac's back, his shoulders, the nape of his neck. Then he brought his hands into it, massaging the stress out of Isaac's stiff muscles. The small growls turned into soft moans as Colton untwisted years of tangled knots. He worked silently for an hour, caressing Isaac's body, kissing him, touching him, savoring every second spent.

CHAPTER 18
ISAAC

ISAAC found himself consumed by the time he dedicated to Colton, entwining their worlds more and more. GSA attendance was about the same, a fair turnout to show support for Colton's latest game. Everyone wanted to see the starting pitcher, and they made no qualms about chatting up his many assets complemented in the uniform. It brought a smirk to Isaac's face.

The fact that everyone wanted the bi batter with a hot jock build only added to the thrill coursing through Isaac. They could want Colton all day, but he belonged to Isaac. And they could make innuendos about his position on the field all they wanted to. Isaac knew Colton might be a pitcher in the streets, but he certainly wasn't one in the sheets.

"What're you up to?" Carlos shoulder-tapped Isaac, ignoring the conversation about hot athletes while focusing on his latest ideas to fundraise for the GSA. He had a list of ideas circled and scratched out and scribbled all over the page.

"Up to?"

"You have a devious smile."

"I'm a devious person."

"Why don't you put that wicked mind to some use and help me figure out a good fundraiser event."

"A live Rocky Horror show?" Isaac's eyes lit up. "I'm not playing Frank."

Carlos crossed out the idea. "Then what's the point."

Isaac continued glossing over the list of overlapping words to the many ideas. Carlos had this tendency to write over his own words, almost with a slight curve or spiral effect. It was difficult to decipher.

"A kissing booth?" Isaac gagged. "How archaic."

"I was going for whimsical."

"Might as well auction people off," Isaac said with a heavy lilt of sarcasm, which he realized Carlos immediately ignored as a fire lit in his eyes. "You're gonna do an auction, aren't you?"

"Hell yeah." Carlos pointed to Colton, who'd reeled in quite the cheer squad of sorority girls from the other end of the stands. "Our newest member would probably bring in quite the crowd. You think you can convince him?"

"Me?" Isaac croaked.

"Yeah, you have a history, right? Went to the same school, now found yourselves at the same college. Have a friendly chat."

"Friends?" Isaac scoffed, feigning disgust so phony even he wanted to roll his eyes at the heavy-handed protest. "Do we look like friends?"

"Well, kinda." Carlos shrugged. "I just figured it was like with you and me. And you and Mina. And you and Jazz. And well, you and everyone you tolerate at a safe distance without actually allowing them to get close because you're like an angry stray cat."

Isaac glared.

"Is there something specific about him you don't like or trust?" Carlos asked. "If there's a problem, I'm here to listen."

"The only problem is how boring these fucking games y'all drag me to are."

Carlos quirked his brow, likely trying to piece together whose suggestion it actually was that the GSA start attending these games regularly. Technically, it was Jazz who brought it up, but Isaac might've whispered in her ear suggestively, playing off her love for sports, the joy of group activities, and the importance of supporting fellow queer friends. Isaac never did something directly, preferring not to be seen as too emotionally invested in anything whatsoever.

"I'm gonna go for a smoke." Isaac brushed past Carlos and out of the bleachers before it was mentioned how he usually snuck his cigarette right there in the stands, rolling the dice on whether or not someone would call him out, fine him, or kick him out of the game.

None of the outcomes seemed like too big a loss, especially the last one, since he needed to downplay his interest in the game. Not only in front of his friends among the GSA but with himself. Isaac had gotten into the routine of studying the rules and regulations involved in baseball, attempting to understand the purpose and entertainment of the game albeit poorly.

He told himself it was only fair considering how much he forced Colton to study things the jock didn't remotely care about. Isaac figured he needed to make an effort himself. But the problem was he didn't know why he felt the need to make such an effort. Okay, that was an easy lie to identify and deduce, but Isaac didn't want to confront the truth yet.

All this time spent with Colton had evolved into feelings Isaac couldn't keep bottled up anymore.

He wandered to the back of the stadium in a hidden pocket between the parking lot and a side entrance where few except other players congregated. Isaac lingered there until the players took a break, and a few found their way outback for some fresh air away from the crowd.

With Colton there, glancing around and dodging chitchat, Isaac knew he was looking for him. It made his heart race. It made him eagerly walk toward Colton.

"Looking good, as usual."

Colton grinned. "Glad you came."

"Well, not yet, but the night is young."

Colton quirked a brow until the joke clicked, and he broke out into a small laugh.

There was so much Isaac wanted to discuss, but he didn't know where to start or if he should. It seemed easier to keep his weird feelings bottled up so things could stay the way they were.

"Well, well, well," Leon's grating voice called out because he hovered around Colton almost as much as Isaac. "You two seem to always be hanging out."

"Could say the same about you." Isaac took a deep drag off his cigarette. "You're always lurking, trying to cling to Colt's ass."

"It's a good ass." Colton winked, trying to diffuse Isaac's hostility.

Leon crinkled his nose and gave a fake smile to Isaac, wishing to hurl an insult most likely, but wary of the goth's gruff attitude and need to escalate an argument. Isaac went out of his way to cut Leon down so much the prick learned not to engage. Unfortunately, he hadn't learned to stay clear of Colton. The envious pitcher still skulked every chance he had in some desperate attempt to steal Colton's fame for himself.

"It just seems you're always here, practically glued to Colton's side," Leon said. "You got a thing for the starting pitcher or pitchers in general?"

There was a curious look from Leon, the type that came with a leading question, and Isaac couldn't gauge if Leon was attempting to discreetly flirt or fishing for leverage on how Isaac was the gay boy with a crush on big, manly jocks. In either case, he didn't care because Leon was a fucking tool hardly worth the breath of conversation.

"It's just what GSA does." Isaac shrugged. "We support, uplift, mildly stalk our queer companions."

"Hmmm. Maybe, but you seem to always be lurking a little more than the others." Leon gestured to Isaac, then to Colton, indicating how much he kept his eyes on Colton, how he studied the patterns of the GSA. Suddenly, Isaac didn't feel like the most obsessive one, finding Leon a bit too unhinged even if he hid it well.

"I just gotta know." Leon's smile grew bigger. "Are y'all a thing?"

Isaac glared, a bit too defensively for a casual assumption that was in fact slightly somewhat sort of accurate.

"Are we a thing?" Colton burst into laughter, giving his fakest and most convincing stunned hilarity before turning to Isaac. "Are we a thing?"

This was Colton's way of playing into the joke while also gauging Isaac's response. It didn't seem like Colton cared much if their arrangement was outed or if there was speculation. After nearly three months of spending so much time together, Colton seemed weirdly committed and open to the idea of being open. But Isaac preferred discretion. The fewer people who knew about this non-relationship, the easier it was for him to convince himself that what they had was purely physical. A fucked up second chance at hate sex turned into…something else. Isaac didn't know what, and he didn't want anyone else to either, which he did his best to convey with a single look.

"I wish," Colton teased, slapping Isaac's shoulder. "Who wouldn't wanna bend over this grumpy goth twink? Maybe pound a smile onto his face."

Isaac snarled.

"Kidding, dude." Colton raised his hands in surrender.

Seemed there were still some things Colton concerned himself over. It was one thing to be openly bi but to admit to being a total bottom with a massive liking for a big dicked goth who railed him without mercy? That was another story altogether.

"But please, start the rumors." Colton shoulder-tapped Leon, feeding into his lack of concern for astute speculation—always the best way to diffuse gossip. "If the cleat chasers hear I'm off-market, maybe they'll stop stalking my every move like some fellas."

Colton winked at Leon, making the rival pitcher's face burn red, before he wandered off toward the sorority girls who'd found their way out back behind the stands. Cleat chasers were some variation of jock junkie fangirls that specialized in locking down a solid baseball boyfriend. Isaac had read that in his meticulous research for the sporting event.

They eagerly huddled around Colton, chatting him up for the rest of the break. One even boldly wrote her number on his forearm. That was something Isaac could live with, but when she proceeded to smack her lips and kiss Colton's forearm, Isaac nearly exploded. Her vibrant red lip imprint popped even from this distance, and Isaac fumed.

Colton must've promised her something ridiculous, like thinking of her with his next pitch, because he feigned throwing a ball and then flexed his biceps, awaiting the hungry flirt's squeal of approval.

Isaac despised blatant and overt flirting, and he hated it even more when the person lusted after Colton. His pitcher.

Thankfully, the break ended, and the game resumed. Colton played even stronger since returning to the field, garnering a louder roar of support from the sorority girls. When the game finally came to an end, Isaac ignored the GSA members, who slowly disbanded and headed out with the crowd. Instead, he lingered around the clearing stands much like Colton did, even as his team headed for the lockers. Colton signed some stuff, chatted with fans, and took his time before making his way to the locker room.

They hadn't discussed it on this occasion, but Isaac had seen this technique from Colton during practices at the very least. He'd take his time, finish last, and make sure to hang out in the locker room long enough for Isaac to sneak inside and join him.

Only when Isaac managed to slip in, he didn't find a shower-fresh and half-dressed Colton like he normally did. Well, normal being the two practices he'd snuck in for. No, this time, Colton remained in the showers, the low grunt of his voice an echoing trail in this empty open space.

Isaac wandered to the showers where he found Colton stroking his cock, feral expression, and eyes entranced on the number he got, on the set of pink puckered lips printed on his hands from an audacious kiss.

"Fantasizing about your little girlfriend?"

"Fuck, man." Colton jumped, nearly slipping in the process. Then he laughed, taking in Isaac, who could clearly see his massive boner. "Yeah, what can I say? She's a hottie. And she'd actually go steady with me. Do people say steady anymore?"

Colton chuckled at his own terrible humor, but Isaac furrowed his brow, practically snarling in the process.

"Are you not content with our arrangement?"

"What? No. I mean, yes. No, I don't have a problem with it—which you didn't ask, hence me correcting myself," Colton rambled nervously, so nervous his erection lessened. "Yes, I'm fine with our arrangement. Why would you ask? 'Cause of the flirting? It's part of the gig. The jerking off? It was half and half. Not that I jerk off to plowing you. But you didn't ask that part either. Damn. Where is this coming from?"

And with that last anxious question, the rest of Colton's dick had turtled up inside him as he awaited Isaac's answers.

Isaac didn't know where to begin and didn't have the energy to respond to all of Colton's random worries. He'd snuck in here for a fun fuck and now found himself questioning his involvement with Colton.

"Come here."

Colton walked from the shower and toward Isaac, who wrapped a towel around the jock.

"I think we're gonna have to review our arrangement and discuss the dos and don'ts once again." Isaac gave a wicked smirk. "Someone's been a bit naughty, breaking the rules, and I might need to give him a reminder of how to behave."

"Broke the rules?" Colton tsked. "How so?"

"Stop by my dorm later, and I'll tell you." Isaac stared with wide eyes. "I'll also punish you, if you're able to handle it."

Colton's expression turned curious. It wasn't like he acted bratty often, but occasionally, he tried to provoke Isaac into disciplining him. There was something so satisfying about it for both men. Isaac would lean into that discipline tonight.

He'd use it to finally express himself, figure out these knotted feelings strangling him from the inside because he feared he couldn't continue casually fucking Colton without putting some type of label on it. Even if that label was only for the two of them to see.

CHAPTER 19
COLTON

COLTON wasted no time arriving at Isaac's dorm suite for a punishment he wasn't certain he deserved. It had never occurred to him that jerking off constituted some violation of their arrangement.

As if reading his mind, Isaac went right into correcting Colton after closing the door behind him.

"It's not the jerking off that has offended me and gotten you into trouble, though I do need you to realize your cock belongs to me," Isaac hissed, yanking Colton's pants down. "You cum when I say you cum."

Colton shuddered in anticipation, the rush of Isaac gripping his semi-erect dick while palming his ass cheek.

"These are not new rules." Isaac glared, expression vicious but touch—oh, fuck, how strong and gentle he was. Each squeeze of Colton's ass, each tug of his dick, brought him closer and closer.

"The fact you fantasized about another is something I can understand. Longing is only natural; curiosity and attraction spark in all types of ways." Isaac continued working, tilting his head to keep his eyes trained on Colton, who could barely stand straight. "It'd be wrong of me to demand you quell those cravings, limit your imagination. These are not things I wish to do."

Colton braced himself against Isaac until he shrugged his shoulders.

The demand was clear, even if his voice was silent. Colton returned to standing on his own.

"What bothers me is the flirting." Isaac's angry façade cracked, and his expression turned somber. "Am I not enough for you?"

"You are," Colton stammered.

"Perhaps. Perhaps not." Isaac leaned in and bit Colton's neck, trailing his teeth and tongue ring along the jock's collarbone, eliciting a tremble. "I don't wish to share you. I don't wish for you to even playfully pursue others."

"I won't." Colton quaked, his dick throbbing. "You're all I want. Need."

Fuck, how he needed Isaac more and more each day. Like the breath he took, Isaac brought Colton to life in the simplest and most extraordinary ways.

"Then you are mine?"

"Yes." Colton let out a breathy groan.

"And I am yours," Isaac whispered; his words ran along Colton's skin like silk.

"Yes," Colton said with a whimper.

"We are exclusive." Isaac worked his hand on the tip of Colton's cock, massaging the head. "Our bodies, our desires, our feelings, are reserved only for each other."

Colton moaned, nodding to express his understanding because that pluralization meant the world to him. *We. Our.* Isaac included himself in such sentiment. Sure, he'd never mentioned messing around with other guys, and with as much time as he dedicated to Colton, it wasn't like he had a lot left over for some other sub, but to know definitively that Isaac only wanted Colton that this little flirtatious action had provoked jealousy, that Isaac sought to lay claim over Colton.

Dammit, he nearly erupted right then and there, but Isaac had released his grip on Colton. Perhaps he'd agreed too soon. A bit longer, and he would've climaxed.

"Now, we can move on to your punishment."

"Being edged isn't the punishment?"

"Only but a step."

Colton grimaced, then grinned, then went to speak but waited for Isaac.

"Strip and lay down." Isaac stepped away, lighting a cigarette as Colton slipped out of his outfit. "Slower."

Grabbing his slacks, Colton stopped their descent and then slowly let them slide to his ankles before easing out of them. Even with his package and ass on full display, he caught Isaac's gaze following the slow lift of his shirt. Isaac very much appreciated Colton's six-pack abs, muscular torso, and broad chest. Colton raised his shirt an inch at a time, swaying his hips a bit as he slowly wriggled out of his outfit.

Once he was fully nude, he lay on the bed face down and ass up, awaiting Isaac's move. It must've been part of the punishment because Isaac took his time with his cigarette before making his way over to his dresser and rifling through drawers.

"This is something I've wanted to do for a while." Isaac's lips kissed Colton's ass cheeks before his hands played with them, spreading them apart and exposing his hole.

Even craning his neck, the position was hard to glean, but he knew what was about to happen.

"I've never..." Colton gulped, swallowing the stuttering moan Isaac's tongue caused.

He immediately went to work, diving into Colton's ass and lapping away with a tongue bath before poking the tip in his hole. Colton dropped his head into the mattress, feeling a wave of heat fill his face and spread over his entire body. A perfect pulse heightened by Isaac's talented tongue. His fingers found their way inside Colton, working him over even more until his dick throbbed under the weight of his resting body.

Colton didn't need to stroke his cock, didn't need to do a goddamn thing other than lay there letting Isaac control the flow of this rim job.

After a few minutes, Colton's body tensed, and he let out a jolt of a convulsion before cumming on the blanket, still lying where he was on the bed.

"This is a punishment?"

Isaac didn't stop. He kept working until his appetites were satisfied.

"To think, I could snack on this ass all night," Isaac said with a playful slap before roughly palming Colton's left cheek. "But that's for good boys. And you're not a good boy, are you?"

"No, sir." Colton trembled a bit, more from the thrill of provoking Isaac than a fear of what came next. A part of him yearned for whatever punishment Isaac sought. He wanted to act out again, just to make Isaac see him, crave him.

"Naughty boys get spankings."

"Seriously?" Colton snorted. "Oh, okay."

And without warning, Isaac smacked Colton across his bare ass with a startling sharp pain.

"Fuck."

"That's one." Isaac wrapped his hands around Colton's thighs, then cupped his ass before he grabbed Colton by the hips and yanked him down to the edge of the bed.

Colton's feet hit the floor, steadying his stance. From this angle, he knew his ass was even more exposed, positioned perfectly for Isaac's rough hand. A shiver of anxious anticipation coursed through Colton.

"Ready?"

Colton didn't respond, just gave Isaac a look that said he didn't oppose what came next. The next few slaps burned, then turned into a piercing sting by the time Isaac hit five.

"Okay, okay, I get it." Colton bit down on the blanket as Isaac continued, showing no indication of slowing.

"Six, seven, eight…"

"Fuck, please." Colton trembled uncontrollably.

Isaac gave one more hard smack and then stopped.

Once it'd ended, Isaac kissed Colton's cheeks, avoiding the tender skin he'd slapped, and prioritized the firm outer glute muscles.

"You going to be a good boy moving forward?"

"Yes."

After the initial shock of the spankings faded and the gentle kisses washed away the pain, Colton realized he'd gotten aroused again at some point. His dick ached once again.

"I think someone likes being punished." Isaac eyed Colton's bulge as the jock attempted to discreetly readjust himself and his boner. "Maybe I need to find another way to teach you obedience."

Fuck, that sent a rush through Colton.

"Oh?" he asked, perhaps a bit too enthusiastically.

But he'd just had his ass slapped damn near ten times which sent a wave of pain that somehow left Colton hard. Not to mention he'd just had his hole licked with such finesse it made him cum all over himself. So, despite Isaac's gruff attitude, Colton couldn't help but lay in a pool of his own sticky mess, a bit eager for what came next.

"Do you trust me?" Isaac asked.

"Implicitly."

"That's a mistake."

"Punish me however you want." Colton lay on the edge of the bed, spread eagle and ass raised up ever so, even if the tenderness ached something fierce. "You wanna spank me again, go for it. You wanna fuck me for fantasizing, do your worst."

"You'd like that, wouldn't you?" Isaac jerked Colton's head back, holding a fistful of hair. "A bratty little sub who's getting too cocky."

"You're gonna have to work hard to pound out that attitude." Colton bit his lower lip teasingly and went a bit further. "Otherwise, I'll just keep being a naughty boy."

The rush of words sent a shudder through him, creating goosebumps of anticipation for Isaac's next punishment. It provoked a stern expression from Isaac, a glazed look of rising to the challenge, and Colton's cock raged against the mattress, throbbing with an ache all over again.

Isaac shoved Colton's face into the mattress, holding him there for a moment before releasing him.

When Colton felt the air shift and Isaac's presence vanish, he went to raise his head.

"Don't."

The order made him quake, and he obeyed. Isaac returned a moment later, slapping his hand between Colton's cheeks and roughly lubing him up before unceremoniously shoving his cock inside him.

Colton groaned into the mattress at the suddenness, the brutal thrust which gutted him immediately.

"You are mine," Isaac said, burying his cock all the way to the base, letting his balls slap Colton's.

Despite the fierce strokes, which made Colton whimper, Isaac's touch remained gentle. His hands caressed Colton's body, running up and down his back to ease him into an arch. They carefully avoided his tender cheeks; even the angle at which his hips bucked barely bounced against the sensitive skin. Isaac railed into Colton faster and harder until Colton couldn't contain himself.

He lifted his head to moan, to tell him he was cumming again, to beg for it, but Isaac pushed Colton's head back down. When Colton convulsed, Isaac's strokes eased, and one of his hands went to work yanking Colton's cock until a jet of cum shot out.

After he'd poured his load, he lay there euphoric and delirious and relishing the heavy panting of Isaac as he growled and raged until finally shooting his seed inside Colton.

The pair gasped and lay sprawled out on the bed, too exhausted to move, to speak, to even think.

"I'll leave it up to you if we go with such a harsh punishment in the future," Isaac said as if he could read Colton's mind. Most of the time, he seemed to always know what the jock thought—even with just a glance.

"Maybe I'll be such a good boy you'll have to think of rewards instead of punishments."

"Oh?" Isaac trailed his fingers along Colton's slick skin. "I think you're far too feisty to be a good boy."

"Hmmm." Colton contemplated. "Guess it'll come down to which you do better."

Isaac raised his eyebrows questioningly.

"Praise or punishment."

"I've got a masters in both."

"Got a masters in being cocky."

"Damn right."

This was everything Colton wanted. Almost. They kept flourishing, but Colton felt like a potted plant that needed to be taken out into the garden. He wanted more from Isaac, and he believed Isaac wanted more, too. Maybe he just didn't know how to express it or ask for it, or maybe he didn't expect it.

"When is this going to turn into something real?"

"It is real," Isaac said, still trailing his fingers along Colton's smooth chest. They looked like little feet wearing fancy shoes because of Isaac's shiny black nail polish.

"I mean something more than just screwing."

"It is something more. We're exclusive. Dom and sub paired together emotionally and physically. If you can't see that that is more than screwing, maybe we need to discuss what your needs are and how I haven't met them."

That sounded like Isaac was on the verge of a lecture, warming up so he could hurl confusing words at Colton, which he had no intention of allowing.

"I wanna hold your hand."

"Okay." Isaac slid his hand over to Colton's and gave it a gentle squeeze.

"In public. And I wanna kiss you. I wanna tell people about you. Show you off. Brag. Make people—well, weirded out because you're so you—but also make them a little jealous because who doesn't want a scary little goth guy they can fit in their pocket?"

"Fit in your pocket?" Isaac scoffed. "You can barely fit me in your ass."

"Stop being so literal." Colton pulled his hand away. "I want more, Isaac. I want you. I know this started weird and not at all how relationships go, but I've never had a right relationship, anyway. You're the happiest I've ever been. You're making me better, brighter, bolder. I want more out of this."

"That type of commitment is asking a lot, all things considered."

"This is about high school, about what I let happen, about..." Colton swallowed the words, the details, the horrors of Isaac's begging and crying

190

and screaming. "I'm sor—"

"Don't." Isaac sat up, sitting crisscrossed. "I don't need or want apologies. I've never asked or expected it. All I've asked for is your submission, your surrender."

"Which I've given in every possible way. I'll give more if that's what you want. I know this arrangement started as just revenge, just a way to regain some of your power, a way to take control and show authority, but there's more to it now. I can feel it in every demand. I've never felt so free surrendering to someone else, giving them the reins of my pleasure." Colton's voice cracked. "But for over four months, you've quickly become my every waking thought. I can't react without your guidance, feel without your touch, breathe without you near me. It hurts to have this much of you and feel like I don't have anything at all."

Isaac stared silently at Colton for almost two solid minutes. When Colton trembled, feeling too emotionally overwhelmed, Isaac reached out and steadied his shoulders, but he still didn't speak. He just took slow breaths, helping Colton mimic them.

"I want an explanation as to why you did what you did," Isaac said quite calmly, his voice eerily level. "I don't want apologies. I don't want feelings, excuses, regrets. I just want a clear, detailed explanation on why you set me up for that. Why you decided to tell the rest of your team about us."

"I never told anyone about us," Colton confessed, ready to unburden himself with the full truth now that Isaac wanted it.

He sat up, and both men sank into the center of the mattress a bit.

"Then, what happened?" Isaac asked. "I know we weren't exactly couple material, and you didn't have feelings for me, but did you really hate me that much?"

"No, never!" Colton did have feelings for Isaac; he'd had them since before he first flirted, before their first hookup. But he was so confused by untangling years of self-loathing coupled with his family's expectations and what his friends, peers, and the world expected out of him, that Colton tried so goddamn hard to keep things simple and casual with Isaac. "The thing is, I was being too nice to you."

Isaac snorted. "Seriously?"

"Yeah. I was so hooked on getting blown by you, spending a little time here and there with you, that I sort of dropped the ball on teasing you, mocking you, bullying the loud and proud queer kid who made everything an annoying cause, who made a town uncomfortable with the way he dressed, the things he believed, and the no bullshit allowed attitude. You had a beacon, and everyone wanted to slap you down for it."

"I remember."

"But I stopped. People noticed. A few guys teased me, started making accusations." Colton almost retreated into himself, looking back on how someone's simple assumption that he liked cock had been the most frightening thing in the world, how he thought his entire existence would crumble to ashes if it was proven to be true. "You remember Gavin?"

Isaac's striking blue eyes turned icy and filled with rage. Of course Isaac remembered Gavin. He was the guy who led the assault in the custodian's closet, the first person to whip Isaac with a belt, the one who encouraged the rest of the team to take shots, to punch and kick and smack Isaac again and again.

"He said he just wanted to catch you trying to do something gay, embarrass you." Colton choked on his words, knowing now how weakly veiled the lie was, and that he just went along with it to prove he wasn't queer, to prove he could trick some filthy homo. "They were supposed to catch you undressing, throw you out of the closet while in your underwear, and laugh. It was supposed to be Gavin and two others. Just them. But then you got undressed so quickly."

"And they took their sweet time." Isaac's gaze softened, possibly recalling the same provocative kisses Colton and he had shared before the team entered.

Not on the lips, Colton hadn't been ready then, but Isaac gave him gentle pecks on the neck, the shoulders, the chest, and he was working his way down until the door flew open.

"I didn't know what to do when the whole team walked in." Colton lowered his head in shame, unable to look at Isaac, realizing more and more as he revealed his part in why Isaac shouldn't date him, why Isaac couldn't date him. "I'm a fucking monster, I know that, and I'm sorr—"

Isaac slapped a hand over Colton's mouth and shoved him back onto the bed. He snarled, nostrils flaring as his squeeze over Colton's jaw tightened.

"I said no emotional bullshit," Isaac hissed. "You're not to blame. I see that. You were young and weak and stupid. Just like me."

Isaac released Colton and went to have a cigarette. Colton wanted to continue, to aim for another apology, but Isaac hated the word sorry—probably because he never heard it growing up, so he taught himself to stop seeking it, to despise it instead of expecting it.

After he finished his cigarette, he returned to the bed and rolled over to face away from Colton.

"I should go." Colton went to slip away when Isaac's hand snatched his wrist and tugged Colton toward him.

Without resistance, Colton rolled onto his side and cuddled up close to Isaac, who wrapped Colton's arm around his stomach. The pair spooned, sitting completely still and remaining silent.

Isaac wouldn't advance their relationship to something public, Colton knew that much, but it did feel a bit more real now that this hidden weight between them had been removed.

"I don't resent you," Isaac finally said, squeezing Colton's hand and guiding it to rest over Isaac's heart. "I don't hate you. I don't want a casual nothing with you, but I'm not sure I'm ready for hand-holding or public fawning or declarations of love."

"Love?" Colton quaked, nearly jolting up from the bed at the idea.

"I won't say it, but I feel it." Isaac pressed his body closer to Colton's, ensuring every part of them touched, from their feet overlapping to the back of Isaac's head pressed under Colton's jaw. "It's okay if you don't feel the same."

"I do." Colton kissed the crook of Isaac's neck.

He stayed up all night, listening to Isaac's light snooze and hugging him tighter and tighter with each passing hour. There was so much more Colton wanted, but he could wait patiently, believing they were on the right path.

CHAPTER 20

ISAAC

ISAAC didn't know what to do with Colton's feelings, with his own, with the continuing shift in their dynamic. Now that he understood what happened in high school, how it spiraled out of control, he'd hoped maybe it would've offered some solace. At the very least, a consolation of no longer eating away at him. But old resentments rarely died out quickly. They clung to life like a virus. Isaac was tired of being infected by such malice.

Still, in the weeks to come, Isaac managed to bury as much of the past as he could. He found himself slowly looking forward to the possibility of what lay in his future. He just didn't have any clue what he wanted in that future.

Colton sat across from Isaac on the other side of the room during the GSA meeting, doing his best not to look in Isaac's direction. Isaac found himself seeking Colton's brief little glances. It confused him how Colton had changed so much since high school, changed so much since their arrangement—their sordid relationship. A relationship. Colton desperately wanted one, making do with the scraps Isaac offered, but ready and willing to take the next step, to make a commitment.

They couldn't date, though, not for the world. They didn't mesh. Maybe in the bedroom, but aside from intimacy, where did they match? Isaac and

Colton didn't like much of anything the other liked, merely made allowances for each other's interests. Was that compromise or compatibility? Isaac didn't have a real relationship to use as a reference, mainly because he never had one and often tuned out anyone he knew in a relationship.

"Ufff. I hate men," Carlos said with a sulk.

Mina tilted her head, laying on Carlos' shoulder to offer sympathy while also spying on his phone.

"I thought you said that app was only for hookups and dating was a waste of time." Mina's curious gaze could only mean Carlos had downloaded the worst gay hookup app ever, the one every guy loathed yet always found themselves diving back into when lonely and horny.

Isaac counted his confusing blessings that he no longer required the assistance of the online fates to quench his lust or hunger for carnal pleasures. While he had no idea what to make of Colton or the blossoming feelings, he'd rather contend with the confusion of their relationship non-relationship than blank profiles, masc4masc dude bros, nude catalogs without a single face pic, kinks without appropriate conversation, random ghosting after addresses were given, and the thousands of other harrowing horrors that came with attempting to grind with another guy online.

"Maybe if you spent less time on g—"

"Do not speak its name," Carlos said with a dramatic hiss, then making a Catholic cross sign as if to rebuke the unholy app. "You only give it more power when spoken aloud."

Isaac snorted.

If Mina kept talking, everyone in GSA was about to hear how Carlos was trolling online for a quick and easy hookup. Carlos had a miserable expression, continuing to scroll through the app, while Mina made suggestions on swiping right even though that wasn't how this app worked.

Isaac recalled how miserable and needy his online experience had gotten when looking to get off while dodging his feelings. He wondered if he'd always dodge them, always shut himself off from the world. Part of that philosophy came from trust broken by Colton—but it wasn't entirely Colton who made Isaac this way. His family and friends all had a part in his need to isolate himself and shut down. He had his own role in it, too, one he needed to accept. He wasn't a kid anymore. If he wanted to change, he had to make that effort.

"Carlos," Jazz said after an uncomfortable silence that Isaac hadn't entirely noticed.

Isaac had zoned out, and apparently, Carlos had fallen down a rabbit hole of blank profiles.

"Yes?" Carlos stuffed the phone in his pocket.

"The PowerPoint."

"Right." Carlos scrambled up front and pulled up the GSA fundraiser event. "This year, we're gonna host an auction date night for all our lovely eligible queers."

"I thought we were gonna do Rocky Horror," someone said with a sigh.

"While that's a lot of fun, given that we'd only be able to book the smaller auditorium, it'd really limit our sales and funds raised," Carlos explained. "But we may still do a performance for GSA Pride. Now, moving back to the planned fundraiser. This is going to help us reach our charitable pledges for the year. Usually, we set a very strong goal at the beginning of each year but struggle to reach that number."

"Aim high," Mina said with a shrug. "It's okay if we miss the mark."

"True." Carlos flicked through the slides. "But here are some samples of other on-campus groups and the numbers they've brought in."

"Would that actually work with our fundraiser?" Isaac asked, attempting to be polite but a step away from pointing out the obvious on how the GSA differed from these other clubs.

"Glad you asked." Carlos flicked to another slide detailing other colleges that had a similar fundraiser. "As you can see, it can draw a lot of interest. It's gonna fall down to how we market it, the date nights we offer, and, of course, our eligible participants."

"I'm in," Mina said, leading the volunteering chain of other members speaking up to join in. "But we need a huge attraction, someone that'll do the heavy lifting for our marketing."

Everyone's eyes quickly fell on Colton. Isaac's blood boiled, finding himself almost as flustered as the jock who tried to laugh it off before the suggestion even left someone's mouth.

"You'd be perfect!" Mina declared. "You're the starting pitcher. You're admired by just about everyone on campus."

"Well, not everyone." Colton frowned.

"Well, everyone who matters." Mina waved a dismissive hand in Isaac's direction, lumping the goth among the rude people who didn't give Colton a proper chance.

"I actually have a small list of reasons why you'd be our ideal bachelor." Carlos cleared his throat and went to the next slide, presenting a headshot of Colton with about a dozen different bullet points about why he should consider it.

Isaac scowled. Talk about manipulating the situation. Instead of asking Colton privately, Carlos decided to rely on the pleading expressions of the entire GSA to encourage Colton.

He grimaced, likely unsure of what to say. And how would he? Because of Isaac, he was locked in a silent arrangement that trapped him somewhere between feeling and fucking, refusing to budge and make a real move.

"I don't know," Colton paused. "This is for bachelors, right?"

"It is." Carlos nodded. "Singles of all kinds. You're single, correct?"

Colton bit his lip, then forced an awkward smile. "I mean, define single."

"Oh?" Mina perked up in her seat.

"Clearly, I am," Colton corrected himself, which made Isaac's insides knot nervously. Was he anxious because Colton almost slipped or because he caught himself from slipping? "But I don't wanna be some cocky bachelor showing up demanding a date for lots of money. That seems um, what's the word?"

"Helpful?" Carlos said, flicking through his slides to show the list of LGBTQ+ programs the GSA was raising funds for.

Dammit. Next, Carlos would cue some sad song while posting pictures of starving puppies. Okay, an exaggeration, but not by much.

"I guess I can't really argue with—"

"He's not single," Isaac snapped, stunned by his own loud announcement. A wave of trepidation washed over him, making his skin buzz and his heart race.

Colton stared, his uncomfortable expression falling away, replaced by a look of perplexed curiosity. That simple smile made Isaac blossom with joy.

Isaac swallowed his doubt, buried his reservations, and finally spoke up honestly about how he felt.

"Colton can't take part because he's not eligible." Isaac fixed his attention on Colton's soft green eyes, knowing he was the only person who could keep him steady here and now. "He's taken. Off the market. He's mine."

Mina stared slack-jawed. "Oh. My. Fucking. God."

"Eeeeeeeee." Jazz nearly fluttered in the air with excitement, having spent the entirety of her friendship with Isaac trying to set him up with someone who would soften the grouch she claimed would be happier if he let someone in.

Isaac didn't feel very happy. Mostly annoyed. Slightly frustrated. And growing more and more queasy as shocked eyes locked onto him from GSA members. He couldn't fathom how he blurted this information, made a public declaration. He scanned the spinning room, looking at Colton and hoping he hadn't made the wrong decision, that he hoped he hadn't overstepped.

The beaming smile on Colton's face suggested he was quite pleased with the gesture.

Carlos tsked. "I knew it."

"How?" Mina asked.

"Haven't seen Isaac trolling the hookup wasteland app since…" Carlos pondered for a moment. "Since Colton became a regular fixture at the GSA meetings."

"Wow, you're like a detective," Colton said with way too much admiration in his expression.

Isaac rolled his eyes at Colton's sincerity and Carlos' bravado.

"Technically speaking, Colton could still participate in the auction." Carlos rocked his head from side to side. "It is for a good cause, after all.

Maybe—"

Isaac's immediate barred teeth and slammed fist silenced Carlos, along with anyone else who wanted to comment. It was rare to see Isaac express anything other than indifference, so when he displayed his affection for Colton, everyone eyed him with questioning faces. He almost regretted the outburst, the reveal of his emotional state, but Colton's happy eyes soothed the doubts threatening to bubble inside Isaac.

Despite his immediate show of ferocity, the joyfully overwhelmed expression on Colton's face cooled Isaac's temper.

"Come over here," Mina slapped Carlos' empty chair, demanding Colton relocate. "I can't believe y'all have been playing the cold shoulder while on the DL. Boys are the worst, I swear."

Colton remained where he was until the awkward silence and strong stares of encouragement finally roused him from his seat.

"Sit down," Isaac said. "We're not putting on a show for anyone."

"Oooooh." Mina threw her hands up to feign offense or fright. "Someone's a bossy bottom."

Isaac stared, unblinking.

"What? I call 'em like I see 'em." Mina leaned closely to Isaac and whispered, "Rumor has it, the starting pitcher is packing quite the bat between his legs. Is that why you've been so mellow lately?"

"Size really doesn't matter."

"You know the guys who say that only do because they're not packing."

Isaac often found the opposite to be true but let Mina believe what she wished.

"We can't all be blessed as dom daddies, I guess." Isaac shrugged with an aloof smile.

"All right, and on that splendid note, can we please try to finish the discussion on our fundraiser? A fundraiser that just lost its star attraction." Carlos cleared his throat, indicating Mina and Isaac's not-so-quiet whispers were heard in the room that Carlos hadn't quite wrangled back on track.

Once the room was settled, Carlos continued but only a few people were engaged with the continuing presentation. Isaac wasn't one of them.

"I'm sorry," Colton mouthed.

Colton had nothing to apologize for unless he meant not correcting Mina. But why would he? It wasn't his assumption or responsibility to fill in the blanks on their sex life. There was still a spark of pride in what people thought about Colton, about him being a strong jock, dominant, and in charge. Isaac understood it to a degree. Personally, he figured taking eight inches on a regular basis made Colton a lot stronger than he gave himself credit for, but whatever he needed to emotionally sort out was up to him, not Isaac.

Isaac never cared when people questioned his masculinity or what position folks assumed. The only time he addressed the topic was alone with a partner before screwing. Then and only then did the conversation matter. For everyone else, they could believe what they wanted.

> Isaac: You know I hate apologies.

Colton: Sorry in advance. I'm gonna be saying it a lot when I drag you places.

> Isaac: No.

Colton: New rules. New arrangement. You made it.

> Isaac: Same arrangement. Just public now. :/

Colton: Nope. You run the bedroom, the book stuff, but you suck at dating. Not in a good way either. ;)

Isaac huffed, drawing attention from others, including Mina, who tried to peek at his phone until Isaac snapped his teeth like a dog giving a warning.

Colton: Yep. I'll be running the relationship portion. Pretty much anything involving human interaction.

With that, Colton stuffed his phone back in his pocket and pretended to pay attention to the rest of the GSA meeting. Definitely pretending. Isaac recognized the glazed look and subtle nod Colton would use when overstimulated during their study sessions.

This wouldn't be the end of their discussion; no way would Isaac allow it to be settled in a handful of texts in the midst of announcing their relationship. Damn. Relationship. It really was a relationship. And already Isaac wondered how much he'd bend his whims to please Colton. He thought about how much he'd already bent to please Colton, to meet him halfway, to see him content. Worse. To see Colton happy. Had he really been whittling himself down to this point the entire time?

Isaac glowered, imagining all the couple things Colton might try to enforce now that they were officially on display for everyone, officially official. What had he done? Allowing himself to become overcome with feelings, worry, jealousy. That wasn't ever part of his plan, ever something he wanted. Yet he couldn't help but bask a little in the attention this drew. The worst part? Isaac liked the fluttery feeling it gave him, the tension, and the anticipation.

He had no idea what the next chapter had in store for them, but he was eager to explore it with Colton.

CHAPTER 21
COLTON

ISAAC announcing their relationship completely stunned Colton in the best way possible. It was unexpected, to say the least. But as expected, Isaac immediately dragged Colton off after the GSA meeting to have a sit-down and privately discuss matters.

"Obviously, that was unplanned." Isaac slowly strolled across campus as the sun set and students went about their business.

Colton enjoyed the casual walk, considering Isaac usually had a tendency of speedwalking everywhere without delay. And that often left Colton rushing to keep up either to meet Isaac discreetly in his car or dorm or some other semi-isolated location across campus.

"So, we're dating," Colton said, not asked.

"If you have to put a label on it."

Colton didn't need clarification. This all pieced together quite soundly in his mind. But he gathered from Isaac's rambles about the reactions in GSA that despite being the one to declare them a couple, Isaac still required more time to wrap his head around things.

Reaching out with his hand, Colton interlocked his fingers with Isaac's and tightened his grip before his skittish boyfriend could retreat. *Boyfriend.* Colton liked the sound of that, the thrill, the rush, the everything!

"What are you doing?" Isaac hissed, his eyes darting about in every direction for onlookers.

"This isn't a hookup anymore. This isn't an arrangement of kink." Colton raised their interlocked hands up and smiled. "This is a relationship. People show off relationships. People show affection in relationships. People—"

"I don't do PDA."

"I wasn't planning on blowing you for an audience." Colton smirked. "But I will hold your hand. I might even demand a kiss from time to time. Just a peck. You won't have to go full tongue in front of a crowd. Unless, of course, you desperately want to shove your tongue in my mouth because I'm just that irresistible."

Isaac glowered, face burning bright red, and it fueled Colton even more.

"We should probably discuss what this means, what we officially are," Colton said, leading them in the opposite direction of Isaac's dorm room. "Like, are we just dating? Are we in a relationship? I know we're exclusive, but that was more for intimacy. Do you wanna be exclusive and serious and..."

Colton struggled to find the right words. He'd never had a real relationship before. Sure, he'd dated girls in high school, but that was often for show. Not so much a cover as a popularity contest. Picking the right partner gave folks clout, status, and access to another inner circle of friends. Most of his time and energy was dedicated to his athletics in high school, so dating really had become a standard thing for him to check off the list. In college, no one seemed to care much about dating. Hooking up was easier than ever before with guys or girls.

But as little as Colton understood about dating, he was miles ahead of Isaac, who still looked like a wide-eyed deer in traffic as they walked across campus holding hands.

"We're gonna need a story on how we met, how we got together." Colton cringed at the idea of the truth. "Neither of our initial get-togethers were that flattering. Between me bullying you nonstop until I switched gears to semi-stalking you until you sucked me off in high school and you threatening to get me kicked out of college unless I let you fuck me, our origin story needs a bit of editing."

"To be clear, you offered yourself up on a dick-sucking platter." Isaac tried to pry his hand loose from Colton's grip to no avail. "I simply asked for an extra side of ass with my order."

"Yeah, being quippy doesn't make our arrangement cuter." Colton strummed the fingers of his free hand. "I say we just keep it vague. Knew each other in high school, reconnected here. My charm was captivating— obvs—and your spitefulness was endearing."

"Is this going to be a regular thing?" Isaac tightened his grip and lifted their held hands. "Parading me around?"

"Maybe." Colton winked. "You look cute flustered."

"I'm not flustered," Isaac said with a crack in his voice. "Or cute."

"You're fucking adorable. Emphasis on the fuck."

Isaac scowled, which only made him that much cuter in Colton's eyes.

"Are we just going to wander aimlessly as we hash out the details of our um, hmmm, coupling?"

"Jesus fucking Christ, dude." Colton wheezed, clutching his ribs with his free hand. "You make it sound painful. Is the idea of dating that scary to you?"

Isaac didn't respond; he just kept studying their surroundings like he was mentally accounting for the unfamiliar.

"And just an FYI, we're not wandering aimlessly." Colton dragged Isaac alongside him toward the on-campus apartments. "Figured since we're officially official, we can have this conversation at my place."

Isaac hesitated. So much of their arrangement required discretion. Avoiding Colton's place had been for his benefit since he shared the apartment with two other players on the team and explaining the angry goth guy slipping in and out of the room at all hours of the night was a lot harder for Colton to do than just dipping out and leaving his bedroom abandoned for the night as he slept at Isaac's.

"Come on." Colton led him toward the building, the much nicer building that'd been built a few years ago unlike the dormitories which were outdated and rundown. "You're about to see why you need to quit the RA gig and live in the apartments."

"They have RAs in the on-campus apartments," Isaac said, still warily taking in the sights. "Are you sure about this?"

"Yes."

"If your roommates are home, they're gonna have questions."

"Cool deal." Colton smiled. "I've got answers. And questions. And stuff to clarify. Which can all be done inside."

In that instance, Colton felt the rush that came with being open and honest slide over to Isaac. Colton read Isaac's expression with ease, watching the realization hit him like a wave. The knowledge that this wasn't some twisted game or private show between a dom and sub anymore but, in fact, something so much better. Colton didn't know exactly what, but the thrill of finding out practically made him soar.

"I've also got some other ideas of what we can do." Colton made his most suggestive face as he led Isaac to the building doors. "And let's just say that my bed is much nicer."

"Oh?"

"Full-size mattress." Colton nodded. "Not that we need all that room, but it'll be fun to see what you can do when not constrained to a small twin size."

Isaac laughed at that and followed Colton inside with ease.

The first few times Isaac came over to Colton's apartment, no one had noticed. Either his roommates weren't home, or they were hunkered in their bedrooms quite possibly enjoying the company of their own guest. When they finally did spot Isaac, the shock wore off quickly. It was possible they were more surprised by Isaac's aesthetic than the fact he was a guy since everyone knew Colton's bi status, and these particular teammates never expressed concern over it.

There was a grand total of one conversation between him and his roommates about it.

"You bagged yourself a bad boy." Tim nodded approvingly.

"Just 'cause he dresses like a freak doesn't mean he's bad anything," Devon snarled, heading back to his bedroom.

"Have you seen the way he fucks around and finds out?" Tim snorted. "He's badder than your bitch boyfriend."

"Leon's my friend, you fa—" Devon caught himself, glaring between Colton and Tim.

When Leon lost his edge to souring Colton's days, he went to work poisoning Devon against his roommates. It made practice and games uncomfortable and quickly made living together unbearable. But aside from that singular setback, Colton's days had a positive uptick, and he focused on spending most of his time with Isaac. Publicly and affectionately.

The pair seamlessly transitioned into a real couple, and Colton quite liked showing off his boyfriend for all to see. Especially since Isaac remained indifferent and rude to just about anyone who pestered him. Colton had never met someone so dedicated to helping people and equally annoyed by the presence of others and in no way afraid of showing that aggravation with a cutting comment.

Still, people reacted positively for the most part, which only encouraged Colton more. In fact, the only person who continued waving a flag of dismay about Colton's queerness was Leon, who became more vigilant after Colton's relationship with Isaac became public knowledge.

Leon's jokes hit harder now. Sure, he'd always mocked Isaac, but seeing how the goth guy mattered to Colton, Leon made more of an effort to rag on him. It threw Colton's focus a bit, and his pitches kept going out of bounds until, eventually, a player managed to hit the worst foul ball off Colton's shitty curve.

"Fuck me," he hissed under his breath as the ball landed in the bleachers, where a handful of folks watched.

"Woooooo!" Mina shouted. "You got this, bitch!"

A few GSA members still had a habit of showing up during practices to support Colton, enjoy their lunch, and watch hot guys run around swinging their bats. Isaac and Mina were among them and often the most vocal. Since Colton's audience had expanded months back, some other cliques started joining in to watch their favorite player practice.

"Damn, man!" Leon shouted from the sidelines, stepping out of the dugout. "Maybe you should call it. Not looking like much of a pitcher at all. Making me wonder what you and that weirdo get up to."

Colton's face flushed. He wanted to say something snappy, witty, mean, but he'd never been great at comebacks. Usually, Colton didn't need them, and frankly, he didn't like belittling people. Even people he didn't like.

"Why are you worrying about what Colton and some other dude are doing in bed?" Tim asked.

"Huh?" Leon's expression hardened. "I'm not! I was making a point."

"Was the point that you're gay or jealous?" another teammate asked.

"It was a fucking joke, you morons!" Leon sneered.

"A shitty joke," someone else said.

Colton released a breath, exhaling almost all his nervousness. There were still players who didn't feel the same as Leon. Nowhere close, in fact. The harder Leon pressed, the more the team supported Colton, especially as Colton became more honest about himself. It seemed they rallied on his behalf, making it easier for him to slip into his identity and almost believe going pro was a possibility.

"Look out!" Isaac's voice barreled through the field.

Before Colton could register the meaning, the baseball hit Leon dead in the face and sent him tumbling backward. Players rushed to help Leon, Colton among them. Not because he cared—he simply didn't need the accusation he'd let his boyfriend assault other pitchers. Thankfully, there wasn't any blood, but the swelling on Leon's forehead was enough to get one of the coaches to send him to the athletic nurse.

"My bad!" Isaac shouted, a gleam in his eye when Leon scowled. "Thought I could try my hand at pitching, too."

Mina burst into laughter, nudging Isaac.

"What?" He played ignorant, as if he could cute his way out of nearly breaking Leon's face. "I thought it'd be easier to aim. If bench warmer over there can do it, why can't I?"

"They should just shine a designated catcher spotlight on you, sweetheart." Mina gestured dramatically to the overhead lights on the field, the ones currently turned off given the daytime practice.

"I guess I should leave the pitching to the professionals." Isaac smirked in Colton's direction, giving him the most mischievous expression ever before letting his face fall to something stern.

Colton almost snorted. Seeing Isaac's dom look usually made Colton shudder with anticipation, but coupled with the awkward humor of the events unfolding, he couldn't help but chuckle. Between Mina's jabs and Isaac's dumbfounded expression, it was hard to remain neutral. Colton couldn't pretend to be sympathetic for Leon's sake if his life depended on it. Either of their lives. But at least he did his best not to gloat at Isaac's actions.

Mina said something out of earshot that provoked a snarl from Isaac. He sucked his teeth, made a loud hissing sound, and shoved Mina.

"Keep it up, boyfriend. I'll show you what a catcher you are." Mina shoved Isaac back, cackling the entire time. "You're about to catch these hands if you're not careful."

Isaac nearly keeled over at that, wheezing loudly as he clawed back the laughter billowing in his chest.

Colton half-smiled, letting Mina inadvertently emasculate Isaac while he played into the bottom twink role, strutting down one of the bleacher aisles as the coaches closed the practice to avoid any more audience participation.

Showing off Isaac was pure joy for Colton. Being honest about himself and his sexuality was exhilarating. There was something so much better about having a partner to show off than simply stating he was bisexual. He hadn't realized how lonely he'd been until he collided with Isaac, until their relationship status became official. But as much as he liked showing off his boyfriend, he still had difficulty bragging about his preferred position.

It was something the other guys on the team wouldn't get. These weren't the comfortably straight allies in GSA who Colton had come to know. Guys who weren't threatened by any perceived notion their manhood was at stake because they didn't abide by gender norms, didn't worry where a partner's finger wandered and didn't feel the need to assert their dominance to prove they liked to fuck. No, Colton found himself anxious because the guys on his team wouldn't see him as a leader, as the starting pitcher, as one of the top players if they learned he was anything but a top.

Colton almost contemplated revealing an interest in being versatile, but Leon's jokes about him switching to the role of team catcher quickly squashed that idea. It was easier for him to lie about bottoming, and Isaac never seemed to mind, which Colton greatly appreciated. In fact, Isaac made a point of saying it was no one's business what they did between the sheets, even if the brunt of assumptions assumed Isaac was the bottom.

"Put your dicks away!" Tim burst into the room with a hand slapped over his face. "It's party time."

Colton snorted at Isaac's wide-eyed stare of aggravation. Isaac had almost grown accustomed to Tim's jovial bullshit, but Colton predicted this would be a few steps backward, given he didn't like barging, assumptions, or cheeriness. Three things that basically embodied Tim.

"I'll be out in a minute." Colton chuckled, turning to Isaac in the process. "It's your last chance."

"Last chance for what?" he asked with the sourest face in the world, like he'd forgotten they were dating and had gone right back to hating Colton. Sadly, that was Isaac's default expression when met with anything he considered hostile. Which was basically everything.

"To sneak away and abandon the party," Colton clarified as he finished checking himself over in the mirror. "Once we get there, I won't be the only one pestering you to have a good time."

Mina, Jazz, and Carlos were meeting them at the party. It wasn't like the frat house bashes were exclusive, but since hanging with the GSA members, Colton realized there wasn't much overlap in their party scenes. He wanted to change that. He wanted to merge his two worlds.

"Whatever." Isaac gave a shudder of sarcastic enthusiasm as his voice shifted from its natural gruff base to a perky, pitchy lilt. "Let's go have fun."

"Oh, God. You're gonna be so awkward." Colton smirked. "I can't wait."

CHAPTER 22
ISAAC

ISAAC managed to make small talk for nearly three hours without feeling the need to deck someone across the face. Most of the partygoers weren't half bad. A bit too loud for Isaac's liking and far too drunk for Isaac's comprehension. Still, he held his own and endured for Colton's sake. Not only for Colton. Mina, Jazz, and Carlos too. Wherever those three had wandered off.

"Surprised you haven't hidden in some corner," Colton said with a laugh, slapping a hand over Isaac's shoulder and pulling him away from a conversation he was only half paying attention to. "Sorry I abandoned you."

"I'd hardly call chatting with your friends abandoning me."

Isaac understood the importance of making his rounds, interacting with friends, the absurd need to make friends, and blah, blah, blah. It wasn't Isaac's cup of tea, but he wouldn't resent Colton for enjoying himself.

"Speaking of friends, where are yours?"

"Last I saw, Mina and Jazz were sneaking outside for some fresh air in the least subtle way."

Colton made a confused face. The party was not the place to elaborate, so Isaac moved on.

"Carlos was playing some drinking game with your roommate. Well, your teammate. Er, or I guess, your friend."

"Tim?" Colton's green eyes lit up with understanding. "All of the above."

"Well, they're around here somewhere with ping pong balls and warm beer at this point."

"I gotta be real," Colton said, steering them away from the partygoers and toward a mostly empty hallway. "I didn't expect you to be so chill and kind of outgoing—well, for you—at a frat party."

"It's not my vibe, but I can handle a little of this if it makes you happy."

"You've been such a good boy," Colton whispered into Isaac's ear, dragging him into the nearest room and slamming the door shut. "I'm honestly shocked by how well you've handled yourself."

"I don't get off on praise like some guys." Isaac smirked, taking in the cramped bathroom space.

"No?" Colton trailed his lips down Isaac's neck. "Thought maybe you'd wanna know just how much I appreciate what a good boy you've been tonight."

"I'm more about degradation."

"Oh." Colton squared up against Isaac, pressing him against the sink. "Mine or yours?"

"Always yours." Isaac bit his lip, staring longingly at Colton, who delicately continued brushing against Isaac.

"Well then, how about you put me in my place for dragging you to the last place in the world you want to be."

Isaac liked the sound of that yet struggled all the same. This wasn't the last place in the world he wanted to be. Anyplace with Colton would automatically rise high on Isaac's list. He'd endure just about anything to spend more time with his boyfriend.

Colton growled, kissing Isaac's neck, then nibbling on his ear and tugging at the cross piercing. He pulled a little harder than he should, and Isaac released an aggressive grunt of irritation, which only provoked Colton to be more playful, more annoying. His fingers tugged at the loops of Isaac's pants. His teeth bit a little too hard on Isaac's Adam's apple. His hips bucked a little too hard against Isaac's, knocking him against the bathroom sink again.

"I suppose since you're offering." Isaac tsked, running his fingers through Colton's black hair. "Get on your fucking knees."

With a firm push, Isaac guided Colton down, and the jock wasted no time unfastening Isaac's pants. The cold sink sent goosebumps across Isaac's skin.

"That's right, boy." Isaac kept his hands on Colton's head, pushing him closer to his cock.

His hands were merely decorative, seeing how Colton needed no instruction on how to take Isaac's massive cock. He'd gotten masterful at sucking off Isaac. Colton knew everything Isaac enjoyed, from the teasing to the deepthroating, and he never let his gag reflex hold him back. Part of Isaac missed the noises Colton used to make, the deep gurgles, the gasps, the choking breaths, but he much preferred the expertise of how Colton handled himself now. And he still struggled, still choked when gripping Isaac's ass and forcing the entirety of the shaft down his throat.

"Fuck." Isaac shuddered as his dick pulsed against the tight, constricting throat muscles of Colton's warm mouth.

If they were in the dorms or apartments or even a bathroom stall in an empty building, then Isaac would attempt to drag this out, savor every pump into Colton's mouth, turn this into a long, brutal face fucking. But Colton's technique was too precise. In all of three minutes, Isaac found himself on the verge of shooting his load. The only way to resist would be to pull Colton off his cock, but he didn't want that.

"I'm gonna cum." Isaac gripped Colton's hair; he squeezed so tightly that his knuckles turned white. "Fucking swallow it."

Isaac pulled back as the first jet of cum released in the back of Colton's throat, but he managed to let the rest of his seed land on Colton's tongue. Isaac's dick twitched, the head resting in Colton's mouth. When Colton gulped, Isaac rammed his dick back into his boyfriend's mouth.

"That's right," Isaac said with an edge in his voice. "Keep it up."

Each stroke as he thrusted in and out of Colton's mouth kept Isaac's orgasm alive a little longer. He knew he'd finished, but the phantom sensation kept him bucking his hips as Colton took in Isaac's dick until it finally softened in his mouth.

"Goddamn." Isaac chuckled, panting with a bit of ecstasy in the process. "If the head's gonna be that good every time, I might have to attend more frat parties in the future."

"Frat guys are hit or miss with their head game." Colton wiped the corner of his mouth and smirked at Isaac.

"Oh, I know." Isaac adjusted his pants, teasing Colton right back at his flimsy attempt to get a rise out of Isaac. The fact was, he'd already sucked that rise right out, and Isaac wasn't about to concern himself with the list of guys or girls who'd sucked Colton off before he locked him down.

"I fucking knew it." Colton gripped the sink, boxing Isaac in place as he pulled himself to his feet.

"What made you suspicious?"

"More than one guy who's given me a brojob was making candy eyes at you."

"It's the lollipop everyone wants to suck." Isaac shrugged, shooting Colton a playful expression. "I got the dick all the boys want."

"Below their belt or in their mouth?"

"Both."

They chuckled as they made their way out of the bathroom and bumped into Tim, who was rounding up guests.

"Well, well, well, dirty birdy boys flapping and fapping in the potty." Tim shook his head while tsking.

Colton blushed.

"Afterparty at our place—hope you're up for it."

"What?"

"Yeah, Devon started talking it up to some of the team. Next thing I knew, Leon was giving folks directions, and here we are." Tim shrugged. "So, I'm grabbing the coolest people to make this bearable."

"All right." Colton turned to Isaac. "Let's grab your friends."

"You can call them your friends, too," Isaac replied in reference to the GSA members at the party. "They like you better than me anyway."

"That's not true." Colton beamed teasingly and probably a little proud of his annoying charm, which Isaac couldn't seem to get enough of these days.

Going back to Colton's apartment was supposed to be Isaac's reward for enduring the frat party tonight. Instead, he ended up in a crowded living room with damn near thirty drunken fools who were one clambering stumbling step away from campus security getting a noise complaint.

It took Isaac all of ten minutes to decide he was over the outgoing party scene and needed to drag Colton away.

"You know, the afterparty is a blast," Isaac whispered, oozing sarcasm. "But I keep revisiting the bathroom blowie."

"Oooooh," Colton replied, playing it off as if he replied to another person.

"Your head game has gotten phenomenal," Isaac continued.

"Maybe later we can revisit that," Colton replied, nodding to someone and clearly about to drag the night out even later.

Isaac hummed. "You know, I kind of wanna revisit it now."

Colton tsked. "It is far too crowded to just sneak off. I'd be a rude host."

"Shame." Isaac nibbled on Colton's ear ever so subtly. "I was hoping to blow your mind this time."

"Wait? What?"

"I didn't stutter." Isaac grinned. "And rarely gag. Something I'm sure you recall."

Colton blinked, probably trying to wrap his mind around the idea of Isaac's proposition.

"I'm going to get us drinks," Colton said, trying to remain calm.

"I'm really only thirsty for one thing," Isaac whispered.

"Oh. My. God. They're gonna be the best to-go drinks you've had in your life." Colton's face burned bright red. "Relax, chat, I'll make us something epic!"

Isaac smirked as Colton darted off into the kitchen. With no interest in small talk, Isaac wandered toward the bedroom while Colton made their drinks. Though, Isaac doubted they'd spend time sipping cocktails when he had big plans for their cocks tonight. As he reached the hallway and turned for the bedroom door on the immediate right, he bumped into someone and nearly stumbled backward.

"Watch it," Leon hissed.

"What was that?" Isaac glared, not backing up an ounce as he took deep, menacing breaths. "Why the fuck are you here?"

"Got invited."

"I don't mean the afterparty, ass cunt." Isaac eyed the door Leon was nearly pressed against, nearly wedged against since Isaac refused to back up.

"Got turned around looking for the bathroom."

Isaac swiveled to stare down the very short hallway and saw the open bathroom door a grand total of three steps away. "How fucking hard were you looking?"

Leon scoffed in response and barged off. Isaac turned back to Colton's closed door and gave the handle a good shake. It was locked.

"Sorry about that," Colton said, moseying over with drinks in hand.

"It's fine." Isaac glared past Colton at the bathroom door where Leon was now holed up and hiding. "Your stalker was lurking around, probably trying to get inside."

"Which is why I always lock my door. He seems to wanna be buddy-buddy with my roomie."

Isaac yacked. "Here I thought Tim had decent taste."

"My other roommate. We're not close." Colton wiggled his hip a bit to draw Isaac's attention. "Keys in my pocket."

Since Colton was carrying cocktails, Isaac reached into his pants and retrieved the keys.

"Uh-hmm?" Isaac made a face and held up the fifteen or so keys.

"It's the third blue key. For homes."

"You have three residences?"

"Four." Colton shrugged. "But we never really lock the beach house."

Isaac counted them out until he'd grabbed the third key with a blue band on it, then opened the door so they could step inside.

"What's with all the keys?"

"Car, baseball, gym, homes, old storage locker, I think, and spares for others."

Isaac directed Colton inside and grabbed one of the drinks. He gulped down the sugary cocktail faster than he should have and belched.

Colton snickered, sipping his own drink. "Sexy."

"Keep it up." Isaac playfully shoved him, waiting impatiently for Colton to down his own drink.

"Speaking of sexy…" Colton set his drink down. "I gotta piss."

"Seriously?" Isaac waved him off and plopped onto the bed.

Colton rushed out, likely realizing Isaac's mood was a rarity. All the same, he eagerly awaited his boyfriend's return. When Colton finally made his way back after the longest ten minutes.

"There was a hell of a line, I swear."

"Uh-huh." Isaac grabbed Colton's shirt and pulled him close before shoving him onto the bed.

"Someone's excited."

"I most certainly am." Isaac flung off his shirt, kicked off his shoes, and unfastened his belt. "You better hurry up."

"No foreplay?" Colton teased, sliding his own pants down.

"I've got a long night planned." Isaac crawled onto the bed. "We can kiss and cuddle after I've tasted your dick."

Colton shuddered beneath Isaac as he lay back on the bed. Isaac did tease Colton with a few kisses, light and guiding, and gentle hands that brushed over Colton's tensed muscles. They could stay like this all night, and Isaac would be happy. But he wanted more. Wanted something he'd craved for years.

Isaac trailed his way down Colton's muscular abs with kisses and licked Colton's inner thigh brushing his face against the erect cock.

"What inspired this?" Colton asked, gripping his dick.

"I won't be outdone," Isaac said, slapping Colton's hand away and taking full control of his boyfriend's cock.

He wasn't joking when he said Colton's cock sucking had improved. Over the last few months, he'd gone from struggling to take half to swallowing all the way to the base with ease.

Isaac licked the head of Colton's cock, teasing and rubbing the pre-cum already dripping. How he'd longed to take Colton's cock back into his mouth, the taste of his dick, the shudder of his body. Oh, how Colton bucked when Isaac swallowed the entirety of his shaft.

"Fuck," Colton hissed with a sharp breath.

He grabbed Isaac by the back of the hair only for the goth to lift his head and straddle Colton's hips.

"What happened?"

"Nothing." Isaac grabbed Colton's wrists and placed his hands higher up, at the head of the bed.

"I might be sucking you off, but don't be fooled, baby." Isaac kissed Colton, leading their tongues. When Colton moved to caress Isaac's body, he found his hands moved back to the head of the bed. "Be a good boy and let me have my fun."

"Yes, sir."

Isaac slid back down, sucking Colton's cock as the jock fought the urge to thrust upward, to bury Isaac's head to the base of his dick. Isaac could feel it in every subtle movement of Colton's body, the twitch of delight as Isaac licked, the moan when Isaac swallowed, the jerk of his body when his hands went to meet Isaac.

"Keep doing that, please," Colton spoke through clenched teeth, desperate for release.

Isaac wanted to bring him off fast, prove he had it in him, and surely wouldn't be outdone by Colton's fantastic blowjob. But another part of him wanted to edge Colton for hours, to play with the dick he'd denied himself in some foolish attempt at maintaining control, keeping his distance, resisting urges that'd lead him back to old habits.

They were well past all that. Isaac had real feelings for Colton, desires that superseded every impulse from when they were teens. Most importantly, while he liked their roles very much, he found himself willing and able to let layers of that fall away to further satisfy Colton.

"You wanna get off?" Isaac asked, running his tongue up the hard shaft of Colton's cock.

"Yes, please." Colton's teeth chattered.

"Then take it." Isaac took Colton's cock back into his mouth and moved his hands up Colton's firm stomach, chest, shoulders—all so he could reach Colton's hands and guide them back down.

Once Colton's hands brushed through Isaac's hair, it only took the simplest direction from Isaac to garner action. Colton took the consent of authority and rammed his dick up and deep into the back of Isaac's throat while holding his head firmly in place.

"Take it," Colton demanded.

Isaac choked from the suddenness of Colton's cock buried deep in his throat. But he pressed his hands to Colton's hips and steadied himself as Colton continued face fucking him. It took more than a moment for him for his mouth to adjust. It'd been far too long since Isaac sucked another cock, stretched his jaw this wide, or felt his throat constrict from the swift thrusts of a cock pushing in and out, deeper and deeper.

Colton couldn't contain himself for long. His breaths became wispy, his body convulsed in Isaac's hold, and his cock throbbed.

"I'm gonna cum." Colton went to pull back, but Isaac took in all of him, holding Colton's cock in his throat as it pulsed, and he shot his load. "Fuuuuck."

Isaac stroked Colton's still hard dick and squeezed out the last drops of cum resting at the head of the cock. Isaac licked them, savoring the drops on his tongue. The taste of Colton. "We'll definitely have to do that again."

"Hell, yeah!" Colton lay back, basking in Isaac.

"But for now, I think I'm fucking you until you cum again and scream my name."

"I will not be screaming anything with this many guests in the apartment."

"Then you better bite down, baby." Isaac sat up and grabbed Colton by the hips, spreading his legs and pulling him closer. "I am feeling quite ravenous."

The smile on Colton's face, the steadiness in his body, and the gentle adjustments he made to align himself to take Isaac only further enthralled the goth. Isaac couldn't believe this was his life.

CHAPTER 23
COLTON

COLTON rode on a high wave the next morning, buzzed from his first social outing in a gay relationship. People saw his boyfriend. People talked to his boyfriend. Most importantly, people liked Isaac. And sure, Colton didn't care too much what people thought. He'd learned to let their opinions of him fall to the wayside. Well, mostly. Okay, he'd learned to focus on not caring what people thought of him. Of course, he still cared a little bit. Just a tiny amount. Not enough to let people's opinions of Isaac determine how he felt.

But Colton couldn't help beaming because Isaac was met with approval. So much so, it seemed like everyone was buzzing about the party. That confused Colton. Lots of eyes fell on him during his classes. Smiling faces turned into shadowy expressions, and whispering followed him well into the afternoon. He struggled to distract himself from the onlookers since he'd forgotten his phone back in his room. It definitely made the day drag on.

"Colton, wait!" Tim shouted as he approached the locker room for practice.

Tim barreled ahead and intercepted Colton, blocking his way inside.

"You don't wanna do that."

"Do what?" Colton chuckled.

"Everyone's seen… They're all in there talking… It's just, Colt, I don't know what to say…" Tim fumbled around, his expression pleading and uncomfortable and reminiscent of the awkward stares around campus that washed away Colton's excitement.

"What's going on?"

"There's a video of you and, um, Isaac."

"A video of us?" Colton cocked his head, trying to recall if anyone was filming at the party or the afterparty—not that he hung around there for long. He'd had a few drinks but didn't struggle to remember the events. "Who cares?"

Colton hadn't done anything embarrassing last night. Isaac had been on his best behavior. Honestly, Colton kind of hoped he would've been a bit ruder. Colton often found Isaac's verbal beatdowns on others a little intoxicating. He had this way about him, this 'no fuck's attitude' that most people strived for but lacked the conviction to handle.

"It's of you guys, you know." Tim shrugged suggestively, but Colton didn't grasp the nature of what Tim was hinting at. All he noticed was the frantic look in his wide bloodshot eyes. "Do I have to spell it out?"

Colton shrugged innocently, always the worst at catching hints. "Maaaaybe."

"It's a video of you two fucking."

"Wait, what?" Colton's heart surged; his entire body crumbled.

Isaac and Colton weren't exactly risk-free, but they were generally careful about public fucking. Public anything hookup related. They'd even curbed that enthusiasm as time had passed, rarely doing more than a kiss or handhold at this point. Had they been sloppy somewhere? Had someone recorded Colton again being indecent?

"Fuck, fuck, fuck!" He didn't know what to think, what to do, how to react. "Where?"

"You two were in your bedroom, you know…"

His bedroom? Colton's mind swirled, spiraling out of control. How did this happen?

"This was from last night?"

Tim grimaced. "There's a video going around everywhere."

"Show me." Colton had to see, had to know.

"You don't want to—"

"Show me the goddamn video." Colton snatched Tim by the collar.

Uncomfortably, Tim pulled up the video.

'Starting Pitcher Catches a Homerun' didn't seem like the most creative name in the world, but it sent a shudder of embarrassment rattling through Colton's core.

He knew what was on the video. He knew exactly what he and Isaac had done last night. And apparently, whoever recorded them picked a particularly intentional point to edit. The video started right when Isaac entered Colton, capturing his groan with a staticky muffle. It'd skipped past Colton's blowjob, glossed over the make-out session and foreplay Isaac usually included to get Colton ready, and jumped right into a scene of Colton getting plowed by Isaac's big dick.

The lighting was bad, and the frame stayed in one position the entire time, but the video seemed to run forever.

"That's enough." Colton turned away.

Tim stuffed his phone back into his pocket.

Colton wondered how many people had seen this video. Not just on campus but everywhere. Strangers. Friends. Family. Oh, fuck, what if his family heard about this video?

He reached into his pocket and froze. It was then that Colton remembered he'd forgotten his phone. Christ, it must've been buzzing all day with warnings, with questions, with a thousand different responses from laughter to mortification.

"You should go home," Tim said, his voice soft. "Everyone will understand."

Colton didn't know what to do, how to feel, but when a few other players walked past them with laughter and whispers as they turned to enter the locker room, Colton's panic turned into rage. With the door to the locker room pushed open, he could hear the conversation, the jokes, the mockery at his expense...all led by the worst human on the planet.

Leon Coleman.

He did this!

Colton didn't know how, but he knew Leon was responsible. Without thinking, he barged into the locker room and stormed toward Leon.

"You son of a bitch!"

"Whoa, whoa, whoa." Leon raised his hands defensively. No, playfully. "We all know how cock hungry you are, but I'm not interested."

"Fuck you!"

"Last I checked, you're not fucking anyone, are you?" Leon snorted. "Well, you're fucking, but not. You know."

"Getting fucked!" Devon said with a bit too much enthusiasm for Colton's pain.

"That's what I was looking for," Leon said with a smug smile.

"I will kill you for this," Colton said, seething rage.

"I didn't have anything to do with your little gay porno. Whatever you and your freaky boyfriend get into is on you."

"I'm not a fucking idiot," Colton snapped.

"No, of course not." Leon nodded. "Just a bottom bitch."

"I know you did this!"

Leon leaned in close to whisper, to taunt, "Prove it, fag."

Colton flipped out, swinging a fist faster than he could think. His anger barreled forward, and he launched himself at Leon, attacking with a ferocity unlike he'd ever felt before. He had a hand at Leon's throat, his body pressed against the lockers, and his fist slamming into him again and again with furious punches.

Before he could break Leon's nose, bash in his smug face, other players intervened. Hands were snatching at Colton from every direction. A sharp pain hit his ribs and his back. People were punching him. Not Leon. No. Leon fell to the ground, gasping like a dying fish once Colton was ripped off him. Other players had swarmed in the mass that was meant to break up the fight and used the chaos to strike Colton without anyone noticing. By the time Colton shook himself free and shoved everyone away from him, he was panting from the pain and confusion and unbridled rage. His torso ached like he'd been stomped on.

"Lennox," Coach Wilson snapped, calling out Colton and waving him over. "Office, now!"

Before anyone could start anything else up by mocking or laughing at Colton, Coach Wilson cursed up a storm and sent everyone off to the field for laps.

"Not a fucking word," he demanded. "Every word is another lap. Let me catch you whispering."

Colton exited the locker room and followed his coach to an office where he sat with all the team leaders. It didn't take long for Colton to sink into the chair offered, awaiting the uncomfortable conversation he knew was about to unfold.

Coach Wilson was an older guy with a never-ending sunburnt farmer's tan and a fat gut made all the bigger by his pencil thin pasty legs. Despite his initial unease with Colton's coming out exposé last year, he proved an overall supportive coach. Colton didn't imagine this video incident turning out the same way.

Despite his best efforts, Colton tuned out almost all the considerate words, the tiptoeing topics, but when the worst part of the discussion started, Colton perked back up.

"It's probably best that you sit on the bench until this blows over," Coach Wilson said. "A few games at most. We're going to evaluate the PR situation—"

"I'm being punished because someone recorded me?"

"No, but we have to take everything and everyone into account." His coach frowned, the hard-pressed face of a man who didn't expect to weather this particular storm. "What happened, the video… It's awful. You're a victim, but I don't think the press is going to care about that half as much as riling up our team, you, the fans, the school. It's a circus right now, and they'll be an investigation, so during that, it's best for you to sit on the sidelines, breathe, and try not to get overwhelmed."

"An investigation?" Colton seethed. "I know who did this!"

But he didn't know how. He just knew in his bones Leon was behind this. And it worked out perfectly. With Colton benched, Leon would be starting pitcher in his absence.

"Not a word." Coach Wilson raised his hand. "Nothing informal right now. Everything needs to go through proper channels. I want this by the book."

"Proper channels? Like police?" Colton's heart raced. Did they even handle stuff like this?

"Lord, no," Coach Wilson said.

"Unless of course, you feel this needs legal documentation," Assistant Coach Adams added. "They can at least look—"

"It's better for you, for your team, for everyone if we keep this incident on campus," Coach Wilson interrupted, glaring daggers at Adams who dared suggest Colton take action. "Something like this, you don't want it dragged out in a courtroom for months or years or anything, right?"

"No," Colton said with a shaky voice.

"Good," Coach Wilson said. "Now, just keep to yourself until we can handle this properly. I don't want you to say something that'll breach your contract."

"My contract?" Colton quivered. "I'm at risk of losing my scholarship, my place on the team because of what someone else did?" Colton stood, panting heavily and furiously. "That's fucking bullshit!"

"No, you're not," Coach Wilson corrected. "Only if it turned out you were involved in it knowingly, intentionally—"

"I would never!"

Coach Wilson reassured Colton that the team had his back, but the longer Colton sat there listening to the strategy plan on how to handle this situation, the more he realized it didn't involve him. He recalled the laughter in the locker room as Leon taunted him. The players who jumped in, not to stop the fight but to get a few hits in themselves. Colton dwelled on everything he'd worked on his entire life as far back as he could remember. Six years old and playing little league with a dream of going pro. Now, it had crumbled away, and he didn't believe there was a goddamn thing he could do to change it.

Unable to attend practice and uninterested in going home, Colton wandered campus, sticking mostly to back parking lots, empty trails, areas not filled with students. He had too much pent-up frustration, confusion, fear, paranoia, hatred, anger, and a thousand other feelings that bombarded him with every step. Soon, Colton was running, sprinting away his energy while hoping to escape these overwhelming feelings that haunted his every thought.

"Colton!" someone shouted.

He ignored it.

"Colton!" they called again.

He ran faster.

If someone tried to ask him questions or offer him comfort, he'd break. If someone tried to mock him, to joke about his pain, he'd break them. So, he did the only thing he could—he ran, ignoring the voice.

"Colton, wait!" they called again. This time, their voice was hoarse, familiar in its gruffness.

He turned to find a red-faced Isaac chasing him.

"What're you doing?"

"Looking for you," Isaac wheezed. "I've been trying to get ahold of you since I…"

The pause indicated that he wasn't sure how much Colton knew.

"I've seen the video."

"What happened is awful—"

"I know, which is why I need space."

"I have a meeting with the dean."

"I might, too." Colton shrugged. "Forgot my phone."

Not that he wanted to look at it.

"How are you handling this?"

"I'm not." Colton ground his teeth.

"I'm here for you."

"I need space from you, too."

"Are you blaming me?"

"No. But we weren't exactly careful. Yes, this happened in my room, but let's be honest, it could've been anywhere. It could've been because I'll do anything anywhere for you."

"And that's on me?"

"No. Don't twist this to make me feel like shit. I already feel like shit," Colton snapped. "It's hard enough not to think you had something to do with this."

"What?"

"Logically, I know this is Leon. There's no one else who would want to do this. He's the only person who wants to ruin me. Who has wanted to ruin me since he got here. But then there's this tiny little paranoid thought in the back of my head that just keeps screaming that's not true."

Isaac listened intently, giving Colton his undivided attention, which made the words difficult for Colton to form, but he had to. There was so much pain eating away at him, so much fear and paranoia and doubt. Speaking it helped purge some of the poison seeped in his soul.

"You would want this."

The look of hurt on Isaac's face made Colton's stomach twist in knots.

"I would never."

"And I believe that. Mostly." Colton sighed. "But I can't stop my brain. Leon had motive but no way into my room."

"He picked the lock."

"At a party with close to thirty people? Leon just randomly learned to pick locks?"

"He could already know."

"Because that's totally a skill people just have on hand," Colton spoke with venomous sarcasm. "How he found a way into my room is a mystery. What, he hid a camera in there and then found his way back outside? Plus, he locked the door again so no one would notice. That's a lot of steps, and he's evil enough for it. But then I think about how you had access to my room. Alone."

Colton recalled the few minutes he'd left to take a piss, to freshen up, to breathe and reel back his overzealous excitement about the blowjob.

"I didn't do this."

"I know."

"I can't believe you think I would!"

"I don't believe you did it," Colton snapped. "It's just a weird, paranoid thought bouncing in my head with, like, a million other thoughts. And honestly, it's not that outlandish. This all started because you hated me."

"This all started because you hurt me." Isaac jabbed an accusatory finger in the air.

"See, it's that right there. The anger and the hurt and resentment you still have for me." Colton gestured between them. "You wanted to expel me. You wanted to hurt me. To use me. To break me. Don't tell me I'm crazy for thinking maybe you were playing some long con to fuck me quite literally for the world to see. My entire fucking life is falling apart. Tens of thousands of people have watched me get fucked in the ass, either jerking off to it or having a good laugh at my expense. I don't have time to tiptoe around your feelings when mine are fucking exploding!"

"I…" Isaac dropped his head.

"I just need space to think, to process, to breathe." Colton fumed, hurt and frustrated and confused beyond measure.

"Take whatever time you need." Isaac abandoned Colton, who wandered campus until he couldn't take the looks anymore and went to his apartment.

Colton got back to his room to find his phone buzzing. His mother was calling. He ignored it. Ignored the dozens of missed calls. Ignored hundreds of notifications. Colton couldn't speak; he couldn't breathe. He stared at his desk, the trophies, the framed photos, the medals hanging on the wall. That little space in his room was where the camera had been hidden. A spot meant to showcase his success, and it'd been used to record his most private moment. All so it could be posted online and fuel Colton's downfall.

His coaches said they had his back, but he didn't believe it. This was the first day of the fallout, and they'd benched him. What would happen when pressure rose? When fans protested? When anonymous fucks called in or sent hateful emails? Colton understood how scandals in sports worked. He was fucked in every sense of the word.

Colton's phone vibrated in his hand.

"Aaaaahhhhh!" Colton screamed, hurling his phone into his trophies.

Watching one tip over soothed the rage and shame eating away at him, so he barreled forward and slammed into his treasure trove of successes. Everything faded beneath the waves of fury as Colton ripped apart his bedroom, unleashing as much as he could. It wasn't enough. His anguish hit like a tidal wave. His shame sent him spiraling to the undercurrents of his thoughts, his fears, his insecurities and doubts.

Colton was broken and alone and afraid.

CHAPTER 24
ISAAC

ISAAC found himself aimless without Colton. So much of his semester had revolved around Colton—controlling him, guiding him, screwing him, loving him. Fuck. When had this hateful obsession turned into devoted dedication? He knew the answer as well as he knew that Colton wasn't wrong in suspecting him, doubting him, questioning if this was all some ruse. How Isaac wished it were, how he wished he could take credit for something so heinous and vile. Being a villain in Colton's story seemed easier than a confused, unworthy lover.

Everything about their relationship was wrong and broken, and this terrible act was the final crack that would divide them. He could feel it in his bones as he lay in bed, unable to sleep, in every nervous breath he took the following morning outside the dean's office.

"Morning, Mr. Parker." Another administrative member of some overpaid board came along and ushered Isaac to follow.

When he reached her office, he found himself in a room with four other individuals, including another student whom he surmised belonged to the disciplinary student panel.

"Oh, fucking joy," he muttered under his breath.

"I'm Mrs. Hyman," the administrator said before introducing the rest of the panel. Isaac didn't bother wasting the brain cells necessary to store their names. "I don't wish to mince words with you, Mr. Parker, but these actions are not how we at Clinton University conduct ourselves."

"Never." Isaac scoffed. "The University of Clinton Lloyd Institute of Technology takes the code of conduct to the extreme."

He recalled how many team building trainings he had to attend as an RA the last two years because of incidents similar if not worse than his own claim to fame through online amateur porn. Hell, he recalled the lacrosse team incident his freshman year, which likely explained why the university acted quickly during any type of athletic sex scandal.

"This isn't a laughing matter or a joke of any sort," Mrs. Hyman said, flipping through a code of conduct book.

"Of course not," Isaac replied, ready to be done with the pretense of this bullshit meeting. "Tell me, is it cause our sex tape didn't include any CLIT merch? Or clits in general? Would you have preferred I railed one of the cheerleaders instead?"

A cacophony of offended noises escaped Mrs. Hyman and a few others.

"I was going to ease us into this discussion, but you're clearly too hostile for civil conversation," Mrs. Hyman snapped, eyes furious and locked onto Isaac.

"Oh, no." Isaac shook his head. "I say pop the hymen, Mrs. Hyman, and just hit me with the bad news."

"Because of this inappropriate behavior and misconduct, you are being relieved of your position as an RA. Filming sexual involvement is against any code of conduct—"

"I didn't film it," Isaac shouted, shouted the way he wanted to when Colton questioned him, when Colton's paranoia made him doubt Isaac's earnest devotion to him. "I had nothing to do with the sex tape. A terrible one at that."

Isaac had watched it, watched every expression on his face, on Colton's, the words they both grunted throughout, and he wished he could undo that entire night. Maybe he should've just rejected Colton's invitation to go partying. Maybe he should've insisted on dragging him back to his dorm instead of the ridiculous afterparty at the apartment. Maybe...

Maybe he shouldn't have dated Colton to begin with.

"Until you have proof otherwise, we have to assume your role in this incident." Mrs. Hyman shrugged, a real 'fuck you' gesture. "Also, given the scandalous choices you've made with a student under your charge, you'll be removed from your TA position pending an investigation."

"Oh, fuck off," Isaac said with bitter disgust rolling off his tongue. Was fucking a student in the class appropriate? Probably not. Was there a rule about it? Nope. He'd read the handbook a dozen times over. And he'd seen enough TAs banging freshmen looking for help in a class to learn that no one gave a fuck who fucked who on campus as long as it didn't make the front pages.

And his relations had. Not by his doing, though.

"Since you're no longer an RA, you'll be required to remove your belongings and vacate the dormitory by the end of the week. Anything left in the suite will be seized and properly disposed of."

"Get fucked," Isaac hissed, then stormed out of the office.

The long trek across campus didn't assuage his rage; in fact, every step only added to his fury when he got back to his building. Anyone foolish enough to speak to him got a curt 'fuck off' comment. When he got to his suite, he started tossing his things into garbage bags as quickly as he could. They were cheaper than suitcases, and he never needed to waste space by storing them when he could buy a new box of bags for any moving needs.

It helped vent his anger, carelessly throwing possessions into keep and trash piles. They'd allotted him a week to collect his stuff and vacate the premises, but he wanted to be out by the end of the day. Every fiber of his being wanted to run away from this campus and never look back, but he didn't know where to go. He didn't know if this scandal would follow him, or worse, prevent him from attending a new university.

With a deep breath, Isaac tried to release his hatred for the campus. It wasn't the school he hated. It was the bureaucracy lotted out by a handful that he despised.

He grabbed his phone and texted Mina about crashing at her place since she was the only friend he had who lived off campus. Well, the only one willing to offer him a couch for who knew how long since he'd lost his job and residency all in one fell swoop.

Mina didn't require an explanation. She texted back with her address and a time when she'd be home.

Since Isaac still needed to clear his head and had a few hours to kill, he texted Jazz to hang at her place. Was it convenient that she lived in the same apartment complex as Colton? Maybe. Was there a chance Isaac would see Colton? Unlikely. Did Isaac want to be nearby just in case the opportunity arose? Definitely.

Jazz didn't reply, so Isaac decided to be the obnoxious friend who showed up unannounced and knocked on the door.

"Dumpster diving?" a cool voice asked with a laugh.

Isaac turned to see his former friend, William, breaking away from a small group and sauntering over. There was an air of arrogance about him, a confidence, a bravado of excitement as he slinked around Isaac.

"How the mighty have fallen." William smirked. "To think, you kicked me out of GSA over a scandalous recording that never saw the light of day, and now, ironically—"

"You're a fucking moron," Isaac said through clamped teeth. "First off, you don't know a damn thing about irony, so don't use pretty words you can't define."

Isaac dropped his trash bags of possessions and closed the distance between him and William.

"Second, I didn't kick you out; we collectively got rid of your sorry ass." William sneered.

"Third, it was never about the video. It was the outing." Isaac glared, seeing only red. Every part of William looked breakable, and he wondered how much hate he could release by hitting him. "Finally, and this is the most important part, I warned you that if you ever showed your face again, I'd rearrange it."

William back stepped. "That was for Pride."

"That was for life, motherfucker. Do I look like the kind of person to tolerate casual mockery?"

William tripped over his own feet, and Isaac cracked his knuckles. Before he had a chance to swing, William scrambled to his feet and ran away.

A pity. Isaac really wanted to break someone into pieces until his frustration subsided.

Isaac grabbed his things and continued walking to the apartments. He waited for someone to leave and then slipped inside since the doors required a key swipe to enter. When he knocked at the door, he could hear scrambling on the other side.

The door swung open, and a breathless Mina answered. "You're early."

Isaac scrunched his face and eyed Mina from head to toe. She was visibly flushed, her braids were tangled, and her shirt was on inside out.

"I take it you heard what happened." Isaac walked right on in without waiting for an invitation.

"It's been all over campus." Mina had an apologetic expression. "How's Colton?"

"Needs space," Isaac sighed. "In the meantime, I got kicked out of my dorm and pretty much got fucked by this whole situation."

"Well, you're welcome to my couch as long as you need it." Mina gestured absentmindedly to the apartment.

"Thanks." Isaac dropped his garbage bags for the time being. "You can tell Jazz to come on out."

Mina's expression turned to phony confusion. "Huh?"

"Didn't realize I was interrupting you two."

"I honestly have no idea what you're talking about."

"Mina, do I really need to embarrass you?" Isaac side-eyed her as he opened the bedroom door. "Is she under the bed or—"

The closet door creaked, and Jazz sheepishly stepped out.

"Hiding in the closet?" Isaac tsked. "Shame."

"Not hiding," Jazz insisted.

"Yeah," Mina jumped in. "We're not hiding anything. We're just taking it slow, like you and Colton did."

"Well, you two clearly need to work harder."

"Oh, please." Mina waved a dismissive hand. "You just got lucky."

"We're in Jazz's apartment." Isaac blinked a few times at them, waiting for the realization to hit.

They'd been so dazed and delirious in whatever the fuck they were doing that they'd literally forgotten whose bedroom they were messing around in. It was such an oddity; Isaac couldn't help but smirk a bit.

"I don't know what kind of pussy power you two are laying down on each other, but y'all might wanna consult a doctor about the memory loss." Isaac's grin grew wider the deeper Mina frowned. "I'm happy for you both."

"Thank you." Jazz beamed. "But also, don't say anything."

"My lips are sealed."

They stood in silence for a few minutes before Jazz asked for more clarification on what had happened. She wanted everything, all the details. This wasn't her being nosy; this was her sleuthing, searching for clues, checking for campus missteps. Already, before Isaac got to the part about his meeting with Mrs. Hyman, Jazz was calling into question the ethics behind Isaac's punishment. If Jazz had it her way, she'd march the entire GSA and other club committees down there right this minute, but she stayed calm and listened to Isaac.

"The worst part is that I know this was all Leon," Isaac said, glowering. "I just have no way of proving how he did any of this. I mean, he's not going to admit to filming us, to uploading it. Hell, I doubt he'd even admit to picking Colton's lock or knowing how to pick a lock, for that matter."

"He wouldn't need to," Jazz said, grabbing her apartment room key and using it on her door. "See, my key."

"Seriously, does pussy pounding cause brain damage?" Isaac asked Mina almost playfully, but he still got a hard smack on the chest and a wicked giggle from her.

Mina smiled. "Only if you know what you're doing."

"Now, watch." Jazz walked over to her roommate's door and used the same key to open it. "Cookie cutter keys."

"Who the hell said you could open my door?"

Jazz slammed it shut as something crashed into it. "She's in a mood."

"Bitch is always in a mood." Mina shot a glare at the closed door like she was ready to bust it wide open again and explain why a nasty attitude wasn't wise.

"Wait. It's the same keys for every apartment?"

"Not every apartment," Jazz explained. "They vary from one apartment to the next, but most of the bedrooms inside an apartment have the same locking mechanism or one so close, a little jiggling is all it takes."

"That's fucked!" Isaac reached for his phone and prepared to text Colton the info before remembering he needed space. "Can you…um… Could you pass that along to Colton? He should be aware."

"Sure thing."

Isaac sat silently, absorbing everything that'd unfolded today, missing Colton and the sliver of happiness he'd carved out this semester.

CHAPTER 25
COLTON

DAYS turned into weeks as Colton took a break for space. Three and a half weeks, to be precise. Isaac hadn't texted once during that time. Colton didn't know if he admired the gesture or envied the attitude. Was Isaac offering him this time to get his head on right, or was Isaac okay disappearing because he never truly cared? Maybe this didn't cut as deep for him as it did Colton.

All he knew was that after almost a month, he was ready to commit to his daily routine again. Classes had been grueling, whether he attended or skipped them. If he went, eyes locked onto him for the entire lecture; if he skipped, he ended up with a mountain of confusing work to handle on his own and a reminder that the scandal didn't make his academic probation vanish. Baseball practice was a joke since he ended up benched the entire time to 'respect his privacy in this difficult time.'

Most days, Colton wandered in a daze, wondering where Isaac had gone. He stopped showing up to the one class they had together where he was the TA. He'd stopped waiting outside of Colton's other classes; he'd stopped everything.

Even when sending news on the apartment locks, that came through the proxy of Jazz. She kept insisting that Colton return to GSA, but he didn't have the energy to be gawked at any more than normal. Yes, he knew they'd support him, but they'd still stare. He was so tired of the staring. He hated people knowing the exact details of his most intimate desires. Colton hadn't been able to work up the nerve to say he enjoyed bottoming, but now tens of thousands of strangers had seen him getting railed.

Despite the mortification that came with people having an inside look at his private sex life, Colton had received a surprisingly high outpour of messages supporting him, condemning the video, hating whoever would do something like this, and a thousand other things that all started to blur together when he scrolled through his DMs.

"You're starting back up again," Coach Wilson said, startling Colton out of his daze.

"Seriously?"

"Too many people are questioning why you're being punished because of what happened," he explained.

Colton scoffed, wondering the same damn thing.

"To be clear, this wasn't a punishment," Coach Wilson said. "We were all looking out for you. We're a team."

Colton left the conversation at that. He couldn't stomach the bullshit, but he didn't want to risk being benched again.

Halfway back to the apartments, Tim hailed him down, shouting from the campus bus that looped the grounds for students who didn't want to walk from one end to the next like Colton, who'd used the nearly two-mile trek as a distraction.

"Colt, are you listening to me?"

"Nope," he mouthed until Tim slapped a hand on his back. "Oh, I didn't see you there."

"Lying ass."

Colton smirked, leading the way into their building where Tim rambled about a half dozen different topics until they reached the end of their hallway and opened the door to their apartment. It was then that Tim got serious.

"Tonight's the night we undo the damage dealt to you."

Colton raised a brow in confusion.

"Very ominous."

"Party at Alpha Tau Omega," Tim said as if Colton should be keeping up with such things.

Yes, they were the go-to athletic fraternity, the default community for sports, but Colton wasn't following any social itinerary as of late.

"I have no idea what you're trying to say."

"It's time you stopped hiding in your room and started reminding folks who you are."

"Oh, they know who I am," Colton said with wide eyes as he opened their apartment door.

"If you plan on getting off the bench—"

"Already am."

"Even better reason to go out and celebrate." Tim wrapped an arm over Colton's shoulder. "It's the perfect time to gloat, just a little. That'll rattle Leon and Devon, which will help with my plan."

"Your plan?"

"To get Devon drunk as fuck so he'll admit to helping Leon sneak into your room and film you."

"Even if he did know something, how do—"

"Devon definitely knows," Tim interrupted. "He's a little ass muncher. No offense, man."

"None taken." Colton shrugged. "I don't really eat ass."

"Seriously?" Tim shook his head and tsked. "Ass is the best part."

"Then why did you say no offense?"

"I dunno. Not sure how gays feel about ass jokes. Or bis. Or other guys. Well, actually, I do. Devon hates it cause he's a little cuck bitch boy ass muncher who I'm about to butter up all night so I can pry every secret out of his cock sucking mouth." Tim smirked. "No offense, dude."

"None taken. Sucking cock is pretty awesome."

"Oh, yeah? Well, if we end up murdering Leon tonight, I'll remind you that when we're in prison."

Colton shoved Tim. "Shut the fuck up, man."

It didn't wash away the shame and exhaustion of the footage, but Tim had a way of distracting Colton from his own pain, his own frustration, and he managed to keep Colton afloat these past few weeks.

Colton wouldn't have had to rely on Tim so much if he hadn't pushed Isaac away. More like shoved him away. Sitting alone in his room for hours, he streamed something for background noise but spent all his energy fixating on whether or not he should talk to Isaac. It'd almost been a month. He was probably tired of Colton, over him, over the drama their sex scandal caused. Or maybe Colton was overthinking it, interpreting it wrong. It wouldn't be the first time.

He sent Isaac a text.

> Colton: Sorry I've been distant. Needed the space. Time. Stuff like that. But I miss you. Miss us.

Three dots bubbled immediately afterward. Typing up a storm of words, or typing and erasing because Isaac preferred to keep his replies short and succinct?

> Isaac: I understand.

If that wasn't the most to-the-point message ever. Colton smirked, slightly annoyed but mostly entertained, especially given how the three dots returned because clearly, Isaac wanted to say more, even if his need to be brief prevented it.

Colton texted the address of the party and a long-winded explanation that Tim was hassling him to get out of his room.

> Colton: Might make the night bearable if you dropped by.

He left out the part where Tim planned on getting proof of Leon's involvement. It seemed unlikely anything would come of it. Even if it did, Isaac wasn't big on drama. Colton didn't want to scare him away any more than he already had.

Without waiting for Isaac's reply, he stuffed his phone in his pocket and got ready for the party.

When Colton and Tim arrived at the party, they stuck together for a bit. It helped with the initial stares and whispers, but soon enough, Tim was off to enact his plan, and Colton found himself drifting to the outskirts of the party. That wasn't his style. Then again, being the center of attention because he liked to get fucked in the ass wasn't his style either.

Colton needed a drink, something to wash away his own second-guessing thoughts and the anxiety that clung to him with every breath.

Two girls intercepted Colton as he reached the drink table in the kitchen.

"Oh my God, Colton!" the brunette called out. She rushed to his side like they were best of friends when he was absolutely certain they'd never met before. "Tell me you're getting off the bench soon!"

She stumbled a bit, and he helped steady her stance. A fan. It'd been a while since he interacted with fans. With anyone baseball-related.

"Actually—"

"He's the best goddamn pitcher they got," she added before Colton could answer her question, talking to her friend, who seemed almost as dazed as her. "And they benched him because of a little… Well, there was nothing little in the video…" She snorted, then caught herself and grimaced. "They need you back on the field where you belong, baby."

"Are you here by yourself?" the blonde asked, her voice pitchy and her steps wobbly. "So brave."

"Not here by myself." Colton gestured at the crowd. "My friend's around here somewhere."

"A *friend* friend or a boyfriend?" the blonde asked with a smile.

"Better not be the same guy from…" The brunette caught herself, eyes wide with embarrassment. She sipped her drink then turned to Colton and smiled. "You can do so much better."

"He's actually a pretty great guy."

Colton regretted coming to this party. Not for the interactions. He was

BEND HIM BREAK HIM

beginning to navigate his way through the awkward conversations with those bold enough or drunk enough to bring it up. No, he regretted being here and wasting his night when he should be with Isaac, making things right.

They'd each kept a healthy distance from each other so Colton could get the space he needed, but he didn't want space to think, to process anymore. He wanted Isaac.

A small group wedged their way into the kitchen, and two of the guys broke away just long enough to mingle next to the girls.

"So brave," the blonde said, reiterating Colton's bravery as she sloshed about, held up by her boyfriend who looked almost as hammered as her.

Brave wasn't the word he'd use, but he'd take it if it meant more people were on his side than he realized. The group wandered off, and Colton poured a beer from the keg.

"Finally coming out of your shell?" Leon materialized beside Colton like a monster from the shadows, slapping a hand to his back in a friendly act but intentionally too hard so it'd provoke a response. "Seems like everything's returned to normal for you."

Colton glared, his jaw clenched, and the desire to punch Leon became more and more palpable. Even if he wasn't behind the film, he had to know Colton despised him, hated him. What kind of person pretended to be buddy-buddy with someone like this? He'd spent the entire year trying to replace Colton on the team, trying to push his way to starting pitcher. Which he'd done successfully, except everything had gone back the way it was, just as Leon stated.

Despite the hell of the video, the embarrassment, the outcry from fans in either camp—pro Colton or anti-scandal; well, anti-queer scandal—Colton would be playing the last games of the season. He'd be leading his team again, and if they made it to the World Series, he'd be the starting pitcher for those games.

Colton studied the strained smile on Leon's face, the glint of rage in his eyes, the tense muscles. He was putting on a show. He was faking it—not surprising—but this recent setback had clearly been too much for Leon.

"It must be difficult." Colton sipped his beer.

Leon gave a questioning look.

"Trying so hard to ruin me and knowing, despite it all, they'd rather have a catcher as starting pitcher than have you."

Leon's face flushed, and Colton laughed. Before he could take another sip of his beer, Leon smacked the cup out of his hand, nostrils flaring.

Getting the truth out of Leon would never happen, but he could provoke him the same way Leon intended on provoking Colton. He could hit Leon with comments to cut down his ego. Hell, maybe he could even incite a fight. Colton weighed his opportunity here, how much damage he could do versus the odds of having it broke up and the chances of getting in trouble if he bashed Leon's face in the way he deeply desired.

"Sorry about that." Leon plastered on a fake smile and went to make Colton a new drink. "Peace offering?"

"Fuck off," Colton said quite matter-of-factly before pushing the drink away with the back of his hand.

It was then that he was able to relax just a bit, enough to let the tension in his shoulders ease ever so slightly and enjoy the blare of music that drowned out the bulk of drunken conversations. Colton checked his phone for any updates from Isaac, and when he saw none, he went to make his own drink, overfilling his cup with mostly foam. At least the beer was cold.

"Didn't expect to see you here," a familiar voice called out.

"Could say the same to you." Colton swiveled around and took in William Cox, former GSA treasurer and occasional hook-up who apparently had a hand in outing Colton.

He scrunched his face, trying to suss out his own feelings. So much of his mind was scrambled by how others perceived him this last month, his longing for Isaac's company, and his current disgust for Leon's presence. It muddled his mind, and not in the satisfying way that booze did. At least Leon had slinked away, disappearing back into the crowd. That gave Colton one less person-shaped obstacle. Unable to determine if he wanted to bury the hatchet or bury it in William's head, Colton turned away, tossed his foamy drink into a bucket of ice, and filled another beer at the keg.

"You know, I'm pretty good at that." William shimmied by Colton, tilting his plastic cup and filling it to the rim with just a splash of foam almost artistically.

Colton huffed and chugged his drink until it left a foam stache on his upper lip, then he refilled it. While he lacked William's finesse with the tilted technique, it did make a difference in the beer to foam ratio.

"Not bad." William tipped his head and slapped his cup against Colton's. The beer sloshed and splashed a bit on the floor. "Whoopsie."

Colton side-stepped and pretended not to have a hand in the spill.

"So, Superstar Colton is finally stepping back out into the spotlight?" William said it more like a statement while he wrapped an arm around Colton's and pulled him out of the kitchen to a quieter hallway intersection.

William wasn't the first person or the hundredth person that Colton wanted to talk to tonight, but he preferred him to the crowded rooms flooded with drunk partygoers and their unfiltered questions.

"You know, your ex really fucked up my life, too." William sighed, heavy and dramatic and grating.

Colton had found himself dragged into a bitchfit conversation.

"He's not my ex."

William's eyes widened, and he practically did a spit take with his drink before nudging Colton, shaking his arm and nearly spilling Colton's drink too.

"After everything he did to you?"

Colton's face reddened until he realized William meant the video. An embarrassment for sure, but that wasn't Isaac.

"You are a more tolerant man than I, good sir." William rambled on forever, trying to explain how Isaac misunderstood him, how he warped what happened, how he'd never out someone.

Colton rolled his eyes and sipped his beer.

"And now, he's turned everyone against me." William's pleading eyes quickly soured as his expression twisted into a snarl. "But maybe it's for the best. Almost three years I've known some of them, and they'd let one misunderstanding, one blatant lie by a liar—yeah, sorry, your should-be ex is a total liar about everything, and many other things. But I digress because, unlike some people, I don't like talking about people behind their back. Which is basically what everyone from GSA is doing to me because they're fakes. And honestly, if they're gonna take Isaac's word—the word of an obvious, attention-seeking liar—over mine, then I don't think I want their friendship."

Colton didn't have the energy to argue or listen, so without a word, he turned to excuse himself without excusing himself. Hopefully, William would ramble on for the next five to ten minutes before realizing Colton's absence.

Colton staggered a bit, and William quickly snatched him up to hold him upright.

"Whoa," William said with a slick smile. "Someone's hitting the beers a little heavy."

No… Colton went to speak, to shake his head in protest, but he found himself nauseous and disoriented. The music faded but the thrum of the bass made that sickening feeling creep deeper in his gut, which twisted and churned as his head whirled round and round, following William.

Colton's feet shuffled, stumbled, and stood their ground for all of two seconds. Each blink blurred his vision, and the room spun through different images until he toppled over on the edge of a bed.

"You should really watch your drink more closely," Leon said.

When'd he get here? How'd he get here? Where was here? Colton fumbled against the mattress but couldn't even roll himself over. His arms lay useless at his sides like leaded weights.

"He was like a hawk, but my chitchat game is top tier," William laughed.

"Whatever," Leon said with an edge in his voice.

"So, what type of team pranks do you have in store?" William asked, still quite lighthearted despite the fact Colton found himself pinned to the bed with an exhaustion he couldn't fathom. "Wait, don't tell me. Deniability and all that. Buuuuuut I'm imagining someone's bat will be landing in someone's homefield. In someone's homerun? Whatever. Just be safe."

"Get the fuck outta here," Leon hissed.

"Yeah, yeah." William's voice grew fainter. "You owe me, Leon. I look forward to collecting."

Feet shuffled, and a door closed a moment later. Soon, all Colton heard was Leon's heavy breaths.

"He's a real creep, but I suppose all you types really are," Leon said, his disgust practically oozing out into tangible form. It was the only thing Colton could really hold onto in the swirling room. "Point is, you're here at the wasteland end of the party circuit where we can start up the afterparty 2.0. It'll be a lot like your last afterparty, only more effective."

Leon snatched Colton by his hair and lifted his head to face him. Colton's vision whirled, each blink a blurring effort to visualize the details of Leon's malicious expression.

"I really thought the last video would've been enough to get rid of you," he said smugly. "When that queer told me he'd filmed you and the rumor of it almost got you kicked off the team, I just knew a vid of you actually fucking some dude would do the trick. Hell, you even took it in the ass. But they still made allowances for you."

"Because of you," Colton slurred. "Not my fault. You're—"

"Tired of playing second to some entitled bitch who doesn't even need his scholarship," Leon snapped. "Coaches and the school might've given you the benefit of the doubt for your last scandalous video, but I wonder how they'll feel when it becomes a repeat offense."

Colton shivered. It took everything he had to jerk away from Leon, to untangle his hair from Leon's locked fingers.

Leon smirked. "Especially with the night I have planned for you."

CHAPTER 26
ISAAC

ISAAC reluctantly made his way toward the party, practically backstepping until Carlos shoulder-bumped him. The gesture encouraged Isaac to move forward, but Isaac proved stubborn.

"Just go inside; you know you wanna see Colton."

Isaac groaned. He did. Desperately. More than he'd let on over the last few weeks among his friends, but apparently, his glum mood had been quite easy for Carlos, Mina, and Jazz to read.

"You sure there's nothing else we can do about the program you made?" Isaac wanted to see Colton, but he wanted to see him with a win in his hands.

While Colton processed the scandal, retreating into solitude and taking space to handle the fallout of their sex plastered all across the internet, Isaac went to work uncovering evidence on who had uploaded the video. Well, Isaac mostly leaned on Carlos to uncover evidence since he was the tech genius.

Isaac nudged Carlos, reiterating his query. "Well?"

"It's damn near impossible to track the original uploader since the video's been reuploaded about a thousand-ish times. I've got my phishing software out there, ready and baited, but they have to take the bait."

"He," Isaac corrected because he knew it was Leon, even if everyone else insisted they needed concrete evidence. "Can't you just hack his computer?"

"I could try if I wanted to break several laws and quite possibly turn up with nothing." Carlos shrugged. "It's not like the movies. I'm not sure if we'll find anything."

Isaac once again contemplated beating the ever-living fuck out of Leon. It'd be a win-win since he could release all this pent-up frustration and get a confession. But Jazz's warnings raddled in his head, how it'd be considered coercion, something about morals or ethics or other legalese bullshit that Mina sprinkled into the conversation to strengthen Jazz's argument. Add to that Jazz's mention of how the act would likely lead to Isaac's expulsion, whether or not he forced the truth out of Leon. No, if he wanted to hit Leon, he'd need him to swing first, which was unlikely since he was a cowardly snake.

"Did he say where to meet up?" Carlos asked as he led them inside. "Mina and Jazz said they'd be circling the bar scene until we got here."

"Just say kitchen." Isaac scoffed. "It's not suddenly a bar just because they drop all their booze in there."

He kept close to Carlos, letting him lead the way while he checked his phone for any follow-ups from Colton. Nothing. Which was surprising since Colton typically text-bombed Isaac with a flurry of messages. Though, he'd gone silent the last few weeks. Maybe it'd changed his attitude on messaging. Or on Isaac.

Scouring the party scene, Isaac couldn't help the twinge of guilt that pinched at him. If he hadn't been involved with Colton, so public with Colton, so hypersexual with Colton, then that video might never have happened. If he had been more vigilant of his surroundings, he might have noticed someone set a phone or spyware or a fucking giant ass video camera in the room to record them.

Unable to spot Colton, Isaac found himself growing anxious. When his gaze locked onto the last person he wanted to see, that anxiety twisted into irritation. William Cox. Isaac still despised Will, especially given his cocky bravado the last time they crossed paths. And that cockiness remained as he strutted through the crowd.

William walked around the party with a swagger Isaac hadn't seen in months. Yes, he'd been brazen when he bumped into Isaac, showcasing phony arrogance meant to taunt, but Isaac knew, for the most part, that William sulked with his new standing. Why? Because Isaac had carefully observed William after the GSA kicked him out. Isaac had silently studied him from a distance over the semester to ensure he didn't inflict his brand of outing horrors onto any unsuspecting fools desperate enough to roll into William's bed.

The glint in William's eyes, the pride in his slick smirk. It sent a chill through Isaac. It told him something foul was afoot. William wasn't putting on a show; he was delighted by something wicked he'd done. Isaac chased that feeling as he chased William down from the other side of the party. After years of ignoring his instincts and finding himself endangered in one way or another, Isaac learned to lean into his gut feelings, read rooms, read people, read situations, and vigilantly search for answers.

When William's attention flitted in Isaac's direction, his eyes went wide and he blanched in horror. Without missing a beat, William beelined in the opposite direction.

That was suspicious. And there was only one way for Isaac to handle things that he found suspicious. Hit them and hurt them until they made sense.

"I told you the next time I saw you, I'd beat the ever-living fuck outta you." Isaac stalked toward William, cornering him against the wall.

"You don't own the campus; I can go wherever I want."

"Sure. As long as I'm not there or anyone I care about."

"You don't care about anyone, you asshole." William shoved Isaac, lightly pressing against his chest and testing the resistance. "You really gonna cause a scene here?"

Isaac glared, fueling the fear in William and savoring the shaky hands as they retreated.

"You think anyone here cares?" Isaac cocked his head, turning to the crowd. "Hey, y'all! I'm about to beat the fuck out of this annoying ass queer kid! Gay on gay crimes! Watch me shove my fist down his throat! No gag reflex if I remember correctly."

No one paid Isaac's shouting any mind except for Carlos, who tried to gently pry Isaac back.

"If you wanna try some screaming, maybe that'll work." Isaac leaned in close, his flaring nostrils nearly pressed to William's nose.

"Just leave me alone."

"First, tell me why you're here." Isaac shook off Carlos and folded his arms. "This isn't your scene."

"And it's yours?" William sneered.

"I was invited."

Truthfully, Isaac avoided parties of any kind—anything involving crowds typically wasn't his scene. William, on the other hand, always preferred clubs, somewhere where he knew his oh-so-charming personality would pay off. Not that there weren't curious straight guys at this party, but Isaac often found William wanted to attend these frat bashes during the wee hours when the crowd thinned and horny bodies were easily swayed.

"Invited?" William tsked. "Yeah, by your desperate boyfriend."

That piqued Isaac's attention.

"You've been talking to Colton?"

"No."

"Funny because I can't get ahold of him."

"I don't know anything."

"Liar, liar." Isaac dug into his pocket and retrieved his lighter, quickly sparking it.

He held the open flame against William's hip. When the boy shouted and wriggled to move away, Isaac smacked him in the face with his free hand. Even as the heat of the lighter sizzled Isaac's thumb, he kept it pressed against the jean fabric of William's pants.

"What are you up to, Willy?" Isaac gently guided the hot flame. "Don't make me set your willy on fire next."

"Okay, okay, okay…" William recoiled, pinned in place but desperately trying to avoid the flame Isaac now waved close to his former friend's face.

"What do you want?"

"I want to know everything that's got you smiling," Isaac said with a gruff darkness in his voice. "And if I feel like you're not being absolutely honest with me, I'm gonna have to burn away that smile and everything else about you I don't like."

Isaac tilted his head, holding the flame so close it created a glint in his sparkling blue eyes. They were icy and filled with malice, which only made his bright grin from ear to ear all the more menacing.

Horror swept through Isaac as he listened to William's confession. Each word further enraging Isaac.

CHAPTER 27

COLTON

THE buzz of blacklights woke Colton, who blinked away some of his delirium. The low lighting and odd angle made it difficult for him to make sense of his surroundings. Colton struggled to breathe, hunched forward with his face sinking into the mattress. The weight of his body came with a strange numb sensation. It was hard for him to grasp, but Colton knew he wasn't just lying out on the bed but positioned. Only, he didn't realize the work Leon had put in angling Colton at the edge of the bed, ready for an evening of carnal savagery.

A gurgle of slurred words bubbled at the tip of Colton's tongue, but he couldn't muster more than confused noises. Leon turned back, his wicked smirk in Colton's peripheral as he tinkered with something on the nearby dresser.

"Just trying to find your best angle, Colt." Leon chuckled. "Wanna make sure everyone gets a full view of your desperate ass going ten rounds."

Leon adjusted the phone he'd propped between books and random knickknacks before he waltzed toward the bed and plopped down beside Colton.

"Well, hopefully, ten rounds. Might try to squeeze a few more in for you."

Colton groaned, garbled mumbles escaping his lips and forming such intangible words, even he wasn't sure what he meant to say.

"Damn, William wasn't fucking around." Leon clicked his tongue with this satisfied sadistic approval. "He might've given you a double dose or some shit. Whatever, it'll wear off enough soon. Not like anyone's gonna mind or notice. That's what matters."

Leon reached for Colton's pants, doing his best to unfasten them without knocking Colton's slumped body over.

At this, Colton screamed or tried to with his weighed-down mind and body lost to a fog of confusion. This couldn't be happening. This wouldn't be happening. But he didn't know what to do, so he screamed and shouted and listened to the bizarre noises that came. He was a dying animal deep in a well, echoing strange sounds.

It gave Leon pause. Not of concern. The annoyance plastered on his face grew the more Colton groaned.

"Shut the fuck up." Leon smacked Colton's head. "I'm just getting you ready. Goddamn."

With that, he went back to work and prepared to yank Colton's pants down. When Colton trembled, desperately attempting to wriggle loose and call for help, Leon stopped and reached into his pocket.

"If you keep moving, I'm gonna give you a real reason to whine and cry, you little bitch." He pressed the tip of a blade underneath Colton's eye. So sharp and cold it roused the muddled senses in Colton's head just long enough to strike fear of the pocketknife Leon wielded. "Is that what you want?"

Colton took shallow breaths, trying and failing to calm himself, to will his obedience for fear Leon might take an eye just for a fucking laugh.

"Guessing you're thinking I'm gonna have a go at you?" Leon cringed, utter disgust on his face as he put his knife away. "That's what I hate about you fags. You think everyone's gay. Oh, if you hate queers, you must be one. No. No, that is dumb as fuck. I mean, I hate spiders. That doesn't secretly make me one. At least spiders are natural. You lot, though." Leon let out a full-body shudder. "Seriously, when I'm done with you, everyone is gonna see just how disgusting you are and the lengths you'll go to get off with your perverted desires."

Colton quaked, eyes glossy, and head tilted just enough he could see the fuming rage and smug arrogance mixed together on Leon's face.

"I thought the last video would be enough to get you tossed off the team, but hey, they wanna make excuses, then I'll just show 'em it's a pattern." Leon retrieved his phone, not the one currently positioned to record Colton, but another. Neither phone looked like Leon's. No, they were cheap and bulky outdated smartphones. "Turns out there are a lot of perverts in the area, and none of them really have questions about the quick in and out I've got planned for ya."

Leon turned the phone to face Colton, revealing a profile with Colton's image looking for anonymous fucks. No strings. No games. No conversation.

"See? Fucking disgusting. The lot of you."

Colton wheezed, desperately trying to wrap his fogged-over mind around what Leon was going to do, going to orchestrate. There wasn't an escape, a way he could find to stop this.

"They're gonna be lined up out the fucking door, running a train on you, and then it won't be a question on whether or not you filmed and posted this." Leon gestured around the room. "It'll be a pattern, coaches will see what a homo slut you are for dick, and I'll be starting pitcher."

All this for his position. All this for Colton's spotlight. All this because he hated Colton's lifestyle.

"All you gotta do is lay there and look easy." Leon grinned. "No one's gonna be asking questions because no one really cares."

"I've actually got a few questions," the familiar gruffness in Isaac's voice sparked hope in Colton.

His body rattled, attempting to move, to call out, to turn and see Isaac's entrance. From this angle, he could hear Isaac approach from behind, but his gaze was still facing Leon, whose expression had dropped to utter shock.

"Now, I've been told not to start shit with you," Isaac said, his feet shuffling inside. "Conflict is never the way to resolution—blah, blah, blah—but something tells me that this right here has just given me a free pass to bash in your fucking face."

"Not another step, you freak fag!"

"Sticks and stones, buddy boy."

Leon backstepped, lost from Colton's sight, only to reappear seconds later with an aluminum bat in hand.

"Oh, sweetie." Isaac took a deep breath, his teeth chattering with anticipation. "You're gonna have to do so much better than that."

Isaac swooped across the room so swiftly, the breeze of his fluid steps tickled Colton's exposed lower back. His shirt had rolled up some, but his pants were still on; he wasn't exposed here despite feeling completely vulnerable and raw. It was a harrowing feeling, a sinking pit that sickened him to dwell on. Instead, he focused on Isaac's manic rage, his calm expression, and his confident body language. Isaac's sharp inhale seemed to swallow all the violence in the air, and his exhale unleashed war.

The cockiness in Isaac's voice soothed Colton, but when Leon swung the bat without hesitation, he gurgled a shout of a warning.

Issac raised an arm, bracing for the impact. He held his position, perhaps stunned by the pain surging through his body from the strike, but he didn't falter. After a deep, seething breath, Isaac stepped forward, arm still raised and shielding against the second swing of Leon's bat. And the third. And the fourth. That was when a feral sound of fury and anguish escaped Isaac. With it came a deranged laughter as Isaac wrapped his arm around the bat and yanked it from Leon's grasp.

"Well, well, well. Looks like I'm joining the team." Isaac cracked his neck, arm trembling—most likely from the throbbing pain pulsing through his muscles and bone from the bat's multiple strikes.

"Get the fuck away from me." Leon raised his hands like he might try to catch the bat if Isaac swung it. But the way his arms shook, there was no way he'd manage such a feat.

"Oh, you think I'm some pussy jock gay basher who needs to hide behind a bat to beat off my foes?" Isaac stared at his confiscated weapon, eyeing the bat before chucking it behind his head and out of view. "Honey, no."

Colton wanted to scream, to demand Isaac retrieve it, to warn him that Leon had another weapon.

As expected and feared, Leon pulled out his knife and began swinging chaotically at Isaac, who darted back, avoiding the erratic swipes.

Isaac didn't remain on the defensive very long. No, his feet moved to strengthen his stance, and his arms weaved in a way that drew Leon into an unsuspecting trap. Colton had seen this movement before, but only in a flash of a few seconds. This was the same technique Isaac had used when Colton foolishly attempted to attack him and ended up flipped over and knocked onto the ground.

But Isaac didn't snatch Leon up and hurl him away. Instead, he pivoted to break Leon's grip on his knife and twisted their bodies around in such a way that, even from the outside, Colton had difficulty tracking Isaac's movements.

One moment, they were swirling, the glint of the blade shining under the blacklights of the room. A blink later, Leon was screaming, and blood was everywhere.

"You motherfucker!" Leon shouted.

"Can we normalize fatherfucker?" Isaac asked, aloof and wearing a twisted smirk. "Because I'd never bang your mom, but I'd one hundred percent bend your daddy over."

"Aaaaahhhh!" Leon shouted, grabbing ahold of his forearm as he stared at the blade protruding from his wrist. His throwing arm. Colton suspected Isaac knew that, too. "What the fuck is wrong with you?"

"I don't know. Maybe it's the crazy homophobe swinging a knife at me and hurling slurs." Isaac shrugged. "Not sure why you're screaming at me. You're the one who came at me. I just returned the weapon to sender. I didn't even charge you postage. Very friendly on my part."

"Stop making jokes!" Leon screamed. "This is serious, you fucking psychopath!"

"Yeah, very serious." Isaac eyed Leon, his injury, the room and the situation. "But I'm not the psycho here."

"You fucking stabbed me."

"Once again, I defended myself against your assault. First with the bat, then the knife. You've already drugged someone. Who knows what other weapons you have on your person?" Isaac's eyes flitted over to the phone propped on the dresser, the one recording everything, the one Leon had at the ready for an awful assault. "Your attack. An attack on me because I interrupted your attempted sexual assault on my boyfriend. Not cool."

Isaac framed his words in such a way that it carefully laid out all of Leon's culpability. Colton found himself awed by Isaac's strategic mind, but he knew Leon had already confessed to his part in tonight and everything else he'd arranged. That phone held all the evidence they needed. Now, he just needed to pray that Isaac didn't do something impulsive like murder Leon on camera.

"I wasn't—" The pain must've hit Leon's nerves hard because he stopped mid-sentence and winced.

"Yeah, you might want to go get that checked out. Like, stat. Before it becomes permanent." Isaac nodded, then held up a hand to count off. "Next thing you know, you won't be able to use that hand to write, to jerk off, to wipe your ass, to throw things at unsuspecting gays, to play baseball, to—"

At that, Leon's eyes went wide, the realization finally sinking in that this pain might leave lasting damage, that it might be a career-ending blow. He bolted past Isaac, his feet stumbling as he ran out of the room.

"Rude." Isaac brushed imaginary dust off his shirt. "Didn't even say excuse me."

Colton gurgled, attempting to say 'excuse me' in a sarcastic snarky way. An utter failure since he couldn't even form the words, let alone the attitude.

Isaac's demeanor completely shifted when his gaze fully landed on Colton. It was as if he'd avoided directly staring at him when he entered the room, and for good reason. Colton saw the calm in Isaac's piercing blue eyes gloss over; he watched Isaac's body become rigid as he fought off a nervous tremble. Soon, he collected himself and swooped over beside Colton, examining him to the best of his abilities.

"You're okay," he said, repeating the words again and again more to himself than to Colton who he repositioned, gently rolling him onto his side. "I'm gonna call help, all right?"

Colton moved his jaw, ignoring the tingling pain, but he still couldn't form words.

CHAPTER 28
ISAAC

THE hours following Leon's deranged plan left Isaac dazed. Between the hospital visit, where Isaac spent more time avoiding medical treatment to check on Colton, and the grueling examination of Isaac's throbbing arm, it was no wonder he hadn't erupted on the poor medical staff trying to help him.

He had two fractures in his humerus bone, on the upper bicep where Leon's bat hit particularly hard. He had another fracture in his forearm but couldn't recall the name since apparently there were a lot of bones in his arm, and his doctor felt the need to review all of them. Surprisingly, Isaac only had one break located in whatever the other forearm bone was called. He could handle the pain, any pain, so long as he knew Colton was okay. That said, he hated the uncomfortable sling wrapped around his arm and the already itchy cast.

While the hospital visit had been excruciating with the waiting, the testing, the waiting again, the lectures, the explanations, the billing information Isaac wouldn't be able to follow up on, he was grateful when they discharged him. Though only after a lengthy review of recovery timelines, physical therapy, and potential surgery. Isaac didn't care. He needed to see Colton, who had an even longer wait time.

As if the hospital wasn't exhausting enough, soon came the questions from the police. Witness statements. Victim statements. A barrage of questions that felt leading to Isaac, so eventually, he told them to watch the video and leave him alone. When they badgered him for clarification, when they insisted he needed to cooperate, when they wanted him to go over the timeline of events for a third time, Isaac told them to fuck off.

"Listen, young man, you attacked another person," the officer said, side-stepping and blocking Isaac's path in the sterile hospital hallway. "It's important you cooperate so we can clear you of possible assault charges."

"For defending myself?"

"*If* your actions are deemed within the bounds of self-defense," the officer clarified. "Some might consider stabbing someone an excessive action, and if I don't feel your story adds up, there might be a need to continue this conversation down at the station."

Isaac swallowed hard.

"So, you need to drop the attitude, sit down, and let's review the evening again."

"I'm sorry, he needs to what?" Mina materialized out of thin air.

Okay, probably not. Definitely not. But to Isaac, she swooped in like an all-powerful force; the stern expression on her face slowed time, and the deep bass in her aggravated voice made the walls quake. Jazz and Carlos appeared on either side of Isaac, checking in on him, but he didn't register a word they said. He didn't register any words, really, just Mina's domineering attitude controlling the situation and bringing the officers to everyone's attention.

Soon, the hall had an audience of curious nurses. Mina ripped into the officer, spouting legal jargon from her courses, and suddenly Isaac found himself soothed by Mina's rant and Jazz's diplomatic commentary. Carlos grabbed Isaac by his uninjured arm and brought him down a few hallways until they reached Colton's room.

"Since we all know you're not going to let the doctors properly examine you until you check in on your boyfriend, we thought we should find you," Carlos explained. "Good thing, too. Knowing your attitude, you would've picked a fight with the cops."

"I'm not an idiot."

"Says the guy who blocked a bat with his arm."

Isaac shrugged. "Better than blocking it with my face."

Carlos led the way, bringing Isaac to Colton's floor, where he slipped into the room without asking for permission. If he had to listen to someone else explain visiting hours or privacy or yet another irritating detail, Isaac believed he might literally explode.

"You're okay…" Colton's groggy voice stirred knots in Isaac's stomach.

He took in the sleepy expression and giggly smile on Colton's face as he lay in his bed.

"I am." Isaac slowly approached. "Are you?"

"Tired mostly." He shrugged. "People kept asking me questions. Then more people tried asking me questions, and other people made them leave, and then those people peopled in here."

Isaac snorted. "I'm glad you're doing well."

"You took a baseball bat to the face for me."

"Not quite my face." Isaac grinned, ignoring the throb from where the second and third swings did rattle a bit against his head. It hurt, but not nearly as much as it would've hurt if something had happened to Colton.

Isaac wouldn't have been able to live with himself if things had gone further. He already regretted arriving when he did, knowing he dragged his feet for nearly an hour debating whether or not he should go to the party.

"I'm so sorry for taking so long."

"No. Perfectly timed." Colton's grin grew wide and goofy. "You missed the villain speech. There's a video online about it."

"It's not online," Isaac said, debating whether or not to explain the entirety of the situation to Colton.

He'd watched the recording while waiting for the ambulance. He'd also sent himself a copy before handing it over to the police, something he credited important now that they seemed to be dicking around with him instead of dealing with Leon.

"Can you stay with me?" Colton asked, pulling Isaac from his thoughts.

"Of course." Isaac dragged a chair close to Colton's bedside and sat beside him.

He leaned over, allowing a sleepy Colton to tousle his hair and whisper adorable nonsense as whatever drugs worked their way out of his system.

Hours passed, and late in the night, Colton shook Isaac awake. His expression had turned serious, his body had gone stiff, and his green eyes had gone glossy.

"You okay?"

"Yeah," Colton replied, swallowing a lump in his throat. "I just needed to say thank you."

"You don't need to thank me."

"I do. If you hadn't gotten there when you had…" There was a tremble in Colton's voice, one likely consumed by all the horrors Leon intended to inflict.

Isaac crawled up and onto the bed, lying beside Colton and easing the anxiety stirring inside him.

"I'll always be here for you," Isaac whispered. "Always."

"Thank you." Colton rolled over and buried his head in Isaac's chest, dozing off to sleep and leaving Isaac awake to gently hold him.

The days that followed turned into an even bigger whirlwind of chaos than the hospital itself. Isaac couldn't go anywhere on campus without eyes falling to him or to Colton, whose side he had kept close to since the party. Isaac was done giving Colton space and had now latched to the baseball player like a shadow.

All the attention, the questions, the whispers, the phone calls, and emails seeking an inside story didn't seem to bother Colton. His coming out story had thrust him into the spotlight last year, and the sex scandal had only finally started dying down before the embers of gossip found a new flame to ignite Colton's unwanted popularity.

At least the truth was out. Everyone knew Leon had a hand in the video leaking. Everyone knew Leon drugged Colton. Everyone knew Leon had a dangerously dark obsession with Colton. The only thing that people didn't know was the reason why. Sure, Colton tried to set the record straight, but rumors blossomed quickly, and every deranged theory was more fascinating to public appeal than the reality of Leon being a homophobic prick with an envious cancer eating away at his insides.

Isaac was partial to the belief that Leon was in love with Colton and attempting to take over his life. Sure, it wasn't exactly true, but it made Leon queer in the public eyes, and that likely pissed the asshole off even more. Isaac had already been warned to keep his distance since his self-defense story wouldn't work as well if repeated. Not that he had to worry about Leon on campus. The expulsion came down faster than anyone believed possible, and with the criminal charges coupled with the medical issues Leon faced in the coming months, he didn't have the time to contest Clinton's swift judgment.

Now came the time when the university would determine how to handle things with Colton and Isaac. Well, with Colton. Isaac was pretty sure his thin ice was going to crack entirely despite his severe injuries. He'd already pissed off the campus enough with the last scandal, and he wasn't sure they'd care much that both incidents were Leon's doing.

Colton had a meeting scheduled first, and Isaac wasn't about to let him go alone. The sting of his administrative meeting, where he lost both his campus jobs and housing all in one fell swoop, still hurt a hell of a lot more than the breaks in his arm from a heavy-handed bat swing. Now, while Isaac suspected this was more of a groveling meeting where the dean would steer Colton toward saying something positive about CLIT University, Isaac didn't want them manipulating his boyfriend and filling his head with drivel.

"Thanks for coming with me." Colton held the door for Isaac, and the pair walked inside the building that led to the dean's office.

Isaac buried his anxiety, his concern, his fear about his own impending meeting. The last time didn't end well, and he didn't hold out much hope for what came next.

"Colton, darling, you're here." An older woman called out, wearing large sunglasses which hid her face.

She wore a tight, powder blue dress that framed her small body and made her long, black hair all the more striking in the sunlight that pierced through the windows. The glint of light reflected against her diamond ring, her sapphire bracelet, her jeweled necklace, and Isaac found himself in awe at the gaudy display, believing those trinkets she wore could pay his entire tuition.

Colton seemed more surprised than intrigued as the woman sauntered down the hallway. The click of her heels carried a thunderous charm, and her outstretched arms came with a smile that craved a hug.

"I'm glad to have run into you."

Without a moment of hesitation, she wrapped Colton in a tight hug. The shock on Colton's face matched the bewilderment on Isaac's, but after a few seconds, the woman's face became familiar to him. It helped that so many of her features matched her son's because Isaac had only seen Colton's mother a handful of times when he was younger. Their mothers were club friends at best and rivals in almost all other aspects.

"Mom, what are you doing here?" Colton finally broke free from the hug, staring at his mother with the most perplexed expression.

"You think I'd let you weather this storm alone?" She scoffed, genuinely offended. "The Lennox family lean on each other in a crisis and conquer it like all things in this world."

Isaac rolled his eyes at that. Colton didn't bad mouth his family, but he'd shared how much they'd distanced themselves when he broke away from tradition to follow his heart and aim to play baseball professionally. Hell, the last crisis he had to conquer involved his coming out scandal, and the way Colton described it, his parents took a very "don't ask, don't tell" stance on their son's bisexuality.

Colton's mother, Mrs. Lennox, turned her attention from her son and onto Isaac. The demure of her sweet smile turned sharp as her eyes locked with Isaac's.

"Mr. Parker, correct?" She removed her sunglasses and delicately placed them in a small pocketbook she'd kept tucked beneath her arm. "You must be the one who's been piledriving my son."

Colton's entire face turned beet red. Isaac choked on the air itself, somehow forgetting how to breathe.

"Ah, yes. News of your scandalous romance reached home," she said with a sigh. "I've been fortunate enough not to view the video, though I hear congratulations are in order."

Congratulations to who? Isaac wondered.

"The ladies at the club really were running their mouths for some time."

"I'm so sorry," Colton blurted as if he had anything to apologize for.

"Nonsense, dear." Mrs. Lennox gave a dismissive wave. "It allowed me a chance to remind the busybodies that they shouldn't mock someone who knows where they hide their bodies. Honestly, it's been a whirlwind of entertainment. I haven't truly aimed to ruin a life with words alone since I was, well, your age."

"You're welcome?" Colton quirked a brow.

Isaac had forgotten how much the town of Straight Arrow thrived on gossip and elitism. It was its own world scandal and privilege and power. His family survived it by blending, which made Isaac a threat because he never tried to fit in with the crowd. It seemed Colton's family thrived by riding the waves of scandal and demonstrating why they differed from the rest of the town. For a few fleeting seconds, Isaac wondered how his life would've changed if his family had more takes like Mrs. Lennox.

When Colton finally composed himself, he gave his mother an almost stern stare. "And what exactly are you doing here?"

"Well, I needed to have a word with your dean. After the audacious way your assault was handled, I reminded him that some families don't tolerate such incompetence," Mrs. Lennox explained. "He squirmed a lot, but we came to an understanding. Truthfully, it was easier talking with your coaches about—"

"You talked to my coaches?" Colton's voice went high and pitchy for a beat. "Mom!"

"What?" she responded, sincerely baffled by Colton's outburst. "They needed to know it's not appropriate to bench their best player on the team because of a tiny scandal. And I made it clear that in the future if…"

It was in that moment, as Mrs. Lennox explained her agenda and expressed her devotion, that Isaac realized she'd kept a much closer eye on her son than Colton ever dared to believe. Most of the time, Colton felt alone because his family didn't approve of how he chased his dreams, and Isaac shared in that pain. He found solace with Colton, noting how their families and lives might've differed, but they were each left to fend for themselves in one manner or another.

But it appeared that Mrs. Lennox was finished with that façade and sought to demonstrate a show of elite family support, something the administrative team at Clinton University likely didn't contend with much. Seriously, Lennoxs, much like Parkers, typically roamed the halls of Ivy Leagues, buying wings or donating scholarships or simply threatening careers.

"I'm meeting with Roger later, but perhaps we can do lunch?" Mrs. Lennox said, finally pulling Isaac from his thoughts.

"What the hell is Roger doing here?"

"Who's Roger?"

"A friend," Mrs. Lennox replied.

"Family lawyer," Colton corrected.

"What?" Mrs. Lennox shrugged. "He's ensuring this tragic excuse of a police department does its job. Three suspects in your assault, and can you believe they only had charges for one of them with the intention of making a deal with another and letting the last one walk away unscathed? Oh, no. I think not."

Isaac wondered which of the two the police or the prosecution intended to use to testify against Leon. Obviously, Leon had a swarm of charges to contend with, especially given the recorded confession. Isaac wondered if William made a deal considering his involvement in drugging Colton or if Devon made a deal since he must've helped Leon illegally film and upload the sex video. It didn't seem to matter who wanted a deal and who intended on slipping away since Mrs. Lennox made it a point of pride to eviscerate anyone who had a hand in harming her baby boy.

"And the absurdity they were wasting resources looking into this one." She waved her hand up and down, gesturing to Isaac. "As if he were any threat."

"Wait, what?" Isaac practically yelped.

"Don't worry, deary," Mrs. Lennox continued. "Roger is expressing how I want this handled and—"

"Mom, you can't just come here and take over everything in my life."

"I can if someone is trying to ruin your life. Now that the dean understands where he sits in the grand scheme of things, this should all roll over soon. Your coaches, God help them, now know to keep an eye out for jealous players and realize the mistake of benching their best. Once Roger's done, we should be able to put this whole incident behind us, and you can enjoy your summer without any hiccups."

Colton stood speechless, seemingly embarrassed by his mother's involvement, whereas Isaac found himself awed and a bit envious. This was something his parents would've never done for him. It was controlling in the most protective manner, unfiltered love, and Isaac wanted to bask in it a little longer. A vicarious sensation that Colton couldn't appreciate at the moment but would learn to value in the long run.

"Can we do lunch?" Mrs. Lennox asked. "I'm famished."

"Um, well, I uh…" Colton blinked away his confusion, which didn't help.

"I know a good spot," Isaac said.

"Perfect," Mrs. Lennox replied.

With that, she led the way to a spacious town car she'd rented, and they all slid into the back while Isaac gave the driver the restaurant name. It was a mostly silent ride except for the clickity taps of Mrs. Lennox's phone. She kept the keyboard sound on as she typed away furious texts that prompted the ping of even faster replies.

Then the driver reached the destination, and Mrs. Lennox stepped out and took a long pause to survey the restaurant.

"Oh, how I do enjoy a quaint place." Mrs. Lennox grimaced. "It allows them to focus on the important things like the menu. Instead of the aesthetic and atmosphere."

Bitchy and refined. Isaac shivered at the way it reminded him of his own mother and her many quick-witted jabs.

After they put in drink orders, Mrs. Lennox eyed her menu for a moment before resting her gaze on Isaac. "You know, Mr. Parker, I spoke with the dean on your behalf as well."

Isaac swallowed his water down the wrong pipe and took pained breaths as he cleared his throat.

"Mom, you can't just do that," Colton said. "You can't mess with other people's lives."

"If he's screwing my child, I most certainly can." She made a face. "At least your taste is better than Charlotte's. Christ, her taste in suitors is more atrocious than mine."

"What did you talk about?" Isaac asked.

"With Charlotte? There's no talking. It's just rehab, screaming, new hobbies she'll never follow through on, and—"

"He means with the dean," Colton hissed, clearly in no mood for his mother's rant about his little sister.

"I merely wanted to ascertain why there was punishment doled out when he was a victim," she said, giving Isaac a polite smile. "Then, of course, I needed assurance such incompetence wouldn't be repeated now that he's gone and protected you from that offish beast."

Colton got quiet. He turned his attention to Isaac, sending a silent thank you. Not that Isaac needed the thanks, but he'd likely find himself receiving a thousand more from Colton in the days to come. It just meant he'd have to find ways to irritate Colton until he stopped being grateful, and they could resume their regular routine.

After they ordered their meals, Isaac checked his notifications to find a few new emails. One canceled his upcoming meeting with the dean. Another came with a message reinstating his TA application for the fall. A third came with a message from the housing department seeking his preference in the dorms. Isaac ground his teeth at that. He wouldn't be living on campus anymore. Though he'd return to his old TA position if Professor Howard would have him. Once he'd skimmed through his emails, he put his phone away and gave Mrs. Lennox the smallest of smiles.

They all ate in silence for the first half of the meal until Colton couldn't take it any longer. Isaac could tell by the antsy tap of his foot, the haggard angry breaths between bites of food, and the confrontational glare he'd shoot his mother for a second before returning to his dish. Isaac had seen that stare from Colton. It was his argument look. It meant he was having a mental argument in his head and preparing to unleash it upon the unsuspecting.

"Mom, I'm glad you're here," Colton said with an aggravated breath. "But why are you here? Why all of a sudden?"

"I'm done playing your father's games," she replied, gesturing with her hand for Colton to quiet himself, which he did almost immediately. "He would sooner see horrors far crueler than what almost happened to you before admitting defeat."

Ah, yes. Isaac recalled Colton's explanation about his family's stance on his college choices. They all but iced him out, forcing him to carry on by himself.

"I'm late when it comes to a show of support," Mrs. Lennox said, her voice quiet. "But I am here now, and I intend on making up for the lost time. Also, if you spent another year on academic probation, I think my head might implode. You're far too bright to fail so many courses."

"That's what I've been saying."

"Isaac's been helping me with the work."

"Well, thank you, Isaac." Mrs. Lennox smiled. "What about all those lost credits?"

"I'll get there."

"There's always summer school." Isaac shrugged.

"Tell me more."

Colton glowered at Isaac, demanding he stop talking, but Mrs. Lennox's inviting smile overruled her son, and Isaac found himself almost enjoying the family bickering as he went on to explain a schedule that could ensure Colton still graduated on time.

CHAPTER 29
COLTON

THINGS had been good with his mom, with the rest of the season, with his credits. Hell, with Isaac ready to advocate—well, threaten—on his behalf at the disciplinary panel, Colton believed he might very well end his academic probation once the school year concluded.

With finals mostly finished and classes wrapping up their last few sessions, Colton could finally breathe easily and relax. At least until he had to start up the summer sessions. He sighed at that, still perplexed how his mother and Isaac teamed up against him during lunch and bullied him into signing up for both sessions so he could catch up on his missing credits.

Whatever. He put that out of his head, dwelling less on the fact his boyfriend and mother ganged up on him and more on the fact his mother not only acknowledged Colton had a boyfriend, but she liked him. Isaac. The least likable person, by choice, in the whole world. Well, Colton's world, at the very least.

"Are you finished getting ready?" Isaac poked his head into the room, scowl at the ready. "It's the easiest costume to slip on."

"It's the skimpiest costume to slip on." Colton scoffed as he slipped out of his boxers and into the tightest, tiniest, glitteriest gold short shorts in the world. That wasn't an exaggeration. His balls were practically hanging out, and there was absolutely no way to downplay his bulge. "Why can't I have a more discreet costume like you?"

Isaac had put some temporary black dye in his hair and wore a black trench coat that went down to his ankles, hiding him entirely. Not much of a costume. He'd finally gotten the sling removed, but his bulky cast caused the sleeve of his coat to bunch up.

"You're the only one who can rock the Rocky look."

"I don't remember Rocky ever wearing this in the ring."

"Ew, not the boxing movie."

"Movies," Colton corrected, adding them to a mental list of flicks he'd make Isaac watch, especially since Isaac was dragging him to go watch *The Rocky Horror Picture Show*. "I just don't see why we all have to dress up."

"Because it's blasphemy to attend undressed," Isaac retorted. "Just be glad we're not going to a live show. They devour virgins."

"Welp, I'm safe."

"Not that kind of virgin."

Colton quirked a brow, perplexed but imagining he'd spend most of the night confused. Mina had been the one to suggest the movie night and poorly attempted to give Colton a synopsis of the story, which didn't make any sense.

"Why are we watching this movie?"

"Because it's iconic, and we've been talking about it all year."

"I thought go-go shorts might be on the GSA's agenda for me," Colton said, playfully popping his hip and strutting a bit. "But I was picturing more Pride parades than weirdo movies."

"How dare you." Isaac tsked. "You will eat those words before the night is over."

"I'm gonna eat something before the night is over." Colton shoulder-bumped Isaac, lightly nudging him and giving quite the suggestive stare.

Isaac chuckled. It was so freeing to see the layers of anger wash away the more they spent time together. Little by little, Isaac transformed before Colton, and the new layers were even more appealing than the person he carried himself as most of the time.

With that, they left Colton's empty apartment and set off for the party. Tim had already left for the night, and Devon moved out after news of Leon's behavior had exploded across campus. Colton wasn't sure if he went virtual for the remainder of the year, if he took the semester off, or if he simply dropped out. Honestly, Colton didn't care. He was just grateful not to have a reminder of Leon in his apartment or on the baseball team. Most of the players—even the ones who'd buddied up to Leon—disavowed him, pretending he never existed.

"Why couldn't we have just gotten ready over here?" Colton asked with a shiver. Despite the summer heat kicking in during May, the nights still held a strong chill which hit Colton exceptionally hard in his skimpy gold shorts.

"Saving you all the annoying pregame antics," Isaac said, leading the way to Mina's apartment—his temporary housing until he signed the lease for his own place in June.

"Saving yourself more like it," Colton replied with chattering teeth and folded arms.

Before Isaac could slip his key into the lock, Mina answered the door, wearing the most bizarre bright pink dress. It wasn't like Mina didn't wear frilly things or pinks, but this had a stuffy, tame kind of look that didn't fit Mina's vibe.

Colton smiled, taking in the look, while she fanned her face and placed a hand on her forehead to dramatically pass out. There was a lot of trust in Mina's fall, which Colton liked and feared in equal measure. He scrambled to catch her, and the pair giggled.

"Oh, Janet, you damn dirty slut." Isaac bit the air. "You best keep your eyes—and everything else—off my man."

Colton almost made a comment, something quippy about Isaac's jealousy, but Mina stood upright and put on some prissy girly voice.

"Oh, Doctor, he's gonna be all over me before the night is over." Mina pursed her lips teasingly, and Colton concluded they were bantering as their characters.

"Well, then I guess I'm just gonna have to take your man for a ride."

Isaac snatched Jazz by the sleeve, nearly knocking her over as he jerked her into a playful squeeze.

Jazz wore the nerdiest oversized glasses with a brown coat and high waisted slacks.

"Now, now, now," Jazz said with an exaggerated mannish voice and a phony nervous stammer. "There will be none of that, you hear."

Jazz broke free from Isaac and eyed him from head to toe.

"Didn't wanna ruin the surprise," Isaac said like he could read her mind. Though, Colton wasn't sure what the question was.

Jazz squinted. "You wore boots, though."

"I've got his *shoes*, hun." Mina nodded, gesturing for Isaac to head to her room.

"Is there more to your costume than I realized?" Colton asked.

"Just you wait," Isaac replied. "The antici…pation is worth it."

With that, Isaac wandered off, a definite swagger in his hips as he strutted away.

"Whatever." Colton sighed. "Got any beers?"

Mina gasped. "Rocky, you're not twenty-one. Dammit. But who am I to judge? Fridge."

Much to his surprise, he spotted Tim in the kitchen, already standing alongside Carlos and having a laugh. It wasn't so much that Tim had shown up. He was there when Mina pitched the idea and sort of invited himself, and Colton liked the idea of his roommate befriending his GSA crew. Sort of merging the two worlds.

No, what left Colton stunned was the costume Tim had gone with. He wore a maid's uniform with a big sloppy red wig while Carlos dressed in a butler's getup and a creepy bald cap with straggly long blond hair.

"Quite the outfit."

"I haven't worn this baby since pledge week." Tim beamed. "Figured why not get my money's worth and show off these *killer* legs."

"Spoilers," Carlos said, reminding Tim that Colton didn't know the movie.

Not that Colton made much sense of the spoiler, but suspected the maid was a murderer. Probably. Or a murder victim. Or just trashy. Maybe that was Tim's messy makeup job.

Colton sipped his beer, keeping an extra close eye on the rim of the bottle, and sort of wandered the apartment before the film started. Mina pounced playfully beside him, a wide smile filling her face.

"You okay, hun?"

"Yeah, I'm good."

"You sure?"

Colton nodded, then took a big swig of his beer.

"We let it lie, what happened, and wanted to give you the space to process or ignore or handle that night." Mina's demeanor shifted entirely, serene and compassionate. "But if you're ever not good, not fine, and want to talk—just know you have a whole crew of friends."

"Thank you." Colton grinned. "I really am good."

"I know, I know. You've got the world's most aggressive attack dog." She waved a hand. "But if you ever want to talk to someone other than Isaac, we're here for you, sweetie."

"Here and queer." Colton chuckled, raising his beer to toast.

"Is there any other way?" Mina cackled as she shuffled away to rejoin the growing party.

After a dozen or so other people arrived, along with one other Rocky, they started the film up, and Colton did his best to pay attention. He'd never really cared for musicals, so the giant lips singing a story didn't really catch his attention. But the sly smile on Isaac's face as he sang along, mouthing the entire script scene for scene, did, in fact, captivate Colton.

He'd never seen such a joyful glint in Isaac's eyes, the pure awe of all his walls falling away as he just giggled and had fun. Colton made a mental note to find more things like this horrible movie to make Isaac smile. He wanted more carefree nights like this, he wanted more nonsense events with his friends, more of Isaac's happiness.

While Colton didn't know what the future held in store for them as a couple, he looked forward to exploring the many facets. After everything the semester threw at them, Colton trusted Isaac implicitly.

Partway through the film, Isaac slipped away. When he returned, his character was making his entrance, stepping off an elevator and through a crowd. Isaac walked with the same flair, his face covered in white makeup and his heels clicking on the floor.

Heels? Colton's eyes went wide.

In a flash, Isaac ripped off his trench coat, revealing a lacy black corset, matching panties, and stockings to cover his legs. He sang to the song, much like everyone else at the party, a kick in his step and a need to steal a sip from everyone's drink as he used their glasses as makeshift microphones while belting the strangest lyrics in the world.

Strangest so far. Colton was in for a long night with this film and the audience participation of far too many people crammed in Mina's living room. Still, he found himself entranced by Isaac's flair, his strut, his sexy outfit.

When the song ended, Isaac collapsed onto the couch. His legs kicked high, tantalizing Colton with a million thoughts, and he was grateful Isaac lay across his waist because Colton's boner would've been quite impossible to hide in the tiny gold shorts he wore.

"I love..." Colton bit his bottom lip. "I love this look."

Isaac responded by maintaining eye contact while he subtly grinded against Colton. When Mina made a comment, Isaac hissed, and she returned to the movie while Isaac finally settled on Colton's lap.

With all the attention back on the movie, Colton wrapped his arms around Isaac's waist and held him in a tight cuddling hug that Isaac sank into with a small smile. It was the perfect night, and Colton hoped for more just as chaotically entertaining as this one. He hoped they could reach love. Real love. He felt it. He wasn't sure how Isaac felt. Sure, he made a point of expressing that wasn't the type of relationship they had, but things had grown and changed and evolved in ways neither of them expected since they first started this relationship.

Hell, it wasn't even a relationship when they began. Tuning out the music of the movie, Colton wondered where their relationship would lead next, and he hoped for the best. He hoped for more days spent with Isaac.

CHAPTER 30
ISAAC

"**UGH**, you're gonna break my back if you keep this up." Colton groaned.

"Oh, you're fine," Isaac said, ignoring Colton's wince. "We're almost done."

"Okay, you can't put that there—I won't be able to see," Colton said, struggling with his grip as Isaac saddled him with another box. "Ah, fuck. That's heavy."

"You got this, you big, strong man." Isaac batted his eyes, pretending to be delicate with his arm cast when they both knew he was the furthest thing.

Colton snorted, nearly making Isaac snicker as he grumbled. But when Colton's annoyance made him lose his balance, Isaac did break out into a giggle as Colton stumbled backward and widened his stance to straddle the concrete.

"Come on! At this rate, we'll only need a few more trips to get everything inside."

"It'd be even less trips if you actually carried stuff!" Colton bypassed Isaac, bumping him with his hip as he swaggered up to the second floor of the apartment complex.

"I'm carrying the team," Isaac professed. "They call me Captain Morale."

"More like Captain Moron," Mina countered, brushing by Isaac as she carried a trove of boxes, too.

Isaac hadn't accumulated too much in the time he spent with Mina, but since he needed to actually get furnishing for his new place, that meant he required lots of help with the manual labor. Who better than the gays?

Much like Isaac, Jazz took on a support role, directing the GSA members she could wrangle into helping and leading them up the stairs with the couch, recliner, and tables.

"Hey, watch it!" Isaac glowered when one of them chipped the corner of the coffee table on the railing.

"You get what you pay for," Carlos teased, carrying nearly as many boxes as Isaac had saddled Colton with a moment ago.

"Someone's gonna pay if my furniture is fucked up."

"Be nice, or I won't assemble this nightstand."

"You wouldn't punish Colton like that," Isaac said. "Imagine leaving my poor sweet boyfriend alone with a feral me as I scream profanities at the directions."

Carlos rolled his eyes and made his way into the apartment.

Thanks to everyone's help, they managed to get the entire apartment set up and organized pretty quickly. Isaac hid the box of glassware in his bedroom as he watched everyone plop onto the furniture to rest after their hard work of moving things and assembling stuff. They all appeared far too homey for Isaac's liking, and Colton's incessant need to fill silence with polite conversation would likely delude the GSA members into believing they had an extended welcome.

Isaac cleared his throat, loudly increasing the gravelly cough until the idle chitchat ceased. Locking eye contact with a few he didn't know, Isaac let his glowering expression rest on them to drive the point home before speaking.

"Thank you all for your assistance. I owe you a cake or parade or drink in the future," Isaac said quite plainly. "Now, get out of my place before I hurt you."

A few people laughed until Isaac's unwavering stare startled them into silence.

Mina rolled her eyes and slapped Isaac on the shoulder. "You owe me big time, bitch."

With that, she took her leave, directing a few of the GSA members with her. Carlos suggested a bar for everyone to unwind with drinks, and Jazz mentioned a restaurant with cheap specials.

Colton spread out on the couch. "I can't believe you kicked everyone out like that."

"Did you really wanna host for the next hour or three?" Isaac huffed. "Seriously, they'd have prattled on until the wee hours."

"Yeah, I'm too tired for that." Colton sighed, dragging himself off the couch. Isaac could see Colton's desire to sink into the cushions and pass out. "I'm gonna take a shower."

"Want company?" Isaac smirked.

"Company? I know what you want." Colton tsked. "And after how you used me for manual labor all day?"

"Maybe I can use you for something sweeter." Isaac squeezed Colton's shoulders.

When Colton paused, Isaac took full advantage, massaging the tension out of his stiff muscles.

"Or you can use me."

Colton kept his expression blank, playing hard to get. The temptation danced across his green eyes, but he remained cool and collected, which only further enticed Isaac. Unwilling to surrender, Isaac closed the distance and slid his arms down Colton's torso. When he reached his waist, Isaac wrapped his arms around and guided his fingers ever so under Colton's shirt. There were a couple of ticklish spots Isaac knew of and how to provoke the perfect smile.

"Okay, okay, okay." Colton wriggled loose. "You can join me."

"Good. I need to get all squeaky clean after my exhausting day of managerial duties."

"Are you this insufferable at work, Mr. Assistant Manager?"

"No, I'm ten times worse."

"Oh, but what I have planned for you and that mouthy mouth of yours is quite filthy."

Isaac growled, snarling in the back of Colton's ear. "Do tell."

"Gah, you're ridiculous. I love…" Colton's eyes darted away from Isaac, and he admired the room for a moment, a small, nervous smile dancing on his face. "This apartment. Christ on a crouton crutch, I love this apartment."

Isaac had seen Colton tiptoeing around the words, almost dropping it here and there but skirting around the L bomb as quickly as he fumbled the grenade. Isaac's expression turned sour. There was probably something very unhealthy about comparing love to an explosive, but he didn't have the time to delve into that level of emotional baggage.

"You okay?" Colton quirked a brow, likely trying to suss out Isaac's expression.

"I love you, too," he said, then furrowed his brow, realizing the error, the flop, the incredible screw-up of three utterly simple words.

Words Isaac swore to himself he'd never say to anyone. Words Isaac practiced in his head a hundred times the night Colton spent in the hospital, a thousand times in the days that followed, and hoped to say properly a million more times over.

Much to Isaac's surprise or disappointment, Colton had an obnoxious, minxy grin plastered on his face. He loved this, the smug bastard.

"I love too…the apartment," Isaac blurted as if that somehow made more sense. Even if it did, his frazzled face definitely gave away his embarrassment.

"Yeah?" Colton puckered his lips. "You wanna kiss the apartment? Wanna spend your days cuddling up to the walls? Maybe dry hump the floor while whispering sweet nothings?"

"Oh, shut the fuck up, you ass," Isaac huffed. "This is why I can't stand you."

"And love your apartment," Colton added, a teasing cockiness in his voice. "It is quite a lovely apartment for sure."

With that, he stripped off his shirt and walked with a cocky swagger toward the bathroom. Isaac dragged himself behind Colton, practically kicking himself for picking the worst time to say the worst words only for Colton to play it off like it meant nothing. Which was the worst thing ever. Isaac didn't know what to make of it.

He certainly wasn't feeling a shared shower anymore or a sexy shower or anything that didn't involve him not crawling in a hole somewhere and dying.

Colton must've noticed the anxiety festering in Isaac as he spun around once they reached the bathroom door and slid back toward him.

"I love you, too," Colton whispered into Isaac's ear, wrapping his arms around his waist much like he did at the GSA party. There was something so comforting in Colton's embrace. Isaac believed he could truly sink into it forever. "In fact, I love you more."

"Not possible."

"Are you challenging me to a love off?" Colton bit Isaac's earlobe, avoiding the piercings.

"No," Isaac said plainly, having finally settled the nervousness that consumed him earlier. "It'd be unfair of someone of my expertise to challenge a novice."

"And you're suddenly an expert at love?"

"Yep. Learned all I needed falling for you."

Colton's cheeks blushed. "You're the worst."

"You *love* it." Isaac tested his hand under the water, finding the temperature a little tepid for him but just right for Colton's liking.

They undressed, and Isaac took in all of Colton, adoring every square inch of this beautiful man that he loved. A man who loved him. Isaac couldn't fathom how he'd gotten so lucky, how the horrors between them had washed away, the past etched in hatred and cruelty had fizzled away. Neither held resentment or rage or regret.

"I really do love you, you know." Isaac wrapped his cast in a plastic bag and stepped into the shower, letting the spray obscure the glossiness of his eyes.

"I know." Colton grinned, goofy and giddy. "But not as much as I love you."

"Insufferable."

Colton stepped into the shower behind Isaac. "Now, why don't you stop telling me how you feel and show me how you feel with that pretty mouth of yours."

Isaac snorted. "Oh, yeah?"

"Don't make fun of me. I'm being all assertive and stuff."

"I'm not teasing." Isaac lightly pecked Colton's lips. "I think it's sexy."

"Damn right you do." Colton smacked Isaac's ass, which created a much louder slap than expected, thanks to the running water.

"But you do realize me telling you how I feel is using my mouth, right?"

Colton scrunched his face. "Don't bring logic into this."

Isaac gently kissed Colton's neck, savoring the taste, the wetness of his skin, the ease of his muscles as Isaac worked his way down. Next, he kissed Colton's chest, licking a nipple while playing with the other. The slight shudder Colton made encouraged Isaac more. Once he'd had his fill of teasing Colton, he kissed his stomach and eased his way to his knees.

Isaac stared up at Colton, taking in all of him as he took in all of him. He gurgled and choked, partially from the full length hitting the back of his throat too quickly and partially from the running water pooling around his face as it ran down Colton's body.

It didn't matter to Isaac; he inhaled through his nose and pushed further down so he could swallow the entirety of Colton's shaft.

"Fuuuuuuck." Colton gripped Isaac's wet hair, looping his fingers and holding tight.

It sent a rush through Isaac, practically feeling the pulse of Colton's knuckles as he squeezed. Isaac bobbed his head up and down, twisting his tongue around the head when he pulled back to the tip and gagged something fierce when he pushed all the way to the base.

Colton's legs trembled, further encouraging Isaac. But he didn't wanna risk Colton tipping over. While the idea amused him for half a second, the reality worried him, so Isaac spun Colton slightly and pressed him up against the wall. This put Isaac under the full blast of the water, but he didn't care. All he wanted was to taste Colton's cock, to feel his orgasm, to elicit pure pleasure in his boyfriend.

Isaac pressed a hand to the cold tile wall and then traced his palm along Colton's bare thigh as he sucked. Colton shivered ever so, his body radiating goosebumps, likely from being pinned to the wall. Clearly, it didn't bother him. Colton focused his energy and controlled Isaac's head, moving him up and down faster and further with a more rhythmic pace.

Isaac relaxed the muscles in his neck, going with the flow. He attempted to relax the muscles in his throat, too, but still gagged when Colton pushed too far too quickly. Still, Isaac relished the sensation, eagerly choking on Colton's cock.

"I'm gonna…" Colton wheezed. "I'm gonna, gonna, fuuuuuu…"

Isaac pulled back just enough to feel the hot load hit the back of his tongue. A second shot hit the roof of his mouth, and the rest sort of splattered all over, nearly spilling out as Isaac held the head of Colton's dick in his mouth and swallowed his load.

Colton braced himself against the wall, euphoric and drained. Certainly no longer interested in cleaning off, Isaac carefully stood up and lathered his hand in bodywash, enjoying every second of running his soapy fingers over Colton's skin.

After their incredibly long shower, Colton and Isaac made their way to Isaac's bedroom, where they plopped on the bed. Isaac read through one of his books, hoping to pass out soon enough, while Colton channel surfed on the television before abandoning it in favor of his phone.

"I'm organizing my summer trip," Colton said, scrolling through his phone. "In case you were wondering."

"I wasn't." Isaac lay back on the bed, his head barely propped by the pillow to see the television.

"It should be a fun vacation. What I manage to squeeze in, of course." Colton side-eyed Isaac, clearly waiting for a reaction. "You know, after the two back-to-back summer sessions you and my mom harassed me about."

Isaac rolled his eyes. Pretending to be annoyed but actually a bit giddy by how Colton's mother seemed to like his presence. Especially the academic influence he had over Colton. Now, he doubted she'd feel the same way if she had an inkling of their sordid past, how they eventually got together, and all the messy details in between.

"There's about two and a half weeks after the sessions before classes in the fall start back up," Colton explained. "So, I'm doing a trip back home."

"And why are you telling me this?"

"I'm wondering if you wanted to join." Colton grinned. "You could crash at my place. I already asked Mom. Figured it'd be a guest bedroom thing, but she's keen on us sharing my room. Pretty sure her and my father are having one of their lover's wars."

"Lover's wars?"

"Yeah, it's where they aim to make the other one miserable until one of them concedes and leaves the country for a few months." Colton shrugged like it was the most normal thing in the world. "How would you like to be really gay and help incite chaos?"

"I think I was born for that," Isaac said with a smirk. "But I have no interest in returning to Straight Arrow. That town can suck it."

"But can it suck it as well as you?"

As much as Isaac wanted to be angry, to show his pure, undiluted resentment for his hometown, that comment kept his smirk from faltering.

Isaac swore to himself to never set foot in his former home again. He vowed to never look back. But he also promised himself to avoid Colton, to ignore the blooming feelings between them. That hadn't exactly turned out how he hoped.

"Okay." Colton made these sad puppy-dog eyes, which annoyed Isaac more than coaxed him.

Isaac huffed, turning away to avoid Colton's expression. When the pitiful jock scooted closer, rubbing his foot against Isaac's under the covers, it nearly squashed Isaac's resolve. They lay in silence, Colton's sad, rhythmic breathing the only noise.

"Fine, whatever." Isaac caved almost immediately because Colton had that awful effect on him, and he didn't want to spend the night with knots in his stomach.

Colton hugged Isaac as he lay against his chest, his head resting over Isaac's heart. A heart that pattered all the faster when Colton snickered with glee. Geez, his boyfriend hadn't even pulled out the big guns, and Isaac cracked. He made a mental note to work on ignoring Colton's future pleas. In the meantime, he wanted to set some ground rules for the summer trip.

"But I'm not going anywhere in town."

"Okay, whatever you say." Colton squeezed him tighter.

"And I'm not doing any stupid parties."

"Of course, only smart parties for you." Colton giggled.

"I'm serious."

"And serious parties." Colton nuzzled into the crook of Isaac's neck.

As much as Isaac wanted to hiss, to protest, to take back his surrender, he simply sank into the comfort of Colton's cuddles and lay in bed as his boyfriend put on some ridiculously absurd show.

"I hate you."

"I love you, too."

Isaac hugged Colton back, savoring these horribly wonderful tiny moments that he couldn't get enough of. No part of him felt worthy of Colton's love, of this life he now led, of the possibility of a real future together, but Isaac intended on working harder each day to earn this life. He wanted more with Colton. He wanted everything.

EPILOGUE
COLTON

Six months later

AS the fall semester came to a close, Colton buzzed with anticipation as he packed up for winter break. For the first time since summer break—the minuscule vacation he squeezed in thanks to all his extra courses—he actually enjoyed going home. Things were changing in his family. His mother was becoming a mom and taking a real interest in Colton. In his identity. In his dreams. In his career goals. She'd even made a point of saying how she planned to attend his games this spring.

Now, the real test would be if she actually showed up or not. But he suspected she would, given it'd offer her a chance to sit in the bleachers with Isaac, whose snippy, snarky, sour attitude meshed well with his mom.

They were like catty gossips together. As much as Colton rolled his eyes at their mean girl antics, he rather enjoyed how Isaac went out and about without making any fuss. Fall break was the same. And Colton was hoping for a nice winter break with his boyfriend. He'd found the perfect Christmas present and was already imagining Isaac unwrapping his gift.

Once he'd finished packing and tucked away his present—in case Isaac snooped through his belongings—he grabbed his things and headed over to Isaac's apartment. Given how long it'd take to get to his folks' place, it saved time sleeping at the same place. Plus, with the stress of the semester wrapping up, they hadn't spent many nights together that didn't involve grueling studying.

Colton knocked on the door when he arrived, and Isaac flung his door open, wearing frost-colored clothes. All white with hues of blue. Given his slender frame and matching dyed hair, he was giving off Jack Frost vibes, and Colton found himself enamored. His long-sleeve crop top had frayed edges and a deep V-cut rip that appeared to be added after the fact, given how the collar hung a little loose and wonky at Isaac's neck.

A neck Colton couldn't stop looking at since Isaac had gotten his new tattoo. CAL was inked in forest green above the flames of Isaac's phoenix tattoo on the left side of his neck. The color choice was picked because Colton considered it his favorite. Not that he spent a lot of time thinking about a favorite color, but since Isaac insisted, he went with his gut and chose the darker, lush green. As for the letters…they stood for Colton Ashton Lennox.

Instinctively, Colton rubbed his neck on the opposite side, his right side, and thought about his matching tattoo that Isaac had convinced him to get. IMP was scrawled across Colton's neck in a deep pink with extra black shading to outline the initials of Isaac's name: Isaac Mathias Parker.

The tattoo was ridiculous and silly and such a jinx on their relationship. Seriously, couples should never get matching tattoos, a sentiment Colton continued believing despite how giddy his made him.

"Well?" Isaac huffed, an edge of annoyance on his face as his eyes flitted up.

Colton followed them and noticed the random bow sitting on top of Isaac's head, nestled in his bleached hair with frosted blue highlights.

"Oh?" Colton raised his eyebrows. "What's this?"

Isaac smirked, tilting his head so the glittery bow sparkled under the Christmas lights. A string of decorative lights Colton had covered the inside of Isaac's apartment with because his boyfriend couldn't bother with being festive. Or so Colton thought, but now this bow look was giving him ideas.

"I suppose you're a present for me to unwrap."

"Yeah." He shrugged. "I might've gotten you a gift card, too, but figured you should be able to unwrap one present early."

Colton chuckled, stepping in close to Isaac. He gripped Isaac's slacks, immediately unfastening the button with his practiced hand as he kicked the door closed behind him.

"You can't open it here," Isaac whispered, teasingly leading Colton toward his bedroom.

This suggested Colton had less of a say in the gift he was about to receive. At first, he figured Isaac wanted a blowjob, which Colton would eagerly provide since finals had kept them both super busy, and Colton hadn't gotten off with Isaac in a while. All studying and no fun.

"I wanted to get you something really, really special," Isaac said, pushing Colton back onto the mattress and taking his time to undress.

Slowly, seductively, Isaac unhooked his suspenders, then let his baggy pants glide to the floor around his ankles.

"Hey!" Colton snapped. "You're unwrapping my gift."

Isaac shushed him. "Did I mention how impressed I was by your final grades this semester?"

Colton rolled his eyes, ignoring the heat in his face. Isaac always did annoying things like that, praising Colton for his work ethic, like any of it had to do with him. Colton knew he wouldn't have passed his finals without Isaac's intensive study regimes.

"Seriously, you aced your exams, passed six classes in one semester."

"Yeah, and I am never taking six classes again."

"Oh, yes, you are," Isaac said with a stern glare. "Especially since you'll be dropping to four in the spring."

With baseball right around the corner, there was no way Colton could balance practice, games, and six classes. Four would be a headache enough. Plus maintaining the B average Isaac continued to insist Colton was capable of achieving.

Isaac shot Colton a look—a very assertive look that told him he needed to start undressing and catch up. As Colton took off his shirt, Isaac slipped out of his slacks, making a little show of it. Hell, he'd even wore a skimpy pair of boxer briefs that looked like something out of Colton's wardrobe.

They definitely weren't, though, considering how skintight they were around Isaac.

"Well?" Isaac slid his thumbs around the elastic band of his underwear.

"I have to undress first?" Colton unfastened his pants, kicking them off along with his underwear and tossing them onto the floor. "This is feeling less and less like a gift for me and more like a you gift."

"That so?" Isaac slowly stripped off his boxer briefs until he stood naked at the end of the bed.

Colton didn't respond; he just waited silently. When Isaac slowly crawled onto the bed, he half expected him to grab Colton by the ankles and roll him onto his stomach. When he reached his waist, he thought maybe he'd spin him around and rim Colton. When his lips nearly pressed to Colton's, he expected Isaac to collapse onto him, grinding and kissing and rolling around the bed until they fucked.

These were all things Colton had experienced and enjoyed with Isaac, yet none of his normal moves came into play. The silence, the anticipation... It excited Colton, making his dick perk up a bit.

Isaac straddled Colton, letting his bare ass brush against Colton's stiffening cock. That nearly made Colton leap.

"For your gift, I thought it was time you showed me what an excellent pitcher you are."

"Wait, what?" Colton sprang up, hands wrapping around Isaac's waist so he didn't jostle him off. "Are you serious?"

"What do you say, not-so-little pitcher?"

Colton gulped. It hadn't ever been something he considered. Isaac was very much nonstop top guy energy, and Colton liked taking on the more submissive role. Usually, when he was feeling assertive, he'd just fuck Isaac's face. They'd grown into a very back-and-forth flow when it came to oral. But with anal... Colton wasn't sure where to begin.

"Are you sure?"

Isaac nodded. "I know it's something I said I wasn't interested in. And that remains true. Mostly."

"But?"

"But—pun intended," Isaac said with a soft laugh until Colton made a sour face.

Colton worried this was leaning on the verge of a learning moment. "No fancy talking."

"Fine." Isaac smirked. "I can't stop thinking about it. Wondering. Craving. Wanting you inside me. I want to feel you in every way, and I want you to feel me, too. If you're comfortable exploring this side—"

"Hell yeah!" Colton playfully tossed Isaac off him and pinned him beneath him on the bed.

Their lips mashed, and Colton rubbed his hands across Isaac's skin, imagining every sensation he'd elicit, every sound. Their bodies pressed against each other, moving rhythmically as Colton lost himself in the taste of Isaac's mouth.

When they rolled back onto their sides, Isaac pulled away just enough to take a breath.

"Someone's energetic." Isaac rolled onto his stomach, positioning himself slightly but leaving room for Colton to make adjustments.

If he were anything like Isaac, Colton would be bending him to just the right angles. In truth, Colton didn't know what to do next. How much he wanted to assert himself.

Delicately, Colton traced his fingertips down Isaac's back. The tremble it elicited from Isaac excited Colton, stirring an eagerness inside him. As his hand reached the small of Isaac's back, he let his palm rest there for a moment, guiding and demanding an arch from his boyfriend. Isaac obediently moved, turning his head so his piercing blue eyes met Colton's.

Resting on his side, he continued running his hand down Isaac's backside. First, he cupped Isaac's right cheek, admiring his little bubble butt. Then, he traced his fingers further, running them along the hairs on the back of Isaac's thigh. Christ, his thighs were so muscular despite how slender he was overall.

Isaac's frame had always been solid, but since joining Colton regularly at the gym, he'd become this compact muscle twink. Well, not a twink exactly, but Isaac certainly wasn't a jock either. There had to be a word for it.

"What's so funny?" Isaac asked.

Colton shook his head, burying his musings and sitting up to position himself behind Isaac.

"It's nothing," he answered. "Just nerves is all."

"Don't be nervous. I'm not."

"You're not?"

"With you?" Isaac craned his neck just enough so Colton could see the happiness in his expression. "Never."

Colton gently adjusted Isaac's hips, lowering him some. Each passing second made his heart beat faster, racing as he anxiously tried to ready himself and Isaac. His knees sank deeper into the mattress than he preferred, and he found himself already breaking into a sweat. Nervously, he fumbled to open the lube bottle.

"Relax." Isaac playfully bucked against him, rubbing his crack against Colton's shaft. That was quite the sensation. It sent a surge of exhilaration coursing through Colton. He squeezed just a bit of lube out, letting it drizzle down Isaac's crack, to which he let out the softest yip from the sensation.

"Relax," Colton teased as he continued grinding against Isaac.

The motion eased the nervous tension, ready to burst inside him. The warmth of Isaac's body, the softness of his skin, and the blissful sensation that came with each stroke helped distract Colton. It helped excite Colton. Soon, he found himself more eager than anxious. Every time he bucked his hips, the heat of Isaac's hole called to him.

"Are you ready?"

"Wouldn't be here ass up if I wasn't." Isaac craned his neck, smirking.

"Might have to rail out a bit of the feistiness tonight."

"Don't get cocky."

"Face down." Colton rested his elbow between Isaac's shoulder blades and pressed his whole forearm against the back of Isaac's head. His fingers gripped his boyfriend's hair as he shoved his face into the pillows. "And arch for me."

There was a quiver in Isaac's body that rippled and sent a euphoric wave of anticipation through Colton. Isaac obediently arched and pushed his ass up against Colton more and more.

Using his free hand, Colton guided his dick into Isaac. The muffled groans Isaac released into the pillow helped steady Colton's approach. Slowly, he pushed the head of his cock past the ring.

"Oooooh, fuck," he said, letting his dick adjust to the tightness of Isaac's hole.

Barely an inch inside him, and already the sensation had him floating. After a minute of allowing Isaac to adjust—and quite honestly himself—Colton pushed further in.

Each thrust made Isaac moan louder into the pillows. Each noise made Colton throb harder as he went deeper. Each inch inside Isaac sent a surge of aggression through him. Eagerness to buck to hump to pound into Isaac. He resisted the urge, if only so he could savor the feeling of sliding all the way to the base and resting with the full length of his cock inside Isaac.

"Fuck." Colton licked his lips, then lifted his arm up, jerking Isaac's head back in a swift motion.

"You're telling me." Isaac's face contorted as he turned to meet Colton's gaze.

His beautiful blue eyes were glossy, and his trembling lips were pouty. They looked delicious and kissable. And fuckable. But Colton didn't want to fuck Isaac's pretty little mouth. He bucked his hips, then pulled back, almost removing his cock entirely before he thrust ahead and pounded all the way back inside Isaac.

When Isaac moaned, Colton swept in and kissed him. Swallowing the sounds, the pain, the building pleasure Colton knew he'd elicit. With each smack of their lips, Colton continued railing Isaac. Soon, he found his rhythm, and Isaac's groans quickly changed.

"Right there." Isaac whimpered, reaching his hands back and holding onto Colton's hips.

He didn't steady or stop them, merely squeezed Colton's hips. The lust in Isaac's voice instructed Colton. He realized he'd found Isaac's prostate, so he kept his pace, the same pounding motion. Each thrust incited him, causing Isaac to moan and whimper and gasp more and more as the seconds turned into minutes, and time lost itself amongst their panting groans.

Colton buzzed, euphoric and near ready to burst. Part of him wanted to change his pace, his position, but the way Isaac's face contorted, Colton knew he'd climax any second. Colton growled, grabbing the back of Isaac's neck and ramming into him.

"Cum for me," he wheezed, desperately trying to hold back his own eruption. "Now."

Isaac jerked his throbbing cock, stroking it in sync with Colton's pounding. A whine of ecstasy consumed Isaac, which further fueled Colton, who rammed harder, taking slow thrusts to relish the sensation that hit his throbbing cock and coursed through his entire body.

"Aaaaah!" Isaac panted.

Colton twisted their bodies just enough to see the pool of cum that had shot from Isaac, and with him already finished, Colton made a few more twitchy thrusts. His pace became erratic as he chased his climax, using Isaac, running his hands along his flesh, grabbing and squeezing and claiming every inch of his body until he finally plunged his cock in as far as he could.

"Goddamn," Colton growled, groaning with a pleasure he'd never known. Never in his life had he fucked someone and felt himself cum so hard. He poured the entirety of his load inside of Isaac, keeping his cock nestled in the warm hole. "Fuck, that was hot."

After a minute or so on top of Isaac, Colton finally rolled off him. It was too far, and despite how exhausted he was, he dragged Isaac closer, holding him to his chest so their sticky skin clung together.

"We are so doing that again." Colton kissed Isaac's forehead.

"Maybe for your birthday." Isaac chuckled. "My ass needs a few months to recover."

"Absolutely not." Colton smacked Isaac's ass cheek and got a firm grip on him. "I'm addicted now. Gotta get my fill on this peach."

"Oh, that so?" Isaac had this curious look, the same expression he got every time he debated something new, considered Colton, and then his face turned surly, which meant he usually conceded. "I'm not vers, but I might dabble a bit more for you."

"Love it." Colton kissed Isaac. "Love you."

"I love you too…as much as I hate it."

ACKNOWLEDGEMENTS

I'd like to give a huge thank you to everyone who took a chance on Colton and Isaac! It really means a lot that you gave my himbo jock and grumpy goth a shot. I hope you enjoyed their journey together and that you'll consider leaving an honest review and/or rating. It makes such a big difference in visibility when readers share their thoughts on a book, and it'll help other folks find these two in the future.

I'd also like to give a massive shout out to my cover artist! Lina did an absolutely amazing job of bringing Colton and Isaac to life. Seriously, this might be my favorite cover thus far (and I really love all my covers).

If you like grumpy/sunshine pairings, I've got another book with a grumpy (former) goth who is now a teacher at a magic school. The Branches of Past and Future is a fun fantasy series if that's your thing. I've also got a series Diabolic Romance between a snarky devil and a chatty mage where they show their affection through casual slaughter. But if contemporary is more your thing, I'm currently working on another contemporary romance (dark-ish) called Politics and Poly. I can't wait to share those boys with interested readers, too.

Thank you again for taking a chance on my story and reading until the end!

AUTHOR'S BIO

MN Bennet is a former high school teacher, writer, and reader. He lives in the mountains of Arizona, which make for really cold winters for a desert state. He's still adjusting to the cold after being born and raised in the South.

He enjoys writing paranormal and fantasy stories with huge worlds (sometimes too big), loveable romances (with so much angst and banter), and Happily Ever Afters (once he's dragged his characters through some emotional turmoil).

When he's not balancing classes, writing, or reading, he can be found binge watching anime or replaying Baldur's Gate 3 for the millionth time.

Author website:
https://www.mnbennet.com

Amazon page:
https://www.amazon.com/stores/MN-Bennet/author/B0BLJJK5NF

Goodreads page:
https://www.goodreads.com/author/show/23017668.M_N_Bennet

Patreon:
patreon.com/MNBennet

Newsletter:
https://subscribepage.io/zUylj7

Find All My Stuff:
https://linktr.ee/mnbennet